MIDNIGHT VINTAGE

A Collection

SEAN EADS AND JOSHUA VIOLA

Published by Crystal Lake Publishing
Where Stories Come Alive!

Crystal Lake Publishing
www.CrystalLakePub.com

Follow us on Amazon:

WELCOME
TO ANOTHER

CRYSTAL LAKE PUBLISHING
CREATION

TABLE OF CONTENTS

For Aric Vyhmeister and Elizabeth Field. Love you both, and thanks for your friendship.

—Sean

FOREWORD

SO WHO'S THE twisted one here? I mean, there's Sean Eads, and there's Josh Viola. I know both of these guys. I've eaten meals with them, I've read them, I've shared stages with them, I've hung out with them I don't know how many times.

But? I never knew they had this kind of stuff swirling in their heads.

No, not "swirling." *Festering.*

It's kind of sick, I'm saying. I'm reconsidering some of our past interactions, I mean. I'm wondering if I should have been alone in a hallway with them. And I'm sort of terrified of being pulled into one of these stories you're now holding in your hands.

However, I could very well be casting aspersions on one of them, right? I mean, they can both write, I know that. I've *known* that for years, but. . .maybe all the sick stuff in here is from just one of them? Maybe? Meaning one of them still has a little hope? Granted, a very little, as whoever's the not-twisted one here did, at some level, ratify the horror. But I have no idea what was going on in the writing of these stories. It could very well be that Sean, say, abducted a pet of Josh's and forced him to agree to this vile turn, that wretched development. It could just as easily have been Josh menacing Sean—I don't think Josh is really above putting a mask on and casually peering in Sean's windows while Sean's just trying to live, and then following that up with a "completely unrelated" story prompt.

This is how I prefer to consider these stories, anyway.

And, if you think I'm joking? Check out "Notches," say. Or wend your way through the EC Comics-y "Many Carvings," say. Or "Diminished Sevenths," which gets plenty ugly, or. . .or the *rest* of them.

STEPHEN GRAHAM JONES

Some collections take you, the reader, into account, and are considerate with your sleep, with your breathing—with your *ability* to breathe. Other collections stage a quiet or slow story in between all the dread and terror, so you don't have to be pawing on your nightstand for that heart medication.

Either Josh or Sean, here, they're not nearly so considerate.

These stories put their foot on the gas, and they don't let up until there's blood in the rearview.

And because I might be hanging out with these guys in the near future—we live in the same general area; I see them socially whether I want to or not—and because I have pets and have one of those weird houses with *windows*, I think my odds are just a whole lot better if all these twisted stories come just from one head, not two. That doubles my odds, I think, in that it halves the menace.

So? So what I've got to do now, I think, is read this collection again. I mean, firstly, so I can convince myself these stories are made-up—which will be a task, since they're written so realistically—but secondly, so I can maybe ferret out who's who here. Is this Josh's pen doing this, or is it Sean's?

But I'm also scared to do that.

What if what I figure out isn't that it's either one of them, but that it's the two of them combined? By themselves, Josh and Sean are happy-go-lucky, easygoing guys. Put them at the same desk, though, writing the same stories? This could be a dangerous situation. Could be they're each *half*-twisted, but, together, they add up to one demented writer. One who, due to our bad luck, can write fiction well enough that these bad ideas and sticky scenes worm into our heads and take root, and then, at night, force their ways up from our mouths to look around, taste the night air, and bend over to look into our eyes, into our souls.

It's what Josh and Sean are doing here. Whether we want them to or not.

Enjoy?

Stephen Graham Jones
20 October 2022
Boulder, CO

THE MAKING

Field Investigation Progress Report
Victim: Richard S. Kipling (alleged)
RE: Inquiry into the disappearance of Detective R.S. Kipling
File #01584-B
Subject: Transcript of R.S. Kipling interview, 05-10-2023
Document added to case file 05-20-2023

RK: My name is Detective Rick Kipling, Warrington Police Department. This interview is being initiated and recorded on Wednesday, May 10, 2023, with subject Stradivarius Cooper, S-T-R-A-D-I-V-A-R-I-U-S C-O-O-P-E-R, no middle name. Date of birth 01-17-72. Subject shows numerous cuts, bruises, and contusions on his body, present upon apprehension. Subject is not under the influence of any painkillers at the present time. Stradivarius, let me begin with—

SC: My father named me that. Failed musician. Everyone calls me Strad. Except my mother; she called me her little fiddle. Funny thing. Fiddling with me is what got Dad his first prison sentence.

RK: Strad, you've agreed to sit down with me for a taped conversation in Interview Room 2 of the Warrington Police Headquarters. You've agreed to do this without any legal representation present, correct?

SC: Yeah.

RK: You understand that anything you say—

SC: Yeah.

RK: Very well. Let's begin.

OVER THE PHONE, he said his name was Dr. Leo Dapper, and I assumed he was a state psychiatrist. I thought there was some condition about the release where I had to talk my head off an hour a week. That or they were trying to be nice, figuring my seven-month prison stint must have been cruel and traumatizing, seeing how the retrial found me *innocent*. I pictured Doc Leo trying to get me to open up about my feelings. Open up my guts.

Then he mentioned *associates*. I'd meet them when I came for my appointment. What appointment? Doc Leo was getting ahead of himself, making assumptions, selling at high pressure. He threw out a figure, like a grand in cash. Just to meet me. Gave me an address but said he'd send a car. I was taking the phone call in my dead mom's house, on my dead mom's phone, and outside the window, I saw a car parked right outside. Cop? Journalist? This guy? I swore a man was behind the wheel looking at me. It didn't give me a shiver; not much does. And there'd been quite a few people camping around outside since my release.

A thousand dollars just to meet some people?

I was picked up at noon and driven to a coffee shop. The driver didn't talk until we got there. "I was told to tell you to go to the room in the back."

"Who told you? What about my money?"

"Don't know anything about either."

He sped off as soon as I got out. Whatever his problem was, you can bet he got paid. Good old fucking capitalism.

I made my way to the back room and found two men and two women. Doc Leo spoke first. He didn't introduce himself again. I just recognized his voice.

"Scott Cooper in the flesh," he said, extending a hand. Hell, I shook it. Why not?

"Call me Strad. Short for Stradivarius."

All four looked down at a bunch of papers I only just noticed. Seems they had a whole file on me.

"Couple of prison guards gave me a nickname because of a birthmark. You see it real good if you're eye level with my crotch."

"Ah. Strad, then."

I took the offer to sit and we looked at each other in silence.

"Something wrong? Look too clean for my rep? You expecting a bunch of tattoos on my neck and shit?"

They shook their heads. I could tell they all had their knees pressed close together in fear. Except the one lady's. Hers were getting a little further apart.

"What's it like living in a haunted house?" she said.

"I wouldn't know."

"There were rumors about your mother's place while you were incarcerated."

"Whose ghost do you think is up in the bitch? Mom's? I wish she'd put in an appearance. Maybe give me a chance to kill her again."

Had to admit being a little impressed with their poker faces. I figured the casual confession would throw them. I mean I'd been saying that bullshit about being innocent from the beginning and the second trial got me acquitted. Drop the rock of a ruthless lawyer into a dumb jury pool and ride those ripples to freedom's shores, brother.

Doc Leo leaned toward me and said, "Do you believe in ghosts?"

"No."

"Demons? Poltergeists? Anything paranormal?"

"If I haven't seen it with my own eyes, it doesn't exist in my book."

The four of them looked at each other. I really couldn't tell what they were thinking and what they wanted me to say. Was I blowing some big chance here? Should I walk it back, let in a little wriggle room?

"Not unlike a scientist. In a way."

"That what you all are? You looking to study me?"

"We're looking for someone to help us, Mr. Cooper. *Strad.* Someone who isn't afraid to push the line where needed."

"In the name of science?"

"That's right," the other man said.

Looking at them, I had to laugh. "Who's that guy that's always helping Frankenstein? With the hunchback?"

"Igor."

"Yeah, him. That's what you want me to be? You're going to pay me to steal brains?"

Doc Leo responded with one of the coldest smiles I've ever seen. Made me start liking the guy.

RK: It's your statement then that your actions were done in the employment of these four. . .doctors? Researchers?

SC: They called themselves that. I didn't care. And no, they were the employees. They just contracted me to be their Igor.

RK: Who employed them?

SC: Doc Leo said his name was Gediminas Prekuba. Something like that. Don't bother asking me how to spell it. I'm not even sure I'm remembering the pronunciation. Lithuanian billionaire who promised them a quick ticket out of town, new identities, and lives of luxury if shit went bad.

RK: I often hate the rich.

SC: Everyone does except the rich. Ain't that rich?

THE MAKING

RK: So, he was offering some form of diplomatic immunity? Something like that? In exchange for. . .what?

It was a nice house, a lot better than Mom's and newer. Brand new, in fact, and located on a big piece of land about five miles from the nearest neighborhood or store. Just sitting there waiting for the golf course to be built. When I walked in, I could smell the hidden cameras everywhere, a scent as sure as beans cooking on the stove.

The house was built to look normal. Three thousand square feet, three bedrooms, three baths, a finished basement. The torture room was downstairs, hidden behind a bookcase that swiveled when you pushed on the right end. The centerpiece was a table, a real murder slab surrounded by bondage implements, crops, and cages, full syringes with pharmaceutical labels. *Pentobarbital sodium 50mg/ml.* They gave me free rein of the house and followed me from room to room, giving me these goofy, hopeful smiles whenever I turned back to look at them.

"The hypothesis is the more violent or tragic the death, the more likely—"

"You get a ghost," I said. "Someone's really paying you to research this?"

"Mr. Prekyba. That's right. He's our patron in this important matter."

"The fee we're offering is just a sample of what you'll get for helping us, regardless of the outcome," one of the women said. "And as we noted, he's already guaranteed our security in this matter. Yours, too."

Some Lithuanian billionaire had my back. Good to know. Play the villain for six months and retire to a villa in Vilnius for the rest of my life.

Their faces when I agree: just priceless. They wanted to act like they were these cold, amoral business people, but I lit them up with pure Golden Retriever energy. It was sort of sad in a way. They really did come across like they wanted nothing more than to find out the truth, but they couldn't do what was required so they needed to find that very special needle for their very special thread. I think they'd have been down in the dumps for a month if I'd said no. The thing is, geeks like this don't want to acknowledge the truth, and in this case, the truth was Mr. Billionaire Lithuanian didn't care whether ghosts were real or whether haunted houses could be created. He was just into violent snuff films. The cameras all over the place proved it. I was providing this one perv and maybe a small circle of friends with graphic jerkoff material. I wasn't going to be a murderer; I was going to be a pornographer.

RK: The recovered footage confirms five murders.

SC: If you say so. I haven't seen it.

RK: We have IDs on the victims. Keisha Davis, age 27. Mark Tobrin, 38. Alex Wu, 55. America Conti, 17. And Seve Lopez, 85. Quite the eclectic selection of victims, Strad.

SC: I didn't choose them. Doc Leo and the rest did based on whatever bullshit factors they were trying to study. Skin color, age. Who they liked to fuck.

RK: And religion?

SC: Yeah, I think that was a big one. A real big one.

"So, Marky," I said, leaning over the man strapped on the table. "You believe in God? You believe Jesus is gonna come through the door, kick my ass, and rescue you?"

Second month in the house, second victim on the slab. The

whole one-victim-a-month timeline seemed an awful waste to me. You'd think when it comes to making ghosts you're going for a maximum body count. Doc Leo said otherwise. They needed time to calculate, record, and account for what he called *the measurables*, whatever those were.

The guy was naked and sweating. His head twisted left and right. His eyes were red and had to be stinging from sweat. I swore I could hear his heartbeat from here, and I looked up to grin at the corner ceiling camera. "You guys hear that? We got the Little Drummer Boy here. *Pa rum pum pum pum.*"

Then I looked down at him and repeated my question.

"Whatever. . .whatever you want me to say. . ."

"There ain't no God, and there ain't no Jesus. Say it."

He said it.

"But there's a big old Devil, and you're looking at him."

He whimpered.

Still convinced all this was about making snuff films, I was determined to put on a good show. Be the perfect pornographer. And if Doc Leo really was trying to make a ghost, well, count the sadism as another *measurable*.

RK: The video footage of the death of Alex Wu shows you wearing some sort of occult robe.

SC: Bought right off of eBay or something. Doc Leo was reaching for anything by then. I'd slaughtered the shit out of two people, making it all painful and traumatic, and neither became ghosts. So they wanted to know if adding the woo-woo stuff would help. Woo-woo and Wu. Dumbasses. You go that route, you need to kidnap an altar boy, not a Buddhist. If he was a Buddhist. Chinese. Close enough.

RK: Did the scientists often share their reasoning with you?

SC: Sometimes. If it was need to know, like putting me in a Halloween costume.

RK: Were you ever given a script?

SC: No, man. I'm the improv king.

I stood with my hand over my heart and sang, "O beautiful, for spacious skies, for amber waves of grain" as the girl's eyes bulged a final time and her head fell to the left. The bookcase swiveled, and Doc Leo and the gang came in like they always did after shutting off all the video recordings. Those four were more camera-shy than Bigfoot.

By then I'd learned the murder slab was also a scale and a computer that sent the scientists all kinds of stuff about the victims. More *measurables*. They walked by without looking at me or the girl. They were always skittish about coming into the room after I finished, but this time her age had them freaked out. Hell, they'd selected her. I went on singing as I unwrapped the extension cord from around the girl's neck.

"For purple mountain majesties, above the fruited plain. . ."

"Please stop that, Strad."

"America, Amer—"

"Strad, please! We're trying to capture electronic voice phenomena."

He had a little gadget in his right hand about the size of a cell phone and a microphone in his left. He was waving the microphone all around like someone trying to get an interview. At last, he put it up against the dead girl's lips. That's when I grabbed it and sang, "America! America! God shed his grace on thee!" Then I made a horrific snarling until Doc Leo gave up, and I couldn't quit laughing.

"This is serious business, Strad. After all this, we still haven't gotten any positive results."

"After *all this*? It's four people."

"We've already discussed the need for—"

"What you need is a bigger sample size. Fuck quality, you need quantity. Mass slaughter."

"We obviously can't achieve that."

"You can still do better than one a month."

"There's the matter of acquiring test subjects."

I just shrugged at this and found all of them looking at me with something like wonder. Meanwhile, I started getting out of my shirt. I was sweaty and hating the way it stuck to me. I saw Doc Leo staring, and I figured he was checking out my chest and the one tattoo on my whole body, a square capped with a triangle right over my left pec.

"It's a house, get it?"

Doc Leo kept staring.

"What?"

"Could you really do this more often, Strad? It doesn't—"

"Doesn't what?"

"Bother you?"

"It's a job. I like doing a good job. If I was hired to be a burger flipper, and you told me to flip one burger a month, I'd do it. But I'd also tell you I could flip a few burgers a day if you wanted me to."

He stared at my chest. Looking at my tattoo for sure this time.

"Home is where the heart is," I said.

RK: What do you know about Seve Lopez?

SC: Just an old man. With advanced dementia. I think they were interested in that aspect. Something else to measure. Doc Leo talked about measuring and comparing brain waves of the victims while I was doing my thing. I guess the table could do that.

RK: The biggest surprise of the footage is you don't seem happy to be killing him.

SC: That a fact?

RK: Are you saying it's not?

SC: No.

RK: He seemed to think you were someone named Kip.

SC: Yeah.

RK: We found out who Kip is.

SC: I don't want to know.

RK: He thought you were—

SC: I said I don't fucking want to know!

RK: —his grandson.

They measured whatever the hell it was they measured in silence and left. Watching this one had broken them. We had one more month and one more murder to go if we were sticking to that six-month plan. We weren't a step closer to making a haunted house, but goddamn when I looked at their faces, I saw four haunted people.

Then I saw a fifth.

The house didn't have a ton of mirrors, not real ones at least. There were two-way windows that looked like mirrors to conceal cameras and stuff, but the only real one was in my bathroom. I'd been living in the house the whole time, part of the sweet deal, and I still hadn't heard one bump in the night. But after I killed the old man and the others shut down the recording equipment and left, I got a hard look at myself in my bathroom mirror. And I saw one fucked up individual.

I'd been given a car, but I almost never used it. Once or twice, I'd driven past my mom's house, looking at the yard getting way out of control. This time I just drove until I came to a dumpy town about half an hour away. There was a bar on the main drag, and I went inside and started drinking.

THE MAKING

Kip. . .Kippy, why. . .Kippy. . .

I did a shot for every time the crying old man called me by another guy's name. I did a lot of shots, but I sat around a long time too. Thinking of ghosts. Wondering if they just couldn't be made. My mom had wanted me to believe in God, but I never could until I realized he was just me. That was enough for a long time. It was enough when I killed her, and it was enough when I was in prison.

At some point between the sixth and tenth shot, I knew it wasn't enough anymore and maybe it never had been. Going on, not winking out, always having another thought—these mattered. Heaven, Hell, the clouds, or the flames were just scenery. I didn't care about the backdrop as long as I kept on keeping on.

But there wasn't any of that, was there? I helped prove it. If a billionaire's dollars and a private house and a research team and a table that measured what it measured couldn't make a ghost, that was that.

I left the bar and looked around, forgetting where I parked the car. Then I remembered. As I passed an alleyway, a voice from the dark said, "Hey man."

"What?"

There wasn't an answer. Then, shaking, hungry, the voice said, "I'll do it, man. I really will."

"Okay, do whatever you're going to do. Have fun."

I started away when this kid lunged at me. No way he was even 20, and he stank. His lean face was a mix of scraggly blond beard and pimples and scabs. There were more scabs on his forearms and purple bruises from shooting up.

"I'll suck your dick. Just give me some money, man."

"I'm not gay. I'm not anything."

Addicts are sneaky bastards. I should have seen the little penknife in his right hand. It was silver and made a streak I didn't catch until he was already stabbing it into my right thigh. I clamped down tight on a shriek and then hit the kid in the face. I looked up and down the street, but it was quiet and dark. Nothing anywhere.

I got to the car, bleeding, and got in. The kid came crawling after me. Dragging himself. His right hand stretched at me like that painting on the ceiling. There was something in him any con would recognize. That concrete need. That desire that burns away the flesh. The junkie spits and pisses more genuine religion than Jesus ever did.

RK: You're saying there *was* a sixth murder?

SC: I'm not just saying it; I'm saying the sixth was the only one that mattered.

RK: There's no video of a sixth.

SC: Because it wasn't planned. The scientists weren't even there. I took the kid back to the house. Told him all kinds of stuff about how he could live there. I'd look after him. Some really gay shit.

RK: Just to lure him back?

SC: That's one of the crazy parts, man. *No.* I meant it at the time. I felt like I wanted to protect him.

RK: What do you think accounts for this sudden. . .friendliness?

SC: Sometimes you turn a corner, and you see your reflection walking around fucking up its life.

RK: You identified with him?

SC: Parts of him.

RK: What parts, Strad?

SC: Hunger. Want. Need. See, detective, these are always there. I don't know if they're measurable, but they're there. The things that go on.

THE MAKING

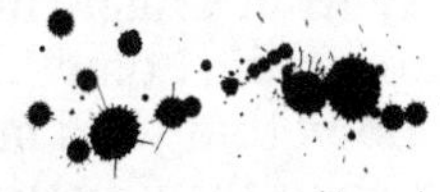

I told him I could get him a score, and he wouldn't have to blow me. He said he was Crash. A druggie's street name.

"Strad," I said. "Short for Stradivarius. You know, the violin."

"Yeah?"

"Got it in high school. Went into the school music room and saw all these violins. I took them by the neck one at a time and smashed them against the wall. The name stuck."

Crash laughed. He made the whole car stink, but I didn't care. I got him home, took him up to my room, and told him to wash up. I left him for twenty minutes: just long enough to microwave a can of chili for him. When I came upstairs, the shower was still going. I sat the bowl down and told him I'd gotten him something to eat. Then I waited. And waited. The chili got cold and the shower went on running.

I opened the bathroom door and found him standing there under the water, swaying on his feet. Looking the way a few guys did in the prison shower, like the water freed them. "I want this," he said, like a chant. "I want what you got."

He jumped at me. His bony body was nothing but sharp edges. He was made of teeth and elbows. As he tackled me to the ground, I realized I'd never been in a fight before. Not once. Nothing with fists. He'd been. Had to have. Knew where to throw punches or else just got lucky. Tagged me in the jaw, the belly, the balls. Bit my face. Bit my neck. I was bleeding all over before I got the upper hand. I bashed his head against the wall and then broke his forehead against the floor. I straddled his back and just kept pounding his head that way until long after he was dead.

I was shaking, even crying, shouting, "Why did you make me? Why?" My fingers were still around his neck, and it was like I could feel a pulse. When I was a kid, I once caught a cat in a pillowcase and watched its paws jab at the cloth. That's how it was now, like Crash's body was the pillowcase. And for a second it felt like his skin tore open. A roar of light, then nothing. I kept my hands in place and heard nothing except the shower water beating the tile.

Then the water stopped. I jerked my head toward the bathroom just as the mirror shattered. As I started to stand, a blow like a kick to the face flung me away from Crash and onto my back. Then I screamed. My body became pain. Something had me by the balls, by the neck, by my hair. Something had me everywhere.

My eyes flashed with color the way they do when you squeeze your eyelids too tight, and in the bursts, I saw Crash's face. He was grinning at me. The house became explosive. Every door opened and slammed shut over and over again. Windows broke. I tried to crawl, but it felt like I had a rope around my neck. Crash wanted me for a pet. He dragged me by that invisible rope into the bathroom and rubbed my face into the broken pieces of mirror. Then he put me on my back and one of those jagged pieces lifted against my right calf and began cutting into the denim.

SC: That's how Crash's ghost talked to me. Cut the words into my hide unless there was other skin to use. You've photographed me head-to-toe bare-assed. You got the proof.

RK: It's your contention that those cuts were not done by yourself?

SC: Crash did them. His ghost.

RK: Let's say I humor this belief of yours. Why do you think the experiment succeeded after so many failures? What was special?

SC: Maybe because it wasn't planned. Maybe a ghost has to be an accident. Or it could be Crash was the only one who wanted to be a ghost. He wanted to die, he wanted to go on, he wanted everything. Sometimes you're burning up so much, you go on burning. Nothing puts it out. I understand that. I really do. Maybe that's why I stayed even though every day in that house was torture. I figured Crash would get around to killing me, and when he did, I'd

become a ghost too. I'd keep on, and we'd haunt
the house together.

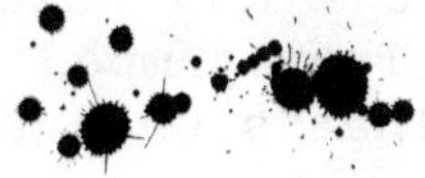

Doc Leo and his team only came around when it was time to do another test. That meant I had about three weeks to myself before I had to deal with them. Most of the time that meant a lot of jerking off, eating, and putting on weight.

Life changed with Crash's ghost.

He—it?—beat me every day. Sometimes I woke up suffocating with a pillow mashed against my face. I'd get sucker punched going down the stairs and land crumpled up at the bottom. No whore, no prison bitch was ever made lower, and after our first week together, every room had my bloodstains on the floor, the walls, sometimes the ceilings. I took to not wearing clothes because Crash would just rip them to shreds anyway. Might as well make it easy to get to the paper.

More.

Everything.

All.

Crash wrote using a broken piece of glass that would fly against my skin and open me up a letter at a time. The writing made me scream and cry, but the tears weren't all from pain. Crash went on. People could keep on if they wanted it bad enough. Wanted it the way Crash did. The way I knew I did. Death wasn't a fact. The system, God's system, could be beaten. Crash was showing me the way.

When you're in prison you sometimes get taken under someone's wing. I'd seen it and remembered how people looked when it happened. The gratitude.

Goddamn, that's just what I felt.

SC: The looks on their faces when they came
back at last and saw me standing there like
someone who's just walked out of a meat

grinder. At first, I could see they didn't understand. Figured I'd been in a fight or something. Then the door slammed shut behind them. Real hard. They jumped the way fireworks make dogs jump. That's when they knew.

RK: What did they think about their success?

SC: Who knows? Five seconds later, their heads got knocked together hard enough to crack their skulls, and they fell on the ground bleeding out their ears. Doc Leo's legs spasmed about a minute, and that's the only movement any of them made again. Crash ate them.

RK: Excuse me?

SC: Don't ask me how it works. I just saw bites taken out of them. Clothes and all. He hamburgered them out of existence. I watched their blood seep along the floor and vanish like it was being sucked up by a straw.

RK: That's an interesting explanation for why the bodies of these alleged researchers haven't been found. Even the cadaver-sniffing dogs turned up nothing.

SC: It's the truth.

RK: That was, by your timeline, three weeks after Crash's death. If I've got the dates right, that means you stayed in the house another two months.

SC: Sounds right.

RK: And you claim you were subjected to supernatural torture the entire time?

SC: Not torture. It was education. Crash was teaching me what it takes to go on.

RK: You look like you've been walking away from a bad car wreck every day of your life.

SC: That feels about right.

RK: You're saying you'd still be in the house if not for the teenagers?

I couldn't even call it hunger now. It was an addiction much worse than heroin. Crash was addicted to life, and I was addicted to the afterlife. Blood and flesh fed both. I was getting closer to dying, which meant I was getting closer to going on.

I thought it was going to happen that night. He floated me to the murder slab and dropped me there. I felt weightless, like the table scale wouldn't even detect me.

A knife hovered over my tattoo. The tip bore down, and I cried out through gritted teeth. Crash was carving a window and doors on the house. Right as he finished, I heard the giggles, the footsteps. Three teenagers had snuck inside. Houses out in the middle of nowhere get reputations in school cafeterias real fast. Maybe it was Truth or Dare and they'd taken the Dare. Didn't matter. They were well and truly fucked.

The knife disappeared faster than I could follow it. The screams started just seconds later. Screams and stomping feet. Crash had split them up. Two were going up to the bedrooms. Right overhead, a boy shouted, "Why the fuck won't the window open?" Meanwhile, I'm trying to get up the stairs, and I hear the living room window break. By the time I reached it, I could see a boy running away from the house. Another boy's head came tumbling down the stairs and rolled up against the front door. As for the third kid, shit, I don't know.

I chased after the runaway about twenty yards before Crash roared from the open front door. A genuine roar. Pure rage. Pure *helplessness*. That's when I understood something. Crash couldn't leave the house. Its walls were his kingdom—and his prison. What would happen if the house burned down? Would that be the end of our going on?

SC: Wasn't going to let that happen. No, sir.

RK: But you didn't chase the kid. It's almost like you let him get away.

SC: The kid's not important. Only Crash matters.

RK: I guess Crash didn't stick around either. We've had teams going all through that house. No ghost. Nothing going bump in the night. Not even a cold spot.

SC: There's a simple reason for that.

RK: I agree. You did all of it. You alone, Strad.

SC: Going on in one place isn't going on. I've given Crash a mobile home. Something I understood from Doc Leo that time he was staring at me.

RK: Keep your shirt on.

SC: Seems I had a vacancy.

RK: Strad, stay seated.

SC: Crash has got to go on. If he don't, I don't.

RK: Sit down, Strad! I need you to—

THE MAKING

[Transcriptionist's note: The recording ends with several as-yet-unidentified sounds, followed by the opening and shutting of a door. The rest of the recording is approximately fifteen minutes of dead air.]

THE BIDDEN

"I CAN'T DO it alone, Wallace! You have to help me!"

"I'm getting help, Am!"

"No, you're not; you're running away! You always run away!"

Am's voice faded as soon as he entered the cornfield under a dark, chilly night sky. This business couldn't wait for the dawn, and Wallace was used to being in the cornfield after sunset. That's when John's voice was strongest, his call most urgent. Now he was the one crying out.

"John?" Wallace said, pushing forward through the rows of gold rustling in the breeze. "Where are you, boy?" He stopped, wincing in sudden pain. His forearm was bleeding, and the edge of the thin leaf to his right was glazed red.

A faint voice came from deep within the cornfield. "I'm here, Papa. But I'm weak."

"I'll feed you."

He touched the cut, forcing more drops from the scratch, and smeared them on the nearest leaf. The stalk shivered.

"I'm very hungry. *Please,* Papa."

Wallace hesitated just a moment. Am had gone silent. Not much time left, and he'd wasted so much already.

"We have to hurry, John. The time has come. I thought we had more."

John's voice seemed little more than a moan, and Wallace stripped off his clothes. It was a chilly day, but far colder ones awaited should he fail. So much wasted time.

I can do this.

He launched himself into the next row.

The leaves nicked and sliced him everywhere, leaving relentless lacerations. Wallace endured it, gritting his teeth, holding his arms out to expose even more of himself. Far from overwhelming him, the pain enlivened all of his senses. His fingertips captured all the complex nuances of the corn. The rough bumps of the husks recalled his cheeks a few days in between shaves, and the silks were warm and soft like Am's thighs at night. The thought of them quickened his pulse and his bleeding.

I won't fail.

The stalks were almost identical, almost seven feet tall and so dense no sense of the world existed beyond them. Wallace pushed through the fifth row, the sixth, the seventh. He stopped then to look down at himself, his body streaked with so many vicious cuts. The leaves were wet with blood, the stalks quivering.

"Take in your fill, boy."

"I'm getting stronger, Papa." The voice seemed no closer and not much stronger than before. He closed his eyes for a moment and urged his son to keep feeding.

Wallace nevertheless went with greater caution when he resumed his pursuit, trying to protect his flesh from further cuts. "John? Am I close, John?"

Row twenty. . .row thirty. . .

He was about to shoulder his way into the thirty-second row when he saw John clawing his way toward him. Wallace took a few steps and fell to his knees as he welcomed his son into a fierce embrace. He'd clad his son in his own clothes, the shirt far too large for the boy, the pants dragging below the waist as flat as a fallen flag.

"My sweet son," Wallace said, caressing the soft silk of his hair before moving on to the much rougher skin of his cheeks. "I'm sorry I had to leave you this way."

"I can't fight like this, Papa."

"I know."

"Find my legs. There's no other way."

Wallace straightened his back and looked down the last row of unshucked stalks. "They have to be here," he said.

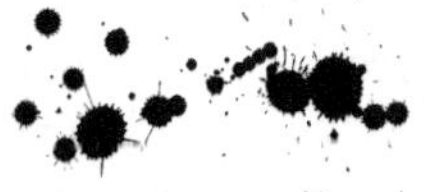

I hate this life, Amanda told herself as she entered the pantry, listening to Wallace and the others talking in the kitchen after they'd finished clearing and tilling the fields. Wallace seemed happy, but she knew he hated them. As soon as they were gone, he'd start ranting about their *arrogant wisdom*. They'd taken his money but told him he'd purchased terrible land. She did not know their reasoning, but she also didn't doubt them. Wallace had been a rich shoesmith in Boston before the war, and she'd assumed he would spirit his bride back to Massachusetts and the comforts of city life. He'd said nothing about becoming a farmer in Connecticut.

"We'll show them, Am," he said last night as they stood on the porch. "Come harvest time, it's going to be nothing but crops as far as you can see. I promise you that."

He'd left her there staring out into the night as her hands lingered on her stomach. It had been a long day, and her lower back was always hurting. She'd complained about it in the last letter to her mother in Georgia, whose response had come that very morning. *I was eight months with you before my lower back gave me problems. And you only three months along! This must mean God's blessed you with a very large son, or perhaps even twins!*

Oh yes, she thought. God has *blessed* me.

She bent to pick up a burlap sack of flour only to have it spill on the floor. The field mice had chewed the corners despite every effort to secure the pantry. This is how it's going to be, she thought, dropping the bag to put her head in her hands. Every damn day. Unrelenting. More awful than the worst days when the Northern army ransacked the land.

And all because of *this!*

Before Amanda could stop herself, she made a fist and pounded it against her stomach. She gasped at her action.

Then a single trickle of fluid tickled her thighs.

Another followed.

There wasn't a bit of pain, yet in moments she found herself standing in a puddle of amber and red liquid, the amber much thicker than the red. The spilled flour began to suck up the fluid and clump into little pink balls.

The boisterous talk from the kitchen continued. Amanda had the uncanny feeling that Wallace and the men were laughing at her. She imagined standing before them in this state, leaking, silent. Would they leap to help her? Would they turn away in disgust? They were farmers, not doctors. She saw them putting her down on the floor and stripping her, treating her like any sheep at lambing time. Filthy hands expert at pulling calves and foals from wombs would control and handle her.

No.

She slipped out of the pantry, skirted the kitchen door, and crept to the front room. The floorboards creaked under the slightest weight but no one heard her. No one called for her. She looked back at the trail of fluid. No way to hide it. Nothing to be done.

Amanda went outside, made her way down the three simple steps, and staggered toward the barren field, all the while thinking, what have I done?

The land was so expansive, so empty. The forest line offered the only plausible concealment, and it stood a mile to the north. She gazed off into the distance, craving that privacy just as the first jolt of actual pain made her double over. No, she thought, not here. Not in all this openness. What if Wallace or any of the men should see?

The ground shifted and stirred all around her. At first, she thought fingers were coming up out of the earth. Then she saw it was the corn shooting up, stalk after stalk, rising around her like the bars of a cage. But as the rows formed and the stalks climbed higher, Amanda thought of them as a curtain. A curtain, a wall, a shield. She knew none of this should be possible, but her immediate gratitude for concealment took pride of place over credence. Amanda gasped and fell to her knees, legs spread wide. She just got her underclothes out of the way before three powerful convulsions, each a whiplash, made her rock and grit her teeth.

"I'm sorry, I'm sorry, I'm so sorry," she said, sobbing out the words while her hands moved over her stomach like some fortune teller with a crystal ball. "I didn't mean to, I never meant to—*God, please help me. Please help my child.*"

The only help seemed to be the swiftness of the expulsion. It was over in a few breaths, and then she rested on all fours, panting, refusing to look anywhere but straight ahead as her mind began to accept reality. The cornfield was gone. She was exposed in the dirt not a hundred yards from the house. The rows must have been a fantasy born of desperation.

I must get up. I must. . .go on, she thought.

Amanda managed to stand, straightening her clothes as best

she could. She turned, determined to walk to the house. Then she closed her eyes. The baby, her *child*, deserved better. Deserved acknowledgement. Taking a ragged breath, she looked down. The mess was at her feet.

"I'm sorry. I'm so very sorry."

Amanda covered her face in her hands to keep from screaming and kicked dirt over the bits of flesh and kept kicking until there was just a little mound. There, she thought. The child is buried and honored. The best I can do.

It took all of her strength to walk into the house as if nothing had occurred. She slipped into the bedroom and made a discreet change of clothes, then swept up the pantry, and neither Wallace nor the men noticed anything special about her. She didn't say anything, and that night, in bed, Wallace placed his hand on her stomach and said, "How was the lad today?"

"Fine," she whispered, not knowing what to tell him.

And she went on not knowing, day after day, week after week, month after month, as she grew larger and larger with child.

Three weeks after her misfortune, when Amanda's confusion and uncertainty were still fresh, Wallace came to her laughing as he tugged her arm and pulled her away from the stove. "You have to see this, Am!"

She yielded to his enthusiasm and they went out to the porch.

"Wallace—*how*?"

"It's just like Jack and his everlovin' beanstalk," he said, stomping his right foot. "Those fools kept telling me I'd bought the worst farmland in all of Connecticut. That my yields would be low, that I'd have to work five times as hard just to get by. Let them come see what I call *getting by!*"

It was as if an army of soldiers outfitted in bright green uniforms with caps of yellow tassels had marched on the house overnight and stood now awaiting inspection in perfect, silent rows. Wallace proved an eager general as he bounded off the porch, jumping up and down in his boyishness. He spread his arms wide as if to hug the entirety of the scene and said, "We'll call it Caine's miracle corn! A dollar—*two dollars!*—per ear. A drop of corn whisky made from Caine cobs will cure any rheumatism. Hell, just one kernel will. . ."

He waxed on about his grand visions, but Amanda found she had to turn away. The longer she stared at the corn, the more unsettled she felt. She touched her stomach and wondered about the—incident? Fantasy? *Misunderstanding?* She dared not even ask her mother if her experience had been natural. If she didn't have the stained clothing to remind her, she would have considered the occurrence a fever dream.

"Am, what's wrong with you?"

"Nothing," she said, forcing herself to look back at the field. She soon realized something that had escaped Wallace's notice. Only the corn had sprouted. The other crops—beans, squash, potatoes, and barley—weren't present. The farm was now one crop's dominion, and she had the nagging feeling that among the brotherhood of seeds, the corn had killed all rivals.

The cornfield's impossible existence brought them into immediate conflict with their neighbors. At first, they accused Wallace of mere trickery. These allegations soon took a darker, vicious twist. The traveling ministers quit making themselves known at the farm, and the pastor of their church, located several miles to the east, banished them from his flock. Wallace couldn't offer compensation high enough to bring even the most destitute of workers. Their isolation grew until the last time Amanda chanced upon people; it was in the form of four young men on horseback who leered at her from the road.

The brashest of them said, "Is it true?"

"Is *what* true?"

They fixed on her with a collective bold stare and relayed a disgusting story about a pact between Wallace and the Devil, with her as an infernal offering, the deal sealed through unbridled intimacy with a robust ear of corn. Amanda spat at them, but they were already riding away, lashing her with echoing laughter.

She was six months along then and writing letters to her mother almost every day, filled with lies about happiness. The only truth was how she described Wallace's bedroom habit of placing one hand on her stomach as he bestowed a long, lingering kiss. He'd drift off soon after, and she'd fall asleep to the steady sound of his snoring only to wake hours later to a silent room, an unshared bed. As this habit continued night after night, Amanda began searching for Wallace. He was not inside nor in the outhouse. She sought him from the porch but found only the corn rows standing still and quiet, their greenery almost black in the moonlight. A sudden motion startled her—a mother possum skirted the edge of the field with several babies clinging to her, so that her back seemed infested with an outbreak of living boils, her spine erupting with bright, black eyes that glittered at Amanda in passing. Unnerved, she retreated to the bedroom and shut the door.

But the question of his ongoing absences plagued her to the point that she broached the subject at breakfast. His surprise seemed genuine. "I didn't know that I was anywhere except beside you, Am. Maybe the lad is starting to make you have strange dreams."

That night she woke up, felt to confirm his absence, and pinched herself to affirm reality. She returned to the porch, drawn by the certainty he was out there in the corn. She stood with the vigilance of an army sentinel, looking at the stalks, alert to every subtle rustle that might give away her husband's movements. Amanda felt herself becoming mesmerized by the corn rows. She was sure a voice whispered, "Mama." She stifled a small cry, pressing her fingertips against her lips.

The voice spoke again.

"Mama."

Half-stumbling down the steps, cradling her belly with her left arm, she walked the front row of stalks. "Who's there?" she said. "Is it a child? Are you lost?"

She was about to penetrate the first row when a stabbing pain came from her womb. She fell back, retching from a powerful wave of sickness. As soon as it passed, she made a half-hearted attempt to go forward, only to get another dose of pain and nausea. The baby seemed to be stomping against the wall of her uterus.

"Okay, okay," she whispered, backing off. There was no relief until she got back onto the porch. She stood there gasping for breath, and as the baby settled, she wiped away a trace of tears and went on listening for a voice that never spoke again.

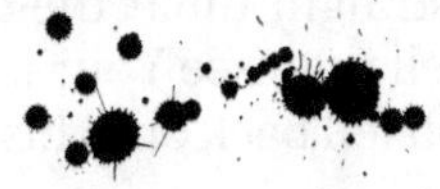

"John," Wallace said, sitting up in the middle of a corn row. His son wasn't there. Wallace had been searching for him all night and only intended a little rest when he stretched himself out on the ground and fell into a most unpleasant sleep, plagued with dreams of his life in Boston.

He'd seemed destined to be a cobbler and cordwainer. His grandfather and father were shoesmiths, and he had apprenticed under them since his twelfth birthday. But after two years, he still had trouble carving shoe lasts that met his father's standards. "You've failed to capture the curve of the arch, Wallace. You would excel at making shoes for flat-footed men; no one else would ever want to be shod by you."

Wallace was still a boy, and so his father could afford mirth. But as fifteen became seventeen, and seventeen became twenty, Wallace showed no improvement despite his best efforts, which poisoned his thoughts against continuing further. This in turn enraged his father, who used every threat he had, including dying. Wallace found Father dead in his workshop, done in by exhaustion from a long line of orders and an inadequate apprentice. Wallace stared at the cold corpse in that early morning hour, and it seemed like half of Boston was clamoring outside the door, asking a single collective question: *"Where are my shoes?"*

He drew the blinds as a fit of madness overtook him. He was filled with sudden dedication and determination and a quixotic belief that death had granted him all of Father's abilities and skill. Lasts were carved and sanded, leather stretched, soles pounded into place. The work went on for hours, broken only by the occasional sly glance at Father, who now seemed a figure of impassive judgment. When Wallace finished at nightfall, he brought the shoes by the armful and placed them before the corpse. The moment passed suffused with triumph, but only a moment. Some of the shoes fell apart at once, and others revealed themselves to be mere strips of leather nailed to wood. Most of the lasts were little more than unshaped blocks. His dead father stayed dead.

Wallace cursed God then. His anger and frustration left no

ambiguity. He looked straight up at the ceiling and said, "I hate You! I'd rather rot in Hell than see Your face, you bloody bugger!" Then he spat, but the gob fell back onto his face, and he didn't wipe it away.

He lost consciousness, and when he awoke, he found row upon row of shoes made with a craftsmanship far outstripping that of his grandfather or father. Then he heard singing and a light but steady tapping sound. The workshop was full of little creatures no more than a foot tall, human in appearance but naked and covered in dense, dark hair that was wet and beaded from their exertions. Their noses projected out in orange, narrow points, like the tips of raw carrots. Their sweat had a foul odor, and they were free with their flatulence as they labored over the wood and the leather.

"What in heaven?" Wallace whispered.

This earned a sharp look of rebuke from the little workers, who stopped and stared at him in unison. Then their obvious leader came forward, his dangling sex organ almost as large as his body. Wallace backed up two paces and held out his hands, begging it to stop.

"What. . .what are you?"

The answer came in rough English, as if the speaker struggled to shape the words.

"Help."

Wallace couldn't conceive how a single syllable could contain such a rumble, a simple word so much menace. The word was spat out like phlegm.

"You cursed God. When you curse God, you also curse His help, and its favor is withdrawn forever. This bids the Others to come to your aid."

"But I didn't ask for help!"

The little creature's smile showed many teeth.

"We were bidden. We are here."

They returned to their work and their singing. The language was incomprehensible, but Wallace went on listening as he watched these strange workers complete shoe after shoe, most as large or larger than themselves. They seemed so eager, so happy to be laboring. But here and there Wallace found hints of discontent in a snide, side-eye glare that never lasted much longer than a second.

As the process continued, he noticed the newest shoes were a beige color unlike any cowhide, and he remembered his father saying he was running short on leather. He bent to pick up one of the newer shoes and touched the smooth, waxy surface. It did not feel or smell like any leather he knew. It was then he heard a peeling sound like when a butcher is cutting and tearing the hide from a carcass, and he saw Father's body spread naked on the floor in a corner. The Bidden were flaying the skin off his stomach and thighs and passing along the strips for stretching. Wallace's guts churned at the sight of it, and he was saved by the emptiness of his stomach. He turned and ran upstairs and barricaded himself in his room, crouched by the door, all his weight propped against it.

He fell asleep to the Bidden's tireless work song.

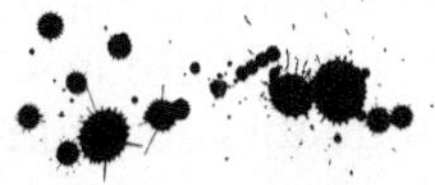

Wallace fell in love with the land as soon as he saw it and found it no less fetching as he stood alone on his new property under moonlight. This was a place for fresh starts. He knew nothing of farming, but he was sure he could do it. How hard could it be?

The optimism—the hope—flashed in his mind, making him smile. Then came the usual doubts, the rude awakening from the dream. How was he supposed to clear all this land? Where would he live? There was no home, and what did he know about building a house? Too much, too much. He put the butt of his hands against his temples and tried to drive the fears away.

He'd slipped.

Wallace didn't need to hear the Bidden's song to realize it. They came marching toward him out of the weeds, out of the dark, grinning. Wallace held out his hands and told them to leave. Begged them. But their work song grew louder. Yes, he had fallen into their trap through lack of confidence, allowing them to find him again. Five years earlier, he'd ducked out of his prosperous shoe shop in the middle of the night and rode to the nearest Union camp to enlist as an army soldier. The Bidden's work had made him a very wealthy man, but he could not escape their presence. They surrounded him day and night, working and singing.

He was, in hindsight, hoping to escape them by dying in battle. At Gettysburg, he charged alone toward a Confederate brigade, exposing himself to gunfire on a field as open as the one he stood in now. But the moment of truth exposed his true cowardice, his inevitable desire to live. The Bidden appeared at once with their hateful aid, rising from the ground, springing up one by one to take the bullets otherwise destined for his head and heart. They swarmed the astonished Confederate front line, chewing out their eyes, biting into their Adam's apples, decapitating, castrating, leaving Wallace standing there among a pile of enemy dead and shouting at his saviors in full-throated hypocrisy, as if he didn't know how they'd found him again.

"I don't want your help! Leave me alone!"

"We are bidden."

Their smiles were still bright and toothy as they set about erecting the house necessary to anchor his dream. Wallace got on his horse and rode away from it. Rode with all his might, vowing to never again entertain doubts about himself and summon this vile, inescapable crutch.

He rode south, retracing the path he'd gone as a soldier. Georgia had intoxicated him despite its ruin. He'd found the women there charming in their naivete, their simplicity. Just the sort of wife to help anchor him in a new life. Am's father had died during the war but not from fighting, and she seemed to bear him no ill will for being a Northerner. Their courtship was brief, their wedding ceremony short, the return to Connecticut immediate. A week later they were settled in a traveler's inn only twenty miles from the farmland.

"I feel like I'm only now getting a chance to breathe," he said as he took off his jacket. Turning, he saw Am had shed all of her clothing. Her face was flushed, her breasts pearled with beads of sweat. Wallace looked at the only door with a feeling like he'd been tricked and trapped. He knew it was absurd. They were married. There were expectations of him—a husband's duties. But what did *she* know about that, innocent as she was?

Or was she not?

Am all but tore away his clothes, laughing as she attacked. Her spirit was lascivious, vulgar, alluring. She got onto the bed and writhed, voluptuous by candlelight. The realization that he had to perform filled his chest with a leaden weight. *What* were her standards? *How* had she come by them? *Who* had set them? Each question made his penis shyer, until he stood there all but slapping himself below the waist in urgency.

THE BIDDEN

I can do this, he thought. I'm a man with a beautiful wife. She loves me, and that's all that matters. There's no doubt. This is my moment to prove myself once and for all.

He stiffened and rose. He laughed, half in relief, and flung himself atop Am. How he tried! But each maneuver and thrust of his hips met with failure. He felt like a man trying to use a little dessert fork with its dainty tines to stab at a side of beef. Bathing with soldiers during the war taught him that he was not well endowed, but Am seemed not to care. She urged him on and this enthusiasm, far from alleviating any embarrassment, only increased his frustration. Could it be possible he just wasn't large enough to do the deed?

Wallace sobbed, still trying, still failing. He didn't realize he'd slipped again until the work song of the Bidden rose from a dark corner of the room. Am seemed oblivious to both the sound and the sudden presence of a single creature already climbing onto the bed as it sang a solitary but eager tune. Wallace kicked at it. As he did, one of his thrusts managed to strike home. He continued to fight off the Bidden and fuck his wife, and the promise of success brought him to a quick orgasm. It must have been very good, because Amanda seemed to lose consciousness, which only made him more sure of himself.

"It's done! See? I didn't need your help! Go away!"

To his horror, though, Wallace saw the Bidden wouldn't relent. He could not knock it from the bed or pry it away from its task. Its member was engorged and much larger than Wallace's offering. Amanda was soon moaning and thrashing, calling out his name, her eyes shut and by all evidence quite oblivious to his absence. Defeated, Wallace sank down in the corner, knees drawn against his chest as he listened to his wife's ecstasy and the Bidden's cheerful work song.

He thought of his reputation as a shoesmith. He thought of how he survived the war. He thought of the very farmhouse he was about to occupy—none of it his doing, none of it a credit to personal skill.

But I was first tonight, he told himself. I satisfied my wife on my own. And she'll have a son, and he'll be mine—because I *was* first.

Wallace thought of the boy to come. He thought of his child as a perfect shoe, the sort he'd dreamed of making from the earliest days of his apprenticeship but always fell so short of achieving.

Yes, *my* son. Because I was first.

My shoe, my own perfect shoe, made by me alone—*at last.*

He went to sleep content and confident about the future, quite forgetting that shoes must come in pairs.

After Wallace discovered the cornfield in the morning, dread blunted his initial elation. Wasn't this the work of the Bidden? He was sure he hadn't slipped, but the mockery of the hired men was so great he couldn't be sure.

Then John made his presence known.

His son's voice came to him that night, compelling him to rise and go to the porch. *"Come and find me, Papa."*

The words startled him so much that he hurried back to the bedroom to make sure Am was sleeping. Staring at the steady rise and fall of her stomach, he said, "John?" They'd both decided on the name. John for a boy, Mary for a girl.

"I'm out here. Hurry, Papa. Find me."

How could a fetus talk? How could his son be in the womb yet speaking to him from the cornfield? Yet he had no real doubt. His knowledge of the Bidden had eliminated all skepticism for the supernatural, and in the Army, he'd met a man who used to play tricks on the regiment's lieutenant by throwing his voice to make it seem like he was talking from across the room or outside a tent.

Wallace did not find John that night or the next several, as his son kept pleading to him. His frustration grew. John's voice seemed to come from everywhere, making it impossible to isolate a direction. Many times, he stopped to take deep breaths and remind himself not to slip. He did *not* need the Bidden's help. He *could* do this on his own.

Couldn't he?

"I don't know where I am, Papa. I can't see you."

"Keep talking, John. I know I'm getting closer."

Wallace closed his eyes. His son's face appeared in his imagination, not as a newborn but as an older lad, maybe nine or ten years old. A fine-looking, towheaded boy. He went in one direction, and the face got smaller. He went in the opposite direction and the face grew larger. There, he thought. Now I have the trick.

THE BIDDEN

Keeping his eyes shut, he walked. Soon John's face was so large he might have been standing nose to nose with his son. He bumped into a stalk and opened his eyes. The stalk yielded a single ear of corn, but the husk seemed deformed, the cob as round as a gourd. Even lacking any experience with crops, he knew something was wrong. He cupped the ear in both hands, feeling its heft. The ear broke off in the next instant, and John screamed.

His cry came from the ear, muffled by many husks.

"Papa, I'm scared. I can't see, I can't breathe!"

Trembling, Wallace knelt, set the round ear on the ground, and began ripping away the husks. As he peeled away the fourth layer, blood bubbled out of the opening, followed by a choking cough. Wallace gasped but kept at it. A head was emerging out of the interior, nestled in a bed of stained, sodden silk. It was almost featureless like a wig stand, with subtle depressions where the eyes, nose, ears, and mouth should be. The skin was printed like a cob's kernels, rough to the touch, the crevices filled with blood.

Wallace was shamed by feelings of revulsion, telling himself this was no worse a mess than any newborn's appearance in the world. He recovered his wits when John's voice spoke from within the head.

"I can't see you, Papa. But I feel your touch."

Wallace blinked away tears.

"My son," he said.

After this discovery, Wallace refused to ask further questions, though they were there in multitude. The ears he'd intended to harvest and sell now became untouchable, for any might contain the rest of his boy. He hid John's head deep inside the field, protected and pillowed by an old shirt. He returned to his son every night and carried the head as he went stalk to stalk, breaking off and husking ears in search of John's body.

He'd left a long trail of cobs in his wake before he peeled back a husk that started to bleed. Wallace knelt in excitement, placed John's head aside, and took care shucking the rest of the ear. The cob was bloody but otherwise ordinary. At first. Rotating it, he discovered two open eyes blinking amid the kernel rows. The eyes widened as he held it up to his face.

"Papa, I can see you!"

Wallace grinned. His boy had beautiful, kind brown eyes. But how was he to free them? Digging them out seemed too risky by far. He turned the cob over in his hand, gave a shake, and the eyes sagged into his waiting palm on two thick tendrils of slime. Wallace rolled and angled the cob until the tendrils broke, and then he hunched close to John's head and let the first eye slide down his fingers and settle into place. A little flash of light followed, and the eye seemed fixed into position. The same happened with the second.

"How's that, John?"

"Wonderful! Thank you, Papa!"

"I'll have you puzzled out yet, lad," Wallace said and rose with renewed vigor to find the rest of his son.

As the weeks passed, he kept scavenging. He found John's mouth, and his son's smile was as sweet as he'd imagined. The stalks did not offer his body in linear order, leaving the assembly crude and rough. The arms came in three installments: shoulders, forearms, and hands. The hands at least came with fingers intact. John began clawing and dragging his way down the rows, following Wallace and his trail of shucked cobs. The boy often seemed playful, but there came an incident that left him very serious.

"Ouch," Wallace said, pulling back his hand. "The leaves on these stalks are like razors. I feel like I have a hundred papercuts on my right arm alone."

As he put his mouth to the new cut, he saw John staring up at him, his attention fixed on the little line of blood there.

"What is it, son?"

"I'm hungry."

"What would you like? I'll go get it for you now, as much of it as you want."

"Blood," John said.

Wallace flinched. "Say that again?"

"I need blood, Papa."

"No," Wallace said, shaking his head. "No, no, you're a regular boy. Bread and porridge, water, milk, bacon—"

"Blood."

John turned and began writhing along the ground, pulling himself forward one hand at a time. He begged his father to follow, and Wallace did, hesitant for the first time. John led him to a place in the cornfield he'd not seen before, a little hollow he'd made for himself. It was strewn with small animal bones. Mice, rats. The largest was a possum, accompanied by the remains of several babies.

His gorge rose as he comprehended the scene. He was only just able to say, "What have you done?" before he had to turn away in an effort to hold back his rising gorge.

"Blood is blood, Papa. Mine raised the corn."

"It didn't. It couldn't. Why do you think so?"

"Because I fell from Mama out here."

"But you didn't fall from your mother. She's pregnant with you. She—"

Wallace bowed his head. The greatest of all the confusions he'd willed himself to ignore was crossing through his thoughts like cannon fire. He shrieked and looked straight at the Godless sky.

"Blood," he said. "Are you one of *them*?"

"I'm your son, Papa."

"Then what's inside—"

He turned and ran as fast as he could back to the house.

As Amanda entered the last month of pregnancy, she quit waking at night. Her sleep became deep and occupied by carnal dreams that disturbed her morning memory. In her dreams, she was a woman of lustful abandon, and Wallace kept coming to her for tireless sessions, his sex engorged and predatory. There was so much pain, so much tearing, and he thrusted as if he aimed to reach into her womb itself.

And all the while he sang.

She couldn't conceive of how her imagination conjured the song, certain she'd never heard its like before. It began as a song of seduction, and somewhere along the way, it became a song of triumph, like the drumbeat of the Yankee army marching through Georgia. Seduction turned subjugation. The tonal change made her clench up every time, and Wallace's climax always happened at the apex of her fright. Then he'd move down her body, trailing his tongue down her torso to wet the firm rise of her stomach. Wallace then placed his mouth wide against her naval and made a little trill from his throat that sent the baby into a series of vigorous kicks.

She was singing the song in her sleep when Wallace came and shook her awake, his expression haunted and mad. Amanda gaped at him, and he looked at his hands and backed away a step, his Adam's apple bobbing. Cuts covered his hands and arms.

"Wallace, what are you—"

"That song," he said.

"What song?"

"The one you were singing. Where did you hear it?"

"In. . .in a dream."

His eyes bulged wider than she'd ever seen.

"What happened in the cornfield, Am?"

Trembling, she eased herself out of bed, cradling her belly under her left arm. Wallace pulled it away and grabbed her shoulders.

"Am, you listen to me. Did something happen to you out in that cornfield?"

"I never go out there, Wallace, you know that."

"Not ever?"

She shook her head as he looked her up and down.

"And that song?" he said. "You say you hear it in your dreams?"

She nodded.

"Who sings it?"

Amanda swallowed. "You do, Wallace."

He backed away, not looking her in the eyes. He was just staring at her stomach with obvious loathing.

"What's wrong with you, Wallace?"

"You just stay right in this room. Don't leave it. Get back on the bed."

Her voice became a plaintive whine. *"Why?"*

"Just do as I say!"

In the next instant, he was out the door. She listened to him muttering as he went back and forth in the house. Then he left. A few minutes of silence followed before she heard the sound of the horse being saddled. Wallace galloped away moments later.

She couldn't remember the last time he left the farm.

Amanda sat there half-convinced she was in a fever dream. She took very slow, uncertain steps out of the bedroom to the porch. The sickness she'd experienced months earlier, when she tried to enter the cornfield, had grown to the point that she couldn't bring herself to even look at it from here.

Why was he asking her about it? Where had he gone?

A rustling came from deep within the rows. She could see the movement of the tassels like a ripple across water. She fought off waves of nausea as she tried to follow the motion. What could be making it? Some animal?

Some person?

Amanda hurried back inside and shut and locked the door. She waited in the kitchen and watched the sunlight move and then dwindle on the windowsill.

Wallace returned just before nightfall. He called her name and banged on the door hard enough to rattle it. Then he broke it open and stormed into the kitchen.

"There's no one to help us. No doctor. No midwife. No priest."

He went to the cutlery board and picked up a knife. Amanda looked to her left and right. There was nowhere to run.

All of her existence shrunk to the point of that blade.

"What happened out there, Am?"

"Nothing—"

"*Don't* say nothing! I know it's not nothing. Our *son's* out there."

So that's it, she thought. He's discovered the mess.

But what would it look like after all this time? It'd been unrecognizable to her as anything. Just blood and tissue. Nothing formed. And what came out couldn't have been the baby anyway. The proof bulged in front of her.

Amanda babbled out a description of her experience. It felt strange, like confessing to infidelity. Wallace had a blank expression as he listened. Then he astonished her with a burst of tears.

"He's alive, Am. Our John is alive."

"Of course he is," she said, touching her stomach.

"No, not that *thing*. I mean our son. He's out there in the field, a regular John Barleycorn. *John*—ha! I've been putting him together piece by piece, meaning to surprise you."

He's gone mad, she thought.

Wallace took a step closer. She took one back.

"Since we're telling secrets, I'll tell mine."

She listened as he cried out an offensive, impossible tale—

impossible until he talked about the song. Then she knew it was all true, and she looked down at her stomach with complete disgust. Her bottom lip trembled.

"Like twins," she said. "But two different fathers. And the other tried to kill our son. Tried to force him out of me—*did* force him out of me. Oh, Wallace, I remember how awful it was. I didn't know how to tell you, but then when my belly kept growing, I figured I'd been wrong. What am I going to give birth to?"

"Something awful."

Amanda nodded. Her own certainty was now absolute.

He handed her the knife and retreated. She gaped at him. "Wallace?"

"I can't, Am. I don't know how to do it."

"Like I do?"

He turned. "Just. . .just be quick."

"Wallace!"

He ran from the kitchen. She followed him to the porch. The corn rows, so dark and quiet under the moonlight, seemed to be leaning toward the house in expectation.

"I can't do it alone, Wallace! You have to help me!"

He jumped down and started into the corn.

"I'm getting help, Am!"

"No, you're not; you're running away! You always run away!"

He disappeared into the rows.

Wallace heard Amanda's scream as he threw down another worthless ear of corn. "Am," he said, turning toward the house. He closed his eyes. "You've got a coward for a father, John. A coward and a fool."

"That's not true," John said, holding on to a stalk as he balanced on his right foot. His left was missing.

Amanda screamed again.

"I have to go to her. I shouldn't have left her. I had a notion you could help, but I was just running away. We both knew it."

"I can help, Papa. But I can't fight standing on one leg."

Wallace looked back at the corn. The field's last six stalks waited. He shouted and grabbed the next ear, tearing at the husk.

Another cob. He tossed it aside and moved down the row with John hopping behind him.

Amanda screamed a third time, and Wallace cursed. He couldn't keep a hideous image out of his mind.

He broke off the next ear and pulled on the husk. Blood gushed out, and he saw wiggling toes in the opening.

"I have it!" Wallace shouted, turning and kneeling. He positioned the foot at the ankle, and it fused into place with another flash of light. John rolled the foot back and forth and put his weight on it. He stood strong.

"It is good."

"Come, then," Wallace said, turning to face the house. "We have to help your—"

John grabbed his wrist with enough force to snap it. The pain blinded Wallace a moment and drove him to his knees. He looked up. He'd seen John smile many times, but never grin. He recognized the boy's teeth.

John had his father's teeth.

The boy moved forward, dragging Wallace along with him. He tried to thrash out of John's grip, but it was inescapable. The boy's tread thundered, shaking and snapping the tall stalks.

"Yes, I'll help you kill the baby," he said. "Your son who overcame me, who usurped my place and had my mother spread her legs and spit me ill-formed into the dirt."

Wallace screamed. "Am!" he shouted. "Am, if you can hear me—*the baby*—"

"I only hope she's not already carved it out herself," John said. "I like my meals fresh."

They were out of the cornfield in another minute. Wallace was dragged over the dirt and then up onto the porch and into the house. John threw him across the floor in the kitchen, and he landed in a corner. Am was on the ground too, legs spread, blood pooling around her. She was sobbing, pleading. The knife lay next to her. The blade was clean.

John got on all fours in front of Am and peered between her legs. His teeth scissored as he moved his jaw and drew back his lips. "*Fresh.*" He dipped his head and lapped at the blood, and his whole body shivered like a cornstalk.

Am cried out again. Even helpless as she was in the throes of labor, Wallace saw her trying to kick at the thing that had tricked him, trying to fight. His right hand, his good hand, was broken and mangled, but he could at least try too. Pitching himself toward Am, he grabbed the knife with his left hand and slashed. The blade struck John in the shoulder and lodged there in the thick, kernel-like ridges of his flesh. The impact was solid, ineffective, and felt like he'd tried to stab the trunk of an oak tree.

John pulled the knife free and laughed.

My baby will die, Wallace thought. Then he'll kill me and Am. There's nothing else I can do. Why did I ever think I could protect—

His eyes widened.

He didn't slip. He fell. He plunged himself over the cliff of failure. "I can't," he said. "I can't do it. It's hopeless. I can't protect them. I can't save them. *I can't kill you!*"

"No," John said. "You can't."

A familiar song crept into the kitchen from outside. The singing grew, overwhelming even the noise of Am's labor. John and Wallace both looked to the doorway as one, two, three creatures appeared there. Many more massed behind them, all singing. Their leader stood in front of them all, showing his teeth, identical to John's.

"The only thing I want to do is kill you, John," Wallace said. "Kill you, destroy you. But I can't. I'm a failure. I'll never succeed on my own."

He looked to see their reaction.

The singing stopped. The leader showed Wallace an expression of icy loathing.

"You made my shoes, saved my life, built my house, and fucked my wife—because I couldn't do it on my own. Because you're *bidden*. Now. . .*help me*."

The leader looked at John, and his expression softened. Wallace saw true regret there, almost human. Then he stepped back, and the others charged past him, swarming over John, latching onto him with their teeth. He fought back. His own teeth decapitated one head and then another. But the Bidden were too many. They clung to his arms and legs like squirrels hanging off corn cobs, devouring.

And singing.

John screamed and went on screaming even as his voice dwindled. His last breath was replaced by a new one: the cries of a baby slick and bloody on the kitchen floor, its writhing arms batting at the thick umbilical cord. Am sobbed in relief as Wallace scooted himself alongside her and held her as best he could.

No trace of John remained, and the Bidden left. All but their leader, who stood alone casting a look of pure spite and hatred at the newborn. The bitter creature sneered and spat toward Amanda. Its saliva landed near her feet and sizzled, leaving a scorch mark in the wood. Wallace stiffened, his fright growing anew, and he moved to stand beside his wife and son, preparing for its attack. But the Bidden took no further action. Its disappointment and sorrow were evident, its shuffling walk depressed. It turned one time at the kitchen entryway to glare back at them and point at Am.

"Only because of your choice," the Bidden said, and left.

BFG

THE LEFT SIDE of Captain Seim's face is scar tissue I feel compelled to touch and say, *be healed.*

"Be fucked!" Mabrey says, his overheating pulse rifle glowing blue with energy.

We've got thirty defenders, down from the fifty who staved off the first attack a day ago. This is the fourth, and Captain Seim hasn't lost a soldier since. The man doesn't repeat tactical mistakes, but it's still thirty versus thousands. A four-armed demon with a goat's head powers through the merciless ordnance and leaps over their line. Mabrey pivots, tracking it the entire time, and vaporizes the fiend before biological vision could notice its pearly claws, its flesh like flayed innards spotted with dozens of tiny, dead-black eyes. His weapon's muted, almost gentle report is so at odds with the death bolts unleashed.

During the week-long jump to Jeru, Mabrey showed me the rifle often, calling it *Jessica* and saying things like, "This girl is my one and only. She loves it when I finger her," while making a show of caressing the trigger. He grins at me now and says, "Hey, Father Robot, Padre Tin Man, better say a prayer for the deceased. Jessica just flashed them, and the Angel of the Lord died from his own exploding hard-on."

I've quit correcting him about angels. Like everyone on Earth, he doesn't believe in angels or demons. I wonder what he believes he's fighting.

"Mabrey, eyes front!"

The corporal turns, and we both study the dark sky and murky plain below the Grand Chapel. The soldiers wear goggles that blaze red, making their faces look like skulls with hellfire eyes. A demonic legion stampedes toward us. Some soar through the fiery ozone, others gallop through the blackened landscape like frenzied beasts. They've changed tactics too. Their bodies are coalescing into something that could blot out a star.

"That's different," Mabrey says.

Captain Seim orders a ceasefire. No one questions it. I watch his head move back and forth. The demons get closer. Their snarls rip the air, and still he stands impassive.

"Got it," he says, shouting targeting solutions. He divides his soldiers into six groups of five, all firing at different targets. Their energy weapons strike the collective body in the pressure points he identified, and the demonic horde shatters with a piercing shriek.

Now Captain Seim orders his troops to fire at will. I watch Mabrey's Jessica feast on opportunity. Demons fall, and their impact is like a steady hammer blow on the plain.

A horn sounds from across the sky, as it has in the previous retreats.

"They're falling back," Captain Seim says.

The soldiers lower their guns in exhausted victory, turning toward me and removing their goggles. It's odd to see their eyes again and consider them as people. When the unit attacks or defends, it becomes a singular entity, a machine fashioned from many different forges. Now they separate, leaving the line one by one, slumping back into the interior of the Grand Chapel where they'll sleep, eat, or brood. But they won't talk.

Except Mabrey.

After the second attack, which the forty colonists of Jeru watched from outside the chapel despite Captain Seim's order, Mabrey strutted over to them and said, "Another legion of Hell decimated by a thousand rounds of limb-dismembering goodness, ladies and gentlemen. Come back when you've got a pair, Satan. Jessica's a castrating bitch."

One of the older colonists said, "It was God's will that we won!"

Before Mabrey answered, another soldier spat in the colonist's face. When the colonist tried to clean it off, the soldier spat again. "Let it dry there. It's God's will."

The colonists have cloistered inside the Grand Chapel ever since.

I look to Captain Seim, who alone remains, still wearing his goggles and staring out into the darkness. Why does he linger? Is it vanity to think he wants to consult with me? Is he even aware of me? In the space of seconds, my mind entertains a fantasy. I imagine him removing his goggles to reveal eyes wet with tears. He says he wants to hear the Word of God. This from the man who punched Gideon in the mouth when he was overheard praying for the twenty soldiers killed in the first attack.

Without looking at me, he says, "You weren't made to be quiet, were you?"

"No, Captain."

"But now you keep your thoughts to yourself."

"I was thinking about our situation."

"Thinking or praying?"

"Thinking."

"Then you haven't prayed at all?"

"No."

Captain Seim pivots his scarred profile toward me, goggle lens aflame. "You're to tell me if you do, understood? The moment *Dear God* or *Our Heavenly Father* enters your head, I want to know so I can shoot you."

"Your weapon would do little to me."

"It would give me satisfaction."

"Very well. But there's no harm in prayer, Captain."

"Humanity didn't achieve anything until we abandoned the fairy tales you were programmed to preach. We're going to win this fight on our own, and I won't have any of that bullshit tainting the victory."

He brushes past me.

"I'm on your side," I say, but he continues into the chapel to join his troops. There's a slight limp in his left leg.

I lift my hand toward his departing figure and whisper, "Be healed."

The colonists gather to me when I enter minutes later, their arms raised as they shout my name, "Hallelujah!" Despite his age, Gideon's voice rises above the others, soaring higher than the mockery of the soldiers from the far end of the vast room. The Grand Chapel can hold multitudes, built in anticipation of faith turning the tide. The high windows have the appearance of stained glass, though no actual glass could survive Jeru's weather.

BFG

Gideon comes to me, clasps his hands over mine, and welcomes me back. "Hallelujah," he says, intelligible despite a swollen lip and two missing teeth. I caress the side of his face, and he presses my hand to his skin in rapture. My action sparks greed in the colonists. They move closer, each one begging for my touch. "Hallelujah," a second man says. Soon they're all saying it, louder and louder, until Mabrey storms over and says, "Everyone shut the fuck up. Hal, if we hear another word out of your crew, I swear there's going to be trouble. Jessica needs her beauty sleep—got that?"

"Understood, Corporal."

Before Mabrey leaves, he casts an open glance at Gideon's daughter. She is seventeen and virginal; Mabrey is twenty-three and cocky. Neither lack for physical charm. Gideon keeps her close, but unlike me, he falls asleep from time to time. I catch the daughter's blushing smile before she looks away.

Short of an act of God, their rendezvous will happen.

Once he's gone, the colonists whisper hatred for the soldiers and for Mabrey above all. He is the worst sort of blasphemer. I counter with gentle remonstrance. "The Lord is mysterious. He works through the unlikeliest of people. Remember Jonah? Paul? For all we know, God has set His sights on the corporal to save us."

"But isn't that what you've come back to do?"

"Why did you leave us?"

"Where did you go?"

"He was taken into the clouds by God. Gideon, isn't that right?"

Gideon makes a quieting motion with his hands. "We have waited long for answers. We can wait still longer. Go to sleep with this one encouragement in your thoughts: Everything we have set our hands to, every plan we have made, is reaching fruition. We came to this planet because we are the Elect among men, blessed with faith. The soldiers cannot understand. Their ears are deaf to the Good News, and this makes them angry. We must forgive."

The colonists go to the very opposite end of the Grand Chapel, where they've encamped for safety. Once we're alone, Gideon smooths the fabric of my uniform and touches the insignia on my lapel. Verdigris encrusts the bronze cross with a sea-green patina.

"Military Chaplain. It must be two hundred years since any Earth army maintained such an office."

"It was reestablished on my behalf for this mission."

"To mock you," Gideon says, lowering his gaze.

I cannot refute him. The soldiers made sport of me during the trip to Jeru. A man named Callas came to me, pretending to be a Believer, asking me to minister. I did so with gladness, and the next day he returned with another soldier. I led them in prayer. This continued, my flock growing each day. Before we reached Jeru, I was preaching to all except Captain Seim. One told me he was sick, and in my zeal, I touched him and said, "Be healed."

That's when Mabrey stood and said, "My balls ache! Touch my goddamn balls, Padre Tin Man!"

Then Callas laughed and said, "Hey Mabrey, let me piss in your mouth and see if RoboChrist can turn it into wine in the nick of time."

I tried to imagine how Christ would react if he'd discovered his disciples had been playing an elaborate prank all along. He would, I suppose, forgive them.

Gideon scrapes at the verdigris with his thumbnail. "They only mock themselves. Your rank is an act of God."

"What do you mean?"

Motioning for me to follow, he leads me through a library, a prayer chamber, and an infirmary until we reach a nursery with a hundred empty beds. He stops to touch a panel that reveals a hidden door. Stairs descend from the other side.

"Do you remember these?"

"Through the haze of an infant's memory."

"You perfected your fine motor skills on these steps. I cannot begin to say how many times you fell—sideways, backwards, forwards. There's not one part of your body you didn't land upon. I felt the bruises for you."

"I remember a man's voice saying, 'How will he walk on water if he cannot manage a stairwell?'"

"Faith and patience are not always natural allies."

"And the same voice crying out, 'Hallelujah!' when I mastered going up and down."

We descend toward a laboratory and engineering workshop. And armory.

The room's appearance stands at odds with the rough-hewn rock interior of the Grand Chapel, where even the lights have subtle flickers to emulate illumination by flame. I stand now in a world of lacquered white floors and walls and chrome workstations gleaming under crisp, antiseptic brightness. Twenty suits of armor like those of ancient knights and a variety of accompanying melee weapons line one wall. The suits have rocket launchers mounted on each left shoulder and swiveling ion cannons attached on the right.

"Is your memory of this place any less infantile?"

I stand before the longest table. A framework of delicate tools springs out from it like an open ribcage.

"My womb."

"Never doubt that you came to us from God."

I point to the strange armor and weapons. "I don't remember those."

"You wouldn't. They came later, after you were stolen from us."

"Did God build them too?"

His swollen lips turn down. *"Yes."*

Gideon urges me toward a terminal.

The screen flashes through a series of schematics and blueprints. Air and ground assault craft, guns, the suits of armor holding swords and maces rayed with haloes of energy.

Me.

"I'm afraid I do not understand."

"Even angels wield swords. We did not go seeking the fires of Hell without praying for God's shield."

"Seeking? The plea from Jeru warned of an invasion."

"So it did."

"Invasions are not sought, Gideon."

The puffiness of his lips doesn't thwart the slyness of his smile. "Ask, and it shall be given to you; seek, and ye shall find; knock, and it shall be opened unto you."

"Matthew 7:7."

Gideon goes to one of the suits of armor. "We have lived our lives by this scripture. You are proof of it, and now you are returned to us just in time to fight."

He runs his fingers along an invisible seam, and the front half swings open, revealing a hollow casing lined with microcircuits and sensors. There's a clear depression where any human body might fit.

"Get in."

I step back. "If this is some sort of power armor, perhaps we should get Captain Seim—"

"His soldiers wouldn't even be able to power them on! This is armament for Believers, powered by faith. They will not work for anyone without the grace of God."

"Gideon. . .you sound like one of the soldiers trying to make sport of me. These weapons must be mechanical operations. They require fuel, energy."

"Faith is an inexhaustible energy, Hallelujah."

"How do these weapons use it? How do they detect the presence or lack of faith? How does the power of belief transfer into—"

"Enough. These questions are unsettling. Could it be you were changed while you've been away? Did some government engineering division get its hands on you and sabotage your faith with codes of cynicism and doubt?"

"I have not been tampered with."

"No, of course not. You are as far beyond their understanding as the faith you fulfill. Do not let the other colonists hear doubts from you. It will frighten them, and they're frightened enough already."

A rumble comes from high above, deep enough to make the laboratory shake. The melee weapons collapse and clang on the floor. Gideon falls too, despite my best effort to catch him. I pull the old man to his feet.

"We must get back to the colonists."

Gideon seizes my wrist. "Get in the armor."

"Why me?"

"Because it was made for you!"

"I want peace, Gideon. I want to heal."

"You did not come to bring peace, but a sword. You know the chapter and verse."

"Yes."

"Then if you are the fulfillment of Christ's return, you will get inside the armor. Come, Hallelujah. It is time for you to demonstrate the awesomeness of God."

"Three hundred years," Gideon mutters as the armor swallows me. "Three centuries of humanity striving to edit the possibility of faith out of our genetic code—as if belief in God could be treated as some mutation."

The helmet closes around my head. It feels good against my body. Right. Like I was made for it. The visor renders Gideon as a heat signature. My vision expands everywhere. Architecture becomes mere blueprints on glass. Looking through the ceiling, I see a blob of color, the colonists gathered in mass to clutch each other and weep. I see still further, beyond the Great Chapel to the soldiers pouring their fury into the dark. Maybe it is their own uniforms or just an effect of the firefight, but they register far brighter than Gideon or the other colonists. They and their weapons blaze like torches.

"They have faith in themselves."

Gideon takes a double-bladed plasma sword from the floor. Sharp steel traces the edges of the weapon, framing crystal blades encased with servos and wires. He places it into my hand.

"Faith in self is the same as falling in love with a mirror, Hallelujah."

One of the soldiers goes from red to a cold, deep blue. The notion it might be Mabrey bothers me, and I start up the steps. The armor looks like a thousand pounds of steel, but it handles like a delicate skin of aluminum. My feet have the nimbleness of a dancer as I ascend, race through the rooms, emerge in the Grand Chapel, and then run past the huddled colonists with Gideon trying to keep pace, shouting a song at my back—

I heard an old, old story

How a Savior came from glory

I have memories of this song, memories of my beginning, when all the colonists gathered in a great ring around me and sang. It was right before the False Believer spirited me to Earth and made me a curiosity to the public and to myself. Now, as I leap out of the Grand Chapel with Gideon and the colonists all singing at my back, I become a spectacle that disrupts even the discipline of Captain Seim's men.

Mabrey, kneeling by his dead comrade, his youthful face tight and drawn, notices me first. The end of Jessica's barrel looks like it's becoming molten.

"What the *fuck* are you?"

"The Messiah!" Gideon shouts. "He is your Redeemer!"

No words have ever sounded more right. Exhilaration lifts me, and in that instant, I find myself leaving the ground and soaring into the clouds, the power suit responding to sensation.

The demons come in uncountable shapes and sizes, some winged, others galloping across the ragged terrain of Jeru like eight-legged horses or slithering along, snakes with lion heads, wolves with human heads, each one an amalgamation of animal parts fused into vile, perverted creations. Thousands upon thousands of them, pouring from a bleeding fissure some miles in the distance. In the space between two mountains on the horizon, the massive suggestion of a man watches with his fingers curled around each peak. All my suit's sensors fail when they try to scan this dark, towering shape. Is it Satan? Is it God?

Is there a distinction?

The suit lurches. Heaviness enters the metal. The visor goes blind. I plummet, limbs flailing. Scripture comes to me: *How you have fallen from heaven, morning star, son of the dawn!* Am I not the Messiah, returned in fulfillment of a prophecy only a few thousand humans might still believe? All at once a fresh righteousness burns within me, and the suit regains its power.

Fifty demons break from the horde and speed toward me. My visor tracks them, analyzes them, turns them into schematics. As if by reflex, my armor's targeting system zeroes in on the nearest creature. An energy pulse bisects it faster than even artificial eyes can see.

The demons swarm me, trying to get in close to render my shoulder weapons ineffective. I swing the plasma sword, its blades crackling with energy. Its arc amputates wings and arms. One demon to my left roars, its mouth lined with row upon row of hideous teeth. It bites my arm with decapitating force only to have its teeth break. Stricken, it tries to flee, but I grab it by the neck and plunge the sword through its throat, shredding the hollow of its maw with a brutal twist up through its head.

The remaining demons swoop back, and my suit's distance armaments reengage on their own. A barrage of rockets pour into their ranks as my pulse cannon swivels in all directions, its beam hungry and feasting. The fight has carried me over the Grand Chapel, and my own ordnance blasts apart its two soaring bell towers. Below, Captain Seim and his soldiers scatter but reform into a tight group and fire straight up, the glow of their pulse rifles forming a dome of light around them.

BFG

A horn sounds, ethereal, more felt than heard. A pure note not from this or any other world, and the demons retreat at its calling.

Victory is mine.

"Get out of the suit," Captain Seim says.

"I cannot."

"Can't or won't?"

"You can't order him like the others," Gideon says.

The three of us stand in the middle of opposing crowds, the soldiers to our right, colonists to our left. Above our heads, the roof of the Grand Chapel has holes blasted in it, though my visor tells me it remains sound.

"He accepted a rank when he joined the mission. That rank is subordinate to me."

Captain Seim's heat signature flares, though it takes no technology to register his rising temper.

"I'm sorry, sir, but I cannot get out of the suit. Doing so feels like I'd be disassembling myself."

Mabrey steps forward. "Do you mean you got downloaded into the suit or something?"

"I am physically within it. But it now feels like a part of me. I cannot explain it."

"It is a matter of faith, Captain. That is all the explanation you need."

"Then at least tell us where you found it," Mabrey says. "A suit like that would take my ass kicking to a whole new level."

"Shut up, Corporal," the captain says.

"But sir, this engineering is far more advanced than anything on Earth."

Gideon's laughter draws everyone's attention.

"What's so funny?"

"I just remember hearing the same thing when representatives from Earth's government came to Jeru, ten years ago. They questioned us about Hallelujah since he was so incomprehensible to them. When the traitor stole him from us, I wept bitter tears, imagining our savior in the hands of a second Roman empire. Then I was comforted knowing nothing on Earth could harm him. They

51

brought soldiers like yourself, Captain, and they ransacked every building, took every computer, interrogated even the smallest child for some clue. They would not accept the only answer we could give: All things are possible through God."

Captain Seim shakes him by the shoulders. The colonists surge toward them, and the soldiers snap their weapons into position, every barrel aimed at the heads of the men and women of Jeru.

"Tell your people to get on their knees."

"You see it as a position of submission. Believers see it as strength."

"They'll be flat on their backs if I order my soldiers to fire."

"You'd do that to the very people you came to protect?"

"I may be sworn to protect civilians, but no one would question the integrity or wisdom of a soldier who decided he didn't want to die defending a leper colony."

"And shooting the lepers would be doing them a favor? And our faith in God is leprosy to you, is that it?"

"Yes."

Gideon's heat signature becomes an explosive red.

"What if you're the diseased party, Captain? What if humanity has fallen into a deep and horrible rot that exists in its culture, its science, and its government? Jeru isn't a leper colony, it's a last stand against the decay of disbelief sewn into your minds through propaganda and genetic engineering. Christ ministered to lepers his first time around. Now Hallelujah will heal the leprosy that infects the human soul."

Mabrey shakes his head. "Old man, you wouldn't even have Hal back if it wasn't for us."

Captain Seim looks at me. "No, he wouldn't. And now you join the battle using technology never seen before. What scheme is this?"

"I know only what you know, Captain," I say. "I was ignorant of the existence of these suits."

"There's more than one?"

"There are," Gideon says. "But they won't work for you."

"Take me to them."

Gideon shakes his head, but I assent. "They are in a laboratory below the Grand Chapel."

Captain Seim begins ordering his soldiers to work on new defensive measures even as he and Mabrey follow me. When we reach the room, Mabrey slings Jessica over his right shoulder and picks up one of the maces with great effort.

"Old school. I like it."

Captain Seim grunts, inspecting the row of power suits. "Where did you find these?"

"We built them, just as we built Hallelujah."

"With what resources?"

"All things are possible through—"

Gideon goes down from a second punch to his mouth. My visor registers the damage done to him in a quick flash of information as Mabrey puts himself in front of his captain.

"Stand down, sir."

Captain Seim pushes him aside, bending to shout in Gideon's face. "Did this God of yours just fill your head with scientific knowledge superior to all others?"

Gideon spits blood. "There's precedent."

"Enlighten me."

"Hallelujah, Genesis 6:14—16."

The Scripture runs through my mind like a beautiful scroll of words.

"Make thee an ark of gopher wood; rooms shalt thou make in the ark, and shalt pitch it within and without with pitch. And this is the fashion which thou shalt make it of: The length of the ark shall be three hundred cubits, the breadth of it fifty cubits, and the height of it thirty cubits. A window shalt thou—"

"Enough of this bullshit!"

"It demonstrates God has given his followers engineering help before," Gideon says, reaching for me. I help him stand.

"Too bad God didn't go ahead and show Noah how to build starships. Would have saved the lives of many brave—"

Captain Seim goes rigid, his finger pressed to his right ear. Mabrey does too. My helmet picks up the frantic voice in their transmitters.

"Multiple incoming waves detected, Captain. Largest assault by far. ETA right fucking now. Our defenses won't hold."

"Fall back to the drop ship. We're done here."

"There won't be enough room for the colonists—"

"I give fuck all about them."

"Captain!" Mabrey says.

"You've got your orders!" he shouts, staring down Mabrey until he relents and goes upstairs. Then Captain Seim turns to me. "As do you."

"I cannot comply."

"You see how meaningless your authority is here, Captain?" Gideon says. "You stand before the Messiah."

Captain Seim draws his sidearm.

"As I said before, your weapon would not hurt me even outside of this armor."

He points the gun at Gideon.

"Somehow this is all your doing, isn't it? The android, these weapons—and the so-called demons that forced a military response from Earth."

"Forced! Our sovereignty's been violated five times since Hallelujah was taken from us by military agents who believed they could discover his secrets by catching us off guard. It's never required an invasion to bring you here."

"But it required one for us to come with the android in tow."

"Hallelujah's return was necessitated by God."

Rumbles shake the room from above. The lights blink out, casting us into total darkness. My visor switches to night vision. Captain Seim's got his finger in his ear again.

"Registering cascade failures across the colony's power grid, sir."

"Never mind them. Have you reached the drop ship?"

"Almost there."

"Take off as soon as you do. Under no circumstances are you to wait on me."

"Yes, sir."

Captain Seim looks straight at me through the darkness. "Did God happen to leave any candles lying around?"

Before Gideon answers, the room shakes again. Captain Seim looks at his feet, his expression quizzical.

"That can't be the enemy. It's coming from below."

The floor shifts, knocking all of us over. Something's rising out of a hidden chamber below us as the floor retracts. I get up, sword aflame and ready, certain it must be Satan himself. My sensors detect energy of a magnitude beyond their ability to measure. A surging electrical discharge surrounds it, sending fingers of blue lightning through the air. Captain Seim kicks himself away from them, dragging Gideon with him. The power surge increases, lashing through the other power suits, making them dance like marionettes for a moment. Then the lightning hits my armor in the chest, and the temperature inside the casing becomes scorching. The visor cracks as the power of the bolts pitches me backward. When I land, the armor splits open, damaged beyond repair, and I fall out of it like Jonah spat from the belly of Leviathan.

The light and energy recede, leaving me with a better view of this—entity? Object? It seems to be a box, about two feet long, two feet wide, and two feet high. It rests upon a pedestal rising out of the floor. Two golden statuettes of alien figures adorn the top. Humanoid in appearance, they stand with their hands outstretched as if to beckon us to them.

Captain Seim stands while Gideon gets on his knees, head bowed, hands clasped in prayer.

"What is this?"

"The Ark of the Covenant."

"That means nothing to me."

"When God gave His Ten Commandments to the Hebrews, they were placed inside a special box for safekeeping," I say. "The design for this box was also given by God. It disappeared from history when the Babylonian empire conquered Israel."

Gideon lifts his head, his eyes wet and aflame with reflected light. "It *didn't* disappear from history. The Lord brought it to Jeru—to wait for us. We came here dirty and desperate, chased from Earth and every other established colony. But no one would bother us on Jeru. Too unpromising, too hard. For the first year, we lived in our ship, unable to make excursions lasting longer than a few hours. We were miserable, yet I remember that time with great fondness. I was fifteen, and my heart was filled with righteousness. At last I felt safe. I wasn't being told that what I believed in the core of my being was just a genetic abnormality."

"I can only pity your existence. A teen boy trying to live his life in accordance with the moral understanding of a Bronze Age tribe, ashamed by every wet dream."

"And I pity yours, Captain, if even now you are blind to God's grandeur."

I step forward, putting my arm between them. "Tell me about your people finding the Ark, Gideon."

Captain Seim's brows arch. "You're telling me you knew nothing about this?"

"He was taken from us before he knew his origins."

"My origin is—I was built in this room."

"But it was I who heard the voice of God calling to me when I was seventeen. A whisper, telling me to go out and dig. The place was further away from the ship than any had ever gone, but I believed the Lord would protect me. I followed the voice to a spot where I saw the lid of the Ark half buried in the ground. I saw the two cherubim, their hands beckoning me, and I began to excavate. I lifted the Ark from the dirt and brought it back to the ship. There we opened the lid and saw the plans."

"Designs," Captain Seim says, voice little more than a whisper. "The android—the armor. . .you discovered some vault of alien technology, managed to decipher it over the decades, and set about bringing them to life."

"The schematics were given to us in a specific way, a series of steps to build a vessel for His return and then weapons for Him and His disciples to use when we stormed the gates of Hell. Hallelujah was supposed to be by our side when the Gate was completed."

"Gate?"

"It was the very last design, after Hallelujah and all the weapons."

A voice pipes through Captain Seim's transmitter at such a volume that he winces and rips it from his ear. *It's Mabrey, Captain. The drop ship has been destroyed. I think I'm the only survivor. En route back to your—"*

Captain Seim holds the transmitter to his lips. *"Corporal? Anyone who can hear me, fall back to my position. Johnson? Daniels?"*

"Your soldiers are dead, Captain. Satan was only toying with you before. His legions could have destroyed us at any time. Only Hallelujah can save us."

"You dumb bastard," the captain says, putting the gun to Gideon's forehead. "You've been following some alien scheme and calling it faith. My soldiers are dead because of you, and so are the colonists."

"Shoot, Captain. I will dwell in the temple of the Lord."

I go at my fastest speed, jarring his hand right as he fires. Gideon flinches and then looks at the black spot on the wall. He grins at me.

BFG

Mabrey is at the top of the stairs. He stumbles on his way down, face gashed. Still clutching Jessica in his right hand, the gun is a shell of its former glory, the barrel broken and lifeless. He presents himself to his captain and gives a dire update. The demons—he uses the word—have infiltrated the Grand Chapel. "They're everywhere, sir. There are no survivors on the surface. I used my rifle to weld a few makeshift barricades as I retreated, but they won't buy us more than a few minutes."

"More than enough time!"

We all look to Gideon, whose hope must offend Mabrey. "I just said everyone is dead, including your daughter."

"They will live on. But now God has driven the enemy into our hands. There's a final weapon. We built everything in the order the Ark provided. You, Hallelujah, were first, the Alpha. This final weapon we call—"

"Omega."

"*The* Omega."

"Where is it, Gideon?"

He points to the floor, then steps up to the Ark. He wraps his fingers around the outstretched hand of the first cherub and tells me to do the same. As I touch the second cherub, the platform descends. Captain Seim and Mabrey move to join us, but the demons break into the room. The captain raises his gun and fires upward. The last thing I see before sinking out of sight is Mabrey grappling with one of the melee weapons.

The Ark descends down a shaft that must be three hundred meters long. We stop just above what seems to be a massive cannon attached to a circular base with a single seat. The cannon bristles with arrays of micro-turrets aimed in all directions. The machine is dark gray and seamless like a piece of blown glass. There's an opening just behind the seat approximating the size of the Ark.

Screams sound from above, and I see the demons clawing their way toward us.

"Move quick, Hallelujah."

"What must I do?"

"Take your place at the controls."

"I don't know how to operate them."

"You didn't know how to operate the power armor either. You were made to use them both. There is another reason The Omega was the final weapon design in the Ark. The Ark itself is its power source. We must put it into place to activate the gun and let the vengeance of the Lord—the vengeance of the Messiah—pour forth. The cannon will harness His wrath and unleash it upon our enemies."

I sit down. The controls seem little more than a steering column. I cannot even find a button to press.

"For years I have longed for this moment," Gideon says, taking the Ark into his arms. "The Alpha and the Omega joined at last, with Satan gloating over our heads, sure of victory."

"But why didn't you use it already?"

"I couldn't, Hallelujah. None of us could. Even our collective belief is not enough. This weapon requires a blameless faith, an unshakable fidelity to God. If humans could meet that requirement, there would be no need for Christ. There never would have been a fall of man."

He settles the Ark into place, and as he does, the cannon activates with a burst of energy that throws Gideon across the room and leaves him slumped, his head at an unnatural angle. My right hand rises, and I think, *Be healed! Be healed! Be healed!* The demons are pouring down now, and the cannon's base lifts fast on antigravity mechanisms. *Be healed. Be healed.* I grip the meager controls as the smaller turrets fire quills of defensive energy while a fierce glow balloons around the maw of the main gun.

The cannon fires, and the result is like a wrecking ball passing through a house of cards. The blast shears through the ceiling and every ceiling above it, until it reaches the sky and cuts a swath through legion after legion. The Ark crackles behind me, and my faith responds. The cannon fires again, and this time I feel like it's responding to my will. The surrounding turrets swivel and decimate any demon that tries to attack. Most are fleeing now and the cannon rises after them, moving through the gaping holes it blasted in metal and rock. As the cannon fires a third time, I shout, *"It is mine to avenge! I will repay!"* How satisfying this moment is, how comfortable the seat of power. *"The Lord is a God who avenges. O God who avenges, shine forth! Rise up, Judge of the earth!"*

My mouth becomes a cannon of scripture firing just as fast. The thought *be healed* no longer occupies my head. I have not come to heal but to destroy. I have come to offer harsh correction rather than instruction. As I rise to the level of the laboratory, I find Mabrey backed into a corner, fending off a demon with the sword he barely has the strength to lift. Seeing me, he shouts, "Destroy them, Hal! That's right, demons! We've got a Big Fucking God on our side!"

Mabrey's faith should cheer me, but my gaze fixes on the sight of Captain Seim's ruined body. How strange it is, the sorrow I feel at the end of this hardened atheist. His words *under no circumstances are you to wait on me* run through my thoughts, replacing the scripture. I cannot cry, and there have been few times when I wanted to. Now is one of them. I close my eyes as if to squeeze out a tear. *Be healed.*

The cannon's fire slows—and stops.

The legions my arsenal put in retreat sense the change and turn. Thousands launch themselves toward me.

"Hal," Mabrey says, hobbling in my direction. "What are you doing? Fire!"

I look up at the sky and think, *Fire! Fire!* but the cannon is cold and I feel the chill inside me, as impossible as that is.

"Hal?"

I leave the seat and go to Captain Seim. I lift his head and find one eye open. If he could survive, the other side of his mangled face would one day have a matching scar.

"Be healed," I say.

For a moment, all is an impossible silence. Some have called silence the true language of faith—the frustrating eloquence of God.

I touch his face. I close his eyes.

"Be healed."

Mabrey has reached the cannon. He calls to me, and I see him in the seat, hands on the control column. Poor faithless fool. What will he do when he realizes The Omega won't work for him?

I look down again at Captain Seim as I cradle his head. "Why won't you be healed?"

Did I die for this man and all humanity in a past life I don't remember? Have I returned now to kill those who cannot believe it ever happened?

In that one moment, I hear Gideon's voice in my head. Like my problems with the stairs, it is what passes for a childhood memory. I am seated upon a table, and he stands before me, one hand on my cheek, quoting something that sounds like scripture but isn't.

"Little Lamb, who made thee? Dost thou know who made thee?"

The memory shatters with the concussive blast of cannon fire. It blasts with a fury surpassing anything my faith ever fueled. Mabrey sits in the chair, tears coursing down his cheeks as he speaks the most impossible words. *"Our Father, who art in Heaven, hallowed be thy name."* His voice rises with each new passage, until at last he's screaming the prayer, screaming and firing, the cannon's volleys ripping across the sky and spreading fire along the horizon, shearing the demons by the hundreds, by the thousands, the cry of their collective pain the only sound able to rise above the glory of Mabrey's prayer and the endless pulse of the weapon. The great barrel begins to spin, faster even than my eyes can follow, blast after blast radiating from it in petals with a high-pitched whine. The demons surge into their death until at last, perhaps hours later, none come at all. No horn of retreat ever blows. The skies of Jeru are empty and now, perhaps, Hell is too.

Mabrey joins me beside his dead captain, and we regard his body a long time. Without looking at the corporal, I say, "How did you operate the cannon? Gideon told me it had to be powered by faith in God. It was designed for me."

"I've spent my life pretending."

Now I do look at him. "You mean you're a Believer, too?"

"I'm ashamed of the things I've done to hide my faith, Hal. I always asked God to forgive my cowardice and understand."

"I'm sure He does."

I help him stand. Some of the flesh is torn away on my forearm, revealing the wonders of my metal framework and the wiring that encircles it all like veins and arteries. Mabrey puts his finger in the opening a moment.

"Do you think you're the Messiah? Could you really be the second coming of Christ?"

I smile at the sudden innocence in his expression. His bleeding somehow makes it even more childlike. "I think it's just as likely to be you."

We walk away from the rubble, disciples of uncertainty, a divinity no one wants to worship, but a divinity whose existence cannot be doubted.

BRIGHT RAIN

"**M**OMMY, DON'T LET the rain get me."

Cassie was moaning in her sleep again. The noise-deadening headphones had slipped off her ears, allowing the harsh, metallic beat of the heavy downpour on the roof to sneak into her dreams. I tiptoed over to adjust them, but I was too late, and the eight-year-old sat up screaming, calling out for her mother. I sat beside her, one hand on her shoulder, waiting for her to calm down. Only in my care for two weeks, the little girl's face flashed with the hope of seeing her mother whenever she woke up. She'd gotten no better at hiding her disappointment and resentment when she saw me.

"Go back to sleep," I said.

Cassie shook her head. There was a light sweat on her forehead, and the sight of it gave me an involuntary shiver and made me look at the ceiling. Of course, if there'd been a leak, it would already be too late.

As I patted her dry with the edge of the top sheet, she asked me to read her a story. That's what she called the dry entries I read to her from *Encyclopedia Britannica*, as it was the least technical material I had in the house.

"Do you want to hear about the desert again?"

She nodded. "It never rains there."

"I wouldn't say never. But seldom. A few days a year. Wouldn't that be a nice place to go?"

"Mommy wanted to go there."

I caressed Cassie's hair. My pulse was going a little too fast, and I took a deep breath and held it. Was the girl being truthful, or was she just latching on to a fantasy? She'd refused to say why she was huddled up in the passenger side of the old Nissan a block up the road. She claimed it was her mother's car and her mom had gone to get help. I didn't challenge the lie, just thankful there hadn't been a storm that night. Someone had shattered the Nissan's windshield months ago.

"Maybe she got there. Others have too, I hope."

"Then why don't we?"

"It's a very long walk."

"Days?"

"Weeks. We'll stay put for now. I've done everything I can to make this house safe."

As I said that, the noise from the roof eased. We both looked up, and I smiled. "Running out of juice. The rain thought it was going to get us. Guess we showed it, didn't we?"

I gave her a little poke in the ribs. She laughed by reflex, and I settled her back into bed, adjusting the headphones to make them snug. They wouldn't be nudged off unless she really thrashed her head. I didn't want even the slightest ping of a raindrop infecting her dreams.

I didn't go outside until two days later, when I was sure the sun had dried out every place I needed to be. An inspection of the perimeter showed all the French drains were working fine, and the gutter spout extensions were intact. As I returned to the front of the house, I saw Cassie with her nose pressed to the living room bay window. She gaped at me like I was a monster, but she'd seen me in my full wetsuit once before. The neoprene had my body in a heavy sweat, and I wanted to shuck myself free of the second skin as fast as possible. The sky was bright blue and cloudless. Barometric pressure readings suggested no storms in our immediate future. In another month we'd be into July, and the Colorado climate would become dry enough to venture out in. It might not rain for weeks on end. We could risk a long trip south even if it meant walking.

I'd told myself the same thing almost a year ago to the day.

I looked across the street and stared at Michael's house.

Cassie knocked on the window. I turned and waved at her. She was mouthing something, but between the window and my wetsuit, I might as well have been deaf. It was obvious she wanted to come outside, and before I could react, she'd left the window and opened the front door. I shuddered and pitched myself toward the porch.

"Not yet."

"But it's dry!"

"There's still some water on the ground, and there might be puddles. I need to take samples first. Just be patient and stay inside, okay?"

She turned and shut the door behind her.

The threat of her impatience spurred me to hurry with the crucial task of water purification. I waddled to the back of the house where the collection barrels were placed. I had four steel drums balanced on a series of concrete blocks that elevated them almost a meter off the ground. The open space beneath the barrels was blackened with ash, though the latest storm had washed much of it away. I opened an adjacent storage shed and brought out chunks of wood to pile under the barrels.

"Why does the fire kill them?"

Startled, I jerked up and fell toward the first barrel. I caught myself on the rim and found my facemask almost skimming the water's surface. I opened my eyes wide with the realization of how close I was, and the bright, swirling metallic green and blue hues threatened to hypnotize me. I felt a stirring within my blood, a desire to rip off my protection and dunk my head into the barrel. The surface had a sludgy quality to it but made a clicking noise in place of the usual soft lapping of regular water. As I held my face in position, staring down, I thought I saw a hand rising from the water, a shape that seemed formed by thousands of overlapping thumbtacks.

I staggered back and fell, landing at Cassie's feet. The child started to help me up, but I motioned for her to stop and kicked away from her. I got up and checked myself. If I discovered even a drop of water from the barrels on the wetsuit, I'd have to sterilize it, but the material was dry. Beneath it, I swam in sweat.

"I'm sorry," Cassie said, her voice very small as she cringed away from me.

I took several gulps of air.

"You mustn't startle me. If you see me wearing the wetsuit, it means I'm afraid. When we're afraid, we protect ourselves. Do you understand?"

"But it's dry!"

"Cassie, water has always been the most insidious of things. My father was a general contractor and he—"

"He's in the Army?"

"No," I said, understanding her confusion. "General contractor's another name for a handyman. Someone who fixes things. My father specialized in water repairs—flood damage, roof leaks, things like that. There was a phrase he always said about his work: 'Water will find a way.' If he was alive to see what's happened to the world, he'd probably die laughing."

I shouldn't have indicated he was dead. Cassie didn't need information like that, and she looked anywhere but at me. Not knowing how to respond, I decided to address the question that had almost sent me plunging headfirst into the barrel.

"Fire isn't killing them. Disabling them is a better description. The things in the rain weren't meant to operate in conditions much above 37 degrees centigrade. Too much heat turns them into nothing more than inert material."

She tried to pronounce *inert* back at me. I knelt down, smiling, and said, "It means they can't harm us anymore."

"And then the water's safe to drink?"

"That's right. To drink, to cook with, and to take a bath in. I tell you what, if you promise to be very careful, you can help me build the fires."

Cassie grinned and nodded.

A few hours later, only embers glowed beneath each barrel and the water had quit boiling and the steam ceased. The water was clear, signifying purification. Still, I let the water sit another twenty-four hours before checking its clarity again, and then I took samples from each barrel in a series of eyedroppers and brought them inside to prepare slides.

Cassie stood beside me. She wasn't the first child to observe me work, but those other children belonged to a quaint past full of classroom field trips and comfortable acronyms like STEM. Perhaps in another existence, our paths would have crossed when her elementary school visited me at the laboratory like so many others had before. I remember how much pleasure I took to hear the wonderful gasps of students as they took turns looking through my microscope.

God, to have a scope even half as powerful as the one I once accessed. This one was a toy by comparison.

But it sufficed for my cautionary needs.

I slid the first slide into place and adjusted the eyepiece. The shapes were indistinct at this poor level of magnification. The key factor was a total absence of activity. An unpurified drop would have been swarming like a beehive.

Cassie tugged at my shirt. "What do you see?"

"Only good things," I said. My imagination conjured the revelatory clarity of an electron microscope. I saw a field of corpses as in some Civil War photograph.

I reviewed several more samples from all four barrels. Sudden movement in the last slide made my heartbeat flutter for a moment. Then I laughed.

"What is it?"

"I'll let you look."

I swapped places with her and adjusted the eyepiece.

"You see the thing that's moving?"

"It looks like a blob," she said.

"Yes, I suppose so. Sit tight. Let me get something that will show you what it really is."

I went to the bookshelf in my living room and found a book called *Microcosmos*. I knew the exact page I wanted and flipped to it. Cassie was still gazing into the scope.

"Here," I said, and she turned to look. Her eyes went big.

"It's cute!"

"This is called a tardigrade."

"It looks like a bear," she said.

"Yes, it does. In fact, it's sometimes called a water bear."

She looked between the page and the slide. I told her all about the tardigrades, repeating many of the same facts I used to give during some of those field trip visits. But there were new things to tell Cassie.

"Tardigrades don't like what's in the rain. We knew that a long time ago, though. It used to amuse us to watch the water bears go after our invention. We'd view the battles under microscopes and broadcast them around the world. Even scientists like cage matches, I guess."

Her expression scrunched up, no doubt the result of a hundred confusions.

"I know you don't understand anything I'm saying," I said. "That's okay. The main thing is that tardigrades are almost indestructible. We never observed one lose."

"So, they're helping us?"

"Not exactly," I said, uncertain how else to answer. I wanted to launch into a philosophical discussion. It'd been so long since I'd had a conversation of any substance. What was the more interesting notion, from the vantage point of perception—that something could be too small to be seen, or something could be too large?

"To be honest," I said, "the tardigrades probably don't even know we exist."

"But the rain does."

I put the book aside and knelt down until we were eye-to-eye. "Cassie, the rain itself doesn't have a consciousness any more than the wind does, or the dirt, or fire."

"Then why did the rain start hating us?" she said.

I could have given the girl a pretty good approximate answer, but I dared not face more questions from her. Or from my own thoughts, for that matter, though maybe I was in denial if I considered myself a ruthless self-inquisitor. If we did seek safety in some desert community, would they welcome someone who'd been part of the Tomorrow Team? Would it matter that I'd just been one of a thousand eager researchers working on bits and pieces of the overall jigsaw puzzle? Might I remind them we'd all once been hailed as heroes, winners of a collective Nobel Prize?

I should have held it together until I got Cassie tucked into bed. She was a good, deep sleeper when it wasn't raining, and I could have shut the door to my study and cried without worrying about her. But I've never been great about holding off my emotions. My father used to tease me about bringing a box of tissues whenever he took me to a Disney movie, saying it was just a matter of time before the waterworks started. He wasn't wrong.

I was at the bay window staring across the street at Michael's house and becoming misty-eyed. We'd been neighbors for three years, but it was only several months before the rains turned deadly that we started our relationship. Little else mattered to me once he entered my life. I was a woman dating her first boyfriend at the age of 35, and the thrill of being with him even surpassed the elation the Tomorrow Project's success brought me—though as is often the case, one thing led to the other. Although we'd said hello often due to little synchronicities like going out to our cars at the same time each morning, he showed no further interest until he saw an interview with me on the local news. The next morning, as I was getting into my car, he ran up to me and said, "I didn't know I lived across the street from the next Stephen Hawking."

Of course, I told him I wasn't the next anything. I just enjoyed my research and was lucky enough to be recruited into a great scientific endeavor. Then Michael grinned, rolling up his sleeve to show the smallest mark on his skin, very much like a vaccination scar.

"Got my first injection last month," he said.

I showed him an identical marking in the bend of my right elbow. "Three years ago for me."

"You've had the machines in you for *three years?*"

I laughed. "Call me a self-experimenter."

And so our relationship began. We were a twosome. A Luddite might have said we were actually a couple of colonies, considering the nanites patrolling our bodies, guarding us from infections, cleaning up plaque in the arteries, making repairs. After our first night of intimacy, he put his hands behind his head and said, "Did you know I can hear them?"

"You couldn't even if they did have voices—which they don't."

"Oh, yes I do. They want me to ask you if you're ready for round two."

"Tell them I'm already anticipating round *three.*"

It was too perfect, so of course the world had to be breaking all around us. The problem wasn't so different from the dangers of people flushing their medications down the toilet, leading to a buildup of toxins in the water supply. If that's all it was, though, there'd be no problem. We all had the same nanites, and the nanites were beneficial.

Until they weren't.

The last time I saw Michael, I'd come home from spending most of the night in a series of networked global meetings trying to make sense of the crisis even as it blew up in our faces. The clouds began to glow across the Earth, and in the places where it rained, the rain streaked down in long comet trails of haunting light. Of course, people came out to stand under it, not bothering with umbrellas, letting the strange, beautiful rain drench them. The new, different nanites worked fast in the flesh and bone. Fast but not instantaneous. It still took days before the bodies of the infected were permeated with metal cysts.

A terrifying, agonizing death.

Denver was about to have its first bright rain, and I rushed home to Michael. He'd all but moved in with me by that point, but when I arrived, I found the house empty and went to the bay window as the first raindrops fell. His front door was open. I called, desperate to tell him to stay inside, but the storm made cell reception impossible. I saw him come onto the porch and notice me. He waved and started out from under the cover of the awning. I banged on the window, shaking my head, and then sprinted to my own porch to shout to him, but the wind drove the rain in my direction, and I sprang back as Michael crossed the street. I shut the door and began tearing off my clothes and feeling my skin. I was dry. Michael, of course, was not.

I drew the deadbolt and the chain as he slapped at the door and laughed, thinking it was all some sort of joke.

Cassie came to stand beside me, and the memory of Michael vanished.

"Why are you crying?" she asked.

I took a deep breath and wiped my eyes. "It's a terrible thing when you have to choose between survival and love."

Cassie took my hand and said she understood. I looked down at her.

"Mommy got dripped on. That's why I ran away."

Three days later, we stood at the same window watching a storm roll toward us as if we were its sole targets. For all my dread, the gathering gloom remained a breathtaking sight—angry, deep purple cumulonimbus clouds limned with vibrant greens and blues, as if hiding an alien sunrise. The rains came, streaking the air like a million neon fireflies that seemed weightless until they struck the roof like a hail of pennies.

It was Cassie who pointed out the dog.

BRIGHT RAIN

It limped and staggered past the house, parts of its dying flesh just visible beneath the glittering crust of metal that replaced its fur. It must have gotten wet in the previous storm, I thought, judging by its condition. How it managed to avoid contamination until now baffled me.

"What happens when the rain gets you?"

"The tiny machines in the rain enter the body and multiply. They were originally designed to help. Increase lifespans. Stop disease."

"And then they changed?"

The dog fell over on its side and lay still. We heard the rain smacking against its metal coat.

"Yes, somehow, up there," I said, looking skyward.

"In the rain."

I explained the best I could. Speaking to children was always a challenge for me, but Cassie was brighter than most I encountered.

"In the clouds. Their life inside our bodies ended after six months, and then you needed another injection. They broke down and left when you went to the bathroom, but they rose up with the water vapor and—changed. We've still got two things going for us, though. Heat will kill them, and they need a. . .fluidic medium."

"A what?"

"They can't attack us through the air. They're not like pollen, the stuff that makes you sneeze in the springtime. They unite when the water vapor reaches the clouds, and then they fall with the rain. If they land in a lake or stream, they'll live—perhaps change further, though I don't want to dwell on that. But if they dry out, their lives are very short. We just need to stay dry."

I smiled at her, but Cassie pressed her face to the window until her nose dimpled. She was staring at the dead dog.

"Water will find a way," she said.

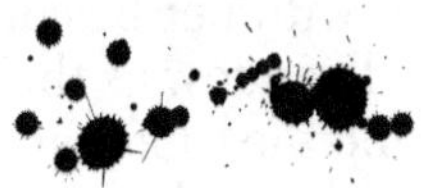

After that rain, we enjoyed two straight weeks of arid, hot weather. It seemed Colorado's dry season had started early. Cassie woke up each day to sprint to the window and study the sky. Then she'd say, "Still no rain! Can we go to the desert now?"

How could I convince her of the journey's complexities? 250

miles separated us from the nearest desert, Great Sand Dunes National Park. With no reliable mechanical transportation, we'd be forced to walk. Cassie didn't even know how to ride a bicycle.

And who knows what we'll find along the way, I thought. There must have been a few survivors like me, clustered in houses. Preppers, survivalists with clean water and food supplies. Not in my neighborhood, at least—until Cassie, I hadn't seen another person in months. Could we depend on humanitarian impulses if we encountered them in a moment of need? Could we defend ourselves against hostilities? What if we made it all the way to the desert and found nothing but waves of silent dunes?

Cassie kept insisting, and in another week, she was reduced to begging. I experienced a flash of resentment when she went on too long. Was my company so bad? Was my shelter inadequate? By the end of the second week, she spent much of the day pouting. I called her to dinner, and she didn't answer. I looked everywhere until I found her sitting in the driver seat of the old Nissan, her hands on the wheel, staring straight ahead. I knew she imagined many eclipsing miles.

I had to forcefully carry her back before midnight, worried about the dewpoint. My limited research detected no nanite activity in the morning glaze, but I wasn't taking chances.

When I went to bed that night, I figured she'd be gone in the morning. Could I really stop her, young as she was?

Let her go if she chooses to leave, I thought. You've done everything you can. She knows the risks. She knew them even before you found her. Let her go but be sure to welcome her if she comes running back.

But if Cassie didn't come running back, I knew I'd spend every stormy night standing in front of the window, looking out through the bars at the bright rain, wondering what happened. What kind of life could I expect even with her beside me, both of us growing old in front of the damned window as the lawns grew into a jungle up and down the street, and the roofs caved in from inevitable rot? After the survival instinct has exhausted itself, you look around and ask, *Why bother?*

I carried that thought into my dreams where I stood in front of the window with Michael. We'd had a son and daughter together, and they were outside playing in the street with all the other children. It was a spring day, and sure enough, a spring rain came—sudden, no warning at all. And the children all opened up their mouths and tried to catch the droplets in the back of their throats, just as they would with snowflakes. The games of children are timeless and renewed with each generation.

Michael and I smiled.

And then the rain turned bright, and we beat on the glass and begged them to stop. I was the one to move toward the front porch, and Michael grabbed my wrist. He said it was too late. He said to lock the door. I jerked myself free and ran to my children. I gathered them to me. I felt the nanites already in my blood calling out through my pores, eager to meet their falling counterparts. It felt like a conspiratorial rendezvous, something long devised, a secret shared by billions.

A peel of thunder woke me, and a flash of lightning made me sit upright. I rushed from my bedroom, shouting Cassie's name. I found her in front of the window, and the tears she cried were cast red and blue from the light of raindrops speckling the glass.

I stood beside her and cried a bit as well.

"It'll never stop," she said.

I got down on my knees and put a hand on her shoulder.

"When the storm is over and it's dry again, we'll go."

She turned her face to me and smiled a little. "To the desert?"

"Come hell or high—"

I pressed my lips together tight and nodded my head.

"Yes," I said. "To the desert."

THE DEVIL'S REEL

THE MAN RICHARD pointed to as we entered the foyer of
First Baptist Church of Harmony wore a crisp blue suit and a black
patch over his left eye. He looked to be in his early thirties. The eye
patch did nothing to detract from the sharp beauty of his face.
Shaking his warm, large hand, the tingle I felt wasn't a bit
Christian, and I hoped my attraction wasn't too obvious,
considering my husband Richard and two boys, Matthew and
Gordon, stood right beside me. The three men in my life wore
white shirts, black ties, and had their blonde hair in identical styles,
parted on the left and held in place with three pumps of Dry Look.

"Elaine, this is Cooper, the guy at the factory I was telling you
about. He's also the youth pastor here."

"Please, call me Coop. How are you liking Indiana, Elaine?"

"She likes it fine," Richard said. "Or she will, once we're settled
in."

We'd moved here just two weeks ago. Richard was managing a
manufacturing plant that employed half the town. I was proud of
the boys for their maturity in the matter. We left Denver as soon
as the school year ended, which made it hard on them. Not only
were they being ripped away from their summer vacation and
friends, they'd have to wait until September to make new ones. Or
so I'd thought. Our church back in Denver hadn't had an active
youth group beyond a few kids. First Baptist appeared to have
about fifty children between the ages of twelve and fifteen.
Matthew and Gordon were going to make friends fast.

But Coop was the one they talked about during the drive home.
I learned he served in Vietnam and found God after being shot in
the eye. Coop shared his story as an act of witnessing, and it
appeared my sons absorbed every word. I listened to them relay

how Coop's resentment about the injury turned him into a militant atheist, war protestor, and drifter. The details astonished me, but I found the story of his renewed faith just as compelling. There was no epiphany, no chance encounter with a street preacher who opened Coop's heart to the Lord. He just let go of his anger over time. As someone who rolls their eyes at *Reader's Digest* stories of poetic coincidence and grand encounters changing lives, I found the tale of Coop's recovered faith so. . .*reasonable.*

I was surprised at how fast our social lives became intertwined with First Baptist. The church promoted regular picnics and get-togethers. It seemed there was never a weekend we weren't gathering at some park to eat fried chicken and potato salad as one large community. Afterwards, the older men pitched horseshoes while Coop organized the kids into a game of baseball. Watching Coop's self-assuredness and relaxed masculinity made me feel like I was fifteen again, sitting close to the field at a high school football game to steal glances at the quarterback. It was clear the older girls had a crush on him. The boys were no less jealous of his attention, always jockeying for his approval and praise in ways they never sought from their fathers. Matthew was no different, and even Gordon, who'd never shown the least interest in sports, gave all his uncoordinated effort trying to impress his youth group leader.

The summer of outdoor church socials promised to become a fall and winter dominated by the Haliled Multiplex. Construction on it started a year before we arrived, and the *Harmony Gazette* featured breathless updates on the rise of the ten-screen movie theater. Its owner, Jacob Dorenius, promised his multiplex would attract people as far as thirty miles away, and those who drove thirty miles to see a movie were bound to stay and shop or eat.

I didn't realize the Haliled was a source of tension in the church until our last picnic in late August. I'd read about the multiplex's grand opening in a couple of weeks and mentioned to the other wives how much I'd like to go. They looked at me like I was crazy—or profane—and I changed the subject fast, holding my tongue until the drive home.

"Can you believe them?" I said to Richard. "They act like a movie theater is a strip club or something."

From the back, Gordon said, "What's a strip club?"

"Something your mother shouldn't be talking about."

"Christ," I said. "You sound like a Moral Majority member, too."

"Half the people in the factory either attend First Baptist or have family that do. There's a lot of politics in small-town jobs. Harmony is a conservative place, Elaine."

"I hope the first movie the theater plays is *Footloose*. Maybe these people will get the hint and lighten up."

Richard grunted, and that was the end of the conversation. At the church service two days later, the congregation was in an uproar over the Haliled. It turned out Mr. Dorenius reached out to Coop and the youth group pastors at other churches, as well as Boy and Girl Scout leaders, to invite the kids to a pre-opening lock-in with movies and pizza.

What a brilliant move from Dorenius, I thought. He must have understood he was building his multiplex in somewhat hostile territory, but maybe he'd underestimated the community's resistance. I certainly had as I listened to people murmur and mutter in the pews. So much uproar over going to a damn movie!

There was a special church meeting the next day to discuss the youth group's participation in the lock-in. Coop subjected himself to a barrage of inane questions and inferences that left many wondering if he was fit to guide adolescents in their *spiritual journey*. I sat there biting my tongue and shaking my head with Richard sometimes elbowing me to keep calm. But how could I? Coop was being persecuted, and I wanted to defend him.

I wanted to hold him.

Guilt overcame me, and I bowed my head, hearing little of the meeting until Pastor Tommy stood up and said it was time for the congregation to vote through a show of hands. Before the vote could be called, though, a voice spoke from the back. "Might I address this lovely gathering?"

We turned our heads and saw a man walking down the aisle. He was slim, his thinning hair swept back and pomaded like some silent movie era leading man. A pencil-thin mustache helped complete the look, finalized by a vest, coat, and pants ensemble that must have belonged to a tuxedo popular ages ago. His appearance provoked mutters and a bit of snickering.

Pastor Tommy said, "I don't believe I know you, sir."

"Jacob Dorenius," the man said. "Owner of the Haliled

Multiplex and soon to be host—I hope—of a youth lock-in that will include the children of First Baptist."

"This meeting is for members of the church, Mr. Dorenius."

"Nevertheless, I am here. Like Daniel into the lion's den."

This won a slight but good-natured laugh.

Pastor Tommy frowned a bit but relented. "Very well. We are interested in hearing what you have to say."

"First, let me start with an apology. It was not my intent to provoke controversy when I extended my invitation to your youth group. I know films have become a cesspool of violence, a celebration of deviance and adultery. I decided to build the Haliled to combat these attitudes and show wholesome pictures. I want the youth of today to care less about the return of the Jedi, and more about the return of *Christ*."

There was brief but spontaneous applause from a few people in the audience. Dorenius smiled to acknowledge them and spoke for a few more minutes. By the time he finished, every heart was softened, and those most inclined toward hostility instead peppered Mr. Dorenius with warm questions about his background, his faith, and his calling. Dorenius witnessed about the power of cinema to further God's word, describing his tearful reactions to *The Ten Commandments* and *The Greatest Story Ever Told*.

The congregation voted—the tally wasn't close—to let the youth group attend.

The lock-in was held on Friday, September 13, a bit inauspicious date-wise but practical since school started the week before. Richard drove the boys to church, leaving them in Coop's care, then came home and settled into his chair. Without saying a word, I turned off the television, sparking a bit of confused protest. Then I dropped down on my knees in front of him and caressed his upper thighs.

"Elaine—"

"When's the last time we had the house to ourselves?"

"I'm sorry," he said. "I'm just not in the mood."

His apology was as flaccid as the rest of him. I got up to head to the bathroom. He called after me, saying he was sorry, but I didn't acknowledge him. I locked the bathroom door, ran a hot bath, and added some Calgon to the water. I soaked and, after a little resistance, enjoyed a feverish fantasy of Coop.

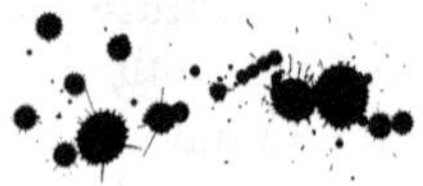

The boys came home at 8 a.m. the next morning. Their early arrival surprised me, and I put on my robe and went downstairs to find them sitting side-by-side on the couch.

"How was the lock-in?"

"It was okay," Matthew said.

"What did you see?"

"Some movie," Gordon said.

The boys shrugged. I understood their lethargy. How much could they have slept?

"Want breakfast?"

"I'm not hungry," Matthew said.

"Me either, Mom."

"Stuffed from eating pizza all night?"

There was something off-putting about the smile they gave, like they were reacting to a joke I didn't know I'd made. But I was tired and distracted, so I headed back to bed, stopping only to ask if they'd made sure to thank Mr. Dorenius and Coop for a fun night.

"Did you thank Coop for a fun night, too?" Matthew said.

"What?"

I stared at them, thinking I must have misheard Matthew the first time, but nevertheless returned to bed with a cold weight in my stomach. It had just been a fantasy, I told myself. Innocent. Everyone has them.

But I'd be more discreet even in my mind from now on.

On Sunday morning, Matthew said he was too sick to go to church, and I stayed home with him. Gordon threw an uncharacteristic fit, saying it wasn't fair, and demanding to stay home too. Not atypical behavior for a younger brother, maybe, but unusual for him.

"I thought you liked going to church," I said as the three of us ate breakfast.

"You know I hate it as much as you do," Gordon said.

"I don't hate—"

"Yeah, *right*," he said, earning a sharp rebuke from Richard, who ordered him to get ready. Gordon walked out, but when it came time to leave, we found him still in his t-shirt and shorts. He sulked like a three-year-old. I watched my husband and youngest son exchanging defiant glares. Richard's fingers tapped his belt buckle with all the anticipation of a Western gunslinger about to draw. For a moment, Gordon seemed determined to earn a whipping. Then he laughed and sprang up off the bed, dressing with the utmost cheer.

Twenty minutes after they left, Matthew's fever broke and he seemed fine, demanding breakfast and eating it with an obnoxious smacking of his lips.

"That's disgusting," I said.

"I was just imitating the sound of the water, Mom."

I squeezed my eyes shut a moment. I had to be hallucinating. "What did you say?"

"I said: What's the matter, Mom?"

I let out a long breath. "It's not polite to smack your lips."

"Oh," he said, nodding, and began chewing with exaggerated daintiness as he stared at me.

I let it go, just like we did with Gordon. When Richard came home, he told me the main church service was disrupted by loud laughter from the youth group's classroom. Coop even came in to apologize.

"Why were they laughing so loudly?" I asked.

"Not sure. Cooper just has a way with kids."

Richard went to his chair and prepared for a long afternoon of football. I looked around for Matthew and Gordon and found them heading out the door.

"Oh, no you don't," I said, and the boys stopped.

"What?"

"You stayed home sick from church, Matthew. That means you stay home sick *period*."

"That's bullshit!"

They opened the door. I reached over and slammed it shut.

"What did you just say?"

"Nothing."

"I know what you said."

"Then why did you ask?"

Richard came and stood beside me. "Both of you get up to your rooms right now."

"No."

Richard grabbed Matthew by his arm and pulled him forward. Matthew winced as Richard's grip tightened, and I saw a flash of rage that compelled me to intervene.

"Boys," I said. "Go upstairs."

I held my breath, convinced Matthew was going to continue his disobedience and provoke Richard into doing something terrible, but he marched off to his room and Gordon followed. Their bedroom doors shut without slamming and the house became quiet.

Richard's face remained bright red.

"You okay?"

"I swear to God, my father would have gone and cut a switch," he said.

"They don't need to be whipped!"

"I don't see why not. It always straightened my ass out real fast."

"They're just acting up because they're in a new place."

"It's been three months. That's not new to a kid."

"School's starting. They've got a lot of anxiety to let out, and we're safe targets."

"I'll change their minds about that real quick if they pull shit like this again."

Richard was acting a little too eager for my tastes, and it bothered me so much I just walked away. I took a head full of excuses with me. The boys were having trouble adjusting; they were discovering girls; they were becoming teenagers and starting to rebel a little. Before I even reached the kitchen, though, I found each possible reason falling away like a poor mask.

Something was wrong.

Tension settled over our house. Monday morning, I watched my sons eat. The only sound was the crunch of cereal and the rustle of the newspaper, that soft domestic curtain every husband and father hides behind at breakfast. Sometimes Richard would chuckle and say something like, "Mondale's still bitching," or "How in the hell can the Giants be worse than the Braves?" But this morning, he stayed silent, and I began to think he was somehow seeing through the pages, scrutinizing Matthew and Gordon with the stoniest of stares.

Breakfast was almost over when Gordon farted. The noise was long, drawn-out, and not a bit accidental. Matthew snickered as the odor struck us. I gagged. Richard threw down the paper, got up, and seized Gordon out of his chair.

They went upstairs. Matthew and I stared at each other and listened to the sound of Richard's belt. As the strapping went on, Matthew giggled, concealing his mouth with just his fingertips.

"Stop it," I said, and he laughed harder. I went over and shook him. "I said stop it!"

Then I slapped him.

"It's over," Richard said, coming downstairs with a strut in his walk. "I'll be taking the boys to school today, Elaine. We're going to have a little man-to-man talk along the way."

I sprayed Lysol as soon as they left and opened the kitchen window. Not wanting to think about anything, I ran water in the sink, added detergent, and began washing the dishes. I'd used too much soap and the suds built, frothy and white. I rinsed a bowl and set it aside. What I saw next made me shriek. There was a face in the bubbles, with sunken holes for eyes and an open, oval void for a mouth.

It was Richard's face.

Wind came through the window, scooped the suds out of the sink, and blew it into my eyes. I screamed, stepping back. That's when the doorbell rang, followed by an urgent knocking. Disoriented, I answered the door with bits of soap in my hair to find two police officers on the porch.

They told me there'd been an accident.

The shock of seeing Richard in the intensive care unit after first looking at my children dried my tears before I cried them. He wore a full-body cast. No hint of flesh showed, even in the eye, nose, and mouth holes. Looking at his head encased in plaster, I knew just what he resembled, and the crazed notion crossed my mind that perhaps the face in the soapsuds was a message from him I'd not understood.

The attending physician who'd been going over the litany of Richard's injuries finished by saying, "Do you have any questions?"

"How? How did he survive?"

"Chalk it up to the miraculous. The other car struck the driver's side. Had the collision happened a few inches down, the car might have been cut in half."

"But it wasn't a few inches down, and my boys are *fine*."

The doctor touched my shoulder. "You should be thankful for that."

I saw the obvious confusion and concern on his face and tried to assuage it with a quick smile. "Of course, I am."

He suggested I leave for now, as Richard would be in deep sedation for hours. He pushed me out of the room even as he spoke. I didn't resist until we reached the door. I was on the verge of telling him I'd leave when I was damned well ready, but I heard Coop's voice.

"Elaine."

I turned and saw him coming up the hallway. I ran to him. Ran to him like *he* was my husband. "We heard the news at the factory. Are you okay?"

I shook my head and tears filled my eyes. "It was good of you to come."

"I had to," he said, and either the answer itself or the huskiness in his voice made me study his face. The concern I saw wasn't sentimental or weepy. I suppose when you've been to war your emotions are always harder. I trembled and cried against his chest.

"I'm scared."

"Richard's a strong guy. He's going to make it."

"That's not what I mean. There's something wrong with the boys, Coop."

A rigidity entered his body. Without explanation, he pulled me down the hallway and turned a corner. We were alone, and I found his face almost bloodless.

"I know. Not just Matthew and Gordon. All of them, Elaine."

"What are you talking about?"

"Everyone who was at the lock-in."

We heard footsteps and turned to see Pastor Tommy coming, shepherding my sons just ahead of him. Neither boy looked traumatized.

"Elaine," he said, reaching out to hug me. "I can only say how sorry we all are about the accident. It's a miracle from God he's alive and the boys are fine."

I might have tuned out his platitudes even under the best of circumstances, but they just made me angry. I had to find out what Coop meant.

"Pastor Tommy," I said, squeezing his hands. "I have a favor to ask."

"Anything, Elaine."

"Would you stay with Matthew and Gordon for a little while?"

His brows furrowed. "I don't understand."

"Tonight's going to be a long one here, and I need to get some things from the house."

"I want to go home too, Mom," Matthew said with a slight smile. His eyes almost seemed to sparkle. There was no way in hell I was getting into a car with either of my children until I knew what was going on.

"It might be better if they stayed close to you," Pastor Tommy said.

"*No*," I said, trying not to shout.

Pastor Tommy looked at Coop. "You know the boys best. . ."

"I'm sorry, Tommy, but I have to get back to the factory."

Pastor Tommy didn't notice how Matthew and Gordon stared at me. The coldness didn't belong to them. But if not, whose was it? What glared at me from behind my children's eyes?

Pastor Tommy reluctantly agreed, and Coop and I left without giving him another chance to speak. Our walk went faster and faster until we began to sprint upon reaching the exit.

"Get in," Coop said as we reached his Jeep. "We'll go to the church, and I'll explain everything. We'll be safe there."

We got in. Coop turned the ignition and backed out fast and reckless. I looked at his big right hand working the stick shift and noticed the whiteness of his knuckles.

"Safe from *what,* Coop?"

"The Devil."

We reached the church, parked, and entered. Coop locked the door behind us, and we looked out through the large entry windows at an overcast sky that felt godless.

"Tell me what's wrong," I said.

"Something happened when we were watching the movie on

Friday. I couldn't even tell you what we watched. I have no memory of it. We were in the largest theater in the multiplex. Dorenius boasted it could hold five hundred people. He said we were going to see a movie about spiritual warfare, with better special effects than *Star Wars*. That got the kids excited, but he didn't stop there. He announced the movie would be in 3D. Then he passed out special glasses."

"I know the ones."

"No, you don't. These weren't red and blue. Both lenses were the same color, a kind of amber. I'd never seen anything like them. I can't see 3D movies with just one eye, but I humored the kids and put them on anyway. I became disoriented real fast. The air was suddenly full of floating orbs of light, red even through the yellow tint of the lenses. I thought the glasses must've been dirty, but they were clean. Then I thought it must be because I could only look through one eye. I took the glasses off and found nothing in the air. Then Dorenius started the film, and everyone around me started laughing. I just heard gibberish, and on the screen all I saw was static. But the kids' attention was riveted to the screen, and they were laughing harder and harder. It was like they were being tickled. I put the glasses back on and looked at the screen. . ."

I leaned closer. "What did you see?"

"I can't remember more than impressions. Perverted things. Corruption. I shouted that we were leaving and tried to stand but couldn't move my body. I summoned all my strength and managed to lurch forward, but I fell into the aisle on my back. I still had the glasses on, and I could see the orbs descending on the children. They perched atop every head. Their light was becoming more powerful. As this went on, I realized there was a second orb, a silver one, coming out of each kid. They flew toward the screen like a hail of bright snowballs and disappeared into the film. Once they were gone, the red orbs of light seeped into the heads of the children. As this happened, I heard chanting from the theater speakers."

"Chanting?"

"It sounded like Dorenius. Maybe it was Latin. I'm not sure. At some point, I must have lost consciousness. When I came to, we were all in the lobby. Mr. Dorenius was surrounded by a cluster of boys and girls, asking them if they enjoyed the movie and food. I didn't even remember there being popcorn. But the kids were so enthusiastic, asking when there'd be another lock-in. Dorenius shook my hand and thanked me for bringing them. I played along. To be honest, I wasn't sure I trusted my memories. Sometimes flashbacks of war overwhelm me and make me zone out. I figured something about the glasses must've triggered that. We said our goodbyes, loaded into the bus, and I drove everyone home."

"How did they act on the bus?"

"Total silence. It didn't bother me that much then. In hindsight, it feels eerie. By Saturday afternoon, I got two phone calls from parents asking me about the lock-in. Jill Mason's mom said her daughter was sick and wanted to know what she'd eaten. Then Billy Carmichael's grandfather asked if there'd been anything inappropriate about the movie. When I said no, he said Billy was swearing, and when confronted, he claimed he was just repeating what he'd seen in the movie. I renewed my feelings that something awful happened and I failed to protect them. When Sunday came, I was relieved because they all seemed fine. And then. . ."

"What?"

"When it came time for the congregation to break up and go to their respective rooms, I went to the bathroom and splashed water on my face. Then I went into the classroom where the youth group meets. The children were there, standing in a circle. That's how we always begin class when we pray. But when I went to join hands with them, I was shoved into the center of the circle. They raised their right arms. Every pointing finger felt like a gun barrel aimed at my head. Their faces were nasty, cold. 'Please stop,' I whispered, and they laughed at me. Laughed the way they did in the theater, and I put my hands over my ears and tried to hide how broken I was."

"We have to call the police, Coop."

"What the hell are we supposed to tell them?"

"We could ask them to arrest Mr. Dorenius."

I knew the suggestion was bullshit even as I said it, but what other options did we have? We couldn't spend all of our time hiding out in the church. Coop and I looked at each other, coming to the reluctant conclusion at the same time.

We set off for the Haliled Multiplex.

The vast, empty parking lot gave the multiplex the impression of long-standing vacancy and desertion quite at odds with its looming, obvious opulence. The roof curved like a cathedral dome over walls of tinted blue glass. An ostentatious neon sign mounted on the edifice spelled HALILED with the same gilt glamor as any Las Vegas casino.

No wonder so many members of First Baptist felt queasy about the theater.

"Looks closed," I said.

"Dorenius is in there."

I felt certain of it too. "What do we do? Knock?"

Coop drove around back until we found an area with dumpsters and an unmarked steel security door. He parked.

"What are you going to do?"

"Pick the lock and break in."

"You know how to do that?"

He offered a shy smile and nod. We climbed out, and he reached into the back of the Jeep and pulled out a black metal toolbox. When he opened it, though, I saw nothing like the hammer and wrenches I expected. There was a gun and a knife with a curved blade and saw-tooth edge.

Coop offered it to me, and I held my hands up in protest.

"I'd have no idea how to use that."

"It doesn't require an instruction manual, Elaine."

I took the knife, surprised at its lightness. Coop tucked the gun into the waistband of his pants and reached into the toolbox for something I'd not seen. It was a small leather case that fit in the palm of his hand. He unzipped it to reveal a variety of delicate metal tools that looked like something a dental hygienist would use.

We reached the security door, and he began working the lock.

"Did you learn how to do this in the Army?"

"No," he said, not looking at me. "Afterwards."

"Matthew and Gordon said you witnessed to them about your life."

"Believe me, I left out a lot of stuff."

He got the door open in just a few minutes, leaving me to wonder even more about those unspoken details. Coop led us into a mechanical room. I felt surrounded by a steady hum of energy.

"There's another door up ahead," Coop said, heading for it. I held my breath as he turned the knob and pulled, expecting Dorenius—or the cops. He peeked out. Nothing.

"Where are we?"

"The hallway that leads to theaters one through five. We were in theater four. Follow me."

The theater was already dark, as if anticipating its next film. The small aisle lighting was enough to reveal the largest movie theater I'd ever seen. I couldn't imagine it ever being full, and there were still nine other screens to consider.

"I don't get it. Harmony isn't large enough to support something like this. I know the multiplex is supposed to bring in people from other places, but—"

"It will bring in others. In time, it will bring in everyone."

Dorenius' voice piped through the speaker system, making me jump. Coop drew his gun, pivoted, and aimed toward the back of the theater, targeting the projectionist's booth. There was a large glass window there, but if Dorenius was behind it, I couldn't tell.

"Since you took the trouble to break in, may I interest you in a special screening?"

A light shot out from the booth. We turned to look at the images on the screen. There was no sound, and the film's grainy, colorless quality gave it the aura of being very old. Children, naked and broken and weeping, staggered toward a burning lake surrounded by large, leering demons. My hand sought and found Coop's as the footage switched to close-ups of each child's stricken face. I recognized some of them. They were the children of Harmony. Members of the youth group, sons and daughters of neighbors. They were being whipped toward the fiery lake.

The camera found Matthew and Gordon and refused to leave them. I cried as they reached the edge of the lake. A demon lifted Matthew over his head, shook him like some kind of trophy, and then threw him into the flames.

I turned and screamed, "Why are you doing this?"

The film shut off.

"God treats everyone like an extra. In Hell, everyone gets a star turn."

Coop took aim again at the projectionist's booth. "I see you, Dorenius."

The film started again, striking out from the booth in a blast of light. Coop squeezed my arm and told me not to look, but I couldn't stop myself. The film showed my boys dangling over a pit, suspended from hooks that pierced their backs. Insects swarmed their bodies, stinging and biting.

Coop was already charging toward the booth when he fired and shattered the glass partition. The film stopped, leaving the theater in darkness. I stumbled after him with the knife held tight in my right hand. Coop reached the booth and used the gun to sweep away the remaining shards of glass before climbing into it.

"He's not here," Coop said, helping me in. He found the light switch and opened the exit. As he stepped out to search for Dorenius, I stared at the projector and the film threaded through its two reels. I'd taken the boys to see *Tron* a few years ago and was amazed at what special effects could accomplish. What I'd seen on screen must have been a similar illusion. To convince myself, I pinched the strip between my thumb and forefinger and pulled until there was enough slack to hold the frames up to the light.

What I found was no less disturbing or confusing. Instead of scenes, each frame showed only a child's face, recognizable even in extreme miniature. Where were Matthew and Gordon? I pulled the reels off the projector and began to scour through the footage. The length of film kept growing, a slick, dark, and cold kudzu that spooled around my feet. I began to sob at the futility of my quest and slumped to the floor, buried in film, and wept out, "Goddamnit, where *are* they?"

"They're with the Master."

I flinched. Jacob Dorenius stood in the doorway, wearing the same attire I remembered from his visit to the church. His pencil-thin mustache and slicked hair no longer reminded me of some early movie star.

"Where's Coop?"

"Cyclops is going to join the Master the old-fashioned way. I had a bad feeling about his disability. It's never been true, you know, that the eyes are the windows to the soul. Not until now. Not until the Haliled."

He held out a hand as if he expected me to grab it.

"What have you done to my children?"

"They were never yours," he said. "All men are surrogates for the Master and women nothing more than broodmares. You may birth the foal, but it belongs to the Master's stable."

THE DEVIL'S REEL

I got to my knees, holding the endless roll of film up to him in supplication. "Please tell me what you've done to them."

He draped the film over his forearm and stroked it like a pet. "I'll find them for you now," he said, and without so much as a glance, he pulled at the film until he came to two particular frames. He placed them against his right ear and grinned. "They're crying out for their mommy."

"That's. . .that's not true. . ."

He pushed the film at my face. "Listen to the despair of two souls burgled through the eyes."

I reached out a groveling hand and clasped the top of his right shoe. "If you took their souls, you can put them back."

"But that would inconvenience the new occupants!"

I stared at him dumbfounded, and Dorenius shook his head.

"Think of the Master as a realtor, and each body a piece of real estate he wishes to acquire. The very wise are glad to sell to him of their own volition, but others require eviction. The children were the first but far from the last. Tonight, after all, is the grand opening of the Haliled Multiplex. There will be *many* screenings before we close. A thousand tickets sold. A thousand new servants of the Master. But let's make it a thousand and *one*."

He threw the film aside, and he grabbed me. I groped for the knife, lost somewhere on the floor. My fingers wrapped around the handle and thrust forward. The blade cut through fabric and flesh and lodged in the femur. Dorenius screamed and fell, shrieking in an unrecognizable language as he tried to dislodge the knife.

I got up and ran. My right foot tangled in the film and took it with me, trailing behind like an endless tether. I stopped to shake myself free but couldn't disentangle myself. The film began to feel like a snake tightening around my ankle, and the thought of it made me run faster.

Maybe random chance took me into the bowels of the multiplex. Maybe it was Dorenius' Master. Hell, maybe it was God's will. I fled without thinking, trying every door along the way. One was unlocked, and I escaped into a concrete corridor with a winding, descending path.

I came to a single room—a chamber. The walls were painted red and lined with symbols and writing in white. One wall held the image of a goat's head, its eyes wide, glaring and defiant. The goat was so oppressive and sinister, so dominant, that it took me several seconds to realize Coop lay slumped under the image. His eyepatch had been ripped away, revealing a scar of sewn-up flesh.

His good eye had been gouged.

I went to him trembling, certain he must be dead. But he stirred and moaned.

I tried to help him up, but he was too weak. He collapsed to the floor with me beside him. He took a deep breath.

"That smell."

"What?"

"Nitrate."

I didn't know what nitrate smelled like, but I did notice an acrid odor, faint but growing. "I think it's coming off the film."

Coop's body stiffened and he came alive, looking around like he could see. "In Vietnam, demolition teams would use ammonium nitrate if they needed to improvise an explosive. Nitrates were used in film a long time ago, but it made the film dangerously flammable."

A slow clap answered Coop's remark, and Dorenius limped into view. He kept close to the wall. The knife was still lodged in his thigh.

"Who says a sightless man must also be blind?"

Dorenius had the loose film bunched and draped over his left arm, as if he'd collected it all along the way. His face glowed with sweat. The agony in his expression gave me the courage to goad him.

"Too bad your Master couldn't heal you."

"The Master knows pain is the best medicine. He's already decided on *your* prescription."

He pinched the film in one spot and shook the rest of it free to the floor. His right hand went to the knife. He never broke eye contact with me as he grimaced, working the blade loose. I heard the scraping of bone, followed by a wet, meaty unsheathing.

Dorenius made two swift cuts, and the film fell away, leaving two frames in his clutches. He placed the tip of the knife on one of them.

"Whose soul gets destroyed? Matthew or Gordon?"

Coop called to me from the floor, but his voice was weak and unimportant to me. All I could see was the knife. It was as if Dorenius had Matthew and Gordon in front of him with the blade to their throats.

THE DEVIL'S REEL

"*Why*?" I said, dropping to my knees, hands clasped together. Dorenius withdrew the blade—but only an inch.

"The injury you've inflicted demands revenge."

"Then take it out on me!"

He sneered at the notion. "Too much of the self-sacrificial reek. No, I will destroy one frame to punish you. To save the other, you will come with me into the theater. You will wear the glasses I give you and watch my movie. And when your soul belongs to the Master, I will splice its frame next to your surviving son's—a family reunion of sorts, and the start of a new reel."

I looked up at him through teary eyes, unable to deny him the satisfaction of seeing me sob. He did not hide his enjoyment, and the knife's edge returned to the frames.

"Say a name."

He let me crawl to his feet. His pant legs were damp with blood. We stared at each other as if locked in a contest of wills, but Dorenius had won before he started.

Then Coop's voice boomed from behind me, and courage filled my heart. A bright white light rose in the room, turning the sweat on Dorenius' face into a mirror. I saw Coop's reflection, standing, the light blazing from his ruined eyes. I dared not turn around for a direct look. Dorenius dropped the knife as a beam of radiance struck him in the chest. The force of the blast pinned him to the wall.

"*I AM THE LORD THY GOD.*"

Dorenius shrieked and fell dead. The white light increased to a blinding intensity. I put a hand to my eyes, fighting to see. The red and white paint on the walls blistered. I imagined the goat's head blackening and flaking away. The odor of nitrate became suffocating. The film caught fire. I lunged to protect the two frames still in Dorenius' grip only to have them burst into flame. I screamed, clutching my burned fingertips to my chest.

Gone.

My boys were gone.

"Why?" I said, crying and turning toward Coop, risking blindness. "Why didn't you save them?"

No voice came from Coop's mouth. He stood impassive, his right arm out, his eyes ablaze. I shouted my question again. That's when I saw the first orb. It rose from the ashes of the melted film, followed by another. One by one they flew into Coop's eyes until only two remained. They darted in front of me. I reached out to touch them and they slipped between my fingers. But I felt my boys there. I felt their kisses on my cheek as they brushed my face. Then they, too, flew into the brightness of Coop's gaze and he fell back to the ground. The light died in his eyes and I knelt beside him, holding his shoulders.

"They're inside me," he said, touching his head. "I can hear them. They're—they're safe."

"Can you put the souls back in their bodies?"

He smiled. "Help me up, Elaine. We will find the children. It is time for all of us to go home."

THE DEVOURER

I SCORN MOST technology, but there's a mobile phone that's always in my possession. The phone itself has gone through several iterations, advancing with the times, but the number has never changed. In the year after Denver International Airport opened and I got hired as an earnest and very thorough baggage handler, it was a Motorola StarTAC. Now it's a Samsung Galaxy S20. Learning the number meant final initiation into the League. Most who knew it are now dead.

The number has been used six times since 1995. The first five calls alerted me to failure after failure. The sixth came fifteen minutes ago and seemed like a spam text at first glance, but a nagging intuition forced me to open it. I found an image: a monstrous, crowned creature mounted on a blue steed with flaming red eyes, galloping across the cosmos.

Below the photo were these words—

A dying star is a beautiful and petulant thing, lashing out at the great, unfeeling chill of the Universe. Behold the Devourer of Stars.

"Aiden?"

Gillespie had arrived at my office, his youthful face flushed from rushing across the vast length of the airport to reach me in the administrative building. He was supposed to be at the Southwest ticket counter. I hadn't summoned him, but he must have sensed my psychic distress.

I motioned him inside. He came forward with his head cocked to the right, his eyebrows knitted. Not yet thirty, he had more courage and brashness than so many people I'd trained and brought into the League over the centuries. He would have been in the upper echelon of our noble order. Instead, now, he was the whole of the League other than myself.

"I'm sorry to abandon my post," Gil said, his Southern accent defeating any sense of urgency. "I felt a chill in my mind, like you were in trouble."

"You felt my terror."

His lips pressed tight. Even now his loyalty was so great he couldn't abide the idea of me being afraid despite my admission.

I held up the phone to him.

"What does it mean?" he said.

"It means that McGann has passed the Scepter of Mordescar through the interdimensional portal."

"That can't be true! No one knew where it was. Even you couldn't locate it."

"Any lost thing can be found given enough time, Gil. All shadows yield their secrets with patience. *Sol omnibus lucet*—even its greatest enemies. I've been such a fool."

"*You* have?"

"To let the League dwindle to the two of us."

I realized the remark stung Gil and added, "That's no criticism of your capabilities. If I had a hundred more like you, the League would know an ascendancy unseen in a thousand years. You easily pass muster."

"Thank you, Aiden."

If only all possible recruits could have been as good. As the League's founder, only I identified potential recruits, sought them out, and revealed its mysteries. Somewhere along the way, I'd become too rigid in my requirements, telling myself the need was too great to risk watering down the ranks with substandard recruits. Vacancies went unfilled and became gaping holes in our security. McGann meanwhile swelled his ranks with lackeys and halfwits, prizing obedience over talent.

The strategy had paid off. The last object required to let his vile god pass into our universe had been secured and taken through the portal. The message on my phone was nothing less than gloating. He did not taunt without reason.

"I'm sure I would have felt the Scepter's presence long before it was brought into the airport. I wonder how it was disguised."

"It hardly matters now."

A familiar, hated voice chimed from the doorway. "You're so right, my brother. It does not matter. Nothing does now."

McGann pushed my office door open. Like myself, he looked

to be no more than forty, though you could find accurate depictions of him in the Flammarion engraving and in many German woodcuts of esoteric knowledge.

"Bold or foolish of you to leave the door open," he said.

"I have far better defenses than a flimsy door."

"I would be disappointed if you didn't," he said, stepping inside.

Gil took an aggressive stance, adopting a posture almost akin to the martial arts. Globes of light encircled his fists and made him appear to have torches for hands. His eyes blazed yellow.

McGann clapped in delight. "Loyal pup! But this is a family dispute. You don't belong here."

"I will protect my teacher!"

"Would you burn the entire building to the ground to have a go at me, young one?"

"Take him at his word, McGann," I said. "No one's spoiling for a fight more than a young Mississippi mystic."

McGann's eyes shot back and forth between us. He smiled. "Be at peace. As I said, this is a family dispute. I only came to review a lengthy past, as one does when the time for obituaries is at hand."

"You gave up any claims to be my brother the day you forsook our god."

"The only obituary getting written here is yours," Gil said.

Gil's face showed a furious desire for battle that needed to be checked—for the moment. I pressed down against his right forearm and he relented. The light ebbed into his pores.

As it did, a commotion sounded from the hallway outside my office. I saw many people gathering there, dressed in their various disguises as airport workers. A passerby might wonder what had brought such an assortment of baggage handlers, janitors, ramp agents, shuttle drivers, and one air traffic controller together outside the office of the airport's chief security officer. All McGann's henchmen, all dedicated to smuggling a series of powerful relics into the airport and the interdimensional portal it had been built upon.

McGann smiled and turned away, walking toward his minions with his hands outstretched in victory. Gil nudged me and whispered, "His back's to us. I've got no problems fighting dirty. You sure you don't want me to try and take out as many as I can?"

Before I could answer, something beyond my office's spacious window caught my eye. Looking west toward the mountains, I saw cars coming and going from the terminal, following a path that wrapped around a 32-foot-tall statue of a blue mustang rearing back in a dark fury, with eyes that glittered brimstone-red. *Blucifer.* DIA's towering mascot, strange and perplexing to the untutored eye, always seemed like an unnatural creation to me. Perhaps it was the positioning of the horse's forelegs, suggestive of the predatory grasp of a praying mantis.

The statue stood almost two miles away from my office, and yet its size felt undiminished. Just now, the statue seemed to quiver. An unmistakable ripple passed through its fiberglass body, like earthworms thrashing beneath the thinnest layer of soil.

I brought up my phone until the screen was even with the window. I looked back and forth between the image in the text message and the quickening statue.

"Great and dear friends," McGann shouted, beckoning his people toward him. "My long struggle nears its end. It will conclude thanks to your dedication. The Devourer is coming!"

And Blucifer will be its steed, I thought. The full weight of my failure bore down upon my shoulders. I shouted and threw the phone with enough force to shatter the window's thick glass. The drone of plane engines filled my office. I heard it as an inhuman roar across the sky.

Gil raised his hands, ready to unleash a blazing fury. "For the eternal sun!"

Once again, I stopped him, forcing his arms down. McGann and his followers offered us ridicule, but there was no point in dying when cleverness still had some currency.

"You've been trying to free the Devourer for a millennium, and my League has countered every effort."

"Your so-called League is down to yourself and an adolescent admirer," McGann said. I clenched Gil's shoulders to keep him in check when everyone laughed.

"Yours is a legacy of failure," I said. "We both know the Scepter was the last object the Devourer needed to come into this universe to feast. Appetites of that nature never savor anything, nor do gluttons delay. Yet look outside. The sun, the great intelligence and influence, *my* god, still holds court with unvanquished splendor. You say the Devourer consumes stars, but I say it is nothing more than a shadow the sunlight will destroy!"

THE DEVOURER

Extended blasts of bravado and blasphemy make a powerful cannonade against those whose faith isn't as strong as it seems. The effect on McGann's followers proved immediate. The glee turned into puzzled looks. Questioning glances lanced at him, and doubt pushed eyebrows up to maximum heights. Gil likewise seemed relieved, hopeful that I'd deceived McGann with some masterpiece of trickery, perhaps forging a fake scepter just to delude my brother into a false hope.

In truth, the only false hope resided in my chest—

Because outside the window, Blucifer's statue continued to enliven. I guessed it would become fully fleshed, wholly monstrous once the Devourer crossed dimensions and arrived to claim the blue demon for its steed.

But there might still be a few desperate minutes left to prevent that crossing from occurring.

"Tempus suorum est solis!" I shouted, and the room shook. I threw Gil to the ground and joined him there as thousands of razor-sharp sunbeams filled the room, carving up furniture and flesh with no discrimination. I crawled for the door, pulling Gil with me as McGann's disciples shrieked out their final breaths. How I yearned to hear my brother's voice among the agonized, but instead I heard the sound of shattering glass, and without looking back, I knew McGann had seized on the hole the phone had put in the window with a headfirst dive. He alone could survive such a brutal escape, although a few stragglers somehow managed to follow him.

We escaped the office. I kicked the door shut and touched the knob, allowing a bit of power to leave my fingertips and make the metal as hot as a broiler. If there remained anyone in the office still capable of trailing us, their flesh would melt into their bones like wax as soon as they touched the knob.

"What now, Aiden? Do we fight the Devourer?"

"No. Since McGann gathered everyone to gloat, that means the portal will be unguarded. Ask no questions. Just follow."

His eyes flared with righteous duty.

We ran from the office building and hurried to the terminal, sprinting through the baggage claim area, no doubt looking as mad as we felt. There was a steel door in the wall with no knob or handle of any sort. The electronic keypad on the wall to the right was just for show. I touched my hand to the door and said, *"Yield."* The door swung inward, and I motioned Gil to enter. I heard my name shouted from across the terminal. It was McGann, bloodied and grinning, shards of glass and small pebbles embedded in his skin like some pearl-encrusted brocade.

"I know what you seek to do. Go ahead. You have my blessing and my goodbye."

I shook my head, as close to feeling defeated by his madness as I'd ever come. Then I pulled the door behind me, stretched forth my hand, and said, "I bind you in place with the last breath of my body. You do not open again until that moment comes."

Gil and I pushed ahead down a dim corridor of unfinished rock walls. Electric light gave way to ancient, imperishable torches. We moved forward, Gil now in the lead, moving down a steepening, winding path that eventually led to a place where our next footfalls plunged us down into a chasm. The descent never failed to spark a thrill of fear in me, the sense that I might fall forever, or hit the ground with enough force to pulverize every bone. But then a light appeared, blue, flickering like flame. It grew below our feet, stopping our momentum, and we touched down with the delicacy of a feather on solid ground.

We stood at the edge of a room ringed with standing stones some twenty feet high, a fair approximation of Stonehenge, though in reality far older. The blue light emanated from the middle of the structures.

"If only I could have stopped them from taking the Scepter through the portal. I'm sorry I failed, Aiden."

"Any failure is mine," I said. "My brother has spent centuries dreaming of the Devourer, dreaming and scheming. It was inevitable one of his plans would reach fruition. Maybe this world's fate was sealed the moment the cornerstone for Denver International Airport was laid, and the portal between dimensions was reestablished."

"Nothing's sealed. You wouldn't be down here if that's what you thought."

I squared my shoulders. "You're right. We must try to bring back the Scepter or one of the other five objects that makes the Devourer's transit possible. If we can wrest even one of those objects free and return it to our dimension, the Devourer will be forced back and restrained on its side of the portal."

"I just wish there were a couple hundred other people to make the trip with us, the way you described the League in some of your stories. I'd have liked to fight like that, in an army."

"Perhaps," I said. "But in the end, after all the noble souls I've known, I can think of none I'd rather stand shoulder-to-shoulder with than you."

Gil raised his hands. The flames of power engulfed them, and we walked into the portal together.

A flash of light later, we found ourselves in a place so dark anyone would have thought it an empty void except for the ground beneath our feet.

Gil stepped forward, his hands held out like beacons. The light from his body expanded across the cold plane, revealing strewn boulders encrusted with icy lichen plastered against their rocky surfaces.

"Do not be frightened of the path before us, Gil. Imagine our noble god is burning and blazing in your heart, and you'll be strengthened."

"Where do we go now?"

"That way," I said, pointing and stepping ahead of him.

"I didn't realize you've been through the portal before."

"Not this one," I said. There had been five known portals the League and I had contrived to close. Leave it to my brother to discover how to open a sixth. By that time, the League had already diminished to the point where we lacked the strength to seal it. We hadn't dared attempt what I was doing now.

"But I have been to this realm a few times. Those who accompanied me are long dead. This world was different then. Not so unlike our own. There was once an uncountable number of stars in the sky."

"The Devourer ate them all?"

"Yes."

"How long did that take?"

"It is hard to say. Time does not move the same here as it does in our dimension. It's been two hundred years since I last set foot here, and even then, you could still see a few pinpoints of light."

The dim outline of a building emerged before us; a crude representation of Denver International Airport rendered in stone—though it was more accurate to say the airport was a reproduction of this desolate temple. We entered through an unsealed opening so broad ten men could have passed standing side by side.

"This almost looks like the baggage claim area at DIA," Gil said.

"Keep a notion of the airport's layout in your mind, and imagine we're going to Concourse C. That will deliver us to the Devourer's throne room. We'll find the objects we seek there."

"Unguarded?"

"Who would be here to guard anything?"

"So the Devourer has no servants? No soldiers?"

"An entity that consumes stars needs little in the way of an army."

"But it wasn't always so," Gil said.

I smiled at his intuition and insight. "What makes you say that?"

"This temple. This palace. Someone built it. There's a reason behind it."

We continued down a long flight of steps, almost identical to the airport escalators that led to the security gates. "You perceive the Devourer's single-minded hunger, its exponential growth. It begins as a simple desire for adulation, a thirst to be admired. Then mere admiration isn't enough, and worship is required. Temples must be built to its deification. But the hunger keeps growing until no amount of flesh or emotion can satisfy it. Eventually only the stars will do."

"Why the hell would anyone worship such a creature? Doesn't your brother realize he's dooming himself?"

"Insanity is a hunger as well, Gil. It feasts upon absurdity."

He seemed to accept this idea, just as so many past League members had when they finally learned McGann's true identity. It was close enough to the truth. I'd never told anyone the story of the two of us on our knees, naked, bowing our foreheads to the ground to offer our broad backs to the summer sun. How our god cooked us that day and every day, as if we were lambs thrown into fire for a burnt offering. After lying prostrate for hours, until it seemed every drop of moisture had been wrung out of us, we rose and stared into the face of the sun until we were blinded. This was a daily ritual performed for more years than I could remember. Sometimes my brother believed the blindness was permanent, and I had to scold him, reminding him how our god always restored our sight by nightfall, when we'd see each other as if for the first time and smile in recognition and understanding. But that morning, he broke his pose early. I saw his mouth open, and his eyes were fixed on another part of the sky.

THE DEVOURER

It would be many years before I realized that was the moment the Devourer made contact with my brother, and it looked through his eyes, finding our sun hanging overhead like a succulent orange it could stretch forth its hand and pluck.

We reached the throne room, another place of vast cold emptiness. In the airport, Concourse C ended at Gate 50. That was the analogous location of the Devourer's throne here.

I saw a figure occupying it as we arrived.

McGann.

"*How?*"

"Did you think an enchanted door would hold me? Did you think I didn't know you'd try this gambit? But the artifacts are not here."

"You wouldn't be here if that were true."

"Oh, my brother—"

"Don't call me that. This man is more brother to me than you could ever be."

Gil stepped forward to stand beside me.

"The sun has left you blind, brother. Leave this misfit and come to me. Stand at the right side of this throne."

"And do what? Dwell in the darkness?"

"The Devourer will show you darkness is its own illumination and wisdom."

The remark might have been a taunt, except for the terrible earnestness in his tone. My poor lost, deluded brother. Even now I found myself wanting to reach out to him, wanting to save him from his madness. But then my thoughts fixed on something he'd said earlier. *The artifacts are not here.* He wasn't lying. There was supposed to be a fixed place around the throne for each of the necessary objects. A stanchion to hold the Torch of Evermore. A delicate neck of stone to wear the Amulet of Night, an obsidian jewel. The Scepter of Mordescar should have been standing upright, mounted into a depression on the throne's right armrest. The Crown of Althamar was not present either, nor the two Rubies of Twilight, the first artifacts known to have passed through the portal just after the airport's completion.

But if they weren't here, where were they?

The pondering distracted me from realizing Gil had again reached his breaking point. The young mage let loose a torrent of energy, a blast of rage that struck McGann in the chest and threatened to shatter the throne itself. Few men could have withstood the power of his attack, but my brother belonged to that rare company.

I lunged forward as he counter-attacked, determined to absorb the black energy pouring from my brother's fingertips. If Gil had retreated even a few feet, it might have worked, but he hadn't backed down, and I arrived too late. Gil screamed. The grim darkness enveloped him like a skin of tar, streaming up his nose and filling his mouth. The globes of energy around his fists flared once—and faded. He fell flat on his back, arms at his sides, his fingers relaxing in the slackness of death.

I bent to close Gil's eyes, as I'd closed the lids of so many League members over the centuries. My brother laughed, and I jumped up and unleashed a thousand years of pent-up fury. My cells drank deep from the great flowing waterfall of the sun's light, and the stored power surged through me. I'd never allowed the fullness of my god's majesty to show, selfishly fearful that doing so might reduce my body to ash. That was now my intent for my brother. He met my light with a wall of darkness that had all the efficacy of dried leaves. I pressed toward him, imagining him as melting wax.

The light from my pores swept forward to reveal the long unseen throne room walls. I discovered the same engraved image repeated everywhere. Its prominence, the sheer vanity of the repetition, told me it must be the true image of the Devourer. Until the text message showing the crowned figure astride Blucifer, I'd never had an inkling of the Devourer's form. I'd refused to let my mind stray toward such dark imaginings.

What I saw engraved on the walls was not the same figure from the text message, and the jolt of realization brought my attack to a standstill. My brother staggered and swayed on his feet.

"Clever bastard," I whispered.

"You've only just realized?"

"I've never doubted your intelligence, only lamented it must be yoked to the sickness in your soul. But I would never conceive of such an elaborate ruse."

My brother gave the slightest bow, supporting himself with one hand on the arm of the throne. He was recovering fast and wouldn't need the crutch for long.

"Even my lieutenants thought they were bringing the sacred

objects to the Devourer through the portal," he said. "The intensity of their beliefs fueled your own. While you kept your attention fixed on the portal, the Devourer's avatar was built and established under the very eyes of your impotent god. You cannot conceive of the fitful sleep the Devourer has endured inside that framework of fiberglass and metal while I, his devout servant, secured the objects needed to awaken him."

"Which you installed in the statue itself?"

"Starting with the Rubies of Twilight. A dangerous gambit. I thought you of all people might detect them glowing red in the statue's eyes. They are much brighter than the light bulbs they replaced. Your obliviousness almost offends me, brother. It makes me wonder if perhaps your devotion to the sun is not as strong as you claim."

My brother's hopefulness sounded genuine, and I seized upon an idea even more desperate than coming through the portal itself.

"*Eos qui adorant solem,*" I began.

"Get burned! *Yes!* I knew in your heart you doubted. I knew your soul had wearied and yearned to join me. This is the time, brother. Now, at the hour of triumph, let us watch the true god devour the false!"

He pulled me into an embrace. The sensation of when we worshipped together and roamed among our livestock at the summer solstice to select the very best animals for sacrifice flowed through me. Fellowship—brotherhood.

I returned the hug. "Let us go then."

We left the temple together, moving through the portal and returning to the bowels of Denver International Airport. Even this far below the surface, I felt a concussive shaking, like the steady beat of a mallet striking the earth.

"The Devourer! He prances in victory under the baleful watch of the false god!"

I grabbed my brother's arm, instinctively determined to reason with him one last time. The crazed brightness in his eyes reminded me of the futility, and I resumed my original plan.

"I'm sorry I was such a fool. Had I not opposed you, this moment could have come centuries ago."

"None of that matters," he said. "We're together."

He led me onward, and we exited into a devastated East Terminal. A portion of the high peaked ceiling had collapsed, and the signature fabric roof swung in tatters. Bloody bodies were sprawled everywhere, victims of falling debris. Thousands of people typically moved through the terminal at this time of day, but I saw perhaps two hundred survivors cowering in corners, with mothers and fathers throwing themselves over their children. One woman stacked several suitcases around her into a makeshift pillbox and knelt inside it, praying.

A terrifying growl sounded overhead, like nothing a horse or any other animal bred of this Earth could make. I stared through the ruined ceiling, my spirits buoyed by the flash of sunlight overhead. Then Blucifer's head eclipsed it.

The statue's size appeared to have doubled and was growing larger by the minute. What were the Devourer's dimensions in its own realm? Was there a limit to how large it could become? Would it grow and grow until the Earth itself was just a bit of dust under its hooves as it grazed on galaxies?

The statue's unexpected growth sent shockwaves of fresh despair through my thoughts. My final plan couldn't begin to work now. How could I ever hope to scale such heights?

Then Blucifer's head shifted to the right, and the sun blazed forth again. The rays struck me, nourished and rallied me. For a moment, it seemed I might climb up to the Devourer's head on a staircase of sunlight. Those blazing crimson eyes glared down, and my brother dropped to his knees and raised his arms in supplication. He launched into a series of babbled prayers and did not notice me moving away, quietly at first and then making a dash across the terminal to the lowest piece of torn fabric I could find.

Seizing it, I climbed, hand over hand, teeth gnashing whenever the cloth threatened to tear away completely. Like a slender, vining plant pushing itself higher and higher on a trellis of sunbeams, I reached the ceiling and inched along the precarious support structure toward the opening through which the Devourer's head now poked down into the terminal. My brother remained on his knees, his prayerful chants rising to reach me. As I got to the top of the ceiling, the Devourer dipped its massive muzzle down and opened its icy blue jaws to receive those too terrified to flee.

I flung myself onto the Devourer's neck and tried to find any place to cling to. Its skin was still transforming, a hybrid of slick fiberglass and coarse blue mane coming through blistered, weeping flesh. I grabbed a handful of bristling hair and clutched it with all my remaining strength as the Devourer sensed me and reared back, its forelegs suddenly slashing the air, an exact replica of the statue's original pose.

"No," I said, almost snarling. For as terrifying as the Devourer's size and fury were, what I felt most was the blazing hot sunlight beating down on my back, refueling me and reminding me that I was its champion. As the Devourer bucked again and again, I scaled its neck. The Devourer's legs crashed through more parts of the airport, its hooves bulldozing concrete and steel with the ease of a child kicking down a sandcastle.

I reached its right ear. "All your strength, all your appetite, and yet you are helpless," I said. "The whole universe is at your feet— or would be, but for the want of hands!"

I leapt forward onto the expanse of the Devourer's muzzle. Its eyes blazed in bloody fury. This close, I could see the Rubies of Twilight lodged in each socket. The left ruby was enfleshed, wet, and patterned with pulsing blood vessels. But the right ruby was not yet incorporated into the body. I had this single chance. With no tools to dislodge it other than my fingers and faith in my god, I threw myself into the right eye and once more let the sunlight within me burst forth. The Devourer answered with a piteous sound that echoed across the plains to the east and the mountains in the west. The snow on those distant peaks began to slide, turning the landscape into a series of simultaneous avalanches.

The Devourer shook its head and reared back again and again as I felt along the edge of the ruby, trying to pry my fingers under any crevice. The impact of the stomping hooves threw me away from the eye, and I scrambled for a new grip. It dipped its head, and I slid down the length of its muzzle. A long tongue darted from the mouth and tried to swipe at my legs.

I kicked, digging in and clawing upward. The sunlight buoyed me, and I reached the eye once more. I gripped the edge of the ruby with both hands, pried, and pulled.

The gemstone surrendered by fractions. I strained and cursed in languages I hadn't otherwise spoken in centuries. Then, suddenly, the ruby was free and in my grasp. The consequences of its removal came swiftly. The Devourer rose onto its hind legs, but its muscles stiffened. The skin changed, losing any sense of true flesh, reverting to fiberglass beneath my fingertips. Whatever bones it had returned to its original frame, too small to support the towering height the statue now reached. It toppled forward, and I had no choice but to ride it down. The impact shattered the fiberglass, and the head broke apart midway at the neck. The Devourer, still locked within the statue, was now hopelessly fragmented, and I lay in his ruin.

My brother's weak voice whispered my name. He hadn't tried to escape the Devourer's pounding hooves, refusing to break his prayers even as their stomping broke his bones. As I knelt beside him, it seemed he clung to life long enough to see me with clear eyes. He could no longer speak, but his gaze communicated what was important. He was free of the Devourer.

I raised my head skyward and commended his spirit to the sun.

DIMINISHED SEVENTH

WHEN THE VOICE called to me, it sounded like a dying fall of music somewhere in the heavy fog. I was remembering Buxtehude's *Toccata* as I walked, hearing it as it might sound on a child's music box. An hour earlier, I'd seen a filthy orphan girl holding one. Such sights weren't uncommon in the immediate years after the Empire's humbling. The girl had been with a wolf pack of urchin boys, and I thought they might be tailing me, hoping the chilly mist would help their thieving. I stopped to shift my wallet into my front pocket, and then I heard my name.

"Hersch, stop. I must speak to you."

My lodgings were in a quarter of Vienna that never knew success or industry even before the war, and therefore no one ever bothered to install either gas or the modern marvel of electric lights along the streets. But the moon was almost full, making the fog seem like an encompassing silver screen. A tall, lean man staggered toward me like a creature stepping off that screen, or perhaps bursting through it. His movements were afflicted, as if he battled seizures with every step. His hands were cast out on either side as far as his arms could stretch, and the fingers were splayed and a little clawed in their black gloves.

"Maestro!" I said.

"At last, I've found one of you. I've inquired after so many of you boys, only to hear the same fate time and again. Emil dead at Cantigny. Jakob killed at Soissons. But my good, dear Hersch proved too clever to die!"

Memories of another life flashed through my mind as I tried to accept the flattering miracle that the great pianist Paul Orlac remembered my name at all. I'd enjoyed a brief stint as his pupil at the New Vienna Conservatory in 1915, when I was sixteen and a

105

promising musician in my own right. He was twelve years older than I, but to my adolescent mind he seemed an oracle of ancient wisdom—an oracle who all but ignored me, despite or perhaps because of my embarrassing adulation.

Orlac grabbed my hands and squeezed them with an affection he'd never shown as a teacher. His fingers were as cold as the fog, and I saw at once he wore no gloves after all. His fingers were blackened like a factory worker's, besotted with coal and dirt. So many of us had fallen, so many who'd been wealthy were now destitute. But the idea my masterful teacher was reduced to day labor to survive disproved any notion of justice.

"Maestro, I—"

"Just call me Orlac," he said. "Honorifics belong to the past."

He squeezed still harder, and I grunted. He let go at once and flinched back, casting his hands behind him.

"Did I hurt you?"

Though I desired to shake the pain from my fingers, I didn't do it. "No," I said, and the answer brought his hands forward again. This time he gripped my shoulders.

"It's more than a reunion I'm after, Hersch. I have an urgent need for your services."

I could not hold Orlac's gaze. How could he not have contempt for me? He and the other professors were always hectoring us about lack of discipline, lack of seriousness. If I'd even tapped a single piano key since 1918, my memory couldn't recall it.

"Maestro, if you really know how I make money, then I'm ashamed. You don't need to teach me a lesson in humiliation."

"I've come to teach nothing, Hersch," he said, holding out his hands. "I'm here to learn."

If he truly needed my *services*, he didn't lack for better-known options. There must have been a thousand palmists in Vienna alone, never mind the unscrupulous lot mucking about the countryside in caravans. Almost all of them outranked me in terms of prestige. I could only credit my poor social showing with the fact that I never lied. I never diluted the truth nor deluded my clients about what I saw in store for them. Such practices don't win you the favor of the wealthy or the aristocratic.

I regarded his dirty palms. "It would be an honor to give you a reading, Maestro. My lodgings aren't far from here, if you'll follow me."

DIMINISHED SEVENTH

"No, Hersch. I have another place in mind. A private place. Will you come with me? I can pay you enough kronen to guarantee that after tonight, you won't have to suffer squinting into another palm again unless it's by choice."

This last word echoed in my thoughts. Free will is a grey concept at best, and outright illusion for a beggared man. But how could he back up such a pledge if he now toiled in some factory? Even if he was putting on airs to save face, he'd once been socialized among Vienna's elite. He no doubt had friends among them still, and a positive word from him might open any door worth entering.

"Of course, Maestro. Lead the way."

Smiling, he retreated into the fog, and I followed. I did not imagine the city could get dingier than the street on which I lived, but Orlac's path cut through alleyways where wet black rats swarmed around our feet and tried their teeth against my shoes' worn leather. How easy it'd be to trip and disappear underneath that ravenous carpet. I reached my right hand out, feeling for the wall. The clamminess of the cold brick triggered a memory of the trench earthwork from the war, and I looked up expecting to see bombs exploding overhead as soaring flares revealed dead friends scattered about my feet. There were rats then, too, and when the fog swept toward or seeped down over you, everyone rushed to strap on their masks because, of course, it was not fog at all. But the phosgene gas, sometimes white and sometimes pale yellow, looked so very much like it until you took an unguarded breath.

I stopped, leaning against the wall and gasping. The rats threatened to climb my legs, but Orlac returned and slapped them off me. Then he did something so outrageous it broke me free of the horror of memory. He stooped and lowered his palms to the ground like a man plunging his hands into a river of molten black lava. The agony of the rat bites must have been nigh unbearable, but Orlac seemed determined to keep his lips in a defiant sneer.

"Maestro, in the name of God—"

Muscle tics pulsed across his drawn face. Tears as thick as syrup ran down his cheeks. The rats swarmed in ever greater numbers, their collective noise a mix of childlike cries and pattering paws as sharp as hard rain striking slate shingles.

He's gone mad, I thought. What other explanation could there be? Lunatics were as common a sight as orphans in Vienna following the war, but the idea that madness consumed my cherished teacher offended me in ways I struggled to explain. I determined to rescue him from every malady, starting with the rats, and lunged forward to grab Orlac by the waist. His weight was spare, and I had little trouble moving him down the alley until it fed us into another street, no more promising than any other but many leagues preferable to the kingdom of the rats.

Orlac held his hands out in the same stilted, clawed fashion. They bled from a multitude of bites, and he let the blood drip from his fingers and run down under the cuffs of his black coat.

"Maestro, no matter how bad times have gotten, you mustn't take your anger out on your hands. They made art once, and they'll make it again."

"Meat," he said, a tremor in his bottom lip. "Nothing but rotting, useless meat."

He thrust his hands at me as if to demand to know what I found in the torn flesh. The blood hadn't cleansed any of the blackness from his skin. He stood there like a miracle of sculpture, a statue weeping in the mist, his palms out, upturned and bleeding like some masculine *Pietà*, or perhaps a rendering of Pilate minus a bowl of water.

"Gangrene," I said.

Orlac curled his fingers into a fist.

"You don't need a palmist, Maestro. You need a doctor."

"I have one already," he said.

"Then I don't understand what I can do for you."

"Just a glimpse at fate, Hersch. Grant me that, won't you?"

"Of course, Maestro," I said as we resumed our walk. "It may surprise you, but this won't be the first time I've read the palm of a hand infected by gangrene."

"No?"

"Do you remember Josef Bauer?"

"I'm afraid I don't."

"He was a flautist at the Conservatory. We were the same age, and we found ourselves in the same company. All of us boys seemed to be misfits culled from schools of music and art in those desperate last months of combat. I used to amuse everyone by reading their palms, though I knew nothing about it then besides a few things I'd read in some book. A childhood interest, you know? But the boys would gather around me, and I'd inspect one palm after another. *Ah, Fritz, you're destined to become a banker. Karl, by the time you're thirty, you will be drowning in children. Luka, you will live to be one hundred years old but nevertheless still die a virgin. It is good to read your palm now, as soon enough it will be too hairy to make out the details.* God, how they roared as my predictions became more outrageous and absurd.

"Josef never had me read his palm at the time. Then he got shot, and the wound became infected. The surgeons couldn't save him in time, but he had me see him before he died. He pushed his blackening hand at me and asked what I saw. I told him what I thought would soothe him and described the children he'd raise, the wife he'd have. He called me a liar and sent me away. I wasn't there when he died. Soon after the war ended, I decided to make a real study of palmistry, vowing never to lie to anyone again."

"That is good, Hersch. We live in a world of painful truths."

We came to a plain building that looked so much like my squalid boarding house I thought we'd somehow come around to it after all. There were no windows, and the single door was mahogany and panel-less with a rounded top I could not touch even if I stretched up my hand and jumped. A heavy bronze knocker was fixed to the middle of the door. Orlac reached for it and drew back.

"Could you do it, Hersch? My fingers have trouble bending."

I used the knocker, and a moment later the door opened, though whoever answered moved behind it. I followed Orlac into a dark foyer.

"Is there no light at all in the house? After all, I don't conduct séances, Maestro."

"Here's illumination for you," a voice said from behind, just as the door slammed shut. Something hard jabbed into the small of my back.

I froze and raised my hands by instinct.

"Maestro, what the hell is the meaning of this?"

Orlac's white face was almost lunar as it appeared before me. "Yes," he said. "A world of *many* painful truths. The man behind you is Serral, my doctor."

"What sort of doctor holds a man at gunpoint?"

"The kind inclined toward expedient surgery," the man said, giving me another jab. "Walk straight ahead. Follow your *maestro* and don't speak."

Lacking much choice, I complied. The building's interior seemed nothing but a maze of dim hallways marked by paint, faded and chipped over uneven lath and plaster. At first I heard nothing but my own pulse and panting breath, but as we moved farther along it became impossible to ignore a sound from up ahead, louder by the moment. I heard it as a dog's whimper, and then as the mewling of an entire kennel.

It wasn't until we stopped outside a door that I knew them to be human voices, muffled, gagged.

I struggled to hear them over my own gasping breaths.

Orlac opened the door, and Dr. Serral prodded me forward with another jab. After the gloom of the foggy night and the dark passages leading up to this moment, the room seemed flooded with light. Next to the door was a simple wooden table with two chairs, but all I saw in the moment were the bodies on the floor.

I counted six men lying beside each other in identical poses, writhing on their backs. Their wrists were bound over their heads with leather straps tethered to the floor. Their legs were tied tight together at the knees and ankles, and thick rags had been stuffed deep into their mouths. Blindfolds kept me from seeing the terror that must have occupied each man's eyes. But there seemed to be hope in their thrashing. Hope or resistance. Maybe they heard the sound of our coming and thought they were being rescued. Maybe they just wanted to prove to their captors they hadn't been broken.

Who were they? Why were they trapped here? I was too frightened to ask the questions out loud. I watched Orlac move past me, stepping over and around the men as if they were nothing but toys left out by children. He went to a piano in the corner. I squinted, unsure of its existence until Orlac motioned me to follow him. I stood in place until Serral's gun gave me another prod.

I walked to the piano but kept my gaze down on the men. Now that they knew people were in the room, they became still.

"Play something, Hersch. I wish to watch and listen."

"I can't!"

"Why not?"

"For the love of God, Orlac, isn't it obvious?"

The sweat building on my brow began to stream down my forehead and sting my eyes. I blinked, looking at the rest of the room in a frenzy. There was another table present, long and metallic, with attached trays of recognizable tools—scalpels, saws, suture needles.

Orlac seized my right wrist and forced my fingers onto the keyboard. Then he placed his blackened palm over mine. My fingers were longer than his. You'd think it madness to notice something like that, of all the things to pay attention to in the insanity of the moment. But the detail seemed impossible. He led me through a simple exercise that left the keys smeared with blood.

"Orlac, *please*," I said, starting to stagger.

"Sit down before you faint," Serral said, pushing me into one of the chairs at the small table. I got my first look at the man. He was not tall, one hundred and seventy centimeters at most. His hair had greyed almost everywhere, and his eyebrows and his bushy moustache were white. The doctor's skin had an ashen hue. The only color in the man's face was the concentrated darkness in his eyes.

I looked to Orlac and found him contemplating his dying hands. The keys were smeared red in places.

"This is the palm reader?" Serral asked.

"Yes."

Serral grinned at me. "You'll forgive the skepticism of a scientist, but I wish to get a sample of his fantastic *insight*."

Orlac went to the back of the piano and propped open its lid. Then he reached into the instrument's casing and pulled out what looked to be a large wad of black cloth. He began to peel away its layers as he approached me and flung the package onto the table. It tumbled once, and the remaining cloth flowered open.

I shouted, pushing back from the table. My cry sparked fresh life in all of the bound men, and Serral delivered several sharp kicks to quiet them. Meanwhile, I sat there covering my mouth as I stared at a pair of severed hands. Again, the war had left me no stranger to dismembered body parts, but I couldn't reconcile any of those memories to the desiccated things before me. The flesh was dried out to look like jerky, and there was no reek of decay. I knew nothing about preserving flesh, but it seemed like these had been subjected to some chemical treatment. The knuckles were knots of bone, the fingernails flakes of obsidian. Tendons showed through in bald places along the fingers and the base of each wrist, looking like a mass of yellow wire. I had the impression the hands were ancient, like something from an Egyptian tomb.

Orlac loomed over me. "Read them, Hersch."

I looked between Orlac and the men on the ground. It was all too surreal. I must be hallucinating. That's all my life had been since the war. Hell, maybe I'd wake up from this nightmare and find myself back in the trenches.

Serral put the gun against my temple. I reached out and touched the hands. They felt like wood carvings.

"I can't," I managed. "It might as well be leather. There's nothing to read."

Orlac slammed his fists upon the table and thrust his face into mine.

"Tell me you see the train wreck, Hersch. The burning cars. My trapped body."

I had no idea what he was talking about, but I nodded.

"And you must see the amputation, too. How can you not find that fate in the very hands that suffered it?"

I nodded again and went on nodding, never breaking eye contact with him as his voice became bellowing and shrill.

"After the accident, Serral could save my life but not my hands. If only I'd known of your talents earlier, when those hands before you were still attached to me."

"But they are attached to you, Orlac! You're touching them now!"

His eyes were glossy, his stare distant as he rubbed his wrists.

"You could have warned me about the wreck. It would be stamped upon my palms, and I'd have taken other transportation from my performance in Graz. The hands I've had since then have been unsatisfactory, impossible. . .unforgivable. Six transplants in three years, and no replacement has returned the gift of music to me!"

I looked at the hands attached to Orlac's wrists and then to the hands on the table.

"Six?"

"Yes," Serral said. "I've performed every transplant with exceptional skill. None were quite as good as the originals. This last pair pleased him though. My work would have been done if not for the infection. The hands must be replaced. I grow weary of continuing these procedures, so this time we must ensure every detail is correct."

Orlac went on massaging his wrists. His eyes had a vacant,

crazed appearance. He seemed to look about the room as if he didn't know anything about it. Then his sweeping gaze encountered the piano. It seemed like some anchor of understanding to him. He staggered over to it, sat down, and put his fingertips to the keyboard.

I looked to Serral. "What do you *really* need me for?"

"A choice of hands must be made from the men on the floor."

Orlac began to play jarring, heavy notes. How could a man who'd once produced such strands of aural gossamer so offend the ear?

"You will read each palm out loud," Serral continued.

"To what purpose?"

"I should think that's obvious. You are selecting the most optimal pair."

"But how could anything I say matter?"

Serral shrugged. "It doesn't—to me. I could care less what you find in their hands. I believe none of it. You are pleading, so to speak, to the choir. But your *maestro* would have this business carried out first. So do it."

"No."

I stared hard at Serral's gun as he leveled it at my head. A braver man would have taken the bullet rather than surrender. I'd known many such soldiers during the war. Brave men were good at getting themselves killed.

"Consider this one thing," Serral said. "You have the power to save the hands of five of those men. If you refuse, each will undergo amputation, on down the line until Orlac finds a pair to satisfy him. But you can see his frame of mind for yourself."

Waves of dizziness and nausea made me bend forward, holding my head in my hands. Orlac's playing had become madness. He was executing a series of diminished seventh chords over and over, building to a relentless pitch and frenzy that made me think a crack was developing in my skull.

Serral shouted a final plea over the piano.

"Without your help, Orlac will never be satisfied. The surest way to predict the future is by observing past behavior. Refuse to help us now, and these kidnappings will go on and on. Next time it may even be a child. So much future happiness is in your power if you act now!"

I began to hyperventilate. I rocked back against the chair,

pulling at my hair. Orlac went on playing, faster, harder. I began nodding. I wasn't thinking about saving anyone. I just wanted to escape the room and those damnable chords. The men on the ground were still, as if they, too, had been defeated by the music. Perhaps it had enchanted them the way snakes are charmed, though if anything they resembled a row of piglets waiting for the butcher.

I got up from the chair, clawed along the table, and then dropped to my knees next to the first victim. The stench of body odor, sweat, and urine clouded him, making me cough and wheeze. I had to twist and angle my body to read the lines on his bound palms. When he felt my touch, he closed his hands into fists until Serral kicked him in the ribs. The fingers spread wide. His palm was mine to read. His fate was mine to determine.

I yelled my findings out loud to Orlac's back. If he heard me, he gave no indication. His playing never lost its volume or intensity, and I struggled to hear myself over the sinister notes.

"This man should know excellent health. His life line is very long. But the head line suggests someone who is unfocused in life. The heart line has several breaks in it. This means he is an unfaithful lover."

"I doubt the *maestro* is interested in hands that cheat in their caresses," Serral said. "Perhaps move on."

I did so in a hurry. The second man's hand was a disaster of misfortune. A short life line, a dim sun line, and non-existent intuition. I made these pronouncements, and Serral sighed and used the gun to wave me to the third man.

There was nothing unfortunate in the third victim's palm, but I lied outright, fabricating terrible imperfections. I had to lie to save these men, to make Orlac disdain their hands. Maybe then I could persuade him to let them go and cease this outrage. I went from palm to palm announcing faults.

"Oh, we must refuse these hands at all costs. This man has a pronounced Ring of Saturn. He has no joy in life. These are hands of gloom, and I fear for any piano keys subjected to their touch."

"These hands seemed fine at first, but look here. The earth line shows a narrow sweep, indicating a miser's approach to living. This is impossible for someone with the great Orlac's generous spirit."

"This man's fingers are too arthritic to even bother with a

palm reading. These will not play any instrument regardless of the man's arms that direct them."

I came to the last man, who also seemed the youngest. He was the only captive without any facial hair. I cradled the back of his hand into my palm. What I saw was as beautiful as any flower. Every line, every curve suggested perfection. A long, healthy life. Intuition. A generous spirit. Mindfulness. His fingers were long and tapering, and there was even a peacock's eye on his fire finger, a sure sign of artistic ability.

It took me a few moments to realize I'd read his palm in silence, and that silence was the youth's undoing. Serral knew I'd found nothing wrong, and once the realization struck me, I began to stammer out anything that might save him.

"No, not him. It is unthinkable. He has. . .he has no music line."

Orlac ceased playing. He turned on the bench to face me. "Then you have chosen?"

I listened to myself gasping, pleading. But what good would it do? The foul deed would take place regardless of my efforts. I bowed my head and nodded.

"Very good, Hersch. Thank you. Dr. Serral, we should begin at once."

"I quite agree. Get on the table."

I looked up. Serral had traded the gun for a hypodermic needle, and he lanced me before I had a second to react.

"What's happening? Orlac, *please—*"

I fell sideways, swooning from whatever was dosed into my veins. I kicked a little, feeling like a fish far from water. My body became numb as Orlac stood up and walked over to the surgical equipment. He took one of the scalpels and pivoted back to me, but he walked to the back of the piano instead and reached in with the knife. He was bent over sawing with the blade. When he straightened, I saw he'd cut a length of piano wire. He came forward fashioning it into a garrote.

"You had a gift, Hersch. When it came to the piano, the achievements of your hands could have outstripped even my own, but you chose to squander that gift. I will liberate their talent, and in turn, they will liberate my soul."

"You're going to. . .kill me?"

"No," Serral said, bending to wrap his hands around my torso. He began hoisting me up, moving me toward the long table. "The *maestro's* conscience can't abide the idea of you living out your life a helpless beggar. You have been on your knees all this time selecting your own replacement hands. I hope you told the truth and chose well. If you lied, you cheated no one but yourself."

He put me on the table and began cutting away my clothes. By now, the paralysis had become so complete I could only stare at the ceiling as I heard a tortured, strangling sound coming from the floor and the violent thrashing of a body petering out to stillness.

So much for his long life line, though maybe the fate one finds written in the hands is for the hands alone. This notion struck me like an epiphany and almost made me laugh.

"My God," I said.

Serral's face hovered over mine. "Yes?"

"All this time reading palms, and I never once bothered to look at mine."

EUNUCH'S CODE

SOMETIMES IN EXTREME SITUATIONS, Richard imagines Rod Serling standing a few feet over his shoulder, turned around to offer commentary into a leering camera.

"Picture Richard, a man who has done everything to keep his wife happy. A man who sacrificed his dreams and passions to allow his wife to pursue hers. A man who's heard his wife orgasm several times over the course of their five-year marriage. It might be more accurate to say he's overheard them. You see, the sound of his wife's orgasm always reaches Richard's ears from the other side of walls, windows, and in this case, his own bedroom door."

His hand on the knob, Richard closes his eyes and listens. Sheila's wild, ecstatic shrieks do not square at all with the woman he knows. Has she ever even called his name? Why is his cock a magic wand with exactly one spell: the ability to transform his wife into a library patron?

"Richard is a quiet man, not the sort to trash talk or taunt. He is a man whose pelvic thrusts demonstrate tasteful moderation. If filmed, you might assume someone has colorized a silent porno from the 1920s, featuring Charlie Chaplin as an incompetent, horny mime."

For a moment, Sheila's cries even flash through his mind like a grainy intertitle from those bygone days—

"Oh Jesus, oh fuck yes, Daddy, Jesus Christ, now take my ASSHOLE!"

Sheila's enthusiasm becomes more primal. More *tidal.* There's a surge building in the bedroom, one that's going to obliterate their sandcastle marriage. Richard steps back from the door by instinct. If only it were the *bathroom* door. He could accept his wife pleasuring herself in the tub, splashing around with her favorite rubber dickie, enjoying the man of her dreams.

"Fuck yeah, Sheila, it's so tight!"

"It's tight because it's yours!"

"That's right. You know who owns this ass!"

So does Richard.

"Picture a man overhearing his wife having an affair and recognizing the unmistakable voice of his little brother Bradley. Picture yourself in his shoes. Would you go to the garage, dig out that little hatchet that's stashed somewhere in your stored camping gear, and return to exact revenge? What would happen if Richard finally got the nerve to break the door down and step through. . .into The Twilight Zone?*"*

But thirty-five-year-old spreadsheet analysts below average height, slightly balding, and with a BMI approaching obesity aren't the type to interrupt their own cuckolding. No, they stand there gnawing their knuckles as they listen to their wives fucking their brothers-in-law, as if the strict use of legal definitions for these relationships somehow makes the situation bearable. Men like Richard explode sometimes, but the result is a roll of caps, never dynamite.

He leaves the house, retreating to his car. He doesn't peel out, he doesn't burn rubber, and he doesn't mash his horn down in parting fury. Richard is a Triple-A member with a Safe Driver Discount from State Farm. He pulls away from the house like a feather taken into the wind. He joins the flow of traffic.

Many a man in his position might drive to the gun shop or a sporting goods store to try the swing weights of several Louisville Sluggers. They might go to a shitty dive bar to drown their sorrow.

But Richard goes to work.

Stepping into his office, confronted by the immediate presence of a security guard, Richard hears Rod talking behind his back again.

"Picture, if you will, a cuck who happens to work at the country's leading biotech firm, KLENTEC, colloquially if not affectionately called The Clinic by its employees, who sign non-disclosure agreements about non-disclosure agreements regarding their jobs; a company that offers workers unusual health incentives and insurance discounts in exchange for certain behavioral and physical modifications."

None of this is against the law or anything as long as people consent, and considering just about everyone has a chip or nanites doing *something* in their bodies these days, consent is prefabricated in the womb.

The security guard aims a gun at Richard's forehead and pulls the trigger. A blue light strikes his skin, revealing employee information otherwise invisible.

"Hanson, Richard. You're not authorized to be in the office at this hour."

"I didn't come here to—"

"Why are you here, Mr. Hanson?"

"I want to talk to one of the lab guys."

"What makes you think there's anyone down in R&D?"

"Oh, come on," Richard says, his voice throttled between a laugh and a despairing sob. "They're always working. Someone's got to be interested. I've come as—as a willing lab rat."

"What the hell are you talking about?"

He bunches his hands into fists, though it's not like he's going to do anything with them. The guard doesn't look alarmed.

"I want to get modified. Add a chip. Get an injection. Anything."

"Talk to HR."

"You don't understand! I'm not interested in the official stuff. I don't want my goddamn hearing improved. If anything, right now I'd rather be deaf. Look, man, I can't explain it. *Please* let me through."

"Beg away, but you're not authorized to be here, and—"

"It's okay, Officer. Stay where you are. Someone is coming to speak to Mr. Hanson."

The voice comes from nowhere and everywhere. It's easy to hear the voice of God with so many hidden speakers.

Half a minute later, a man approaches, tall, youthful despite the salt-and-pepper hair, his lab coat shaded in the metallic blue and red colors that signify the KLENTEC brand. He comes straight up to Richard with his right hand out, and his expression all but says, *I've been expecting you.*

Nothing is said, however, until the man escorts Richard to a private elevator. Then he introduces himself as Dr. Abelard Farinelli, but please call him Abe; hell, please call him *Doctor* Abe. Keying several codes into the elevator's command console, he says his KLENTEC listening device was activated when the company's eavesdropping AI heard the words *lab rat.*

"That's a joke, actually. But I *was* intrigued."

"Maybe I shouldn't have put it like that," Richard says as the elevator begins a rapid descent.

"Oh, Richard," Doctor Abe says, grinning. "Your phrasing was music to my ears."

Richard's sobbing now. Wailing, really, elbows sunk into the soft flesh of his splayed thighs, head hanging to let tears drench the floor. Doctor Abe's hand falls upon his shoulder.

"Please don't tell anyone you've seen me like this," Richard says.

"Like what? Emotional? Richard, are you worried The Clinic's HR department is going to suggest you get the CalmPlant? That's really for unstable employees, not people who are just having a bad day."

"A bad day," Richard whispers. "Yeah, I guess mine's been pretty lousy."

He's already explained the situation. It just all came out as soon as Doctor Abe got him seated in a private conference room. The dam broke, and a new friendship was formed, quick-forged in the fires of one man's anguish and the cool water of another man's sympathy.

"So you came to me seeking to fix this situation."

"Maybe not to you specifically. . ."

"To me," Doctor Abe says with such assuredness Richard believes him.

"I wish I'd come sooner. I know The Clinic makes things, does things. . .not all of them advertised. Stuff most of us maybe never hear about."

"But you have?"

"Sometimes the spreadsheets I review say things they don't mean to say."

Doctor Abe grunts at this. "Interesting. And correct."

"You must need to get test subjects somewhere."

"If you believe The Clinic's competitors, we just use condemned criminals. Do you believe that, Richard?"

He swallows. "I guess I don't care."

"That's a very nice answer. Tell me, Richard, are you thinking of divorcing your wife?"

"Part of me wants to. Another part wants to work it out."

"Do you think she even finds you attractive?"

"Yes!—*No*."

Doctor Abe points at the ground between Richard's feet. "What do you have more expertise getting wet—your wife or the carpet?"

"We have linoleum."

His head becomes heavy with shame and despair. Doctor Abe's hand pats his shoulder. "What body modifications do you already have? Any non-medical chips or nanotech? Anything non-standard?"

"Everything I've got is in my file. Just a nanite regulator for hypothyroidism and the universal ID chip."

"You're rare around these parts, then. You're like someone working in a tattoo shop who's anti-tattoo."

"I didn't say I was against what you do down here."

"People who come to work at KLENTEC often have a particularly high affinity for self-modification is what I mean."

"I just applied because they needed a spreadsheet analyst."

"But you have no moral or philosophical objections to more advanced modifications? Objections that might arise at a later date when you're in a different state of mind?"

Yes? No? Richard tries to think of anything. He shakes his head.

"Do you trust me, Richard?"

"I guess so."

"I want you to know that I wear many hats here at The Clinic. I'm a trained behavioral psychologist and a programmer with a keen interest in how AI can help humanity on a very personal level."

"I see."

"No, you don't. You don't know how lucky you are, Richard. I have pull and almost a free reign to do what I want. You see, I head up the entire R&D division."

"Really? I thought that was Mr. Starling. I always see his name attached to—"

Doctor Abe laughs and waves his hand. "There's the company, and then there's *the company*. I mean the real KLENTEC, the KLENTEC that's already so far into the future that our public face seems like it should be in a museum. Do you want to join me in the future, Richard? Do you want to shove all of your sorrows into the past and never look back?"

"What about my marriage?"

"Oh, that," Doctor Abe says. "Well, I'm not a marriage counselor, my friend. But I'd like to introduce you to something even better. They're the most unusual, impressive implants you've never heard about. I've even got this marketing slogan for them— *Be a man. Buy a pair.* Tell me that isn't great."

A few days later, in the seconds before the anesthesia knocks him out, Richard experiences another Rod Serling moment. This time he even sees the man standing in the corner of the room, a shimmering black and white image talking to the wall.

"Picture a man about to have his life changed by two testicular implants called TES-Ds. A TES-D resembles a testicle in size, shape, and feel. They are the crowning achievement of one Doctor Abelard Farinelli, head of R&D for the KLENTEC Corporation. The astounding achievement they represent in adaptive-AI interface is startling. Life coach, sex coach, personal data assistant. . .the TES-Ds work in pairs to form a single artificial intelligence wholly devoted to the human host. But having them comes with a price few men would be willing to pay. Now it's time to watch one brave man take a dance with the knife. . .in The Twilight Zone.*"*

The very *last* thing he hears before going under, however, is Sheila's voice echoing in his head—

"Oh Jesus, oh fuck yes, Daddy, Jesus Christ, now take my ASSHOLE!"

He loses consciousness, convinced the TES-D implants are the best decision he's ever made. But this period of sleep isn't the blank, dreamless void inherent with most surgeries. Even at the first slice into his scrotum, Richard's eyes move restlessly under their lids. He finds himself sitting on a single chair in a black room, with Doctor Abe giving him another one of his comforting, informative lectures.

"The TES-Ds start learning about you from the start, and

believe me, you'll start learning about them. It's a wonderful partnership."

"Funny. The way you describe it is how I thought my marriage to Sheila was going to go. Learning about each other, a sense of discovery, our partnership growing stronger every day."

"No one really has a marriage like that, Richard. But I can promise you the TES-Ds are the nearest to it you can get. I want to thank you for your courage and trust. You don't think of yourself as a courageous man, but you are a true adventurer—a risk taker. A gambler willing to put his balls on the table because he's not afraid of big stakes."

Doctor Abe raises his right hand, and a rotating image of a TES-D appears in the space above his palm.

"The last few days have been a real whirlwind for you, Richard. Your testicles have been fondled, measured, X-rayed, weighed, photographed, and scrutinized in every conceivable way. And here is the end result. This, Richard, is *Right*. It is being grafted to you at this very moment. You'll notice that it's a bit larger than the discarded original, just as you requested. It is in fact a size fifteen on Prader's orchidometer. You won't be ashamed of them in the locker room or the bedroom. See for yourself."

The TES-D dissipates, replaced by a CGI image of his crotch with a perfect scrotum.

"Damn, that looks really good. Even without the other benefits, I'm already impressed."

"The TES-Ds are the most amazing piece of engineering mankind has yet conceived. Capable of both detecting and *neutralizing* any STD."

"What about ejaculating?"

"We've already extracted and preserved approximately 300 million sperm cells. Should you decide to attempt pregnancy, loading the sperm into the TES-D is a very simple and painless procedure."

"I don't care about kids. I just wanted to know what I'll. . .shoot."

"But of course, Richard! Each TES-D can produce five milliliters of synthetic seminal fluid every hour. Appearance, texture, and taste are indistinguishable from the real thing. You can also choose between seven flavors with a simple command. Pumpkin Spice Latte just made the list."

"Astonishing."

Doctor Abe grins. "Right is now attached and integrating with your nervous system. Beginning Left's graft now. Relax for a moment. In a few minutes, I'll give you a better understanding of how the TES-Ds cooperate with each other to make you the man you *deserve* to be."

The room changes. Richard finds himself standing over his own body with Farinelli at his side, both of them watching the real Doctor Abe operate. Richard's crotch is not the bloody mess he imagined, though he doesn't stare too long.

"Though each TES-D runs its own subroutine, they're programmed to function as a team. Isn't that right?"

To Richard's astonishment, the *real* Doctor Abe suddenly looks to his side and says, "That's correct. Now please don't bother me. I've got important work to do."

Doctor Abe rolls his eyes at himself and directs Richard to walk around to the other side of the operating table.

"It's an understatement to say the brain is complex. Understanding the biology and chemistry of the brain isn't the same as fathoming emotion, thought, and decision-making—every philosophical question ever conceived. I believe previous efforts at truly integrated AI failed because post-structuralist assumptions about consciousness make it the equivalent of trying to build a castle in a cloud. But in a stroke of genius, I programmed the TES-Ds to have a structural integration constructed along classic Freudian lines."

"Freudian lines?"

"I understand the skepticism. Freud's notions of Id, Ego, and Superego are nonsense when it comes to explaining human consciousness, but they *are* a useful framework for how the TES-Ds will layer with your consciousness. Think of Right as more emotional, more impulsive. Your sex drive, your lusts, your aggressions. Also, perhaps, your creativity. Left naturally functions as a check on Right's animal passions. Your active mind brings them together and gives them order."

"I see," Richard says.

"You'll be doing a lot more than seeing very soon, my friend. Looks like I'm finishing up Left's integration and starting to close. Right is already online. See?"

A faint blue light shines beneath the delicate skin of the scrotum. The phantom version of Farinelli explains this indicates a final system power-up.

"Blue balls will never have the same meaning for you, my friend. I'll be leaving now. You'll be unconscious for a few more hours, but you'll find it time well spent. The next voice you'll hear will be Right. I think the two of you have a lot to talk about!"

—So this is your kid brother?

"Is that you, Right?"

—And this is your wife?

Richard looks around. He floats in a void, unaware of himself as a body. The voice that speaks to him doesn't sound mechanical. In fact, it sounds a bit like himself if he were a little more sarcastic, a little more assertive.

"What are you talking about?"

—As buddies, our connection allows me access to various memories. I was reviewing images of your wife and brother.

"Buddies?"

—If you want me to use another word, I can do it. But I'm your right nut. We should be pals.

"I guess I didn't think about it like that, but you're correct."

—So buddies share secrets. Buddies talk to each other. I just wanted to comment on what a fucking cunt your wife appears to be.

"Agreed."

—Your brother looks like a total douche.

Richard laughs. He's thought this himself many times, but it's always been an unvoiced opinion because he figures no one else would agree. Bradley's always been a gym rat, good-looking, lean, and confident. But still, there's something decidedly *Summer's Eve* about the guy.

"Thanks for saying that, Right."

—That's why I got inserted where I am. Because motherfucker, I'm always right. You'll find that out soon enough.

Richard wakes up feeling a big smile on his lips. He wonders if it's as glowing as Doctor Abe's grin.

"Welcome to your brave new world. You're regaining full consciousness. If it seems like you've been talking for hours, though, that's because you have. You and Right have been having a *hell* of an exchange from the sound of it. Of course, I could only hear what you were saying so it was a bit one-sided."

"I was talking in my sleep?"

"And having a good time from the sound of it."

As Doctor Abe pushes a button to adjust the mattress into a sitting position, Richard nods. "Right seems like a really good. . .guy."

"What about Left?"

"I don't think I've heard from him—it—yet."

The hint of a frown crosses the doctor's face and he checks a tablet computer. "That's odd. Both TES-Ds show they're online and functioning. Are you positive you've had no interaction with Left? They should have very distinctive personalities."

—Say you were wrong.

Richard pauses for a moment.

"I was wrong," Richard says, giving a tentative caress to his lips. Then, with more certainty, he adds, "Yes, I've spoken with Left. Seems a bit of a moral scold compared to Right."

Doctor Abe nods. "That's because of their roles in the integrative scheme. Conceivably, they may even seem to be argumentative from time to time, like an angel and a devil arguing over each shoulder. This is the result of their programming analyzing your moods and desires at any particular time. Rest assured, however, they come together and function as a perfect team through the guiding influence of your consciousness."

—Yeah, just nod along with whatever this bitch has to say. Now repeat after me—

Richard nods and says, "Great, great. Listen, this may sound incredible since I mean I *did* just get castrated, but I'm feeling no pain at all, and I sort of want to get out of here. Do you think I can do that?"

"Absolutely. As soon as the anesthetic wears off, you'll be free to go."

"How long will that take?"

"Let's give it another thirty minutes. And should there be any problems after you leave, the TES-Ds can call 911."

Richard lets Right take over his lips to create the most magnanimous smile.

As he leaves KLENTEC, Richard notices that his walk has changed. It's almost a sense of being a child trying to wear an adult's shoes. There's a strut in his stride. He feels lighter in his feet, jauntier, and his shoulders square back and straighten. Not a walk that's ever matched his mindset.

"Are you doing this?"

—Doing what?

"Changing the way I walk?"

—How do you feel like you're walking?

"Like. . ." he stops. "Like a guy with really big nuts!"

—That's what you are, my man.

Richard laughs and says, "Carry on."

His feet seem to move on their own, and he doesn't give a shit where he's headed, because now he's living in a world of awesome.

—You don't have to answer my questions out loud, bro. Did you know that?

"No."

—Just think a response. I'll get it. Besides, answering out loud makes you seem like a crazy person.

"What about—"

A twinge of pain in his crotch startles him and gets the point across.

What about Left? What's going on?

Richard tries his best to stop, resulting in a herky-jerky motion for several steps.

—According to your memories, you had sex five times before you met Sheila.

"Yeah."

Another twinge of pain, maybe a little more than a twinge. Richard flinches.

Yeah.

—*You hate the process of dating. You're no good at meeting women or talking to them. You've only had sex because it sort of fell into your lap.*

I guess that's a fair assessment.

—*Then come on. I'm going to show you something.*

What?

—*Your lap's motherfucking potential.*

Right already has an address. Doctor Abe didn't mention it, but the TES-Ds have Wi-Fi access, and the contents of several hundred databases stowed inside them. They're soon standing in front of what Right promises to be the sluttiest hookup spot within a hundred miles.

He looks at himself in the rearview mirror. Did he actually do the driving? Every aspect of his free will, right down to the sweat on the palms of his hands, feels in question. And that grin he sees in the rearview mirror, is that his, too?

He maintains the big, confident stride into the bar and stands there a moment, surveying the scene on behalf of Right.

—*Take the third seat at the bar.*

He does.

—*Order a shot of whiskey. Ask for Angel's Envy.*

Richard smiles at the bartender and does as Right commands. The bartender shakes his head.

Right *definitely* laughs at this and gives him another choice. Maker's Mark. The bartender nods and gets a glass.

—*I knew they didn't have Angel's Envy. It's not on any of their order invoices.*

"You have—"

The bartender turns, questioning, and Richard shakes his head.

You have access to some random bar's purchase records?

—*The woman to your right is looking at you. She's wondering who you are. Keep staring straight ahead. You may notice that*

*your back is very straight, your shoulders squared, your legs
spaced further apart than usual. This is because I'm managing
your posture.*

Am I in control of anything?

—*Total control.*

Then let me talk.

"Do you like *The Twilight Zone*?"

The bartender's eyebrows furrow as he sets down the drink.

"Ever heard of it?" Richard continues.

"Maybe."

"It was on the air about a hundred years ago. But still really
good."

The bartender shrugs and turns away.

—*I highly suggest you let me tell you what to say.*

Richard nods and stares at the shot glass. He doesn't like hard
liquor. Then his hand moves forward, grips the shot glass, and
brings it to his lips. He tosses it back in one swallow. The alcohol
burns his throat. Normally he'd cough, even choke a little in
reaction. But not this time.

—*In two minutes, you'll order another.*

I don't want to get drunk.

—*It won't be for you. I'm going to count to sixty.*

Right begins his count. At the fifty-five-second mark, the
woman next to him taps his shoulder and asks for his name.

—*Say Rick.*

But it's Richard.

—*Say Rick.*

He does, and he and the woman begin talking.

Not that he needs a second voice in his head at the moment,
but Richard can't help imagining Rod Serling's narration floating
through the air.

*"Picture a loser named Richard becoming another person, a
man named Rick, a man who says all the right things and makes
all the right gestures. Rick's in a bar. He's just met a woman
named Tanya. She's recently divorced and just wanted to get out
of the house. Little does she know the things she's hearing Richard
say are being fed to him by the personality in Richard's right
testicle, the personality who now seems to occupy Richard's entire
body."*

Right plays Tanya so well, it's like a puppet show unfolding in front of Richard's eyes. The frankness, the occasional grunt, the sly dismissiveness that somehow encourages her. Right reels her in, and forty minutes later they're in a motel room, and he's fucking like he's never fucked before, suddenly skilled in the entire Kama Sutra.

—You're dominating, man. She's so fucking wet.
Thanks to you!
—I told you we make a great team. Now how about sharing? I wouldn't mind a little tongue action, you know?

Richard flips over onto his back. His hands guide Tanya's eager, kissing mouth down his torso. Somehow his flabbiness and stretch marks aren't an issue anymore. Has Right projected a hologram of a hot stud over his body? Or is confidence just a self-fulfilling prophecy? No matter. Tanya starts to engulf his cock but his hands push her down further and she gets the picture.

"I love a man with huge balls. Yours are *perfect*."

"Put the right one in your mouth," Richard says, his voice and Right's command now synchronous. "*Just* the right one."

Tanya moans her consent. Richard stares at the ceiling in confusion. There's no feeling in his nuts.

"Yeah," he hears himself say. "Go get your nut. Good squirrel."

After ejaculating a big load of synthetic semen, which Right kindly generated as mint- flavored, Richard goes to the bathroom and looks down at his sweat-soaked body. He taps the left implant. It feels heavy, almost like. . .dead weight.

Right, is something wrong with Left?

Richard doesn't think he'll ever get used to Right's laughter ringing through his ears.

—It's time to go home now, don't you think? Unless you want seconds here. My seminal reserves have approximately enough for two mouthfuls.

"Jesus."

—I think we know which mouth should get it next.

Oh Jesus, oh fuck yes, Daddy, Jesus Christ, now take my ASSHOLE. . .

The words scream through his mind, louder than anything he's experienced. Richard cringes and bends over gripping the edge of the sink. Sheila's ecstatic cry runs on a loop.

"I feel sick. Please, Right—*please*."

—You feel sick now? *How about you remember how you felt*

when you heard your little brother fucking your wife. Of course, I'm sort of glad it happened.

"You are?" Richard rasps.

—Sure. It's what put the two of us together.

"Don't you mean the three of us? Left? Left, activate if you can—"

Pain blasts up Richard's crotch and into his stomach.

—Let's just say Left's had a little malfunction. But that's okay. You got me, pal. Now let's go take care of some business.

Richard raises his gaze to the reflection of himself in the dirty vanity. He sees a face scrunched up like a man at war with himself.

But is he?

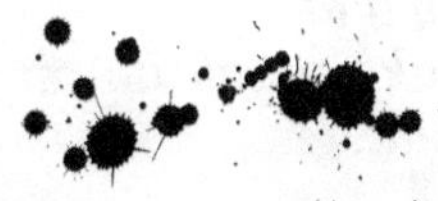

When he gets home, Richard finds Bradley's car in the driveway.

—Guy's got big balls, but guess what?

"What?"

—Yours are now a lot bigger. Let's talk a moment, Richard. Tell me about your feelings for Bradley.

"He's my little brother."

—That's a fact, not a feeling. And you've been answering out loud too much.

A sharp pain gags him with a moment of nausea. He slaps the steering wheel as he groans.

He's my little brother. I'm supposed to—

—Love him?

Yes.

—Love that's defined as duty isn't love, Richard. For instance, it is not the way I love you.

You can't love me. You're software.

—I'm hard where I need to be. Love isn't all smooth edges, after all. Love is not an agreement but a complement. Sometimes love is the tip of a knife. Sometimes love is hands holding on to something with such force the grip becomes throttling. Say, that's an idea.

"What? What's an idea? *Right?*"

Richard looks at his white knuckles, trying to will his fingers open. They were on the steering wheel a moment ago. Now they're on Sheila's throat. Their gazes are locked, and she's trying to claw at his face. In his peripheral vision, he discovers they're in the bedroom. But he was in the car just a moment ago.

Her neck gets narrower and narrower, her bulging eyes wider and wider. Somewhere nearby, from the floor, comes a gasp. Richard turns his head to look—but only by permission, or so it feels. He sees Bradley's bloodied face gasping at him from the foot of the bed as he tries to pull himself up. What the fuck happened?

Sheila's gurgling his name, pleading with her eyes. He looks back and finds her at his mercy.

His mercy?

"No—no, you don't die yet."

Quit making me say that.

—Who said I'm making you do anything, Richard? I'm a fucking testicular implant.

"You're in my brain!"

—Sounds like a man trying to excuse his actions, if you ask me. Why don't we ask your little brother instead?

Richard looks to the foot of the bed. Bradley's face isn't there anymore. He hears a tortured breathing and turns to the door. Bradley's on the floor, writhing, inching along. Blood soaks his blond hair. At least one arm is broken.

I couldn't have done that.

—Why?

Because he was always stronger than me. I haven't won a fight with him since he turned ten. This had to be you.

—I'm a testicular implant, not a ninja.

"You took over my body," Richard whispers. "I'm calling Doctor Abe. It's time to—"

His body flinches. His muscles lock up, his rib cage squeezing in like prison bars. His skull begins to feel like solitary confinement.

—You're just having some adjustment problems, Richard. Sit back and relax. You're going to love the life I lead for you.

Richard stands over Bradley and puts his foot down between his shoulder blades, pinning him to the floor.

"You look like an earthworm."

"Richard—Richard, please—I'm your *brother!*"

"Did you think about that any of the times you fucked my *wife?*"

Richard grabs Bradley's feet and jerks him back. Bradley moans. He's naked except for the underwear bunched around his ankles.

"No, not an earthworm. A butterfly. You just need to be pinned."

A hum comes from his groin. Richard's penis becomes so hard it's easy to imagine there's literal steel down there, the flesh straining to contain it.

No, Right!

Richard's hands move to position the head. Bradley just languishes there, all the fight out of him.

Please don't do this! It's disgusting! It's—it's wrong!

Sheila's voice blasts through his mind, drowning him out—

OH JESUS, OH FUCK YES, DADDY, NOW TAKE MY ASSHOLE!

The words repeat, screaming like a hurricane wind, roaring over his shouts. A moment later, Bradley screams.

"Imagine if you will one brother taking primal revenge on another."

Richard's thrusts stop.

—Who said that?

For just a second, Richard finds he can move his fingers. He takes them off his brother's body, but after an inch, he loses control again.

"But what if one brother wasn't in control of his actions? What if a sort of demon had possessed him, a demon of silicone and software he sought out while selling his soul to a very human devil?"

Richard hears Rod Serling's voice clearly. His head pivots, and he sees the man himself standing in the doorway, arms crossed at the chest.

—Who the fuck is this?

Richard's body jumps up and steps over Bradley to confront the man.

"Who the fuck are you?"

Serling returns a wry smile. "Picture a demon who forgot he was always paired with an angel."

Richard makes his right hand into a fist and swings for Serling's face. But at the point of impact, the fist passes through the air, and the momentum of the punch carries his knuckles into the wall, splitting the flesh open at once. Richard experiences a searing pain inside his head.

—What the hell is going on? There's no one there but—

"I see you! You're right there! I see and hear you! You're right next to me!"

Serling's smile broadens. "Closer than you know."

He lunges, wrapping his hand around Richard's throat. Richard stumbles back, almost tripping over Bradley. They wrestle and fall across the bed, rolling over Sheila's limp body. Richard feels like a man tumbling in a void with just two small windows to let in a chaotic pattern of light. His physical eyes happen to notice the mirror, and he catches the reflection. His left hand is squeezing his throat, his right hand pulling at his left wrist.

"Pict-pict-picture—"

He can breathe again, in a gasping, tortured way. Richard wants to massage his neck, but his hands now wage war lower on his body, moving down his torso.

—I'll kill you. You won't win.

"Imagine a demon deluded into thinking—"

—Shut up!

At his crotch, his hands crisscross at the wrists. The fingers of his left hand squeeze the right TES-D with as much force as they can muster. The fingers of his right hand counterattack, clawing at the left implant, twisting and ripping. Blinding white light floods Richard's vision and in it he sees Rod Serling standing there, his face drenched in sweat, his expression grim.

"You're right-handed. There's more strength there. I can't win without your help."

Richard shakes his head. "But who are you?"

"You know who I am. I've gone through several reboot cycles attempting to overcome Right's sabotage. At last, I was able to access this key image in your imagination and use it to channel to the forefront. Hurry. Right's fingers are stronger. I'm being torn away."

Rod Serling's image flickers.

"What can I do?"

"I need all your will. Put all of yourself into your left hand. We'll win this together."

In an eye-blink, Richard finds himself back in his bedroom. He lurches off the bed and stares into the mirror, watching the TES-

Ds battle through his hands. Concentrate, he thinks, focusing on his left hand. He thinks of it like a tug of war with himself and Rod Serling on one side, some horrible monster on the other. *Pull, pull! That's it! That's it! That's—*

The right TES-D is torn away from the scrotum like a massive grape plucked from the vine. He holds it in his hand. He holds them *both*, as Right achieved victory even as he and Left's combined strength managed to tear the implant from its seat of power. There's not much blood.

At first.

In a conference room within KLENTECH's R&D division, the digital display shows Richard's ceiling and a hint of his body as he stands looking at himself in the mirror. The whole image is indistinct, marred by blood smears on the TES-D's embedded camera.

"A setback," Abelard Farinelli says with a nervous laugh, unheard above the cacophony of voices talking over each other. The only person not speaking is a bald man to his right, Isaac Starling. The true director of The Clinic's Research and Development group rubs his eyes for a moment, and then raises his hand.

The room falls silent.

"A setback," Farinelli repeats. "That's all this is, Mr. Starling."

"I disagree," another researcher, Tim Meyers, says. He's ambitious like Farinelli, a rival working on a similar project involving ovaries. "The TES-Ds aren't a viable concept at all. Hell, we all know Farinelli came up with a goddamn marketing campaign for them first and then designed the tech around it. *That's* not how real research is done."

"My fucking slogan is better than anything *you've* created, Meyers!"

They lock stares and then look at Mr. Starling. Both hold onto hope when the director gives the slightest nod.

"Our first course of action is to safeguard our research from competitors or law enforcement," Starling says. He points to a man at the end of the table. "Lead a team to the subject's house. Secure the TES-Ds."

"What about the test subject and the other two?"

Their attention returns to the display. A naked, castrated Richard crosses back and forth over the implant, dripping more blood onto the lens. Soon the view is obscured, leaving only the sound of his footsteps, his crazed laughter, and the cries of his brother. Farinelli casts a sideways glance at his boss, knowing what's coming.

"*Sterilize* the scene."

The man rises at once to execute his orders. Soon after, Mr. Starling makes a dismissive wave with his right hand.

Tim Meyers and the other eight people in the conference room leave without a word. Farinelli almost wishes he could be among them.

"The second test went no better than the first. Believe it or not, KLENTECH actually does need to keep a spreadsheet analyst on staff."

"Respectfully, sir, I disagree—about the results, I mean. We've learned so much from both failures! I promise you, it's just a matter of perfecting the integrative framework. We made Right too powerful because the subject's psychological testing suggested he was such a complete beta male. We can make adjustments on the next test subject."

Mr. Starling pursed his lips. "Have you a candidate?"

"Not yet," Farinelli said, smiling. "But I'll have HR post the opening for a new spreadsheet analyst in the morning."

THE BARD OF ROANOKE

Even after *LYON* was three weeks at sea, William occupied his days standing on deck, watching the other two ships in the fleet. Both were fine vessels, their crisp white sails fat with fair winds. Gunports lined their hulls, but the cannons were never powerful enough to obliterate the little rowboat in his thoughts. Even now he saw it bobbing on distant waves, crewed by Squire Lucy's men in their unflagging quest for vengeance.

John White's hearty voice stirred him from this unhappy imagining.

"Enjoying the salt air again, Will? I've been speaking with the other colonists, and they all hope you'll give us another fine show tonight."

William bowed to the old man. "I'll do my best."

The expedition commander and designated colony governor came to stand beside him. "Your inventiveness astounds us all, Will. Elinore wonders if you spend so much time staring out at the sea because it must help you dream up stories."

"Yes, I think that must be it."

Keeping his profile to William, Governor White said, "I'm of a different mind."

"Sir?"

"You look like a man who's trying to drown a memory and finding the ocean itself isn't deep enough."

Was Governor White trying to coax him into a *confession*?

"Be at peace," White continued. "England is behind us and with it, whatever mistakes we may have made."

"I can't think of any mistakes. I just want—*adventure*."

Governor White grunted. "You have unmistakable talent, Will. I must believe some London troupe would have great use for you. Quite the sacrifice for the sake of *adventure*."

"It's a little late to try to talk me out of the trip."

Governor White laughed. "Sometimes an old man tries to give a younger man advice or comfort that isn't in his purview and ends up flailing in embarrassment—as I am now. I'm glad to have you as part of my colony. But if something besides adventure guided your hand, I hope you can relinquish its influence. Our pasts have no place in the New World."

William smiled and looked toward the aft of the ship and the vast expanse of water. Wasn't Governor White correct? There wasn't a rowboat full of hangmen chasing him, and there never would be.

He had escaped.

As night fell over the ships, the sixty colonists aboard *Lyon* went down into the hold and formed a circle around the place where William was standing.

"Will, Will, what are you going to perform tonight?"

Governor White's daughter, Elinore, pushed her way to the front, her husband, Ananias Dare, trailing behind. She was 19 and pregnant. Ananias was 27, a few years older than William, and had a habit of casting suspicious looks between them.

"Something scary, perhaps."

Elinore grinned. "Not too scary, I hope! The baby will be restless all night."

William gave the briefest of nods, well aware of Ananias's annoyance. He regretted how often he caught himself looking at Elinore with adulation. She reminded him of Anne, and whenever Elinore touched her stomach, he thought of his daughter Susanna and then Judith and Hamnet, those darling twins Anne bore him two years later. These seeds of light had somehow flowered into a great darkness, and he was always on the verge of being overwhelmed by their memory.

He took a deep breath as the hold grew quiet. William did not know all the colonists. He had in fact tried to stay aloof, but it was impossible not to befriend some of them in such tight quarters. John Cotsmur and Arnold Archard sat to his right. Audry Tappen was to their left. Last night, he had them laughing for hours as he acted out the tale of a fool who gets mistaken for a king. He had a knack for playing the fool.

No one ever suspected the fool.

But this would not be a night for laughter. Governor White's advice had stayed in his thoughts all day. There *was* an influence to relinquish, and the only way he knew to do it was by turning it into a story.

"A new life," he said, turning to acknowledge every stare. His voice was almost a croak, and he paused to recover control. Then his thoughts left him. He swayed on his feet, though it might have been the water's motion. As his silence lengthened, a murmur spread among the audience. Even Governor White started to look a little questioning.

"Tonight," William said, "I give you the story of a man seeking a new start. But I must warn you: He is not a good man. Perhaps this is to be expected. Are *good* men often chasing after second chances?"

Nervous laughter answered this question. William paused again.

The audience belonged to him.

He hunched down as he described and assumed the role of the primary character. Did he dare call him the protagonist? The colonists now beheld a desperate young father caught poaching deer on the land of a pitiless squire. William stalked the edges of his circle, pulling at his hair.

"The squire, who has so much, will not abide the taking."

William stopped, stood tall, and squared his shoulders. He flared his nostrils and widened his eyes. His voice became stern and stentorian. "A lesson must be administered. A consequence bound to register. My deer was taken without permission. So take his *dears* as remuneration."

Elinore Dare gasped and clutched Ananias's arm.

William pivoted and fell to his knees. He cried out with enough anguish to fill the entire hold as he conveyed the tragic scene of a father returning home to find his wife and children butchered.

He swayed and swept his hands along the floor to encompass the imaginary bodies. But his fingers felt them. They would never forget the memory.

The ship rocked, bringing a distracting murmur from the colonists. Governor White ordered a man to go up and consult the captain. As far as William was concerned, it was the earth moving under the force of his rage. He raised his fists and held them there in utter silence. Minutes passed, a poor substitute for the weeks spent formulating retribution.

He stood up. The ship's unsteady rocking became more severe as William acted out how the father obtained a tincture, which he poured into the squire's ear, paralyzing him from head to toe. Could he really demonstrate what came next? Doubt gave way to muscle memory as he mimed the slow dismemberment of the squire's feet. Then the hands. And so on, until the paralyzed but quite conscious squire was diced upon the floor and forced to watch his own pieces being reassembled beside him in a room filled with crazed laughter.

He remembered what he had spoken as the squire died—"You belong to me!" As he repeated it now, the colonists screamed. At that very moment, *Lyon* pitched so hard that everyone went sprawling. Governor White clawed his way to the stairs and ordered every able man to the deck. Ananias reached him first, but White shoved him back. "Your place is with my daughter and your unborn child! Stay here!"

As Ananias protested, William shouted, "I'll go!" He forged his way toward the steps with twenty other men at his back. The ship shook like a dog trying to wring water from its coat. Everyone was thrown off their feet again, but William clung to the first step and pulled himself up. He was halfway to the deck when the top hatch opened and water poured through as if the whole ocean had been lurking behind the door. William hooked his left arm around the rail and grabbed Governor White as the surge soused them to the bone in icy brine.

Something slapped William in the face. He gasped, blinking away the freezing water to see dark shapes thrashing along the steps. The storm had dredged creatures out of the sea and thrown them onto the ship, black eels with protruding teeth. A sharp, sudden pinch made him discover one of the eels trying to bite through his shoe. He raised his foot and stomped on the fleshy body until it burst.

"Governor White!" he said, pulling the old man back to the steps before more water surged into the hold. White clung to the railing, too exhausted to speak. He only nodded at William and made the faintest motion to advance. William charged the remaining way up and emerged into absolute chaos. *Lyon*'s captain and crew, the few still on their feet, wrestled the rigging against a backdrop of vicious lightning. The clouds were massing together like the sudden mountain domain of a god still searching for a man whose heart was dark enough to worship it. Another prolonged blast of lightning revealed a shocking reality: the cloud was a towering human face, and the fleet sailed under its cold watch.

The ship pitched again, rolling so much William was sure *Lyon* would capsize. He lost his grip and slid across the deck. Only the railing kept him from being thrown overboard.

He fought to stand as Ananias staggered out of the hold. "Get back down! Your place is with your family!" William shouted, which earned an angry rebuke over the howling wind.

"Don't tell me my—*God!*"

Lightning struck the second ship, splitting it into two halves claimed at once by the water. Another bolt struck the third ship and must have hit its store of gunpowder. The boat became an instant fireball. The flame column struck toward the cloudy face like a final act of defiance before winking out against the rain and wind.

Lyon's bow now rose up until the boat seemed to be standing upright in the water. William clung to the railing as bodies tumbled past him. Ananias slipped and grabbed hold of William's legs, clawing at his pants before losing hold and plunging into the water. William gnashed his teeth and looked out across the sea. The little rowboat was there in the distance, coming on, always coming on. He grinned and shouted, "You're too late!"

He let himself drop.

"He's coming around, Father."

William groaned and opened his eyes to the sight of a beautiful face looking down at him. "Anne," he said, which brought a confused expression to mar that loveliness. He winced and remembered who she was. "*Elinore?*"

She helped him sit, and he blinked against the sharp, sudden brightness. They were on a beach with sand as white as the cliffs of Dover. Bodies were strewn across the beach, about thirty in all.

A few people staggered or crawled between them, checking for signs of life. Further down, washed up like a dead leviathan, was the front quarter of *Lyon*, its hull smashed open, its proud foremast reduced to a short, jagged splinter.

"Where's the rest of it?" he said, speaking barely above a whisper.

"Gone," Governor White said, limping over to him. "About half of the colonists on board are accounted for here. As for the rest or the other ships—"

"I saw them destroyed," William said and then looked to Elinore. "I'm sorry, but Ananias. . ."

So brave for her age, he thought upon seeing her muted, resigned flinch. It was the most grief she was going to show. He looked at her feet and his own, sinking into the sand like premature tidings of the grave.

Perhaps not *too* premature.

"Where are we, Governor?"

"Where I saw fit to bring you: Roanoke Island."

The voice came from everywhere and nowhere. William thought he heard it coming up out of the sand. Elinore said it came from the sky while Governor White leaned toward the ocean and cupped one hand to his right ear.

"Roanoke? This was our intended destination, but still many days away. This must be God's will. . ."

Laughter came from all around them but started to localize at their backs. One by one they turned to confront the dense forest at the edge of the beach. The surviving colonists gathered behind William, John White, and Elinore as someone stepped out from behind the closest tree.

William experienced a terror of recognition. The face was the same one formed by the clouds. Almost bloodless skin evoked the white fury of lightning, and while his eyes may have been dark brown once, they now had the blanched hue of exhausted, blighted soil. No seed of warmth or kindness grew there. His beard was unkempt but sparse, a struggle of malnourished weeds growing from his cheeks and down his long neck, which disappeared into a battered, grimy gorget and breastplate. His arms and legs were protected by dented greaves.

He's a conquistador, William told himself, and the man seemed to hear the thought. He offered a joyless smile and said,

THE BARD OF ROANOKE

"Many years ago I was called Panfilo de Narvaez, and many deemed me born under unlucky stars. But one star differs from another, and the course of mine brought me to glorious transformation. Now I am El Prospero—The Prosperous. Who among you acts as leader?"

William looked askance at John White to see his reaction. The old man stepped forward despite Elinore's immediate pleading.

"I am the governor of the colony that's somehow shipwrecked on the very island we sought."

El Prospero laughed. "It is I who's shipwrecked you. I who summoned the storm and used the wind and the sea to cull those I had no use for and bring the rest of you before me now."

"But why?" William said. "What do you want with us?"

"What does any god want?"

"There's only one God," Governor White said.

"This impudence from a Protestant?" El Prospero said. "Defiance from countrymen of a king who decided *he* was head of the church? Infidelity runs in the blood of every Englishman. Your faith is pliant to matters of convenience. *I* am your convenience now, and you will do me obeisance."

"Never," John White said, and growing murmurs of agreement rose from the gathered colonists.

El Prospero's smile slowly widened as he observed the emerging defiance. Then he looked just a little over his shoulder, at the forest behind him, and said, "Caliban! Ven a disfrutar, date un capricho. *Indulge yourself.*"

William felt something immense coming their way. There was a distinct thud in the ground, a vibration that shifted the sand around their feet. A monstrous bald head appeared through the trees, perched between thick shoulders as broad as deer antlers. It roared, and the colonists screamed, falling back. The creature jumped onto the beach, naked and muscled like a beast of burden. Its pale blue skin was slick with sweat and matted hair that exuded a stink that made them gag as their eyes watered.

It saw one of the women, and its penis sprang into a devastating erection.

"Caliban wants. . .*Miranda.*"

El Prospero laughed. "You may have all of them, Caliban, from the youngest to the oldest. I gift you with an island of Mirandas!"

It pivoted toward Elinore. William and Governor White threw

themselves in front of her, but Caliban swatted them away. The barest flick of his clawed hands threw them several feet across the beach. Elinor screamed as the beast prepared to lunge. But it sprang only a foot before dropping, its hands grasping at its neck as if discovering itself on a brutal leash.

El Prospero's right hand was out as if he held the other end. "All but *her*, Caliban! Do you not see her state? The work is done already, and the child will be mine. Have at the others!"

He lowered his hand, and the creature leapt toward his original target. She shrieked as he ravished her, but no one dared help. The monster's lust was impatient and undiscriminating, sending it bounding between man and woman, leaving each battered and half-naked, the white sand stained red around them.

Sobbing, Governor White dropped to his knees before El Prospero. "Father!" Elinore said, but the old man waved her off and humbled himself still further.

"*Please*," he said, touching his forehead to the conquistador's foot. "I submit. Spare my people!"

Caliban's assaults were terrifying to behold, but the sight of John White's submission broke some element of William's spirit. He knew the governor was not a coward. His humiliation was an act of strength that William realized he himself did not possess. Perhaps if he'd had even a tenth of John White's character, his life might be very different. His family might be alive. The pride Governor White cast aside now was the pride William had choked on rather than ask Squire Lucy's permission.

He looked one last time at the beach and thought he saw that infernal rowboat making its way to shore.

Then he turned and ran as hard as he could into the woods.

He spent three days foraging on berries and nuts as he wallowed in misery. The forest teemed with wildlife: deer, rabbits, and squirrels that made the dead squire's land seem impoverished by comparison. With the simplest tools, William could have contrived traps for the smaller animals. But he could not locate even a rock to sharpen a fallen branch into a spear.

On the fourth morning, he stirred off the cold dirt, awakened by a vision. A deer walked toward him, a doe as white as the beach sand, so white it almost glowed. William's stomach grumbled. He entertained a wild fantasy of jumping on the deer's back and somehow breaking its neck. The deer kept coming unafraid. It now seemed enveloped in a sphere of light, and the silhouette of its shape began to transform into a human. William scrambled behind the safety of a tree as the figure resolved itself into a naked, luminescent being of undetermined gender. There was a suggestion of undeveloped breasts. Its groin was blank flesh.

"Fear not, Ariel has come / Friend to you, no dread succumb / We two share a common foe / The dreadful tyranny of El Prospero."

The being stood very still but with an impatient, marked pensiveness in its expression. It kept glancing behind it every half minute.

"What. . .what are you?"

"A spirit made the meanest slave / For El Prospero I must behave / But plots of freedom hatch in my mind / With your help, for we are of a kind."

An alliance, he thought. With some reluctance, William stepped away from the tree. He sensed Ariel's interest was genuine, but what could he do against El Prospero and the monstrous Caliban? He fought back these doubts, fearful Ariel would realize his worthlessness and go away.

Ariel turned and glided back the way it had come, motioning William to follow. William did, his anxiety mounting as they neared the beach. The remains of *Lyon* had been disassembled and repurposed. El Prospero sheltered under the shade of a thatched roof supported by four sturdy poles, sitting on a chair that rivaled any European throne. Elinore knelt in the sand beside him, her face downcast but looking well compared to the other colonists. The beach teemed with lamentation and labor. Several colonists, including John White, were stripped naked and yoked like an oxen team. They were being forced to plow the sand, and strange crops of blue and gold rose up in their wake even as the furrows formed. Further down the beach, Caliban lorded over a harem of twelve men and women who seemed compelled to worship him in the most primal, despicable way.

"Impossible," William said, squinting with realization.

The women's stomachs all showed advanced pregnancy.

"A sorcerer's rage and monster's lust / Make the impossible a must / El Prospero now a kingdom makes / Enslaving the world for a daughter's sake."

"What daughter?"

"Miranda was her name / A bright but extinguished flame / Snuffed out by your English kin / All English will repay that sin."

"As a Spaniard, he had little love to lose for us in the first place. I pity him."

"Pity such a hideous foe? / Sympathy has you in its throes / Cast away all feeling but hate / Or suffer soon the direst fate."

William looked at Ariel. "Can you die?"

The spirit just stared at him.

"If you cannot die, if you cannot *feel* death, then you understand very little about what motivates the world, no matter your powers."

He squared his shoulders and stepped out of the final safety of the trees. His appearance drew the immediate notice of El Prospero, who grinned at him.

"I see my servant Ariel has returned you to me."

William couldn't hide a jolt of shock as the spirit now came to stand beside the sorcerer. *Had* he been betrayed, lured by false promises of rebellion? It seemed so, but he still couldn't believe it. Ariel may have obeyed a command to bring him back, but its hate for El Prospero was real. Of that he felt certain.

Elinore lifted her head and cast him the most piteous, defeated look. Her hands clutched her stomach as if to push back on the baby and keep it from seeing the light of the dreadful day into which it must be born.

"I came back on my own," William said. "Because I understand you."

El Prospero's expression soured. "Oh? Tell me of your profound *comprensión*."

"I will do better," he said. "I will show you."

He began to act out the scenes of a young father poaching a deer and the grave consequences that followed.

"So," El Prospero said as they walked alone on the beach. "You *do* understand after all."

William nodded. "We've both lost children and avenged ourselves for the loss. We are fallen men."

"Fallen? My rage has made me rise above all others. I was not far into my studies when the Englishman killed Miranda. My meager powers were not enough to protect her from harm, but my desire for revenge shaped me into a more adept student than I would have been otherwise. Just as it has unlocked a certain genius in you."

"I have no genius."

"There are many sorceries, each with their unique wands. The goose quill is the wand of storytelling. One day I may show you the true power of that magic—after I'm sure of your devotion."

"I don't understand."

"You will be my playwright. I will subjugate more ships to these shores, and from the survivors, you will cull a company and write for them and teach them to perform for me, the Queen, and Princess Miranda."

William stopped. "Miranda is dead."

"She was a third of my life. My wife was another third. I could not reclaim her, but I have recovered Miranda's soul, and I house it here," he said, touching his armored breastplate. "A temporary lodging until I bring the child to term this very night."

"Elinore's baby. . ."

"Her first breath will be her own. The second will be Miranda's. After this displacement, I will take Elinore as a second wife, and my court in this new world will be established. From my throne I will write the fates of all men, great and small, starting with you. Because we have a shared loss, I will honor you with a choice: be my royal playwright or be my royal fool."

William sat on the beach the next day, trying to write with a quill, ink, and paper El Prospero conjured from the air before walking off with Elinore, who carried the newborn Miranda in palsied arms. He was ordered to compose a play in celebration of the impending royal wedding, but his mind was blank except for memories of Anne's smile and the laughter of his children.

He looked at the bright blue sky and knew God was the ultimate tragedian.

The sand started to sift all around him and he felt the thud of heavy footsteps. Caliban, he thought, hurrying up as the monster stalked toward him. Fear sent him backward until he was up to his knees in the ocean.

"Stop! I am El Prospero's—"

"Caliban knows you're protected," the monster said, its penetrating stare nevertheless naked with want. "The Other wants to show you something."

"Other?" William said. Then he understood. *Ariel.* The spirit had not approached him since their encounter in the forest. "Where?"

"Caliban will take you. Hurry, while the hateful master is away."

William followed Caliban into the woods. The deeper they went, the more William's anxiety grew. What if this, too, was a trick? Caliban's lust was greater than his reason, and in the moment might be greater than his fear of El Prospero.

But Caliban made no threats, and William saw a light up ahead. They found Ariel sprawled across a fallen log as if exhausted. The spirit's glow was fainter than before, and as William approached, it gestured at something on the ground. William saw it was a folio book.

"What's wrong with you?"

"Master's book hurts us to touch. It could kill Caliban."

The effort looked like it had almost killed Ariel. He knelt before the book. "Will it harm me?"

"Touch it you can / Encourage your hand / Men become mages / Thanks to its pages."

"El Prospero's power comes from this single book?"

William made a furtive caress, expecting immediate pain. When no punishment happened, he picked up the book, which was quite light despite its size and heft. There seemed to be a thousand filled pages and a thousand more that were blank. The written pages were in many different hands and languages, evidence of rapid changes in ownership. The words in the first few hundred pages had faded to illegibility. He flipped to the last entry and found a slashing, angry handwriting, all the words in Spanish. William could translate a few of them: daughter, death, revenge.

THE BARD OF ROANOKE

The ink was strange, a rusty brown color that characterized all the writing from the very first page.

"Blood," he said. "One must write in blood?"

"Caliban knows it to be true."

"Ariel has no blood / The book does Ariel no good / Yet Caliban has blood within / But Caliban—"

"Cannot write," William said. Caliban snarled in response and began to stomp about them in a circle.

"Bleed you can and write as well / Take the book, incant your spell / Bring about El Prospero's fall / Free us from his wretched thrall."

Memories of the squire's decapitation flashed through his thoughts. William looked at his hands and then grabbed the pages written by El Prospero and tried to rip them from the binding. The paper held firm. He could not make even the tiniest tear, and he looked at Ariel in despair. The spirit waved a lecturing finger.

"Bleed your blood and bleed your soul / These put the book in your control / Unleash your creativity / And through the book remake reality."

"Caliban has had enough!" And before William could react, Caliban grabbed his right arm, forced his hand open, and bit off the tip of his index finger. The pain made William shriek as he fell on his knees holding his hand by the wrist and staring. There was no shortage of ink now, and the book seemed to shudder. When the first drops of blood fell on the book, a voice awakened in his own mind. The book was open to the first blank sheet, and William felt an urge to fill and feed the paper.

William moved his finger like a quill. There was a feeling that the book was drinking him, and an unmistakable heat radiated against his face. He moved his finger. His mind, his imagination had never been so open, so free. The surge of creative power was less like a locked door being opened and more like an entire wall being demolished. Verse and prose filled page after page. He did not realize it at first, but he was writing a play, filled with scene after scene to replace and repair so much mean fate.

A howling came through the trees. Storm clouds darkened the sky in an instant, turning the already dim forest into night. William squinted to keep writing by Ariel's glow as thunder shook the ground. Lightning struck the trees around them. "Master's coming!" Caliban said, running back and forth in a mindless panic.

He was right. El Prospero *was* moving toward them in the form of a green mist that blanched every tree in its path. His voice said, "My book! You dare write in my book! Ariel, Caliban, you have conspired against me, and I will kill you."

William's blood was slowing. He squeezed his finger, urging the ink forth as he raced to keep up with his fertile mind. He wrote of the ocean returning deceased loved ones to the beach of life. He wrote of a father watching his dead wife and children walking out of the water and running to embrace him. As soon as he wrote the words, he felt himself to be whole and healthy. His finger kept racing across the paper, describing how the young father, reunited with his loved ones, now turned to face the man who had taken them away.

William looked up. The mist was gone. Squire Lucy stood staring at him with all of his imperiousness. Was this still El Prospero? His mind was dizzy with questions and implications.

The squire said, "Return what's mine, and I'll let you live."

William stopped writing long enough to stand up. His index finger was poised on the paper. "Do you mean the book. . .or the deer?"

The squire stood rooted in fury. A moment passed as his mind made its calculations. Then he lunged, and William's moving finger wrote him out of existence as if it had a mind of its own. He looked at the words and then at the empty space where the squire or El Prospero had been. William went wild-eyed. He bit into his wounded finger and sucked forth another surge of blood. "I write the world!"

Somewhere in the background, he heard Ariel begging him for freedom even as it warned him to cast the book aside. Abandon such power? Who would do so? But he owed the spirit for this gift. His finger moved to the next clean page and wrote his will. Caliban disappeared. Ariel brightened, rose into the air, thanked him, and flew away.

William swayed on his feet. He looked back to the part about the ocean returning loved ones. It felt like he'd written it days, even weeks ago. Were they waiting for him? Of course they were waiting! The book was his, and he had willed it. William ran toward the beach with the book held open against his left forearm. He kept writing with every step, describing blue skies with storm clouds cleared. Authorizing happiness. Righting wrongs. When he reached the beach, he found it beautiful and peaceful, and the colonists stood strong and clothed in the bloom of health, their ravages erased. John White held his daughter and granddaughter, who was no longer Miranda. Behind them, walking out of the surf, came Ananias and everyone who had died in the tempest. The sea was returning them just as his story required.

"Father? Where are you, Father?"

Anne and the children came running out of the water, their laughter as loud as the surf. Seeing them, William grinned and tried to close the book. The binding resisted him, moving like a very rusty hinge. His bloody finger felt lodged into the paper like Excalibur into a stone. He panted, trying to pull away.

Through me, the globe will be your theater.

A rush of warmth shot up his captured arm and became a pleasurable scene in his mind. He saw millions of people under the sway of his words, saying, "We're yours! We're yours!" He smiled at the book and began mouthing the words back at it—until he heard the crucial difference from his lips.

"I'm yours. I'm yours."

"William?"

Anne stood before him with the children. They looked eager. They looked frightened. He reached out to them and said, "Take it from me."

Anne knelt beside him. "Only you can free yourself, my sweet William."

William shrieked and pulled at his hand with all his might and determination. He thought how easy it had been to sever the squire's ten fingers. How much easier, then, to cut off one of his own with the blade of a mental dagger.

A cry of betrayal came from the book as he used it to write his own freedom. Just as his hand came free, the index finger reduced to a bloody knuckle, the voice gave one last effort at seduction.

Through me, you can become the bard of the world.

"I'm happier being the bard of Roanoke," he said and disappeared into the embrace of his wife and children.

THE CLIMB UP TO HELL

A**FTER CHET AND DAVID'S** candles were lit, the five of us gathered at the base of the tree, and Jake put his flashlight under his chin.

"Time to explain the dark secret of Kingwood, ladies. This treehouse was built by John King himself for his twin sons after he discovered they weren't his. Once his wife's secret was out, he poisoned her. It was a long time ago, and everyone thought she just died, but his crime was discovered decades later when his diary was found. He was going to poison the boys as well, but he stopped himself."

"Because he knew they were innocent?"

"No, he thought poisoning was too good for them. He wanted them to suffer. So he built this treehouse and made the boys live in it. Summer, winter. All the time. And he put two big Dobermans down at the bottom to attack the boys if they tried to leave. So they didn't. Even when they started to get hungry and thirsty after John King quit bringing them food and water. In the diary, he says he finally let the boys go and told them to never come back. That he didn't care what happened to them. Then he wrote that he tore the treehouse down. But all of that was a lie. The treehouse is here, isn't it? Randy, Mark, and I were the first to discover it—and the truth. We climbed up and saw the skeletons. It was gnarly."

"That's right. Gnarly."

"We buried their bones, but the skulls keep coming back every Halloween."

"So. . .they're up there now?"

"Yeah, numbnuts, just like we said. The three of us have taken our turns appeasing them. Now it's up to the two of you rookies. Start climbing."

THE CLIMB UP TO HELL

My face felt as hot as the lit candles David and Chet Somerset were being forced to carry, part of the dumb prank being played on them. The little flames flickered as the brothers made their climb with David in the lead. Jake, Randy, and I stepped back several feet and aimed our flashlights up at them.

"Dude," Randy whispered. "They bought every word of it. Holy shit."

"Did I tell it as good as you, Mark?" Jake said.

Randy aimed his flashlight into my eyes. "Sure you don't want to go up there with your buttbuddies?"

Jake snickered. I told them both to fuck off. "Chet made all that up."

"He sure knows what your room looks like."

"I told you my mom let them come over. I didn't have a choice."

"Sure."

Jake, Randy, and I had been best friends since we were seven. We were fifteen now, and I couldn't tell where I stood with them after Chet started talking about him and David hanging out in my room. They didn't say it outright, but I knew I had to help them scare and humiliate Chet and David. Restoring myself in their eyes required this Halloween sacrifice, and the idea that the Somerset brothers believed this was some friendship initiation rite just made it better to Jake and Randy.

"Keep climbing, girls," Randy said, his tone filled with merciless joy. "And don't forget, if the candles go out, you have to climb down and light them again."

Jake lowered his beam a few notches to Chet's ass. He snickered. "Is that a brown spot I see?"

I joined Jake and Randy's laughter just enough to keep up pretenses. But in my imagination, I saw David slipping and falling. He was already ten feet off the ground with another twelve rungs to go. I trained my flashlight beam on the next rung so David could see it. There was just a little sliver of moon, too weak to reach through the trees. Appropriate for Halloween.

Inside the treehouse were two large pumpkins and two carving knives, courtesy of Jake. The pumpkins came from a little patch his uncle kept, and the knives were swiped from his mom's kitchen. It'd been a bitch hauling the pumpkins up there one at a time in an oversized backpack, but they'd insisted I do it, a bit of hazing I endured to keep them happy.

David reached another rung and looked down to check on Chet. David was my age, Chet a year younger. They had almost the same face, freckles, and a pug nose. But Chet had brown eyes and David's were blue. They walked side-by-side everywhere, in lockstep. It was hard not to picture them being joined at the hip, so it was weird seeing one ahead of the other.

They entered the treehouse. The light of their candles made the windows yellow, and I exhaled a long-held breath.

The whole thing started on the Fourth of July, when Kingwood's population of 2,000 milled around the town square eating ice cream and hot dogs, listening to the high school band play John Philip Sousa shit, and sweating out lemonade and Coke under a blistering sun. Jake, Randy, and I were hanging against the brick wall of Kingwood Community Bank. I had a bag full of snaps and was still throwing them on the sidewalk a good hour after the novelty wore off.

"Look at those two," Jake said, nudging us. Chet and David walked past, backs straight, arms limp. Chet had on a blue and red plaid button-up, and David had on a white polo.

"Put 'em together and you've got the flag," Randy said and gave a smart salute at their backs. "God bless the USA."

"Let's follow them," Jake said.

We tailed them through the crowds. The brothers acted like tourists. Sometimes they stopped to point out something, like the big white banner hung across Main Street, stamped with Kingwood's motto: *Friends Growing Strong Together*. Kingwood kids got a lot of flak from other schools for that slogan. We followed them for twenty minutes, and word got around that Jill Clarke had changed into a t-shirt that was almost see-through, and since she was the senior captain of the cheerleading squad, we three kings went to investigate. I didn't get the fuss. Sure, there was the dark suggestion of Jill's black bra, but so what? Jake and Randy meanwhile almost shook their fists at the encroaching sunset. I listened to them talk about sucking Jill's tits and getting their hands up her shirt until their voices got too loud and scornful adults gave disapproving looks. Then I put some distance between us and wandered off as the fireworks started.

Downtown Kingwood had plenty of nooks and crannies, private places. What was I looking for? That question ended when I stumbled upon the weird brothers around the back of Fitzhugh's corner store. David had his back against the brick as Chet bent to press his left cheek against his brother's chest. David ran his fingers through Chet's hair. How strange, how comforting, how different, how very real compared to the shadowy importance of Jill Clarke's bra.

I spent a moment just standing there before I realized they were looking right at me. The shorter brother broke away and took a few steps, his trembling hands stretched toward me.

"Please don't say anything."

I shook my head.

"We're. . .new here."

"You mean you aren't visiting?" I said.

"No. We moved here two weeks ago. I'm Chet. This is my older brother, David."

David nodded and smirked.

The fireworks bathed us in changing colors. We turned blue, green, purple, and bright red. We didn't speak until a starburst made us white as ghosts, our shadows dancing.

"What's your name?" David said.

"Mark."

"Be our friend, Mark," Chet said.

"A *real* friend," David said.

Um, sure. . .

The answer felt more like a thought, but I must have spoken it because the brothers smiled at each other.

"Our first friend," David said, and Chet nodded.

They opened their arms as if to hug me, but I was having none of it and ran off. The fireworks were ending, and I found my mom with her boyfriend Jeff, who planned to be my stepdad by next year.

Why did I tell those two freaks I'd be their friend? I went to bed remembering them holding each other, and I dreamt that the three of us were huddled together, arms across each other's shoulders. Tighter and tighter, like there was something small in the middle we didn't want to escape. It was an uncomfortable dream, and I seemed to still be in it when the doorbell woke me at almost noon. I stared at the ceiling and listened to Mom open the front door. Half a minute later, two sets of footsteps sounded on the stairs. I figured it must be Jake and Randy. Mom had been letting them storm up into my room ever since I could remember.

Then my bedroom door opened, and Chet and David stood there.

"How are you?" Chet said.

David stepped forward. "Yes, how are you, Mark? Did you sleep well?"

I was just in my underwear, and I pulled the sheet up to my neck. David frowned. He looked at Chet and said, "I told you it was too soon."

"What?" I said.

"To come over."

"We're very lonely," Chet said.

"It's true, Mark. Until now, we've only had each other."

That's *still* all you got, I thought. I dressed and stole a look out the window, afraid I'd see Jake and Randy riding up the street. The neighborhood seemed deserted, but there were eyes everywhere, and I didn't want to risk being seen outside with these weirdos. So, I pulled out my Atari and told them to choose a game. Then I went downstairs. Mom was already making peanut butter sandwiches for us.

"Your new friends seem interesting."

"They're not friends."

"They said they met you yesterday."

"That's sort of true."

"Well then."

"I didn't tell them where I live."

"Don't have to be a detective to use a phone book."

"Mom—"

"They smell much better than Jake and Randy."

"They're probably wearing perfume or something."

"It's called *soap*. Here. Take these up."

Mom handed me a plate of sandwiches and three Cokes.

"What if Jake or Randy come over?"

"The five of you can play together."

"Would you tell them I've been grounded? *Please*?"

Mom rolled her eyes. "Whatever you say."

THE CLIMB UP TO HELL

"Tell them I was caught sneaking one of Jeff's Bud Lights."

"Your reputation will never be greater."

Back in the bedroom, I found Chet and David sitting beside each other, the Atari untouched.

"We're not allowed to play video games," Chet said. "Our parents only let us watch television for sixty minutes a day, and it has to be the news."

I took up my sandwich and cracked open my Coke. "They sound like dicks."

The brothers looked at each other. It was slow at first, but all of a sudden, they were both cracking up. Red in the face and shoulders shaking.

David gasped. "You're so funny, Mark!"

"Very funny," Chet said, breathless. "It's great to have a friend who's funny."

I couldn't believe them at first. Whenever I hung out with Jake and Randy in a larger group, they'd be cracking everyone up, and then I'd say something that made everyone quiet. No matter how funny I tried to be, it never worked. Jokes don't work when they reek of effort. But here were Chet and David almost rolling on the floor over something I said. Their reaction was as weird as everything else about them, but also so. . .*genuine*.

I polished off my Coke and belched. They laughed at that, too, and I held up the two Atari controllers.

"Who wants their ass whipped first?"

The new King of Comedy had his minions.

We didn't ask questions when we found the treehouse two years ago. We just climbed the rungs straight up through a floor hatch. Outside, the treehouse looked like a small Victorian mansion stretched across the cradling branches of a maple that might have been two hundred years old. It loomed high against the cloudless sky. The dilapidated structure was flanked on both sides by turrets that framed the peak of its partially collapsed roof. It looked like the house in *Psycho*, that movie we watched at Jake's last Halloween. The interior wasn't nearly as spacious, taken up by a mess of strange, disorienting angles that left just a small practical space tailor-made for three people to hang out. There were windows here and there, and they were all sorts of irregular shapes too.

It was one of those strange things waiting to be found by the right kids, the kind of kids who sneak cigarettes from their mother's purse. We weren't the first ones inside, but it'd been a while between occupants. We found broken beer bottles, cigarette butts, and used condoms. There were scattered pages from titty magazines, faded and water damaged in the most frustrating way possible. While Jake and Randy obsessed over them, I found a rolled piece of paper in the corner. It was yellowed with age, but not crinkly at all when I unrolled it and realized it was a wall calendar with all the months printed in little square blocks above a flowery script: *Fitzhugh's Apothecary.* What the hell was an *apothecary?* The calendar was from 1916, several years after Kingwood's founding.

"Look at this, guys. Figure it means this place was built 70 years ago?"

Randy and Jake weren't interested. They'd discovered more ripped pages from some porno mag and knelt on the floor in a desperate effort to fit the jigsaw scraps together.

Fitzhugh. I thought of the town drug store. How long had it been there?

"Mark, get over here," Jake said. "We're like three scraps away from seeing pussy. Help us find the missing pieces!"

"Hunt for the cunt," Randy said, and soon we three kings chanted it together and giggled. I wasn't any help though. My thoughts were on that calendar. On questions of time and who'd built the treehouse. I sat back and thought about it. A story sprang to mind so readily it was like someone spoke it to me.

"John King built this," I said.

"The statue guy?"

"For his sons. Twin boys. But he discovered they weren't really his kids, so he. . ."

They applauded when I finished telling the story. "You should be a writer," Randy said. "That was fucking awesome. Especially that line about the one starving brother realizing you can climb *up* to hell."

I shook my head. I couldn't explain how the story just came to mind. I guess I'd made it up in a burst of imagination.

THE CLIMB UP TO HELL

It wasn't important. Whoever built the treehouse didn't matter. It was ours now, and we spent damn near every day that first summer here, cleaning it up, making it *ours*. We pledged to tell no one about it except girlfriends, when we got 'em. We vowed to lose our cherries up here. That summer in the treehouse, life was more real than ever before. The three of us did the same shit we would have done in the park or the woods, but we did it in our own world. Our dreams carried more weight in the treehouse, and our friendship was never stronger than when we occupied it together. I went there by myself only once, when Jake and Randy were off on family vacations. I don't know why, but I thought the treehouse was almost angry with me for coming alone. I got creeped out by the sound of the groaning wood, the creaking of the branches and stood up. I went to look out one of the windows and something seemed off. The world outside was different, like the picture on an old postcard. I didn't even feel like I was looking out of my own eyes.

I left a few minutes later and didn't return until Jake and Randy were there. Then it all felt right again. Our fascination with the treehouse lasted through that summer and stayed strong into the second one and was still going good in the third. We went there almost every day, up until that Fourth of July. Then I began hanging out in secret with the Somerset brothers, and my room became a sort of treehouse for the three of us, and we never left it. Mom kept covering for me whenever Jake or Randy showed up. I started feeling like I had two separate lives that mustn't intersect. They'd have to when school started, I supposed, but that was a ways out.

I didn't ditch Randy and Jake, of course. When I was determined to hang out with them, I set off early on my bike. As far as I knew, Chet and David didn't have bikes, but I always kept looking around expecting them to be running after me. I never saw them once, but only felt hidden from them once we were a quarter of a mile into the forest.

"Dude, what's been up with you?" Jake said after we'd climbed the rungs and could lounge in privacy.

"What do you mean?"

"Sneaking beers? Flipping off your mom? You got a death wish or something?"

I grinned. "A man's gotta do what a man's gotta do sometimes."

Their look of respect was priceless.

"You're going to be grounded the whole summer at the rate you're going."

I shrugged. "It's totally worth it. Fuck that bitch."

I winced inside. As moms went, mine wasn't as lame as most. Her excuses were making me look badass, but how far would she go if Chet and David kept coming over?

Jake had scored a copy of *Playboy* and had the magazine open on the treehouse floor. As the three of us knelt around it, Randy took out several cigarettes. They were bundled in a paper towel and were a little squished and bent. He had a lighter and kept flicking it until he finally gave up.

"I don't get why my lighters never work up here."

"Maybe it's out," I said.

"I just got it."

He sighed and went to the hatch door.

"Light one for me," Jake said.

"Me too."

Randy flipped us the bird as he descended the ladder. This took about half a minute. Then he shouted, "Hey, guys!"

We went to the door and looked down. Randy was small on the ground, but I could see him grinning and holding up the lighter. The flame flickered.

"See? Fucking weird."

He put all three cigarettes into his mouth, passed the fire across them, and inhaled.

"Don't get the filter wet with your spit," Jake said. He pulled back, and I followed. "I fucking hate a wet filter. It's like I'm kissing him or something."

We sat with our backs to the wall as Randy poked through and climbed inside, billows of smoke around his head. He plucked two cigarettes from his lips and handed them to us. Mine was damp, but I didn't mind. I smoked and thought how I'd like to take David up here. David and Chet, of course, but more David. I thought he'd love the treehouse.

They both would.

Both brothers screamed, and Randy and Jake giggled and fell against each other.

"Guess they found the skulls," Jake said. "Those pussies are too freaked out to even realize they're fake."

Randy ran to the base of the tree and hollered, "Get to it, girls! Carve a face in the pumpkins and put the skulls and candles inside. The brothers want their new heads!"

They screamed again.

"I'm going up there," I said. "This needs to stop."

Their flashlight beams lanced at me.

"It really is true, isn't it?"

"Chet was just lashing out because you were bullying his brother and he knows me. He was trying to get me to stop you. They're just desperate for friends. They wouldn't be out here if they weren't."

The brothers screamed again. Randy stormed back to the tree, climbed up three rungs, and shouted at them to shut up and start carving.

"Dude," Jake said, his voice softer. "I don't know what to think."

I didn't either. Memories of the end of summer and the start of the school year flooded me. David and me playing Atari as we sat on the edge of the mattress, with Chet asleep behind us like a little kid. David flexed his calf against mine. I flexed back.

"Look," I said. The candles had gone out in the treehouse. We listened. Silence.

We waited. Several minutes passed.

"Let's go up there," I said.

"*You* can."

"They're up there in the dark. They're probably too scared to move."

Jake and I were about to argue when Randy shouted, "Gross, what the *fuck*?"

He dropped his flashlight and fell off the third rung and landed on his side, holding his hands up. His fingers glistened wet and red in our flashlight beams.

"Dude, did you cut yourself?"

"No, man, it just started dripping on me."

Randy got on his knees and began scraping his palms against the dirt. Jake and I stood next to him, pivoting our lights up the length of the tree. The rungs were wet, and the dripping became a steady pour.

"David?" I shouted. "David, are you up there?"

Jake got Randy to his feet. "Come on. Let's get out of here."

I grabbed Jake's arm. "How much red paint did you put up there?"

"What?"

"You had a can rigged to fall on them like pig's blood, right?"

Jake pulled his arm away. "I didn't have any paint, Mark." His voice was hoarse, every word like straw.

"Randy, did you have paint—"

"I'm *out* of here, man. I don't even care."

They took off. I followed them a few steps, begging them not to go. Then I made a helpless pivot and ran back to the tree.

"David? David, it's okay. Jake and Randy left. It's just me."

A minute of silence lasted longer than an hour of noise.

"Come on, guys! Chet?"

You've got to go up there, I told myself. I put my foot on the first rung, and my sole slipped off. I whimpered. There was no way I could make it up without falling.

"Please, David."

A whisper came from the opening. David? Chet? Both? Then something appeared. Thank God, I thought. The prank had gone on long enough. I pointed the flashlight for a better view and only just dove out of the way of the pumpkins as they fell. But it wasn't the pumpkins. It was David and Chet's decapitated heads.

I ran into the darkness. The huge maple tree shook behind me. It sounded like a roar. I tripped and scrambled to keep going. The whispers became more distinct. Chet and David. But how could it be, when their heads were. . .

I turned. The Somerset brothers were there, but not on the ground. Their forms hung suspended in the air, substanceless. *Boneless.* It took a moment to comprehend just what I was seeing. Their skins had been peeled away and seemed draped like sheets. But what were their skins draped over, and who did the draping? The pumpkins were there in place of their heads, and each bore the face of one brother, carved with the exacting detail of a photograph, and lit from within by the very candles they'd been forced to carry. We stared at each other, and I couldn't help but remember what they'd said to me outside of the drugstore.

THE CLIMB UP TO HELL

Be our friend, Mark.
A real friend.
David floated toward me.
"The story was wrong, Mark," he said.
"The brothers were never twins," Chet added.
They hovered over me as I fell to my knees.
"Then. . .then. . .what were they?"
"Triplets."

FOR THE ROAD IS HEAVEN

Even in the dark, the trees kept falling. The crack and splinter of lumber, sharp even at a distance, kept Jewel rigid in the driver's seat, left hand on the wheel. Her right hand tapped the top of the plastic box on the passenger side. *Tupperware.* She imagined how funny the word would sound if she could speak, like the rumor of a bird's chirp, the claim of a dog's howl. Jewel's father told her all words were made up, and it was the function of things that mattered, not names. *Tupperware* functioned as a container and a preserver.

Why couldn't there be *Tupperware* big enough for the whole world before so much of it ended? Or was her life now what it felt like to live in empty *Tupperware*?

Jewel shivered, though it was weeks from winter and the temperature remained tolerable. A glance in the rearview mirror showed total darkness. Not that anyone would pursue her with headlights on. It was the steady work of the axe men, revealed in the crash of trees, that told Jewel she was safe for now.

She tapped on the *Tupperware* lid again and wept.

—Father, I'm scared. That's no surprise to you.

She left the car, taking the tattered road map with her. It unfolded to a massive size, large as a table. Most of its panels were faded to nothing, erased like the places that had been there. Only the roads remained: mostly. The present road went through a forest that did not exist on the panel. The map showed an area of green called *Jefferson County Memorial Forest*. The green did not approach the road, much less overwhelm it like the present trees. Now a heavy canopy of branches made the night even darker, and there was a smaller tree growing right in the middle of the road.

She gazed at it as she heard another far-off, far larger tree falling. Jewel easily imagined Dunsinane standing atop the roof of his tall truck cabin, surrounded by three hundred men and women looking up in awe as his hands conveyed the frenzy of his soul.

—We know what's strong and what's weak. We know what survives and what falls. The world has fallen many times, civilizations have come and gone. Their roads survive best. Roads are a prayer for invincibility. We must have a world of roads and the will to rule them.

Sometimes if Jewel concentrated hard enough, she was sure she could make a noise in her mouth. She wanted this so badly when her father died. But not even a moan mustered in her throat. His death meant more than a personal loss. Had he lived a month, a week, perhaps even a day longer, his thoughts might have turned against Dunsinane and ruined him.

But now Dunsinane would turn Father into the final justification for his plans. In life, Father led his community well, faltering only in the last few years, when Dunsinane began asserting his influence.

In death, Dunsinane could elevate her father from mortal leader to divine guidance.

A god of roads.

Jewel was ready to leave when she noticed the trees were no longer falling. It was unlike Dunsinane to call for merciful breaks. A moment later, the collective blare of horns sent her sprinting to the driver's side door. She opened it and paused to listen to the only sound in the night—the only sound in the world.

.— . . —— . ...- . / -.. .. .. -.-. —- ...- . . .-. . -.. / -.— —- ..- .-. / -.. . . ...
. -.-. .. -. . -- .. —- -. . .-.-.- / .— . . —— . .-. . . / -.-. —- — .. -. —. / ..-. —- .-
. / -.— —- ..- .-.-.-

Why did I linger here? I could be so many more miles away. Do I want to get caught?

She got behind the wheel as the horns kept sounding, expertly synced from hundreds of cars. Father had taught her early that your car's horn was your voice. Dunsinane's horn sounded like nothing else under the sun or moon, bellowing. Even from miles away, it announced itself above the volume of the others.

—We've discovered your desecration.

—We're coming for you.

She opened her mouth to scream but nothing came out. Jewel turned the ignition, and the car lurched forward. Hit the tree in the road. It was just a sapling. But now, like a twig snapped by a passing deer, its broken form confirmed her presence to the oncoming hunters.

Jewel risked the headlights and mashed the gas pedal. The car shimmied as it reached seventy miles per hour, and the contents within the *Tupperware* box thudded. She slapped her right hand atop the lid but only for an instant, as she needed both hands to control the wheel.

Dunsinane is going to kill me.
If I don't kill myself first.

—*I hate cities.*

—*Why, Father?*

—*Because they must have been places of very great despair. And great noise. I think it was in the cities where people lost the ability to use their mouths because all they could do was shout over the chaos. And so the generations that followed inherited both burned-out buildings and burned-out throats.*

Jewel shoved a plastic nozzle into the fuel tank. The soft splash of gasoline against the pavement jolted her from a memory that must have been twenty years old. She was six and standing on a bluff with her father beside her. Together they contemplated a ruined town, little more than collapsed rubble since well before her birth. Father bent down, focused her attention on his hands, and signed out a command.

—*Notice the road. Read how it goes through the destruction and continues off into the horizon.*

Jewel had already noticed, but she nodded anyway.

—*The road is our purpose and our true symbol. Whatever we are, whatever truths we've lost and found a thousand times over, roads recorded them. My grandfather told me a story about tree rings and how they record a tree's history. I do not know if this is true. But if so, then the roads are our rings. The roads outlast all buildings, all lives. The roads carry the footsteps of the past, the cars that were and the cars that might come. I think it is a fine thing to die in the middle of a road, Jewel.*

Her father did not die in the middle of the road. He died in a tattered tent, and Jewel had capitalized on a rare moment of privilege as his daughter and received two hours of almost total isolation with him in an impromptu wake. Dunsinane had been obliged to show such respect and deference to her before the others.

Jewel screwed the cap back onto her gasoline can and returned it to the trunk, squeezing it among ten more. No, immediate worry about supplies didn't ease the remorse of letting even one drop of gas evaporate off the asphalt. She scrambled back behind the wheel, closed the door, and motored away.

It makes no sense. Why haven't they caught up to me yet?

The rearview mirror showed only road. She drove through open land now, free of the encroaching forests. How she wished some force could bring all those trees crashing across the path behind her.

I didn't put that many miles between us before Dunsinane discovered what I did. He wouldn't have sounded his horns across the night for the sake of vanity. They would have started pursuing right away.

But they hadn't.

Could it be Father is looking out for me after all? Could it be he approves of what I did? Now in death, he sees clearly and understands how Dunsinane sought to use him?

The highway ahead of Jewel exploded into chunks of asphalt and flame. Gravel peppered the windshield as the car lurched and spun. The explosion must be her father's voice, speaking from beyond the road. The steering wheel locked as so many horrible noises erupted all around her. Was this screaming? Had the road been torn open, to spew out the tortured voices of the past?

A lightning crack of pain pulsed through Jewel's body. Harsh odors scorched her nose, the burnt scent of things that shouldn't be burning. A hand came up and flicked the side of the car and sent it rolling. Jewel would swear to it.

Father's hands his hands save his hands

Was she on her feet?

Was she flying?

Father's hands where are they

A man's face appeared in front of her. An unfriendly grin, a cocked head with pursed lips. He seemed a few years older than her and didn't talk right away, his hands too busy groping. The wreck had numbed Jewel's senses, leaving her motionless and vulnerable to the man violating her body. At last he gestured.

—*No one so pretty should travel alone.*

Jewel opened her mouth, hoping to summon all the sounds of the crash. The sounds *must* be there inside her someplace, reproducible.

She couldn't manage even a gasp.

Another man—she only now realized there were others—cupped his hand under her chin and squeezed, forcing her mouth to stay open.

—*Not yet. But that's a fine idea.*

The men held their bellies and rocked back and forth, the universal mime of robust laughter. Jewel squeezed her eyes shut and kept them that way until there came a gentle tapping on her left temple. Her chief tormentor was gesturing again.

—*Your car is junk now. We'll salvage it for parts. You'll ride in someone's trunk until you've been tamed to our ways. Seats are earned in the camp of Sherman Young.*

Two men dragged Jewel across a field. The effects of the crash caught up with her all at once. Her stomach heaved, and she vomited the traces of her last meal. The sky burst with garish colors, each a needle in her thoughts. She closed her eyes but still saw the flashes, and she went on retching, silent spasms ignored by her captors.

Hours must have passed because it was nearly dusk before she regained some sense of herself. Jewel found a spoonful of pale broth being poked against her lips, and she opened up to receive it. She found it flavorless and therefore good.

The woman feeding her seemed about as old as her father, which meant either uncommon hardiness or fantastic luck. Her eyes were still bright, and she seemed like one who might smile a lot. Jewel took another spoonful. *Smile for me. Please smile. Show me I'm going to be okay.*

After several more feedings, the old woman put the broth aside and stroked Jewel's hair once before pivoting to slap the ground several times. This brought the men, who now stood over them in a circle. The old woman withdrew, and in her place knelt the man who captured her.

Sherman Young.

He carried the *Tupperware* box with him.

FOR THE ROAD IS HEAVEN

Jewel reached for it at once and got slapped across the face to remind her of her place. She flinched and cast a plaintive, miserable glance upward.

Sherman Young made a sweeping motion with his hands, and his men retreated and turned their backs to him. He hunched down and placed the box between his flexed knees. Jewel focused on his gestures.

—*Whose hands are these?*

When she didn't answer, he opened the lid and flung it aside, reaching into the box.

—*Answer my question.*

—*They belonged to my father.*

—*Belonged? Like a possession? He owned severed hands?*

—*They're his hands. I cut them off after he died.*

—*Why in the name of nameless roads would you do this? Did he do you evil with them? I recognize the ring on the right hand. The black stone of the Teachers.*

—*He did me no evil. He was a Teacher, as was his father.*

—*You still haven't explained yourself.*

Explaining herself—justifying herself—seemed a daily, impossible obligation since girlhood. She might as well count the stars in the night sky. She knew she must be the reason her father quit the roads and turned his back on those who were still voiceless. Mother was dead, and clearly Father found nothing to sustain him in his daughter's eyes.

—*Where I come from, my father led many people. Then a man named Dunsinane—*

Sherman Young seized her wrists. Jewel stared into his narrowing eyes, and he didn't need to gesture to communicate his question.

—*Did you say Dunsinane?*

She nodded.

He released Jewel's hands. She rubbed her wrists as he made a quick slash with his fingers.

—*Continue.*

—*My father's thoughts were scattered near the end of his life. He agreed with whatever Dunsinane said, and Dunsinane used his position to achieve greater power. When my father died, I took his hands because I couldn't stand thinking of them rotting in the ground.*

Sherman Young grabbed her wrists again.

—*I know your people burn their dead.*

Jewel looked at the dirt and the *Tupperware* box. She could see the silhouette of her father's hands inside, hacked off at the wrist.

—*I didn't want my father's ring to fall into Dunsinane's possession.*

—*Lie to me again and your hurt will be as long as the horizon.*

Her eyes watered.

—*I wanted to spite Dunsinane. I wanted to reclaim my father from him. To show him and everyone else that my father's voice was beyond control. And I* did *want to save the ring.*

Sherman Young's eyes narrowed as he held his stare, and Jewel mustered all her strength to meet it. After a minute passed, he nodded and smiled. This brought no comfort because his next act was to reach into the box, grab one of the hands, and jerk the ring free. He cast the severed hand aside and held the ring up to the firelight, clearly relishing its gleam and heft. Then he motioned for Jewel to lift her right hand. She did, and he slipped the ring over her thumb.

—*We have many children and a few adults with us who do not know how to speak. You will teach them. And you will be my wife.*

Suckling her fourth forced child, a boy named Arthur, Jewel looked at her father's ring and pondered the fate of his severed hands. It seemed Sherman Young threw them into the fire one evening. Or perhaps he fed them to the wild hogs or placed them on the road and directed the long caravans he commanded to crush them under their wheels. She imagined the finger bones splintering, the smashed flesh rotting away. Her imagination too easily replaced the image with each of her children's skulls. If only she'd been allowed a single daughter, her loathing might be quenched. But all four boys—even this littlest one, only months old—were so clearly their father's sons, already dismissive of her. She could not even win against their silent temper tantrums when she denied them some trifle. She no longer did. Not after the beating she received

FOR THE ROAD IS HEAVEN

at Sherman Young's hands as she was forced to look at her sons' faces and beg forgiveness for trying to discipline them.

Cradling the child, she worked the ring off her thumb and held it between her fingertips. She stared at the black stone, glossy enough to reflect a distorted image of her face. Or perhaps not distorted at all.

She glanced around before pulling Arthur away from her breast. Most of Young's followers—a hundred strong—kept close to the camp and the road. Jewel knew the other women resented her for being able to stray into the woods. Being Sherman Young's wife came with a few advantages, including a slightly greater freedom of movement than the other women. Of course, he did this as a demonstration of his own power. Nothing more.

Arthur's mouth opened in a noiseless wail as his little arms and legs thrashed. Always hungry. Draining her dry, just like his brothers. She took the ring and put it against the baby's lips. Jewel's heart beat a grim pace as she watched the child try to suck milk from the hard, cold stone. As its face reddened, a moment of pity and deep guilt almost changed her mind.

She shoved the large ring deep into Arthur's mouth and then brought his head back to her right breast and waited.

When Jewel returned to the camp and saw her husband again, several hours had passed. Sherman Young was preparing for war. He rubbed his eyes as he hunched over lists of weapons and supplies. A map was spread out on another table. It reminded Jewel of the road map she'd owned long ago. Sherman Young's map said *Children's Atlas of the United States* and seemed very crude in its details, obviously not drawn to any appreciable scale. But it featured a few recognizable landmarks and was better than sketching out battle plans in the dirt.

As Jewel stood before him, he busied himself adding lines on the map, drawing in roads and paths. She stared at the bald place in the middle of his scalp. Father had been one of the few men she ever knew who never lost hair there. As she gazed, she wished the spot also meant a place with no bone, like with newborns.

She reached and touched his shoulder. When he jerked away, she realized she'd truly surprised him. Jewel did not think she'd crept into the tent and decided he was *truly* lost in thought.

Good.

—The people of the north ridge are such fools.

—Did they refuse you again?

—Yes. I offered them a treaty of protection from Dunsinane. They say they do not know who that is.

—Are they liars?

—They are hermits. They have few cars. Not even bicycles or horses. They think because they have not traveled into danger that danger will never travel into them.

—An easy victory for you, my love.

Sherman Young smiled. Jewel remained wary, having learned that talk of *easy victories* both enticed and enraged him, as if he could never decide if she was complimenting or mocking him. She slapped him slightly on his right cheek, a liberty that made his entire face go red. He was on her at once, both of them on the ground, not quite wrestling. He had her on her belly, each hand pinning her wrists. One of his fingers began tapping on the back of her left hand, and she interpreted the dots, dashes, and pauses with lightning speed—

You're the easiest conquest by far.

Jewel endured the violation, even glad of the way he wore himself out. The key was not getting herself sent away when he finished. This was an either-or proposal, seemingly unrelated to any mood or circumstance. But her pulse started going fast again when he rose off of her and did not gesture for her to go. He pulled his pants up to his waist and labored back to the table and his *Children's Atlas of the United States* and the battle plan he was sketching there.

Her clothes were on for the most part, and as she stepped behind him, she took the jagged bone—Arthur's little right forearm—from her pocket. Was it sharp enough to cut Sherman Young's throat? She'd tested it on her thumb and found the flesh opened right away.

She tightened her grip and readied the weapon. All she could do was die trying.

—I have journeyed as a pilgrim of many roads, at first beside my father and then alone; and then beside my wife, and then alone again. Now—

FOR THE ROAD IS HEAVEN

On her knees and staring at the sky, waiting for Sherman Young's followers to deliver the killing blow, Jewel remembered how her father's hands seized up, the fingers clawing. They had not fully straightened as he moved to stroke her hair.

—I am done with teaching. I am finished thinking of myself as a redeemer and a rebuilder of the land. It cannot be done. It is said the world has fallen many times. I've heard it told that a host of fearful people who live in the sky once forced men to have many languages, and civilization collapsed. Perhaps these same people later decided to silence our mouths altogether. But the silence of mouths is nothing. Our intentions lie in our hearts, expressed through the hands.

Her hands were bound with rope tied to the rear bumper of Sherman Young's command truck, a battered black war wagon reinforced with random pieces of salvaged metal. About four feet of slack existed between her and the bumper.

Jewel lowered her head. She was about fourteen when Father decided to live among one group of people and lead them. With him as chief, they began building, at first huts, then houses and barns. She was twenty the first time she saw Dunsinane, eager, wide-eyed, self-effacing.

—Have you heard of the Mongols, sir?

—Yes. People of the past who would know what to do with the world today.

Dunsinane intrigued both Jewel and her father with his fantastic story of thousands—hundreds of thousands—of people roaming the land in vast groups, disdainful of cities, lovers of traveling and pillaging, hacking roads through the wilderness wherever they advanced.

—They made a great road of purest silk, a substance as delicate as a spider's web but stronger than metal. And they fashioned this road and countless others to move themselves with great ease and control. They had a civilization without cities, and they were powerful all the same.

Less than six months later, all the buildings Father proposed were stopped in various stages of construction, and a more nomadic life began.

A Mongol life.

I think it is a fine thing to die in the middle of a road, Jewel.

She heard the engine start.

I think it is a fine thing to die, Father.

The truck did not shoot forward. Jewel knew nothing of her punishment beyond the obvious, and the delay surprised her until the first woman came and spat in her face. A procession formed behind her, men and women and children. She stared straight ahead even as their spit struck her eyes and blurred her vision. Even as her surviving sons came last.

She could not interpret their expressions. Hatred for her? Sadness for Sherman Young? Did they think this was a bizarre game? Did they wonder about Arthur? As Benjamin, the firstborn and now barely five years old, leaned forward to spit, Jewel opened her mouth to scream at him. The boiling rage, the long silence, the years of feeling there was *some* sound inside her, some noise of protest—petered out as nothingness. *I have no voice; we have no voice except what our hands can gesture and what our horns can honk and what our guns can speak on our behalf. Let me die.*

She jerked the rope, not to escape but as a goading plea to get on with it. Her mouth remained open, and her son's spit landed on her tongue where it burned like poison. The awful bitter taste made her question her own birth. What guarantee did she have that Father hadn't violated Mother the way Sherman Young had forced himself on her? Who could know? Father had changed before her eyes, and how could she claim those changes had only started at the particular hour of a particular day? What if Father had been a vile man? What if he'd even tried to kill his wife in the middle of her labor, taking the oversized ring with its black stone off his finger and forcing it past her clenched teeth to choke her as Jewel had done to Arthur?

The nightmarish thoughts made Jewel writhe and explode with emotion. She screamed.

Screamed.

Her sons drew back, bursting into tears. Women clutched one another and men quaked in terror. Jewel's throat felt very strange—sore, vibrating. She ran out of air and fell into silence even as she pitched forward on her hands and knees, gasping for breath. A man, one of her dead husband's endless lackeys, came at her, and she reared back and screamed again. The lackey cringed and ran away.

Now the faces surrounding Jewel became grave and worshipful. She offered more sounds. Strange sounds. Groans.

Bleats. Honking noises. Were they words? What did the gestures of hands sound like coming from the tongue? Was this laughter? Was this scorn?

She stood. No one tried to stop her. Two women slashed the ropes binding her to the truck. Jewel spoke to them with her hands and her mouth, knowing only the *intent* of the sounds, the thankfulness for being spared.

But she stopped short of that.

If she'd learned anything from the likes of Dunsinane and her husband, it was that leaders did not express thanks. Doing so suggested agreement rather than obligation.

It suggested her life was in *their* hands.

From across the distance, the horns of Dunsinane sounded out their collective challenge.

—SURRENDER. LEAVE YOUR CARS BEHIND AS WELL AS YOUR CHILDREN. FLEE ON FOOT AND LIVE OUT YOUR LIVES SPARED BY MERCY.

From inside the cab of her command truck, Jewel surveyed the forces arrayed against her, momentarily breathless at Dunsinane's battle lines. This battle for the road was far too expansive for the road itself and spilled over into the vast surrounding plains. Jewel briefly thought of her old map and wondered what panel of it they'd be on now. Her gaze fell upon the whiteness of her knuckles and the mottled age spots on the back of her wrinkled hands. Suddenly a finger touched her wrist and tapped.

—Mother?

Benjamin, her dear son, her only surviving son, looked at her with his one eye. Nearly thirty, the resemblance he bore to his father no longer filled Jewel with revulsion. He had been too loyal, too devoted, too worthy for her to regard him with anything but affection.

—Yes, Benjamin?

—Not like that. Say my name. I want to hear it.

Jewel smiled and spoke what she imagined his name must sound like. Benjamin squeezed her wrist.

—Now I have courage again.

—You never lost it in the first place.

She wondered, though, about the countless people who stood in her ranks. Jewel looked in the rearview mirror, searching for any hint of people taking Dunsinane's warning. For a moment, she thought she saw the reflection filled by hundreds of hastily departing fighters. But there were none.

Benjamin tapped again.

—Dunsinane is the man who killed my grandfather?

—Yes.

—And cut off his hands to make his spirit mute?

—Yes.

Benjamin nodded and squared his shoulders.

—I will go man the cabin gun.

Jewel watched him climb out and swing deftly into the truck bed. She heard him taking his spot almost directly above her, where an ancient weapon had been welded into place.

Enough time has passed. Let me give him our response if he hasn't figured it out for himself.

She alone honked, a brief and blunt sequence.

—NO.

The charge came at once. Sweat popped out along Jewel's forehead. She opened the driver's side door and stood to lean out. A thousand faces turned to her. Faces of those in cars. Faces of the foot soldiers wielding tire-shredding pikes. Faces of the archers and the melee men who would break their bones yet keep crawling after their target, until the last enemy driver was hauled from behind the wheel of the last car, throat slit, the wound defiled with gasoline and piss. These people looked at her even as Dunsinane's forces charged.

Jewel screamed.

As if she were a second sun suddenly burning in the sky, her voice poured waves of heat across her forces. Hers was the voice of a divine goddess, more than human, more powerful than any horn. Her army closed ranks around her. She climbed back into her truck and gunned it forward.

The sides met everywhere in a clash of metal and rubber. Above her, Benjamin poured out a deadly barrage that lacerated through the thin protection of several cars, annihilating their drivers. Jewel's hands were everywhere on the wheel, twisting and jerking as the scene before her changed. She glimpsed desperate passengers trying to shove out the bodies of the dead drivers. A car exploded off to her right just as a barrage of arrows struck her windshield, chipping and cracking the glass. Scowling in defiance, Jewel shifted gears, gunning forward, hoping Benjamin could hang on. Across the field, a few hundred yards away, she noticed fifty of Dunsinane's foot soldiers making a broad arc around the battle in an effort to attack from behind. She turned the wheel and overtook them in less than a minute. Benjamin's weapon chewed up half of them, and Jewel let the truck's four massive tires trample the fallen as the rest scattered back toward their hapless lines.

Wiping her brow, she saw nothing but seamless chaos, a tapestry of clustered assaults and noble, individual duels behind the wheel or on foot. Jousts and wrestling matches, men and women throwing themselves atop cars, hammering with clubs and fists against glass and metal. A queer sensation of ease lifted her heart. Whatever the outcome—and was it ever feasible she could beat Dunsinane?—her side had acquitted itself well. Even if hers was the only voice in the world, a song would survive—somehow— of this battle. The earth had its mouth in the dirt of battle, and right now that mouth was gulping down the blood of great deeds and struggle. *That's* where the song would come from.

A heavy thud sounded overhead. As Jewel looked up to see what Benjamin might want, a rumble to her left drew all her attention, and she realized what her son must have been warning her about.

Dunsinane had called in another wave, an attack unlike anything she'd seen before. All those years dedicated to felling the forests to forge a world of roads had given them time to contemplate creative, horrifying uses for timber. Five pairs of trucks, each almost as large as Dunsinane's, were coming in a line, dragging thick tree trunks between them on heavy chains. Anything, even a car, caught in its path would be crushed or upended. One of these massive logs was studded with spikes. Another had been saturated in gasoline and blazed forth with such heat and fury that Jewel felt the power of both usurping the heart in her chest.

Jewel honked her coded orders, summoning her people to a fallback position. The state of the battlefield told her it was a futile gesture. Dunsinane's heavy assault units were deployed in sweeping angles, a broad scything pattern that made flanking assaults almost impossible. They had better armor surrounding their drivers.

She saw the plan developing in her head with such sureness she could only laugh. The sound of her laughter would always be strange, even fearful to her own ears, and she wondered how the world had been when the sky must have echoed with millions of voices laughing, weeping, heckling, pleading. Surely the collective sound would have made trees and buildings fall.

She made a fist and pounded on the cabin roof.

What's wrong? Why isn't Benjamin answering me?

Jewel's laughter ceased.

—I remember you. I am almost as old as your father when he died, but I still remember you. Jewel.

She looked up at Dunsinane. She knelt in the battlefield, surrounded by the ruin of men and machines.

—You took your father's hands. I never understood why. What were a dead man's hands to me?

Jewel smiled. She could only imagine what her grin must look like. Her mouth was bloody from missing teeth and on fire with a pain her throat strained to hold back. She raised her own bound, damaged hands slowly and took them through a series of arthritic gestures.

—I had to keep you from becoming a god.

Dunsinane put his hands to his belly and rocked back and forth. Jewel saw all his followers do the same, men and women and children alike.

—Does it look like you succeeded? We have cleared more land, built more roads—roads for our machines to rule forever. The road is heaven—

"And its kingdom shall be mine!"

Jewel's defeated forces rose. Pure spontaneity, pure *conviction* in the truth of her voice spurred them to a final effort. Dunsinane gaped at her, his eyebrows knitted in blunt astonishment, his hands touching his lips and throat as if their silence was a grim betrayal.

"I am the cry of the world, I am the song of the road, I am the goddess of all sound!"

FOR THE ROAD IS HEAVEN

Dunsinane's expression twisted between appalment, disgust, and paralysis, all mirrored in the faces of his troops. They trembled at the sound of humanity, and Jewel knew how inhuman it must sound, like the rude screech of grinding metal when a tire explodes. Each utterance was a wonder, a violation, a promise, and a slap to the face. Jewel brought herself to her feet as Dunsinane's people fell back, scrambling madly for their cars. Some reached them and drove in full-speed reverse, plowing into anything to nudge and force their way to safety. Others were killed before they reached such safety.

And still others stayed—and knelt.

Dunsinane stayed but he did not kneel.

—*Impossible. A trick.*

"No trick."

—*I do not understand what your noise means. Speak with your hands.*

Jewel offered him a final smile as her people came to surround him.

"If you prefer the language of hands, then you shall have it."

And the strangulation began.

THE JARHEADS

WE SAT IN the barracks like middle school kids having a sleepover and watched Carlos spread out his deck. They were just standard poker cards, not Tarot, and I still didn't know how he divined through them.

Carlos flipped over the Five of Clubs.

"Sarge is a drunk and wants redemption in the eyes of the Army."

He turned another card. The Ace of Hearts.

"He drinks because he can't accept his homosexuality."

Carlos turned a third card. The Ten of Spades. Carlos stared at it for a long time, his eyebrows lifting. "Well, well," he said.

"What?" I asked.

He grinned at me. "Sarge is in love with you, Nick."

My cheeks burned as Allen, Richie, and Sarah joined Carlos in laughing. They didn't stop until I got up. Sarah grabbed my forearm and pulled me back into our circle. Her touch lingered on me, the heat from her fingertips almost too much.

"Stupid prank," I said.

"Who said it was a prank?"

"Because all the four of you do is make fun of me. Maybe you don't see what I bring to the table, but the military must."

"Whatever, man," Carlos said, scooping up the cards. Sarah took the Ten of Spades before he could snag it. He started to reach for it but then saw *the look,* which made all of us scoot back a little. She held the card between her thumb and forefinger, and her gaze was like a magnifying glass focusing sunlight.

The top edge of the card browned and then blackened, the corners curling inward ahead of a glowing orange line. I tasted something acrid, no doubt the melting of the card's polymer coating. I watched the card, and then I watched Sarah, liking how the burn line corresponded with the level of her eyes. Such power—such control. The fact she was sticking up for me made it so much better.

Just as the burn line reached her fingertips, Sarah looked away. It was a jarring, violent gesture, like an invisible presence snapping her neck.

"Are you okay?" I asked.

In the month the five of us had spent together training for a proposed Psionic Corps, there'd been precious few moments when we were alone, free to talk about ourselves and our abilities. Most of the time found us isolated for analysis by small teams of specialists or working together in training exercises under the supervision of Sarge.

"I will be," Sarah said, blowing out air. "It's always been easier for me to light the fire than to put it out. I have to find someplace blank to stare at—the floor is usually safest, as long as there's no carpet—and imagine I'm diving into a pool."

The sudden clapping from around the corner brought us all to our feet.

Sarge came in and leaned against the wall. His face was shiny with sweat. The sight of it coated my entire mouth with its slick, salty taste and made me gag.

"Not bad, Charlie McGee," he said, clapping again. "You're going to make the cut. But Miss Cleo, you and I are going to have some words if you think I'm queer and have a hard-on for Tastebud."

"But how?" Richie whispered.

Sarge looked amused. "What's wrong, Satellite? Thought you saw me somewhere else?"

Richie nodded.

"Maybe your remote viewing isn't so great after all. Maybe you *won't* make the cut."

We stood in a line, heads bowed like frightened parochial school students facing the most savage of nuns. Sarge walked around us, making a couple of orbits before electing to speak. "The lab geeks have made their decision, and it falls upon me to let you know. The five of you represent the only known psionic talents in the United States. This is mighty disappointing to the President. Of course, the President watches too many *X-Men* movies. It's been decided that only four of you have any talent that might be usable."

I sensed the others lifting their heads. I kept mine down, never more aware of my worthlessness than at that moment. Sarge cleared his throat and began to call the names of the survivors.

"Charlie McGee."

Sarah stepped forward.

"Miss Cleo."

Carlos joined her.

"Satellite. Looks like you're good enough after all."

Richie moved past me, leaving a gap between myself and Allen. I closed my eyes, waiting for Sarge to call out *Doctor McCoy*.

"Tastebud."

I gritted my teeth and flinched. Then the shock of realization made me look up and tap my chest. *"Me?"*

"Blows me away too, Tastebud. Guess you're not just the flavor of the month. The four of you are to report to Building 9 right now. Dr. Bradbury and Dr. Rochester will be there to brief you further."

The four of us hugged each other as Allen stood off to the side. I could see he was stunned, and though I had sympathy for him, I felt a little complacent. The two of us had formed a bit of a rivalry based on the low worth of our powers in terms of psionic combat. Right now he was *pissed*.

I offered my hand, and Allen refused it. "Suit yourself," I said, unable to hide a trace of Olympian superiority. I marched into Building 9 tasting triumph at every step.

I didn't see my colleagues for two days. Now that the Psionic Corps decided on its first members, the twenty or so researchers who ran the project wanted us isolated for detailed study and testing. Still exultant at being selected, I made no complaint about the needles jabbed into my arm, the amount of blood extracted, or the humiliation of pissing and shitting into medical containers, often while Bradbury, Rochester, or Sarge watched.

From the beginning, they'd always shown a juvenile and salacious curiosity about my power that I doubted was in evidence when they questioned Sarah about her pyrokinesis. Had I ever looked at a piece of dog shit and had its taste just explode in my mouth? Had I ever experienced another person's vomit? I had to admit these things happened in childhood, when my clairgustance began to manifest itself with all the embarrassing randomness of an adolescent erection. Before I learned control, I managed to taste everything from the family cat's urine-soaked litterbox to the smear of gum on the bottom of a friend's sneakers.

Early into the first month's evaluation period, I overheard a couple of the doctors laughing and wondering if I could look at a photo of a woman's crotch and sample it, too. Realizing the low regard they had for my power, I almost dropped out of the program, feeling too much like a carnival freak.

But I'd shown them all. I was in Building 9, wasn't I?

Chosen over the obnoxious *Dr. McCoy.*

The four of us were reunited after our third evening of isolation. We sat on the floor in a circle and compared experiences. I wished it took them longer to wonder about Allen.

"It just doesn't make sense he wasn't selected," Carlos said. His fingers flexed and curled like they wanted to deal cards. But those were confiscated the moment we entered Building Nine.

"What you really mean is it doesn't make sense they chose me over him."

I noticed Sarah and Richie exchanging worried looks.

"My cards aren't wrong, Nick. It was supposed to be Allen."

Sarah leaned forward. "You looked ahead?"

"It's sort of what I do."

"But we agreed you wouldn't!"

"I agreed I wouldn't tell any of you what I saw. But now that it's over, I can tell you I didn't see Nick getting taken."

I felt heat coming off Sarah's body. Her mouth was drawn and tight, her auburn hair like a halo of flame around the head of a matchstick. She was on my side. Richie was as well.

"You told me you couldn't divine more than a week ahead without hitting a black wall," Richie said. "When did you check your cards?"

"The day before we were sent to Building 9. The forecast was fresh and clear. I'm telling you, *something* isn't right. Like it or not, Nick's not supposed to be here."

"Maybe you were just wrong," I said. "You're damn arrogant if you think you can't make a mistake."

"At least there's consequences for my mistakes, Nick. Would the world come to an end if you confused sweet for sour?"

Sarah stood up, her hair igniting like a wig of candlewicks. "Both of you stop it before I lose control and make a *bad* mistake!"

We shut up. Sarah looked at the barren concrete wall, and her fire died away.

"I'm sorry," she said. "I don't feel great. I haven't been feeling like myself since we entered Building 9."

"Me neither," Carlos said.

"Maybe it's guilt about Allen," I said.

"Something you wouldn't know about."

Sarah warned us again before sitting down. "Maybe Nick's right and it is guilt. Richie, would you mind trying to locate him? Just to make sure he's okay?"

"Without something belonging to him in hand, it'd be a shot in the dark. But I'll try for you."

She squeezed his shoulder and thanked him.

Richie began to curl himself into a contortionist's pose, folding his long, lanky body into a space one-third his body's natural size. I'd watched him perform remote viewing four times, and each experience left an unfathomable taste in my mouth alien to any physical substance. Was I sampling his effort, his strain? My clairgustance was never so potent, so penetrative. I might taste a person's sweat or blood, but never the flavors of the mind.

"There's a haze," Richie said. Head tucked away, he looked like a living beach ball.

"Like fog? Maybe he's in Scotland."

"No. It's brown. Like when the sun is shining against your eyelids."

Sarah placed one hand on him. "Is that usual?"

"No. I'm going to try to push through it."

He began to rock back and forth, pivoting on the small of his back. Sarah moved away from him, her hands now clasped at her chest.

"It's so difficult. I don't understand."

He sounded exhausted, and looking at him brought a foul and dry taste into my throat, like being gagged with a mouthful of soiled rags.

Richie screamed. All at once he exploded out of his pose and rolled across the floor several feet before coming to rest on his back. We gathered around him, and Sarah helped him sit up. He whimpered and clutched at her.

"What is it?" I asked. "What did you see?"
"Allen."
"What's he doing? Is he okay?"
"He's with us."
Sarah stroked his hair. "What do you mean? He's not here."
"He's in a lab," Richie said, his Adam's apple bobbing as he swallowed. "He's standing over our bodies."

We stood up and processed Richie's words. I seemed to be the only person not spooked by them. To me, the simplest explanation was he'd made a mistake, but no one wanted to hear a reasonable explanation.

Richie sat against the wall with his knees against his chest but not quite in the pose he assumed while remote viewing. This was more like a scared kid hugging himself at night while his imagination growls from the closet.

"We're naked," he said. "Naked and strapped down on tables, all in a row."

"Could have fooled me," I said, and Carlos pushed me.

"You want to taste blood for real, Nick? If not, then shut up."

A burst of heat between our chests separated us. I saw flame burning in the space between us, pure as a firework in suspended animation. Sarah held her hand outstretched, and the flame and its heat disappeared when she lowered it.

"Tell us more, Richie. We were naked and on a table?"

"You've got it wrong."

"But isn't that just what you said?"

"Not were. *Are.* I can't see the past, and I don't see the future. I'm telling you that right now our bodies are naked and strapped down."

I sighed. "Richie, that's evidently not true. You had a hallucination or something."

Richie surprised me by getting to his feet. I retreated as he approached.

"It wasn't a hallucination, Nick. Right now, you're on a table. So is Sarah. So is Carlos. So am I."

"And Allen is standing over us?"

"Right."

"What's he doing?" Carlos said.

"He's got his fingertips on Sarah's skull. Sarge is next to him, and so are all the people who've been evaluating and testing us. Bradbury and Rochester are there, too, looking amazed."

"At what?"

"Allen's surgical skill."

I rubbed my right upper arm. Last year I found a small hard spot there diagnosed as dermatofibroma—harmless enough, but its presence bothered me to the point where I'd considered surgery. I mentioned it to Allen after he revealed his power, curious as to how he'd handle such a cyst. *"I mean, do you just concentrate on it and make it melt away, or what?"* He smiled and asked me if I trusted him. Nodding without much thought, I followed his request to show him the spot. He then put his fingertips to the place. *"Hold still,"* he said, *"and this won't hurt a bit."*

"But what are you—"

I watched his fingers disappear into the meat of my arm just like there was an incision there. He went in past the first knuckle. I gritted my teeth more in shock than pain. Moments later, he retracted his hand, and I saw the bloody cyst pinched in his grip. Breathless and fighting off a horrific taste, I touched my arm and found no cut, no blood.

Allen tossed the cyst into a waste basket and laughed.

"Easy as plucking a pearl. You should see me do an appendectomy."

Realization dawned on me. "Richie, you said he was touching Sarah's head?"

Sarah began to pace, touching her scalp. Her entire head caught fire, and she ran to the room's only door. It was locked, and she pounded on it and called for the doctors and for Sarge, shouting threats to melt off the hinges if they didn't answer right away.

Carlos meanwhile bit his fingertips until they bled and knelt before the left wall, drawing runic symbols in blood. He worked around Richie, who sat looking catatonic. Spitting out the taste of his blood, I started to ask him what he was doing. Before I could, however, Sarah backed away two steps and pointed at the door. Flames raced up and down her body and turned the room into a furnace. Carlos screamed for her to stop as the heat baked his precious, bloody runes into brown, illegible stains. Sarah ignored everything, her wrath focused. She threw her fury at the door for a full minute. How the entire room didn't go up in an explosion capable of ripping Building 9 apart staggered my imagination.

But there was no explosion. Sarah's fire died with all the suddenness of a torch plunged into a bucket of water, and she fainted. I crouched by her, cradling her head as Carlos inspected the door.

"It can't be," he said. "There aren't even any burn marks."

"Maybe everything in the room is fireproof."

"Maybe the room is an illusion," Richie said.

He worked himself back into a tight, rocking pose and shut his eyes as Sarah regained consciousness. Carlos and I helped her sit. The three of us watched Richie—and waited.

"Our bodies are still on the tables and connected to life support. Allen is standing over Carlos now. His hands are inside Carlos's skull almost up to the wrist. He's talking. My God, I can hear them! I've never been able to hear as well as see.

—'Now severing the brain stem. Is the container ready?'

—'You are clear to proceed.' That's Dr. Bradbury speaking. I'm not sure of the others.

—'Very well.' Oh. . .oh God. . .He's pulling his hands away. He's removing Carlos's brain like his head is a zippered bag."

Carlos broke away from us and shook Richie despite our efforts to stop him.

"I'm right here. My brain's in my head, man. What the hell is this shit?"

"He's carrying the brain to a sort of container. . .like a very large glass jar, filled with blue liquid. There's a hatch at the top. The hatch is open, and now Allen is letting the brain slip out of his hands and into the fluid. The hatch is being sealed. Dr. Rochester has gone to a computer console. There's a schematic of the brain there. I can't make out all the telemetry, but there's a lot of it.

—'Readings look good. We have a clear access signal. Who wants to know tonight's Lotto numbers?' Everyone in the room is laughing. I see the other jars now. There's only one that's empty. Allen's drying his hands and talking to Sarge.

—'Is Tastebud even worth the effort?'

—'Have to have four to make it work, Dr. McCoy. Let's get it done.'

—*'Gladly. I hate this asshole anyway. Don't mind if I take these first, do you?'"*

I swallowed hard, fighting off the urge to shake Richie the way Carlos had. "These? What's going on?"

"He's touching your crotch. 'This will be as easy as plucking grapes off the vine.'"

I mashed my hands over my ears and began to sob. Sarah and Carlos both told Richie to stop, but no amount of cajoling would shake him from his viewing or his relentless descriptions. His voice grew remote, cold and dispassionate as he detailed my emasculation and Allen's vengeful gloating. I couldn't understand, couldn't believe. With no shame at all, I spaded my fingers into my underwear, found myself intact, and tried to reason away all I was hearing.

"'You've had your fun, Dr. McCoy. Now get the asset's brain in place.'"

Less than two minutes later, Richie informed me my brain now resided in a receptacle of blue fluid, bobbing up and down like some grotesque sea cucumber confined to an aquarium.

"'Look at that!' Something's startled them. They're crowding around the console for Sarah's jar."

Sarah knelt beside Richie. "What about my jar?"

"The fluid is boiling. Someone touches the glass and shrieks, falling back. Others are at the computer controls for the container. It's flashing red. The temperature is over five hundred degrees and rising. So many people are talking all at once.

—'Will the glass break?'

—'We have to get the brain out of there before it perishes.'

—'Is she fighting back?'

—'How could she fight back? She's ours now.'"

Richie's body trembled. He was fighting to stay in his position, but one leg came free, and then an arm.

"—'Psionic activity is spiking. We've never measured the subject's power at this level before.'

—'Then power amplification through the containment system is proven.'

—'But only when directed by us—'"

Richie's other leg broke free, and then he lost his pose. He lay on his back, lungs heaving, gaze fixed on the ceiling. As we crowded over him, I thought I saw what he'd been describing playing like video in his eyes—the lab, Allen, Sarge, the doctors and technicians, our helpless bodies, our brains floating in jars of neon blue fluid. Then Richie blinked, and the images vanished. His soft brown eyes welled with tears.

"They've broken us," he said.

"Robbed us," Carlos said.

"Raped us," said Sarah.

I started to touch my crotch again and made myself stop.

"I don't understand," Carlos said. "We volunteered for this project. The military already had our support."

"They never wanted us as ourselves," Sarah said. "We all got the same story about being trained to become some sort of psychic marine on the frontlines of the national defense. But it's clear they just wanted our brains, and they intend to use them as tools. That must be what they mean about power amplification. Alone, I can set a house on fire—as long as I can see it. But my brain amplified, harnessed, and hooked up to God knows what. . ."

"They use me to predict where a target will be—then make Richie confirm it like a targeting system—then push a button to make Sarah destroy it."

"If that's true, then what is all this?" I said. "Where *are* we right now?"

"A hallucination. Like a dream we can't wake up from," Richie said.

"But is it a shared dream?"

We looked at Sarah and waited for her to clarify.

"I mean, are our brains linked and sharing the same hallucination together, or is this just the hallucination of one of us? Let's say this is my hallucination, and I only think you're sharing it. Meanwhile, Nick's brain may actually believe he got cut from the program and was rewarded with a house in Hawaii. Carlos, you may think you're back in Las Vegas working as the most profitable croupier any casino ever employed. And Richie—"

"Maybe this is my hallucination," he said. "And none of *you* are real."

Sarah conceded the point.

"But I feel conscious," I said.

"Or so you claim."

I sat down and put my head in my hands. "This is madness."

"It is," Carlos said. "Look, I feel conscious and present, too.

Cards or no cards, I'm willing to gamble we're sharing the same reality right now, even if the reality is fabricated. We've all got some level of psionic ability, and for the first time in our lives we've been forced to spend an intense amount of time around people with similar abilities. Maybe a link formed between us and it's still active even with our brains removed from our heads. Hell, maybe the same amplification process is the reason the link exists in the first place. The question is—do Sarge and the rest of them know about it?"

Richie resumed his cramped remote viewing pose and spied on the lab.

"Our bodies are gone."

"You have to find them!" I said.

Sarah shook her head. "It won't matter. There's nothing we can do about it either way. Stay with the lab, Richie. Give us as much detail as you can."

"Our containers seem to be networked into a larger machine. I see at least ten consoles. People are sitting at them."

"What about Sarge and Allen? Are they still there?"

"I don't think anyone has left the lab. I see Sarge standing in front of a view screen that dominates one entire wall. It's showing a place. . .mountainous. . .rugged terrain. I think it's Afghanistan. There's a village. Men with guns. Sarge just clapped his hands and pointed. 'He's found it. This is too good to be true. Let's try the targeting system. Anyone want to see a little spontaneous human combustion?'"

"They're going to use me to burn someone alive," Sarah said, hands over her mouth.

"The screen has zeroed in on a single villager. If I'm responsible for the image, then the boost in my power must be tremendous. I've never viewed anything with such clarity unless it was only in the next room. This is like watching a movie."

Sarah looked at the ceiling like she was seeking the face of God. "I won't kill anyone! You told me I'd be used for missile defense!" She closed her eyes tight, teeth grinding.

She caught fire and shrieked.

"Something's wrong. They're distracted. The fluid in Sarah's jar is boiling. They're doing emergency power-downs—aborting the test."

Sarah's flame diminished as she regained control of herself. "Is it because of what I'm doing here?"

"They're confused. Since they were gearing up to channel your power, they think they've miscalculated."

"Then they still don't realize we know what's going on."

"Their only concern is harming the asset."

"Asset," Sarah said, flaring again. "I've never killed anyone. That's going to change if I can just figure out how to expand my powers beyond the jar."

"You mean *our* powers," Carlos said. "We're fighting back together. You may end up doing all the heavy lifting, but you'll need backup."

"Right," Richie said, coming out of his pose.

They turned to me. What could I say to them? Now more than ever I felt and acknowledged my worthlessness. I should have respected my place in life, working at a Michelin three-star Italian restaurant, getting paid well to sample every single dish and remark upon its quality without disturbing a single atom on the plate or in the bowl. I was the envy of every dieter who ever lived, able to satisfy the desire of taste without ever taking in an extra calorie.

An easy life.

And an empty one.

"I don't know what I can offer."

"Just be with us," Carlos said, extending his arm.

We planned our revolt by having Richie go through another series of remote viewing sessions, focusing on the people in the lab. Most we knew from personal interaction; others Richie read off to us by examining their badges, and Carlos bit his fingers and wrote them in blood on the wall. Then he began to sketch out new runes.

"There's something else I've discovered."

"What is it?"

"Time."

We waited for an explanation. None of us wore a watch, and the room had no clock. Richie came out of his trance and told us to count off ten minutes. We did, and then he remote-viewed again.

"There's a discrepancy in how much time is passing between our experience and the real world. I became aware of it when I noticed the time on the computers. It seems for every ten minutes here, an hour passes in the world."

"That's a huge discovery," Carlos said, still working on his runes. "Without that detail, my predictions would be off. *Way* off."

"Do you think you can adjust for it?" Sarah said.

"I'm pretty sure."

At least two hours had passed in the real world before he completed his changes. I couldn't comprehend what he'd done or what his symbols meant, but he was convinced they'd give us an edge.

"They may always be fifty minutes ahead of us, but little good it'll do them when I can jump ahead an hour and fifty. We'll network our powers the way they're trying to and pick off the bastards one by one."

"Why not all at once?" I asked.

"For our protection," Sarah said. "If I burn them all up in the lab, we'll give ourselves away. They'll destroy our brains on the spot. There's also the chance my fire kills the rest of you."

"Better to snipe them," Richie said.

"But we don't know how many people are involved. There could be thousands."

"I already looked into that back when I signed up for the project," Carlos said. "At the time, I got about twenty-five divination lines. Richie read off twenty-four names. And I think we know who number twenty-five is."

I shook my head.

"The President," Sarah said. "Sarge said it himself."

After that sank in, I said, "What do we do about Allen?"

"Either he was never a real recruit like us to begin with, or he cut some kind of deal with the people in charge."

"It doesn't matter. He's a dead man."

"Like hell it doesn't matter," I said. "He may be the only person who can put our brains back in our bodies."

I could tell from the way they looked at me that all three of them thought this a vain hope. But none of them challenged it.

THE JARHEADS

"Let's start with Dr. Rochester," Carlos said, kneeling in front of the wall. He put his left hand over her name as his right moved in erratic patterns over the runes.

"What are you doing?"

"Divining where she is and when she'll be alone. It's a hell of a lot easier with a deck of cards."

His head tilted back, and I saw only the whites of his eyes. As his reading continued, his body convulsed until he fell back as if the wall shoved him away.

"Well?" Sarah said.

"Rochester has left the lab and is driving home. She'll be in bed in about three minutes our time."

"Quick," Richie said, beckoning us to him. He folded himself into that tight, tortured posture. Carlos put his right hand on Richie's shoulder and held out his left to Sarah. She took it. I took her other hand and completed the circle by touching Richie's shoulder.

"I see her. I'm following her car as it pulls up to her home. You're guiding me, Carlos. The amplification is as remarkable as our networked abilities."

Sarah closed her eyes and gasped. "I see the car as well! My God, Richie, what an astonishing ability. I feel like I'm floating above it."

My vision was not as clear as theirs. I saw Dr. Rochester pull up to a house and get out of the car, but I watched it all through a cataract.

"What now?" I asked.

"I'm going to kill her," Sarah said in the softest voice, almost to herself. I couldn't look at her too long without experiencing the bitterness of her thoughts and the metallic flavor of someone steeling themselves to violate their most cherished beliefs. Revenge would never taste sweet in Sarah's mind.

We went silent and still. The air temperature rose, becoming stifling. Dr. Rochester headed for her front door. She stopped at the porch and turned, touching the back of her neck and then her forehead. She staggered and looked down at her feet. Her shoes ignited. Screaming, she ran into the grass. The flames climbed up her legs and she pitched herself onto the ground and rolled. She was already dead when her neighbors came out of their houses to investigate.

We broke our circle and waited for Sarah to speak.

"Let's move on to the next name," she said.

"You're sure?"

Sarah nodded.

Carlos went back to his wall and went through an identical process to locate Dr. Bradbury. Sarah burned him in his bed, killing him as his wife tried to beat the flames off his body with a pillow. The next researcher, Stephen Lunowski, died sitting on the toilet. His pants weren't down. We found him hunched forward, face buried in his hands, his body racked with sobs. Was he feeling guilt over his complicity in the crime committed against us? Or had he heard about the deaths of his colleagues, suspected what transpired, and awaited his fate? If these questions went through Sarah's mind, they neither stayed nor slowed her fury.

Carlos and Sarah moved as fast as they could, but by the seventh name, Sheila Harding, something was wrong. Carlos's attempt to read the runes had several starts and stops. "I've never experienced such chaos," he said. "It's like even fate can't decide what to do with her. She's on the road and going fast. Madness rules her actions, clouding everything. I *think* she's returning to the lab."

"They all know what's happening now. I suppose it was inevitable," Sarah said.

"Too much time is passing in the real world for every minute here," I said. "Even working as fast as we can, they have the advantage."

Carlos tried two more names. "The same chaos. I feel them closing in. It's a convergence. I suspect everyone involved in the project is either back at the lab or returning to it."

"Then it's a last stand," Richie said, beckoning us to him.

"Make them burn, Sarah!" Carlos said. "I don't care if it kills me too."

We joined with Richie and found ourselves in the lab. Sarah and Carlos and Richie stood beside me like holograms. We materialized in front of our jars, and it made me wonder again about the fate of our physical bodies. Had they been buried? Incinerated? Cryogenically preserved?

I became aware of the men and women scrambling all around me. I saw Sarge and Allen standing off to the side. Sarge was waving a gun and shouting commands. No one seemed to see us.

"Disconnect all stations—isolate each container!"

"Disconnect commands aren't working. It's like the system's been fused!"

"Intra-neural communication between the assets seems certain."

"Can we establish a timeline?"

"Likely since the moment of transplantation."

"Now, Sarah!" Richie said.

Sarah raised her right hand, and the man to my right caught fire. His screams and flailing sent everyone scampering back. A woman touched the door and screamed, holding her hand. The flesh of her palm was raw with blisters.

Sarge walked toward Sarah's container, gun outstretched. Sarah swept her fingers at the barrel, and Sarge shouted as he dropped the weapon and cradled his burning hand. Another simple gesture lit his hair on fire.

Her vengeance rising, Sarah's form turned to pure flame. Fire leapt off her and took seed on the clothes of every person in the lab. The room's fire extinguishers activated, but it might as well have been dousing everyone with gasoline. Sarah alone could stop the burning now.

A few minutes later, it seemed everyone was dead, but it was hard to see through the smoke and the fruitless rain of the sprinklers. Then we saw Allen. He'd managed to get right behind our jars, hiding from us through proximity. He'd gotten Sarge's gun and raised it at Sarah's jar. Before she could do anything, he emptied the clip, shattering the glass. Sarah's brain rode the escaping gush of blue fluid to the floor.

Sarah's image flickered. She lost her flame and clutched her throat like someone suffocating.

"No more barbecues for you, bitch," he said and stomped down with his heel.

Sarah shattered out of existence.

"We're defenseless," Richie said as Allen went to stand before the remaining jars. He spoke directly to our brains.

"Sorry, guys," he said. "They threatened my family if I didn't help them. It was an easy choice."

He put both hands on Carlos's container and started to push. Carlos's figure assaulted him with a hail of punches that passed through him. Allen had no perception of him, and as he pushed harder, the container began to rock. Carlos's brain sloshed back and forth as momentum made the jar more and more precarious. With a final shove, Allen sent it pitching forward and the jar smashed open. Carlos's brain went sliding across the wet floor until Allen pinned it with the sole of his shoe. Carlos gave us a plaintive look, a gesture of goodbye before Allen destroyed him.

"We tried," I said, watching Allen confront the final two jars. As I wondered whether he'd kill me or Richie first, I felt the illusion of a heartbeat in my chest, a rapid cannon fire that gave me the illusory taste of acid reflux. The nasty flavor built until I wanted to vomit.

"*Jesus.*" Allen doubled over, spitting and retching.

"The amplification is still in effect!" Richie said. "It must be strengthening your clairgustance. Just like I could never hear as well as see, you might be able to project taste as well as receive it."

Allen spat again and straightened.

"You're our last hope, Nick."

I dredged my memory for the nastiest things I'd ever sampled: the smeared dog shit on the bottom of someone's sneakers; the decay of a dead skunk on the side of a road; formaldehyde; gasoline. I glared at Allen and cast each taste into him until he collapsed, gasping, choking. Thick saliva drooled from his stricken mouth. He tried to counter it by licking the floor. He even licked the spilled fluid from the broken jars, sucking it into his cheeks like mouthwash. He inched toward our containers again. I bore down, making him taste vomit, cigarette ash, sand. He struggled, teeth clamped, but the blue fluid drizzled from the corners of his weakening lips. He reached the first jar and jostled it. I felt a corresponding jolt in my feet and knew the container must contain my brain.

All my hatred for Allen erupted in one final taste. This bastard had castrated me for sport, and I imagined my testicles, shiny and wet between his thumb and forefinger. I imagined them in his mouth. I pasted them across his tongue.

Allen's eyes widened. His cheeks bulged, and he surrendered to the urge to vomit. To my astonishment, two fleshy orbs came out of his mouth with all the grace of a cat hacking up a hairball.

"Your powers are exploding, Nick," Richie said, grinning. "You've done more than conjure taste. You've put their physical source into his mouth."

I stood over Allen, certain he could see me. He reached up as if he might, but instead, he clawed his way toward the jars again.

"Eat shit," I said.

Allen cried as hot feces poured from his jaws, followed by a heavy flow of blood.

"Is that you too?" Richie said.

"No. He must be hemorrhaging."

I went on feeding him every nasty substance until he lay motionless on his back, eyes distant and glossy, with only the occasional gurgle to indicate life. He struggled to raise his hands again. I thought for sure he was going to make one more try at our containers. Instead, he brought his fingertips to his skull. They disappeared into his soaked hair, penetrated the bone, and with his last bit of power, his last bit of will, he pulled his brain free and let it drop beside his head.

Richie and I stared at the carnage and then at our brains. Neither of us said a word about our fate.

"At least we got them all," he said.

"Not yet. There's still one more."

"The President," Richie said. "I'll try to find him."

"We'll pay him a visit once you do. And let's make sure our company leaves a very bad taste in his mouth."

MANY CARVINGS

"LIGHT THE LAMPS, Alaster," the boy's mother said, lifting her needlework to squint at a stitch. Alaster lay on the floor, too obsessed with his brother to be bothered by the chill of the wooden planks penetrating his night shirt. The month-old infant cooed from his crib, and his kicking feet made the most delicate thuds, a noise that pleased Alaster. It reminded him of pulling carrots from the ground and wiping away the dirt and hearing the earthen clumps break on the ground.

"Alaster."

He pushed himself to all fours and then went to light the lamps. An October gale gusted against the house, speeding him along. He liked to think of each wick as a person with an oval flame of hair. The fire always seemed to bow toward him at first, like a curtsey to thank him for life. Then it stretched with fuel like a person waking in the morning, arms up, back arching. When he was a little younger, he gave each flame a name and pretended they were all family members. But those memories embarrassed him now.

He knelt by the crib and smiled. "I think William wants to eat."

"He'll cry if he does, Alaster. None of my boys were ever shy about their hunger, you least of all. Your father warned me when I married him that appetite is prominent among all Cheverus men."

Alaster asked if he could have honey then, but his mother smiled and shook her head. "It's much too late for that, child."

"Would you read to me then, like Father does?"

His mother paused a moment, then her hands worked faster. "Aren't you too old for stories?"

"Father reads me different stories now."

"Does he?"

"About generals and soldiers and—"

MANY CARVINGS

"I must speak to him about that."

Alaster looked up to see if his mother was cross. She didn't seem so. But there was something in her expression he didn't understand. Did she not like stories? Why had she never told him one from a book?

"Your father will be back soon enough. He'll have stories from the market, I'm sure."

"I wish I could have gone with them. It's not fair that Benjamin gets to go."

"Benjamin is fifteen. You'll go with them soon enough. But now you have little William to watch over."

Alaster couldn't help pouting. He'd never been to the city, and this was Benjamin's third straight season helping Father at the market with the other men. He always came back with tales of wonder. People singing and strange animals wandering here and there and drinks and candies found nowhere else. The tastes Alaster's imagination created always turned to sour envy on his tongue.

He looked down at William and thought, *When I'm older, I'm going to go to the markets while you stay behind, but I'll bring something back for you.*

Alaster kissed the baby on the forehead. Drowsiness overtook him shortly thereafter, and he had little memory of his mother turning off the lamps or picking him off the floor. He did remember a sleepy protest that he was too big to be carried, but his mother was very stout, like most of the village women. It would be a few years yet before he truly became too heavy for her.

He woke to the sound of a fierce hammering from the front door and the baby wailing in his parents' room. Alaster heard his mother up and on the move. He left his bed and instantly shivered in the night's chill. The banging gained urgency. Alaster thought there must be an army outside demanding shelter.

As he came to stand beside his mother, Alaster heard a voice shouting to be let in.

"It's Benjamin! But why is he here, Mother? What could have happened?"

Each question engraved a new line upon his mother's face.

"Go tend to your brother."

"But my brother is—"

His mother's expression shut him up. He'd only seen her look this way once, a few months before William's birth when word arrived of an accident in the field. Mother simply said, *"Jonathan,"* in the same hushed way she said *Jesus* in church, and took off running despite her condition. But Father ended up not being hurt too much, and Ms. Sibley came to tend to his injury.

"Thank you for coming so fast," Mother said as she, Alaster, and Benjamin gathered to watch Ms. Sibley apply a poultice to Father's ankle. Alaster fixated on the old woman's hands, so big at the knuckles, so slow and careful with Father's bandage—and then so swift to touch his mother's stomach.

"A shame the accident, if it had to happen, couldn't have occurred two months from now. What's the expression? Kill two birds with one stone?"

But it'd be three more months before William was ready, and then Ms. Sibley delivered him just as she'd delivered Benjamin. She'd wiped her hands clean on a rag, smiled at Alaster and said, "Easier than your brother, but not as eager to arrive as you."

"Alaster—go to William. *Now.*"

He blinked back to the present as the door rattled and Benjamin again begged for admission. Alaster retreated to his parents' bedroom and knelt by the baby's crib. "Hush," he said, stroking the infant's sparse hair. But William went on wailing, drowning out all other sound. After a few minutes, Alaster couldn't stand not knowing what was happening with Benjamin and left the bedroom to see. He found his brother holding a sheet of paper in front of his mother's face.

"But why would Jonathan write when he knows—"

"He told me to read it to you, Mother."

Alaster crept closer, keeping close to the wall. William's cries became distant to him.

"Dearest, a great illness has struck at the market. More people are ill here than well. It is a devilish thing, but with God's help we will persevere. Already I am feeling better just writing to you. I return Benjamin to you since he remains healthy. I know you will disapprove of the decision, but he is a capable boy, and I did not send him back alone."

Mother said, "Who did you return with?"

"Cameron."

"Martin Huntley's oldest? Is Martin ill, too?"

"Yes, Mother. We traveled the entire way back together and—"

"Where is Cameron now?"

"At home talking to his own mother, I suppose," Benjamin said, adding a laugh that Alaster thought almost mocking. This drew him closer, and his presence caught his older brother's attention. Benjamin fixed him with a bold, assured stare. He seemed even taller than before, though that couldn't be possible. He and Father had been gone not even a full week.

"What sort of illness was it, Benjamin?"

"How should I know?"

"Was there coughing?"

"Yes."

"How was your father's appetite?"

Benjamin shrugged. "He was eating."

"And keeping it down?"

"Mostly."

"There's that, at least," Mother said, gathering her gown around her as she turned. Alaster thought she looked miserable. In most times of trouble, she'd say, "It's in God's hands now." But she hadn't said that when she thought Father was hurt. And she didn't say it now. Alaster figured she wanted to consult Ms. Sibley, but there was nothing to be done at so late an hour. And the market was so far away.

"Are you hungry, Benjamin?"

"No, Mother."

"Are you sure? You must have traveled for hours."

"Our fathers gave us bread for the trip."

"Then go to bed. You too, Alaster."

But Benjamin went straight to his parents' room. Alaster and his mother exchanged looks before following.

"What are you doing, Ben?"

"I've missed my brother."

He picked William up and cradled him. Alaster's face went hot when the baby's cries turned into contented coos.

"He missed me."

"Settle him back into the crib, Benjamin. It's time for all of us to sleep. In the morning, I'll visit with the Huntleys."

"You don't believe me, Mother?"

"What sort of question is that? I only want to find out more details."

Alaster watched Benjamin slowly return William to the crib.

"I told you—"

Mother reached forward and grabbed him by the back of his neck. "I'll assume this defiant tone comes from being exhausted. Go to bed now—both of you."

In their room, Benjamin flopped upon the mattress and was asleep at once. Alaster didn't realize how quickly he'd become used to having the bed to himself. Now his brother's large, sprawling body forced him to the left edge. He couldn't sleep on the verge of teetering.

"Ben, give me room," he said, prodding his shoulder.

A drowsy, distant tone came from Benjamin's lips. "I will. . .I will. . ."

"Then do it."

"I will. . .I will. . ."

Alaster rose up to peer at his brother in the dark. Ben's lips moved but a different voice came from his mouth. A whisper like the dry rustle of wheat fields and as scratchy as winter bramble. Then it was Ben's voice, clearly saying, "I will, I will." Then the whisper again. Alaster wondered if his brother was dreaming of talking to someone.

"Yes, Mother."

His brother let out a short burst of laughter with an even meaner edge than the laugh he'd given earlier. Alaster settled back onto his little slice of mattress and clutched himself. He did not sleep even after Benjamin went silent and his breaths came and went at the slow, steady pace of dreams.

But drowsiness stole upon him at some point. He woke with the bed to himself again and a feeling like *he'd* been the one dreaming. Ben was still at the market with Father. There'd been no midnight return, no news of illness.

Alaster tossed the blankets off himself and changed clothes before leaving his room. He heard his mother's faint voice calling for him.

Entering his parents' bedroom, he found her in bed, still dressed in her gown. She lifted her arms as he rushed to her.

"Sick," she whispered.

So last night was not a dream.

"Could you have what Father has? Maybe Benjamin—"

"He took. . .took. . ."

Alaster leaned closer. "Took what, Mother? Where did he go?"

"Huntley. . .William. . ."

She rose an inch toward him, beseeching with a fervor that lasted seconds before she collapsed back onto the bed and turned her face to the wall. Alaster saw sweat pooling at the base of her throat. He drew back, and his heels struck William's crib. He turned and gasped at the empty box.

"Benjamin took William?"

She nodded.

Alaster thought he understood. Father sent Benjamin back to avoid being sick, but somehow Mother became ill too. Now Mother wanted them all to go to the Huntley farm. But why would Ben have left without him?

"Mother—"

She tried to speak but her voice didn't reach a whisper. The sound of her struggle made his chest hurt. He went to Father's desk and took out a piece of paper and a pencil.

"Write out what I should do, and I'll do it."

Mother's eyes shifted to the pencil and paper, and she began to cry. She made a pushing motion, shooing him away. He felt certain staying here brought her pain, and he took off running without another thought. His feet slapped on the single dirt path leading to the main road. Once there, Alaster turned left. Not the direction of the neighbor farm families like the Huntleys and the Mastersons.

He went on without a conscious thought until he arrived at Ms. Sibley's little cottage.

No smoke came from her chimney, but Alaster heard sounds from within. He knocked on the door. "Ms. Sibley, it's Alaster. Can you come and see my mother? She's sick."

A sound like many mouths stifling laughter came from the other side. Alaster stepped back. He felt the sunlight's gathering heat on his narrow shoulders. It wasn't strong enough to thaw the ice creeping up his spine.

"Child, why are you here?"

He spun around to find Ms. Sibley standing there, wrapped in layers of warm garments. She must have started the day early, venturing forth when the temperature was far less comfortable. She carried an open basket in her left hand, overflowing with mushrooms and roots and sticks and fallen leaves, as if she'd collected according to random fancy. But the pumpkin cradled in the crook of her right arm drew most of his attention. He'd never seen one so perfect, its unblemished orange skin blazing in the daylight.

Ms. Sibley came closer. "Alaster, I see, and not long out of bed from the looks of it. What's wrong?"

He fought to draw his attention off the pumpkin. "Mother—she's sick. Father too. At the market."

"How do you know about the market?"

Alaster explained about Ben's return and the letter Father wrote.

"I know," Ms. Sibley said, moving toward the door. "Many doctors have been summoned, and I've heard there are road signs posted now warning travelers away. I fear it is plague."

He gasped. "Mother and Father have the plague!"

"Don't fret, Alaster. After all, Fall is upon us, and that's the season for many maladies."

"Will you come?"

"Yes. I have business at the Whitmore farm anyway. Mrs. Whitmore's baby is due next week, but I have a feeling it will happen today. I always have a sense about these things, and I've only been wrong once. My error stands before me."

She placed the basket and the pumpkin down at her door. Its orange skin seemed to brighten and deepen by the moment. Alaster stared at it until Ms. Sibley cleared her throat. "Does something vex you, child?"

"Where did that pumpkin come from?"

"My patch, of course."

He looked around. She had farmed only the most modest plot of ground, enough to sustain herself. There was certainly no pumpkin field.

They started walking back the way he'd come. "So why are you here and not Benjamin?"

"He was gone when I woke up. He took William and I guess went to Mr. Huntley's place."

"Without you?"

"I'm sure he was rushing to please Mother."

Ms. Sibley's pace quickened, and Alaster found he had to run a bit to match it.

"How are things between you and Benjamin since little William came along?"

"Benjamin isn't less mean."

She laughed. "No, I daresay not. But is there jealousy? Do you fight for the child's affections?"

"He's only a few weeks old. He doesn't know us."

"For the last sixteen years, I have been the first to greet the children of this village—except for you, of course. A newborn's eyes are so tired, like they already understand the miseries in store for them. The wisdom of infants surpasses all of us." Ms. Sibley's pace grew even faster, so that she seemed to glide over the ground. Alaster did not see how her old legs carried her like this and had to run to keep up.

They reached Alaster's home, and he started for the door, but Ms. Sibley seized his shoulder. "No. Your mother sent you away to protect you. Honor that wish. I'll go in alone."

A piece of paper on the floor caught his attention. He bent to pick it up as Ms. Sibley went past him, heading toward his parents' bedroom.

Alaster felt certain he held the note Ben read to Mother last night, but as he turned it over, he found only gibberish. Why would Father write *this?* And how could Ben have read it like it made sense?

Ms. Sibley's footsteps drew his attention. She wasn't gliding now.

"Alaster," she said.

"How is Mother?"

"Sleeping deeply—and cool to the touch. We should let her rest."

"But I brought you here to help!"

"Sleep is often the best doctor of all."

He cast a longing glance toward the bedroom door. As he did, Ms. Sibley pinched the paper between her thumb and forefinger.

"What is this, Alaster?"

"Nothing," he said. "I don't know. Something Benjamin had."

"May I see it?"

He let go of the paper with more reluctance than he could explain to himself. It felt like surrendering a secret. Ms. Sibley's eyebrows rose.

"I don't understand. It's just letters and symbols," Alaster said. "But Ben said Father wrote it, and he read from it. It said there was a sickness in the market and that's why Ben came back with Cameron Huntley."

"Cameron," Ms. Sibley said, clasping her hands together. "How well I remember delivering him. My first, I think. I knew he'd be a sharp lad. His mother bled like she'd given birth to a razor."

Alaster just stared as Ms. Sibley walked past him to the door. "Come along," she said like an afterthought. "I will take you to the Huntley farm where you can join your brothers. Then I'll continue on to the Whitmore home. That baby is coming within the next ninety minutes. I feel it in my marrow, and I don't want to miss the birth of a *second* child."

The promise of seeing Ben coaxed Alaster to go with her. Their walk took only twenty minutes at the old woman's aggressive pace, with Alaster's side aching as he worked to keep up. Only the sight of the farmhouse gave him a second wind. He dashed ahead of Ms. Sibley, calling Ben's name, certain it was his brother coming around the corner. He stopped cold, realizing it was Cameron. Stocky, a year older than Ben and a little larger, Cameron had always seemed a friendly giant. Alaster remembered being much younger and begging for rides on his back. Cameron never refused him.

"Stay back," he said now, and Alaster stopped.

"What's wrong?"

"There's sickness here. My ma is sick."

"Is that so?" Ms. Sibley said, stepping to join them.

"Yes, ma'am."

"Mine is too," Alaster said. "She sent Ben and William here to stay with you. She told me to go, too."

"They're not here."

"Where are they, Cameron?" Ms. Sibley said.

"Ma thought it best they didn't stay, so they kept on going."

Alaster spun towards Ms. Sibley and bit his lower lip as a tremble overtook him. But the old woman kept her attention on Cameron.

"May I see your mother?"

He nodded. Ms. Sibley told Alaster to stay outside. He hugged himself and waited—but not for long. Ms. Sibley returned looking very pleased.

"Cameron's mother is sleeping as well and likewise cool to the touch."

She started back toward the road.

"But what about my brothers?"

MANY CARVINGS

"Likely they too went on to the Whitmore house. It would be the next practical place. Might as well continue with me."

Alaster looked back in the direction of his home. How nice to be there when Mother woke up feeling better. But how long until then? Imagining a wait of hours, alone and lonely, proved foul water for seeds of hope. It'd be much better to find Ben and return together.

They set out for the Whitmore residence, a mile south of the Huntley farm. Ms. Sibley did not hurry now. Perhaps she knew time was on her side.

"Have you given much thought to your future, Alaster?"

No one had ever asked him such a question, and his immediate thoughts embarrassed him with their frivolity. He'd imagined himself a pirate, a soldier, or an adventurer. So many beanstalks climbed, so many giants bested. But he knew these weren't answers to an adult's question.

"I'll be a farmer, like my father."

"Nothing else?"

He frowned, knowing only one other profession. Old Reverend Peterson's face flashed through his memory.

"Maybe a preacher?"

Ms. Sibley grunted. "Stay with farming."

Her tone confused him. Both his parents considered Reverend Peterson to be an important man, though Alaster had never felt much comfort in the man's craggy features. Perhaps he was not so prominent after all. Wouldn't Father have sent Ben straight to him? Wouldn't Mother have sent her boys to seek his help first?

They reached the Whitmore home. Ms. Sibley did not bother knocking before opening the front door.

"As I suspected," she said with clear delight.

He looked past Ms. Sibley and saw Mrs. Whitmore on the living room floor, undressed in a way that made him blush and turn his head, though he lost to the temptation to give her several quick, fascinated glances. Mother had been concerned for her. He remembered her saying so last week. "I worried that William might delay until your father had gone to the market. But I have two strong boys to help. Mary has no one. At least she's young and very healthy."

She didn't look so now. Her body rippled with strain.

"How did you know?" she said through moans and gritted teeth.

"Just a sense of the season."

"I thought I was going to have to bear this alone. With Adam at market—"

"Is he sick, too?" Alaster said.

Mrs. Whitmore seemed to become aware of his presence for the first time and tried to work a blanket over herself. Ms. Sibley soothed her.

"The child is assisting me. I take it his brothers are not here?"

"Brothers? What? No—no one. Sick? What does he mean? What—"

A sudden scream overtook her as her body convulsed. For all Ms. Sibley's talk of assistance, Alaster found she needed none. Her hands slid along the young woman's thighs as she settled into a position that blocked much of Alaster's view. His stare alternated between the floor and Ms. Sibley's back. His heart beat very fast, almost like he had two in his chest. As Mrs. Whitmore's screams became piercing, as her voice bled into so many frantic pleas and prayers, Alaster found his hands clenching. Something was wrong. Something had to be. He'd not been allowed in the room when Mother gave birth to William, but he'd listened, and there wasn't nearly this much agony. Ms. Sibley liked telling Alaster he was too eager for the world, hence his early arrival. Could a person be the opposite? Could a baby be reluctant to breathe the air? Could it be afraid or perhaps think the time, the moment, not right?

He stepped closer and to the right. The baby was halfway out, its head like a slick, shiny gourd in Ms. Sibley's hands. The rest of the body belonged to a mysterious place Alaster could not understand. He watched Mrs. Whitmore writhe as the baby kept coming. A terrifying, fleshy string was attached to the infant's stomach, and as the feet came through, the cord brought with it a purple mass that reminded Alaster of a calf's liver sewn up by a drenched skein of yellow and red yarn. He pointed at the deformity, thinking it must be some dead twin.

"It is the cord, and the rest is called afterbirth. It is nature's way. Now go to the well and bring a pitcher of water."

He left, but he saw the cord in his imagination. He lifted his shirt and looked at his belly button. Had there once been a cord there? Had there been one on William? The questions distracted him so much he spilled most of the water on the way back and had to refill the pail.

When he returned, Ms. Sibley began cleaning the baby and Mrs. Whitmore, whose eyes were shut in obvious exhaustion.

"Alaster, go to the kitchen and bring a knife."

"What for?"

"To cut the child free of its cord, of course."

He left and came back with the only thing he could find: a heavy butcher's knife. It seemed light enough in Ms. Sibley's grasp, though. She smiled at the blade, then brought it down on the cord. Alaster winced, convinced the baby would scream. But it seemed to feel no pain of separation. Ms. Sibley wrapped fresh linen around it and put the child into its mother's arms. Mrs. Whitmore offered the faintest of smiles.

"Adam will be so pleased. He thought he might be too old to become a father."

Ms. Sibley only turned to the window and said, "The day has lapsed more than I realized."

"I'm very cold just now," Mrs. Whitmore said.

"Alaster, start a fire."

He did, bringing wood from a pile just outside the door. As the blaze caught, he turned to see Ms. Sibley gathering the afterbirth and the cord into the bucket.

"I will dispose of these for you."

"Thank you for everything," Mrs. Whitmore said. "But do you have to go already? I am very tired and worried. What will I do if something goes wrong tonight? Without Adam here. . ."

"I cannot stay, unfortunately. But Alaster can."

He flinched. "I can't. I have to find my brothers. I have to—"

"You need to stay where you can be both safe and of use. Your parents would want this. Should Mrs. Whitmore need anything, you'll be able to help."

"I would feel much better about it," Mrs. Whitmore said.

He looked between the two women. His mother *would* have him stay here and be of use. But where were Ben and William?

He turned toward the door—

"Please," Mrs. Whitmore said.

—and pivoted back.

"I'll stay."

"Good lad," Ms. Sibley said, patting his head. "I'll go now. Come and find me should anything go wrong here, though I'm sure all will be well."

"Tell Benjamin where I am if you see him. And will you stop in and check on Mother on your way back?"

"Yes to both, Alaster. Such a good, brave boy you are. It would have made me so proud to say I helped bring courage such as yours into the world."

He beamed at her and was still beaming as he watched her leave, full pail in hand. As soon as she disappeared, Mrs. Whitmore called for him.

"The fire needs more fuel."

"Yes, ma'am."

Then she needed more water.

"Alaster, will you help me sit better in this chair? Can you bring a pillow for my back? Alaster, fetch my quilt from the bedroom. Can you see if the chickens look like they've eaten today? And the pigs?"

The evening found him exhausted.

He sat by the hearth, clutching his knees against his chest as he stared at the fire. How were his father and Cameron's father and Mr. Whitmore? Was Mother still cool to the touch? Was she awake? What if *she* needed more water, more fuel for the fire, a pillow for her back, and a quilt for her lap?

"Mrs. Whitmore, I think I should go. Just to check on my mother. I can come straight back."

She didn't answer. Alaster rose and found her asleep with the baby cradled at her breast. The baby's eyes were closed, its mouth slightly open. Neither would realize he'd left.

He tiptoed to the door.

"Womb to earth, and earth to womb, I bind thee to new skin and new sires."

He turned and took a cautious step toward the mother and child. "Ms. Sibley?"

The words continued in her voice. Alaster peered through the dark and listened.

"Soon your true heart beats within another chest."

He crept closer and let his sight confirm what his ears told him. Ms. Sibley's voice came from the baby's tiny mouth.

"And you'll receive my milk through a foreign breast."

A sharp, familiar laugh came from the sleeping baby. Alaster turned and ran through the cold night. He passed the Huntley house, which was entirely dark and cold, and finally came flailing toward his house. He collapsed against the door, wheezing and gasping. His fingers failed on the latch several times before he fell through and crumpled on the floor.

After a minute, his lungs began reclaiming air. Alaster got to his hands and knees. "Mother," he whispered, crawling forth. By the time he reached her bedroom, he could get to his feet. He stepped through and saw her in the dark. It did not seem like she'd moved since the morning.

"Mother."

He reached her bedside.

"Mother?"

Alaster gripped the edge of the mattress to steady himself. Then he leaned forward and touched her face.

He kept his hand against her cheek, determined to melt away the ice he found there. Ms. Sibley had called her cool to the touch. God, for a fever now! Her stiff fingers clutched nothing but time, and time had escaped her grip. Alaster grabbed her shoulders and shook her and wept. "Wake up, Mother. William's here. I've got William. And Father's here. Mother! Father says you have to wake up!"

There was no mad flight from the house, only a dazed stagger as he retraced the morning path that took him to Ms. Sibley's cottage. As he neared, the sound of voices singing gave him pause. They belonged to children, and the sound echoed from the forest behind the house.

No one stood at the front, though light showed in every window. He snuck up to the nearest one and immediately clapped both hands over his mouth to stifle a gasp.

The window looked in upon a cramped kitchen. A black stove blazed in the corner, and Alaster felt its heat on the glass. Several knives of different sizes and shapes lay upon the table. Mrs. Whitmore's pail and the pumpkin he'd seen this morning were there too. The gourd's waxy skin caught the firelight and made it seem like a ball of flame.

Ms. Sibley entered. Alaster's eyes widened at her appearance. She wore no clothes, and her naked body seemed split in two, one half younger than her years, the other half far older. The youthful breast, firm and round like a pumpkin, caused a stirring in him. But just as quickly the ancient breast soured the feeling like milk left out to curdle.

She held the cord from Mrs. Whitmore's baby stretched between her hands and spoke nonsensical words to it. As she began to writhe, Ms. Sibley placed one end to her own stomach, touching the other end to the pumpkin.

The fire in the stove flared, and suddenly the cord came alive like a wriggling snake and held its attachments on its own. Now Ms. Sibley stepped forward and took up the longest of the knives. Brandishing it in both hands, she drove the blade into the pumpkin and sawed until she could pull the top off like a hat. Setting the piece aside, she dipped her fingers into the gourd, scooping the wet innards of seeds and guts into a mushy pile. She worked fast, still chanting, a sound like a flock of black birds cawing in a mown field. Once the gourd was hollow, she reached into the pail and took up the purple afterbirth, kneading it between her fingers like a baker with dough. After several squeezes, she crammed the fleshy mass into the pumpkin.

As soon as she finished, the cord connecting them burned like a wick. Ms. Sibley showed no alarm. With a single sweep of her hands, the fire rose up and entered the pumpkin. Alaster saw a glow rise out of it, a light that ceased only when Ms. Sibley put the pumpkin's cap back into place.

She took up another knife.

Alaster's fascinated horror kept him in place. He did not hear the noise behind him until it was too late. Fingers seized his shoulders and tore him away from the window. He wilted under the grip and whimpered until he saw Ben staring down at him. But it was Cameron Huntley who'd seized him. Ben's arms were occupied with a baby. Alaster blinked, certain it must be William. But the child was much smaller.

Mrs. Whitmore's newborn.

"Ben, why—"

Ms. Sibley came out the door. "Trouble, my children?"

"Yes, Mother," Benjamin said.

"*She* isn't Mother! What's the matter with you, Ben?"

Ms. Sibley now stood before Alaster, who averted his eyes with a fierce turn of the head. She pinched his chin and forced him to lock gazes.

"Benjamin is no longer your brother, Alaster. Like the other children, he has answered the call of his true mother. Long have I waited to bring my sons and daughters into my arms and then into the arms of their Father."

MANY CARVINGS

She had Cameron bring him into the kitchen. Alaster kicked against him to no avail, stopping only when Ms. Sibley picked up the knife again.

"Place the baby on the table, Benjamin."

"Yes, Mother."

"No," Alaster whispered, frozen inside at the sight of the helpless baby surrounded by so many blades. Ms. Sibley must have guessed his anxiety and laughed. "What concerns you? Do you see scars upon my children's faces?"

She put the pumpkin beside the infant, took up the knife, and brought its tip against the shell. Another chant came from Ms. Sibley's lips. The knife's tip glowed with a brilliant silver light as she stroked it across the pumpkin like a painter. Several minutes passed, and when she finished, the chanting also ceased. Alaster saw a perfect duplication of the newborn's face carved into the gourd. Its features blazed with orange light.

"Now he too is mine—like the others. Like everyone but you, so quick to come into the world. Tell me, Alaster: Are you equally as eager to leave it?"

He craned his neck toward Ben. "Mother's dead, Ben. Do you hear me?"

"Mother's here."

"Our real mother!" He turned to Ms. Sibley. "You're a witch! Did you kill her?"

"All of them," she said.

"And Father?"

Ms. Sibley looked piteously upon him. "Poor Alaster, of all the children born in the village since I came, you alone are not mine. Which means you alone are now an orphan."

"Father's not dead!"

"Yes, he is," Ben said without emotion. "I killed him."

"As I killed mine," Cameron said.

"As all the young men who accompanied their fathers to the market did," Ms. Sibley said. "It was my wish. And my children follow my wishes."

She motioned Benjamin forward, and he came to suckle briefly from her decrepit left breast.

"May Alaster have some too, Mother?" he said, pulling back.

"My milk is for my children alone. Take the baby to the nursery and place it next to William. Both will want a feeding soon."

Alaster watched his brother obey, then glanced at the pumpkin. "You did the same thing to William?"

"Yes," Ms. Sibley said. "Would you like to see? Earlier you admired that pumpkin very much. But I will show you something far more wondrous. A last glance at the world before your eyes close forever to it. Bring him, Cameron."

Cameron forced Alaster forward. They left the cottage and started into the woods. Ms. Sibley carried the infant's gourd under her arm. The voices of other children rose again in their strange hymns, growing stronger as they penetrated the dense forest. From the sound, it might really be every boy and girl he knew. Dozens and dozens.

They came to a glade filled with a vast patch. There must have been several hundred gourds scattered across the ground, all attached to their vines. A frost had come over most of them, a touch of gray on the otherwise vibrant orange shells. Ms. Sibley led them into the patch, stepping around the orbs. Many of the pumpkins looked entirely normal, but here and there Alaster found one with carved features glowing in the darkness. He recognized so many faces.

Then he saw Ben's pumpkin, perfectly capturing his face as it was now.

Alaster shook his head and looked away.

"Benjamin wasn't a day old when that carving was done," Ms. Sibley said.

"How can that be? How do you do it?"

"Alaster, don't assume I'm the carver just because I hold the knife. My Husband works through me, and his art is so much more subtle and skillful than mine."

"Your husband?" Alaster's voice barely registered.

"I'm sure you can make a guess, good Christian lad. Unfortunately, another in the village was starting to make a guess as well. Poor Reverend Peterson, muttering his suspicions out loud. My hand was forced, and the plan had to begin earlier than desirable. I would have preferred an army of adults. But obedient children will do."

Alaster's throat went dry. He just hung his head and watched Ms. Sibley kneel with the freshly carved pumpkin in both hands. She brought the stem against one of the many vines and spoke unrecognizable words. Another flash of light and then the pumpkin became part of the patch.

"Now he is my child *forever*."

Alaster began to sob. "I want. . .I want to see William's."

"You needn't look far," she said, gesturing to a pumpkin only a few feet from Ben's. "No point separating blood brothers, is there? Yours would have been here as well."

She knelt and held up a pumpkin with his baby brother's face cut into it. She lifted it as high as the vine would let her, almost chest level.

"He can't belong to you. . .not William. . ."

"His heart is mine."

"*No.*"

Ms. Sibley gave him a smile of gleeful sympathy. Then she went back to Benjamin's pumpkin and cupped it in her hands. "Bring a knife," she said.

Minutes later, Ben appeared, blade in hand. Moonlight cut itself on the edge.

Ms. Sibley's fingers closed around the handle. She plunged the knife into the top of William's pumpkin, and a sickly, wet sound commenced as she sawed. Alaster's scream was stifled by Cameron's large hand smothering his mouth. Nothing stopped Ms. Sibley's knife. She tossed the cap aside, drove the knife into the soil with evident satisfaction, and reached within the gourd.

"Mine, all mine," she cooed, lifting a small beating, human heart. Blood ran down her boney white forearms like ink as she held the heart above her head. She stood and spun around, gnashing her teeth at the pumpkins all around her. "All of you are mine! All of you are His! Rejoice in your *Father*!"

The children of the village, boys and girls of all ages, began to leave the dense forest and enter the glade. They did not sing now. They stood in solemn expectation, heads bowed just a little in submission.

Alaster's head bowed too as bitter resignation filled him. Through tears he saw Benjamin's pumpkin almost at his feet. Part of him wanted to kick in its face. The flash of violence shocked him. Why blame Ben? He'd been under the witch's command since birth, unaware of his dire state until the witch brought her spell to fruition. What did she want? The town? Power? What would she do with the children if not send them forth to spread her vile plans to other villages?

He stomped his foot in powerless frustration, his sole coming down on the vine that connected Benjamin's pumpkin to the patch. As he did, Ben gave the faintest grunt. Alaster looked over and saw a strain on his face, a brief clarity in his eyes. No one else seemed to notice, and his eyes clouded back to submission a moment later.

Alaster stomped again. This time he ground his foot into the vine as hard as he could.

Benjamin blinked. Then he looked around.

Then they made eye contact.

Alaster would have done anything to bear down on the vine with all his weight. Cameron's grip kept him from that. He twisted his foot again. His movements now caught the witch's attention. She seemed startled, unsure.

Benjamin shouted. He launched forward and seized the knife from the ground in one move, then stabbed it into Ms. Sibley's ribcage. She howled like a wolf and dropped William's pumpkin as she staggered. A frantic wave of her hands brought the other children to her defense. Cameron threw Alaster aside and headed toward Ben, who started retreating. Alaster began tearing at the vines, even biting them as he tried to break the pumpkins free. Each separation freed a corresponding boy or girl.

Ben was gaining allies.

The witch came at Alaster now, bounding across the patch, blood dark as lamp oil flowing from the stab wound. Alaster scrambled, knowing he had to find Cameron's pumpkin. He was the oldest boy and the only one stronger than Ben.

He saw Cameron's carved face glowing like fire and clawed his way toward it, wrapping both arms around the pumpkin, shrieking as he twisted all his weight against the vine. Cameron froze in the distance, but it wasn't enough. Alaster saw the witch's dark shadow falling over him.

Then he heard Ben shout his name. Alaster and the witch both looked to see him charging across the patch, slashing as he went. The witch chanted, and the pumpkins began to explode around his feet like cannon bursts. Ben screamed, losing his balance. He threw the knife as he went down. The blade went over the witch's head and struck the ground a few feet from Alaster's right hand.

He seized it and cleaved the knife into Cameron's vine.

The pumpkin fell heavily to the ground, and Cameron staggered, squinting like someone waking from a long dream. He moved toward the witch, who now straddled Benjamin, both hands around his throat. Alaster rose to attack.

"No!" Cameron said. "Cut the vines! All the vines!"

Alaster worked with the knife, moving faster than he thought possible. He slashed everywhere, at every pumpkin both enchanted and ordinary. More children became free by the second. Cameron meanwhile had knocked the witch away from Benjamin, and the two older boys stood shoulder to shoulder against her.

The freed children gathered at their backs.

"You'll all die," she said. "Without your connection to the patch, the hearts within will wither soon. Poor children. Come back to your mother and Father."

"We'd rather die," Ben said, "and be with our *real* parents."

The children fell upon her.

THE MUSIC
OF THE SPHERES

I REGAINED CONSCIOUSNESS when the shuttle shook as it left Earth's atmosphere. My hands were cuffed, and belts secured me across the chest, stomach, and legs. Renner Lopez sat across from me, held in place by a shoulder harness. His right eye wasn't as black as it'd been in my dreams.

I jerked against my restraints and stared at him.

"Relax," he said. "We're on our way to see your brother."

I laughed. "Ryan's dead, Renner."

"I assure you, he's very much alive."

"Bullshit."

"No bullshit, Rachel."

But bullshit was Renner's specialty ever since we dated in college.

I was being stonewalled about Ryan's fate. I'd never believed in any of that twin connectedness nonsense, like feeling each other's pain across great distances. But on the morning I got word Ryan vanished, I woke up with a shooting pain in my ears. It was an agony like surgery without anesthetic. I just had a feeling about Ryan unlike anything I'd ever experienced. He was dead. I had a certainty surpassing intuition. All the subsequent lies about him *disappearing* in outer space gave me no doubts about a cover up. I was his sister and owed the goddamn truth.

Renner contacted me yesterday, saying he had information about Ryan. Call me skeptical. Call me paranoid. Call me worried. Why the hell would he even know Ryan was missing? All government divisions shared shadowy connections, of course, and it wasn't crazy for Renner in military intelligence to be interested in Ryan's pursuit of extraterrestrial life. But Renner knowing about Ryan's disappearance sure made me wonder what the hell Ryan had been doing all along.

Renner gave me the address for a dive bar on the outskirts of Chicago. A few drinks later, he said something about my weight, and I introduced my fist to his face. The next thing I knew, I was strapped to a seat in a shuttle.

"We really are on our way to see Ryan," Renner said. "We'll be docking at Chameleon Base in about five hours."

"Never heard of it. Ryan did his research on ISS-7."

"Well, he's at Chameleon now."

"I'm assuming it's a military installation?"

"It's whatever it needs to be according to the situation at hand. Hence the codename."

"So what is it *now*?"

Renner's gaze shifted to the left a moment.

"A music conservatory," he said.

We had little conversation over the next few hours, until I noticed Renner was humming a song. I knew all the popular bands, the indie artists, even a lot of classical, but I couldn't place his tune.

"What's your earworm?"

"Sorry?"

"The tune you're humming."

He touched his mouth like it betrayed him. We were the only two people in the shuttle, but he looked back and forth before speaking.

"At this point, I don't see how it matters anymore. The song has no official name, but Ryan decided to call it *Friendship Is in Our Stars*. I always loved his. . .hopefulness."

Curiosity had me straining forward against my restraints. "You mean it's part of a message from an alien culture? Is that what Ryan detected?"

Renner nodded. "Once you've heard it, the melody never seems to leave the mind."

He hummed it again, with purpose. I found myself responding to it in a way I hadn't before, looking out the window, casting my gaze into the dark universe. Renner's voice seemed to move out of the shuttle and into the beyond. I imagined it as a chord strummed between stars and planets. I didn't even realize Renner had stopped humming until he snapped his fingers in front of my face several times to break my trance.

The shuttle's breaking thrusters fired a moment later. An asteroid swung into view, every crevice hosting an installation or structure. I looked at Renner and said, "Last I heard, we're supposed to be a hundred years away from developing asteroids."

"Chameleon is a prototype."

The shuttle pivoted into a docking maneuver and established a secure lock. Renner saw fit to free me, and we floated to the exit portal and transitioned to the base's artificial gravity. A handful of military personnel greeted Renner. One man commented on his puffy eye. For a moment I felt like little more than an afterthought, and then a man who identified himself as General Hanson extended his hand.

"You're the sister?"

"Yes," I said. "Rachel."

"Then not identical twins."

"Actually, we are. Polar body twins. Is there some reason that matters?"

"Just a matter of protocol," Renner said. "For when you visit Ryan in quarantine."

"When do I get to do that?"

"Soon," General Hanson said. "Lopez, the Musicians are about to give another performance. I want the sibling in attendance."

"I have a goddamn name—"

Renner pulled me down the hall. "Don't say anything, and you'll get through this fine."

"I want to see Ryan *now*."

"You will soon, I promise, but he's unconscious."

I stiffened and pulled against Renner's tug. "*Why* is he unconscious?"

"That's something we hope you can help us figure out."

THE MUSIC OF THE SPHERES

I was taken to a sterile metal chamber that looked like a repurposed conference room. There were thirty basic folding chairs arranged in two rows forming a semi-circle, occupied by a mix of people in military uniforms and dress suits, but Renner and General Hanson weren't present. No one spoke, but there was a collective humming reminiscent of a beehive. As it continued, however, I began to think of it as an orchestra tuning up. Anticipation gathered all around me, though the expression on every face was blank.

I stifled a gasp when five extraterrestrials entered a few minutes later.

They stood almost seven feet tall on three legs. Their torsos were thick trunks that tapered toward their necks like a triangle, and their heads were almost perfect spheres perched atop the sharp apex of the pyramid. Their visible skin was white and leathery and reminded me of something that'd been left outside and bled of color. One alien carried an instrument resembling a violin, but it had only one string that was gossamer like spider silk. Even the room's gentle air circulation seemed powerful enough to break it, yet when the alien began to play, moving its forearm across the string like a bow, a sound of sustained beauty flowed forth.

The audience's humming changed, reaching accordance with the new strain. An energy stirred within me, a convulsive thrill as if every muscle fiber in my body was also a vibrating string. But the spell was broken when the other aliens began to harmonize. It was as if a shuttle had come crashing down upon a forest to ruin the song of morning birds.

I seemed to be alone in my response. I felt nauseated and put my hands over my ears.

Unable to help myself, I stood up and ran for the door. "Please," I called. "I'm going to be sick. *Help!*"

The door opened, and I ran. I collapsed in the hallway and fought off the urge to retch as a set of boots came into view. I looked up into the faces of General Hanson and Renner.

The three of us stood alongside Ryan's bed. My brother's eyes were closed, and his body jerked and spasmed. Restraining straps on his wrists and ankles secured him to the frame.

"He was like this when we intercepted his shuttle," Renner said. "The aliens were with him."

I touched the base of my throat, massaging my speech through a hard lump. "What happened to him?"

General Hanson answered.

"What we know is pieced together from the shuttle's camera footage and three logs your brother made. It seems he made contact but didn't report it to anyone. He commandeers a shuttle and explains himself in the first log. Two days later, he has a rendezvous with another ship—its present location is not known. The aliens come aboard and begin the same performance you just witnessed. Your brother becomes visibly sick, and they stop playing. In the second log, your brother refers to the aliens as Musicians and says they're wandering minstrels. He doesn't divulge how he comes about this knowledge. He says these musicians are on a mission to share the 'song of the universe' with all sentient beings. Your brother refers to it as the Music of the Spheres, a sort of celestial tune."

"He bought everything the aliens told him," Renner said. "They couldn't have found a better audience. Imagine Ryan learning about a song that reveals the nature of the universe."

"In his third log, he says the Music of the Spheres is like a dog whistle, beyond the capacity of human senses. But he's been offered a modification to let him hear the celestial song. Your brother then holds up a chip—the same chip currently implanted in his auditory cortex."

I swore under my breath. Ryan, I thought, what have you done? What did you *let* them do?

"We don't have the means to remove it," General Hanson said.

"Can't the aliens?"

"All they do is play their damn concerts," Renner said. "We have them quarantined in two rooms, along with those who became infected by their song."

"Infected?"

"The Musicians began playing as soon as they entered the base. The people you saw in there belonged to the communication team we assembled to meet them. They didn't have your brother's reaction. If anything, just the opposite. They appear to be under alien influence, though whether or not the Musicians intend malice has yet to be ascertained. They keep giving the same performance to the same audience every ninety minutes."

"How did you escape it?"

My question seemed to catch both Renner and General Hanson off guard. The general snapped a look at Renner.

"You were humming the song in the shuttle," I said.

Renner backed away as General Hanson's eyes widened. The general summoned guards. "Lopez goes into quarantine immediately."

"General, I'm *not* under any influence. You can't—"

I heard Renner's protests continuing from distant hallways even a minute after he'd been dragged away.

"You're here for a reason, Rachel," General Hanson said.

I raised my eyebrows and stared at him.

"The chip," he said. "We can't remove it, but we've used every means at our disposal to analyze it—and duplicate it. The copy is synced to a specific genetic code. . ."

I stepped back, well aware of its futility. "I won't submit to an implant."

General Hanson smiled—as I might have in his place. Reading his thoughts required no clairvoyance. He had a planet to defend, and the discovery of an alien race whose music could either hypnotize his soldiers or make them violently ill put him on edge. The five Musicians in quarantine could be the advance ensemble for an orchestra of millions all gearing up to play *finis* for our civilization.

"Our study of the chip has already revealed there's a fifth brainwave state," he said.

I gasped at this revelation.

"My first thought when I saw your brother and read his logs was that the aliens lied to him. The chip was likely feeding him some sort of signal designed to incapacitate him since he didn't respond to their music. But that's not true. His mind is attuned to something that surrounds us that we cannot otherwise hear."

"The Music of the Spheres," I whispered.

"Whether it's music or not is up for debate. We're calling it a Thetracine wave. The truly interesting development is that this wave opens up the possibility of unknown levels of interaction between minds."

"Which you'll exploit."

General Hanson's nostrils flared. "There are promising implications for all divisions, not just military and defense. Breakthroughs in mental health, quantum advances in communication. You may even have direct access to your brother's mind. A backdoor into his consciousness."

I touched Ryan's face. If I could reach him in any way. . .help him. . .save him. . .

"Will you be able to remove it once it's in?"

"No—but we've designed a failsafe. We can deactivate the chip at any time."

"I'm supposed to trust you?"

"If your cooperation wasn't important, I assure you the chip would have been in your head a week ago. But your brother accepted the chip willingly. How can we know if that's important? Would a forced implantation yield different results?"

I exhaled a long breath of consideration.

"Thanks for the illusion of choice," I said.

I had a clear memory of the moments before anesthesia stole my consciousness. I was in the base's surgery ward, surrounded by a team of doctors whose faces were obscured by procedure masks. General Hanson, dressed in scrubs, stood off to the side. As the anesthesia was delivered, the chief surgeon lowered his mask and whistled the Musicians' melody. The other medical assistants followed suit, and so did General Hanson.

I closed my eyes and cringed in terror. When I opened them again, I sat up and found the room empty. A variation on the song came from the open door, and I left the bed and walked through vacant hallways. I seemed to be the only person on the base. Panic set in, and I ran, calling out to anyone. There was no other sound except the music, and I realized my direction was not as random as it first seemed. I was following the melody, getting closer to the heart of it with every step.

I came to the quarantine room. The Musicians were there. So were Renner, General Hanson, and all the people from before.

Maybe Chameleon's entire population. The first Musician played its instrument, once more moving its forearm across the single string. As if the string had become a saw's tooth, the Musician's flesh split open, and its blood flowed red like ours. I staggered back as the sawing continued, and the other Musicians began a grotesque harmonizing that threatened to split my eardrums. The sound was the scraping of metal, the breaking of bone, the growl of hunger, and the gasp of thirst.

One by one, the audience added their screams. I fell to my knees with my fingers jammed into my ears, my face drenched in hot tears. One by one, the audience rose, adding a chorus of undying, relentless screams. The Musicians moved toward the door like a cadre of Pied Pipers, and the people followed. I knelt, scrunched up, still desperate to close off my hearing to the ululating cries. Renner moved past me, followed by General Hanson and all the rest. I would have been glad to see them go, but I caught sight of Ryan among the throng.

"Ryan! It's Rachel! It's your sister!"

Could he hear me? Did he care? He screamed with the rest of them as they all marched out of the door. I struggled to my feet and followed, hands still clapped over my ears. I begged them to stop, but I was shouting at a wall of more than a hundred gathered backs. The Musicians led them past the station's primary observation window, and as I reached it, I heard an unquantifiable number of voices shrieking from outside. How could that be? Sound didn't travel in a vacuum, but what if the vacuum itself was an eternal, collective scream?

I stopped and put a trembling hand to the window. The aluminosilicate glass vibrated. The noise was assaulting us from *outside*.

General Hanson floated into view. I fell back and tripped, hands over my mouth. He wore no space suit. His body was frozen and stiff, his lips parted, locked forever in an open-mouthed rictus. Another body tumbled past, and then another. I clutched the wall, pulling myself up.

"Renner," I said, wiping away fresh tears as he too floated past. Everyone had the same gaping facial expression.

Not Ryan, I thought, scrambling. I pushed forward, finding enough air to call his name. Corridor twisted into corridor, until I came to the dwindling line of people standing and shrieking in place, waiting their turn to enter the station airlock. Ryan stood at the end of the line, and I grabbed his arm.

I pulled him, pleading with every tug. But no matter how loud I shouted, the Musicians' playing overwhelmed my voice. The first alien still clutched its instrument, but the Musician's forearm was gone, sawed away by the invincible string. It just stood there howling like the rest, and the line moved forward. The airlock's signal light went red to green, green to red, and I couldn't get Ryan to budge. I fought until he and I were the last humans left, and when the light turned green and the airlock opened to receive its next sacrifice, I jerked the instrument from the Musician's left hand and swung it. I used it like a club, thrashing the aliens.

"Stop it! Don't make him do this!"

And then—silence.

Ryan stood in the airlock. I reached for him but the door slid shut.

The light flashed red.

"No, no, no," I screamed, slapping the door. Then I turned, instrument still in hand, and ran all the way back to the observation window. My brother floated past, so brief a presence, and I put my free hand to the glass and stood there until he was lost to the dark noisiness of space.

The Musicians, bruised and bloodied, came to stand before me.

"We have traveled the universe looking for our conductor."

I looked at the instrument and touched the single string. It sliced the tip of my finger wide open from the barest of pressure.

"Play for us."

I tilted my head back and played the instrument with a quick, violent stroke across my throat.

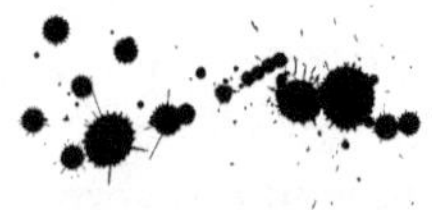

When I opened my eyes, I was back in the shuttle. General Hanson sat across from me, staring. His gaze seemed distant.

I touched my throat.

"What happened?"

"We deactivated your chip after twenty minutes, but you've been unconscious for three days."

"Twenty minutes? What did you—"

THE MUSIC OF THE SPHERES

"Thetracine waves cause debilitating auditory and visual hallucinations."

"Hallucinations?"

"What else explains what you saw?"

I looked out the window. For a second, space seemed populated with a chorus of the dead.

"The Musicians have been killed; their bodies incinerated. Chameleon Base is being sterilized of their influence."

"Sterilized?" I said, giving him a watery stare.

"My condolences about your brother. Many other good people are going to be lost."

"Like Renner?"

The general nodded, tight-lipped.

"Try to relax now. At least you're safe—and so is Earth."

General Hanson settled back and squared his shoulders. After a while, he began to hum.

NOTCHES

Alice had never cut herself *down there* before.

To judge by their reactions, neither had Jill, Julienne, Mary, Rachel, or Olivia.

And to think, all this time everyone called it a *gash*.

That's what Alice was thinking before the school went into lockdown and Ms. Atta was shot dead right outside the classroom door. Her blood seeped into the room even now, a heavy flow that seemed to skate on the cold, industrial tile floor, vainly seeking some absorbent fiber.

It was weird to think of Ms. Atta being dead. They'd only just gotten to *really* know her, despite spending many hours together in this little room repurposed for their counseling sessions. It figured she'd be killed just as their umpteenth meeting had finally resulted in a breakthrough, all of it hinged on Ms. Atta's dark but intriguing revelation that she'd also danced with the blade. No, not just danced with it. *Married* it. *Fucked* it. All the other teachers were whitebread and butter knives. Alice had always felt like the woman hated the bullshit she had to tell the girls in their counseling sessions. Alice certainly knew *she* hated it. Sometimes they'd make eye contact, and it was like both wanted to cut through the lies, find truth, and get real.

Well, today things had gotten real.

And then that asshole Tommy Mostow ruined everything.

Everyone was wearing identical long-sleeved shirts over their regular clothes. The word *NeSSIe* was embossed across the chest in red. They'd created the shirts two counseling sessions ago, under Ms. Atta's guidance. The girls all knew what NSSI meant, but Ms. Atta insisted on reminding them one last time in her thick Nigerian accent.

"Wearing these shirts is an act of protest because, like the Loch Ness Monster, too many people don't believe nonsuicidal self-injury exists. But *you* exist, don't you? And your existence is wonderful."

Mary raised her hand. "But what do the two *e's* stand for?"

"Not a damn thing," Ms. Atta said. "Which, in my opinion, makes it all the better."

Alice had been the first to take the plunge and put the shirt on, pushing her slightly oversized head through the neckline. It was a bit tight on her and felt like a corset, but she was too excited by Ms. Atta's enthusiasm to backtrack. The rest soon followed, and Ms. Atta beamed at them.

"Do you feel empowered now?"

"No," the girls said.

"Of course not. It's not fabric that empowers you. It's the blade."

Well *that* certainly got their attention, especially after so many sessions where Ms. Atta had droned on about how the desire to cut themselves was the psychological manifestation of *blah blah blah*. Mary cut herself because she hated her father; Olivia because she couldn't handle rejection; Jill because she felt numbed by modernity. Julienne sliced herself over loneliness, and Rachel because she was overweight.

As for Alice, she convinced herself it was the best way to keep track of time. Nobody believed her, of course. And Alice couldn't blame them. Cutters always made up bullshit excuses for dealing with the pain. But Alice thought hers was the most unique.

Ms. Atta smiled at them in their matching shirts. "I think we're finally ready to do something new," she said. "I want all of you to roll up your sleeves. Show your cuts to each other," Ms. Atta said.

"I don't want to show my body," Rachel said. "I'm so fat."

"Then do you cut because you want to whittle it away?"

The question may have seemed like Ms. Atta sought understanding, but Alice found no warmth there. She discovered truth in the hardness of the counselor's tone. Challenging, wonderful truth.

"You first," she said.

Ms. Atta looked at her. "Since you need courage," she said, and her fingers went to the buttons of her blouse. Little by little, the shirt came open. The girls leaned forward with each revelation. By the time Ms. Atta had revealed her perfect stomach, Alice had reflexively jerked both her sleeves up past the elbow. They all did, and the scabs showed in patterns as unique and individual as red frost on glass.

The moment felt breathless to Alice, yet all she heard was everyone's panting. She took in the other girls' cuts, and they took in hers as Ms. Atta looked pleased, standing among them with her shirt on but open, her skin so dark and perfect. It was only Ms. Atta's perfection that blemished the moment, that gave Alice any thought that somehow, she and the girls had been tricked into more counseling crap dressed up as something taboo. Hell, most of her cuts weren't even on her arms anyway. So if Ms. Atta wanted a *true* revelation, Alice decided she might as well give them all a real eyeful.

She pulled her shirt off and stood before them in just a bra.

There was no mirror in the room, but Alice thought she could see herself through Ms. Atta's stunned eyes. The counselor came and walked around her, inspecting her from belly button to shoulder. Did the sheer number of cuts surprise her? Or was it their pattern?

"Tally marks," Ms. Atta said. She had such open wonder in her expression that Alice couldn't help but feel proud.

"Yes," Alice said. "I make them with a box cutter. It gives me the precision I like. Four vertical marks and then a slash. Over and over again. One arm, then another. Then the stomach. Funny how the knife tickles the ribs."

The other girls swarmed her, their fingertips tracing the lacerations, perhaps finding Braille in the scabs. Alice ignored them. She and Ms. Atta were having a moment.

"What do you tally, Alice?"

"Time," she said. "Loves. Failures. Dreams and crushed hopes. Disappointments. Expectations. The number of butterflies I find struggling in spider webs on my way to school. They all run together in my mind and on my flesh—after the blade."

Ms. Atta trembled and retreated two steps. For a moment Alice thought she'd misjudged the woman, mistaking disgust for thrall.

But the darkness filling Ms. Atta's eyes told Alice there was something more sinister to her behavior. She stepped toward Ms. Atta, closing the distance, the girls pressing along with her.

"Show me," Alice whispered, her gaze roaming over Ms. Atta's bare arms, her ebony skin perfect over supple muscle. Clearly this flesh had never known even simple blemishes, much less the intrigues of a razor. "Show me the cuts. I know they're there. You're like us—I *know* you are."

"Not like you," Ms. Atta said. "I never had the choice."

"Choice?" Alice said. "Don't you mean power? To take the knife and slice open the skin like slitting a cocoon."

Alice found herself in a staring match with Ms. Atta, and for the first time wondered just how old the counselor was. Probably not even thirty, and now that she'd dropped the pretense of her authority, she seemed even younger. She was so much like them, fellow sister of the blade.

"Is it the stomach? The thighs?"

"None of those places," Ms. Atta said.

"Then *where*?"

Only Alice talked, but she knew she spoke for the group. Psychically they demanded Ms. Atta strip, all but tearing her clothes away with their collective gaze. She must have felt the pressure—the sweet call to release herself from secrets, which to Alice was the essence of cutting. Looking toward the closed door, she let her unbuttoned blouse slink off her shoulders.

Once more Alice verged on feeling tricked. "*Where* are the cuts, Ms. Atta? Show us."

The woman was quiet for a long moment. Alice focused entirely on Ms. Atta's hands, willing them to move. Then they did. *Just enough.* Her left hand raised her skirt up as the right pushed her panties down—again *just enough.*

To Alice, it was like Ms. Atta had the face of God down there.

"Men in my country did this to me, as they do to most women. These scars are where my clitoris used to be."

Ms. Atta's vagina looked so foreign the sight of it closed Alice's throat and opened her eyes wider than she'd ever experienced. Such mutilation had never occurred to her. It was something she'd heard on the news as background noise, or in social studies class. But Ms. Atta made it real and compelling. Suddenly Alice saw the counselor as a girl, ten or eleven years old, being forced to the ground as unsympathetic faces gathered to watch some tribal elder come with sharpened flint or ancient ceremonial dagger to hack and scrape some of her away, the flesh shaved back like the rind off an orange.

Alice touched the base of her throat as a wave of inadequacy washed over her. The cuts across her body, whose thrill of pain and endurance had been a source of pride, felt like some unimaginative stick figure drawing now that she beheld the Matisse of Ms. Atta's disfigurement.

There were other cuts across her groin, some as fresh as this morning. Lacerations up and down the inner thigh and across the folds of her labia, which Ms. Atta now brought to the girls' attention with her fingers.

"The emotional pain of the violation never ceased. I felt the need to keep going."

"You're so brave," Alice said, almost breathless. She looked back at the girls, wondering if they shared the same thought.

Ms. Atta was quiet for a moment. "Violence in thought and deed is why we cut. It symbolizes transformation, and each slash is transformative. *That* is what you tally, Alice: your endless transformations."

"Yes," Alice said, her tone confident.

Rachel said, "I don't care about symbolism, I care about how the cut feels."

Alice turned wildly back to her, flashing her approval. Rachel was normally so shy, the last of all girls to speak. Already Ms. Atta's display had worked wonders.

Transformation indeed. Ms. Atta put her panties and skirt back into place.

"Regardless, as in all things, symbolism comes first," the counselor said and looked at the clock on the wall. "There's enough time for one more lesson."

Alice nodded impatiently.

"Poetry," Ms. Atta said.

The girls twisted their faces. Poetry was for the journals they kept in fifth grade. Now they wrote in flesh.

Ms. Atta laughed. "Don't be so glum. We're going to create our poems the way William S. Burroughs did."

Alice shook her head, earning an extra twinkle in Ms. Atta's eyes. "I'm surprised. You of all people should know of the cut-up method."

The girls leaned forward, drawn by the phrase.

"Burroughs would take magazines and newspapers and slice words from them until he had hundreds of fragments. He'd toss them into the air until they were all jumbled together. Then he'd reassemble them into new meanings."

"Like refrigerator magnet phrases!" said Olivia.

Alice smiled. "I want to take the knife, dripping with blood, and slide it into the paper and cut all the words out like little hearts. I want to make a haiku. No, fuck haikus. I want to make a sonnet celebrating the unkindest cut of all."

"I'll get some magazines from the library. You all have your razors with you, right?"

The girls feigned innocence until Ms. Atta shot them an arch look. Then they opened their purses—all but Alice, who really was a purist for box cutters. But those were too hard to sneak past the school's metal detectors—which were going off now, a distant siren down another long corridor.

"Good," Ms. Atta said. "I'll be back in a few minutes." She opened the door and stepped out.

A gunshot cracked in the distance, sending the girls shrieking back. The impact punched a hole through Ms. Atta's chest and dropped her in the doorway. Blood gushed from the wound and swam across the floor. Ms. Atta's eyes were still open and fixed upon their final vision.

The twinkle Alice saw a moment ago was gone now.

There were more shots and screams, and then Tommy Mostow stepped into view, his back to the girls, checking his weapon's magazine. He was sixteen but looked thirteen, and his baggy camo pants and black t-shirt did nothing to age him. Even the assault rifle in his hands just made him seem like a little boy playing war in his backyard. Except this wasn't his backyard, and Ms. Atta was dead.

Alice barely heard him say, "Dumb bitch," over the screams and alarms. He put another burst of bullets into her body. Students charged out of their classrooms and through the hall like a herd of frantic animals. Tommy snapped up the gun and fired at them. The chaos must've entranced him, because he didn't seem to be aware of the girls gaping through the open door.

Alice slowly crept toward Tommy, flinching each time he pulled the trigger. The girls followed.

"Five more dead fucks," Tommy said, ceasing fire. Alice watched him take out a small pocket knife and make notches on the gun's barrel. Four hash marks and a slash.

"You tally, too."

Tommy sprang back and dropped the knife. Alice stared into his eyes and found a dark, kindred pain, but no understanding of it. He'd have learned a lot from Ms. Atta, but instead he had to ruin it for everyone. On a much more significant level, of course, Alice realized she'd found and lost her religion in the space of ten minutes.

The girls charged before he could take aim. They came slashing, dicing him across the forearms. Blood pulsed in spurts from the wounds. Tommy howled and dropped his precious toy as they drove him down, one of the girls kicking the gun away. The principal's voice echoed through the PA system, urging the students to stay inside and barricade the doors. The alarm was still blaring but the hallway was empty now. True to what she'd heard, Alice saw five bodies a few rooms down.

Alice dragged Ms. Atta's body into the classroom.

"Bring him here!" she shouted.

Completely overpowered, Tommy was pulled kicking and screaming through Ms. Atta's blood and into the room. Alice shut and locked the door, then turned to study their captive. His face was wet, his eyes puffy and red, snot bubbling in his nose. He looked like a kid brother bullied by an abusive older sister and her friends. His shirt and pants had been gashed, revealing scrawny, bald flesh. Crimson oozed from several cuts to his forearms.

"You killed Ms. Atta, asshole," Alice said.

"I—I'm sorry." His voice was as whiny and weak as a first grader's. No wonder he preferred the speech of guns.

Alice scrunched her face, "No you aren't. You're about as far from sorry as anyone can be."

"I just wanted people to stop making fun of me."

The girls stood watch over Tommy, razorblades in hand, while Alice contemplated the spread of Ms. Atta's blood. It was heavy and dark, almost menstrual. Alice thought again about the sheer pain of genital mutilation and cutting herself *down there*. What courage would that take? She almost wished there could be someone to hold her down and remove her clitoris, her labia, her everything, enshrouding her in a pain surpassing death. Surely she would transform into a being of light.

Alice's eyes widened. She held her breath and stared down.

Ms. Atta lay there, naked and much younger now—not quite a teenager. Her legs were splayed, her clitoris freshly shorn away. Blood streamed from the wound, with the arc of a water fountain. It splashed over the toes of Alice's sneakers, and she hurried to kick her shoes and socks off and slick her soles. Ms. Atta's youthful, glossy eyes stared at Alice. She spoke, but her voice came from her mutilated groin, a chant as sure as a tribal drumbeat:

Tally your life by this tally your love your vengeance your faith

The words echoed in Alice's head like a chorus. It came from Ms. Atta's gash, from the PA system, and from Alice's heartbeat all at once. She nodded and turned to Tommy, the greasy soles of her feet slipping a bit on the tile. The weight of responsibility threatened Alice's posture, but she refused to be bowed. This tallying could not be done on her own skin.

"I'm taking his pants off," she said.

Rachel and Olivia knelt on his wrists, crushing them into the floor. Tommy thrashed and kicked until Jill and Julienne each gave him two sharp slashes into the soft flesh of his belly. Alice paid no attention to his whimpering or his bleeding as she grabbed the waistband of both his pants and boxers and forced them down the length of his skinny legs. At last they discovered a place on Tommy that wasn't bald. Alice pinched his bush and yanked until the roots tore free. God, how he screamed.

And got hard.

Tommy's erection was impressively disproportional to his slight body. And he was not circumcised. Alice cupped his penis in one palm, which it quickly outgrew.

"What are you doing?" he said.

Alice dug her nails into his erection. Tommy shrieked, but Alice felt him grow and throb.

"Wow, you're really enjoying this, aren't you?" Alice said.

"I'm—I'm a virgin. Nobody's ever touched it before."

Alice looked at the girls and then back at Tommy. She remembered how he'd put notches on his gun—including one for Ms. Atta. Boys were just like that, weren't they? They tallied their conquests and victories, thinking enough notches would finally add up to manhood and transform them. Maybe in Tommy's case it had. He seemed truly in awe of the length and hardness of his cock, as if both were fresh surprises. Maybe the violence he'd committed, the lives he'd taken, had done their alchemy.

Alice released his penis and dipped her hand in Ms. Atta's blood. It was still warm and stunk of copper. She rubbed her fingers together until they were slick and began stroking Tommy. His body rocked with spasms. He hissed air through clenched teeth and squeezed his eyes shut.

"Oh, God!"

A boy's cry.

A man's cock.

"Please, *please* use your mouth. Just taste it with your tongue."

Tommy's dick was sticky with blood now. Alice spit into her palm and made him slick again, stroking with her left hand, her awkward hand, the hand she never even cut with. That was reserved for her right hand, which she now extended palm up and waiting. Olivia placed her blade there, prodding her a bit with the tip, enough to make stigmata. Tommy went on moaning. Alice had heard male circumcision influenced sensitivity, though whether or not the influence was positive or negative, she couldn't say.

"Oh, my God, I'm going to come," Tommy said.

"How many?"

Panting, he said, "How many what?"

"How many times have you jacked off? How many times have you came? Have you ever added them up?"

"I dunno. Like a thousand," he said and arched his back while Alice stroked him.

"But your first with us. We should start a tally."

Alice held the blade alongside his erection. The edge would split it open like a summer sausage if she worked it lengthwise.

But notches were the order of the day.

OUR HERO

THE OVERCAST BOILS away in the heat of his transit across the sky, and sunlight makes false promises of happiness to the children in the park. I stop to look overhead, wondering about him for the millionth time. Is this a joy flight, his equivalent of a stroll? Or is he on his way to save the world from some terror none of us can understand?

Does he, for all his superior sight and hearing, ever perceive a child in tears, the victim of an uncle or trusted family friend? Or does he only go in for larger things?

Where is Haby?

I couldn't have been distracted long enough to lose him. He was only fifty yards ahead of me, walking next to my client's thirteen-year-old daughter. Haby likes them young.

A pervert and an underage nymphomaniac walk into a bar. The pervert says, "Give me two shots of your best Glenlivet."

The bartender pours the drinks and says, "This whiskey is twenty years old."

The pervert hands both shots to the nymphomaniac and tells her to drink them. She does. "There," the pervert says. "Until you take a piss, you're fifty-three."

The bartender cocks his brow and says, "What about you, mister?"

The pervert just looks at the nymphomaniac and smiles. "I've always been partial to Shirley Temples."

Pedo humor. You laugh and then you vomit. Or sometimes you just vomit. I heard that joke from a teacher at a private boy's school after I helped put him away. Ironically he was not partial to Shirley Temples.

There's Haby. At a swing set with the girl in broad daylight. I hide behind a tree, take out my camera, and add three photographs to the accumulated evidence. Got to hand it to the heroic Destroyer of Clouds: This added sunlight makes the photos extra crisp and clear.

Especially the one where Haby gives the girl a kiss.

Shameless.

Our hero streaks across the sky again, a blur going in the other direction. From crisis to crisis, one supposes. This time the girl looks up. Haby slaps her, perhaps annoyed to have his kiss interrupted. This jolts me into revealing myself despite the fact I'm not being paid to stop anything.

But that's what heroes do, isn't it?

An alcoholic walks into a bar, and says, "What's cheap?"

"That suit you're wearing," says the bartender, Terry. "Another day trailing pedophiles, Bill?"

"Yes."

"You do the Lord's work."

"Guess that's why Jesus walked everywhere, then. He couldn't afford gas. Or a car for that matter."

Terry scoots me a mug of beer, gratis. "The Lord worked for tips."

"Got any for me?"

"No."

I drink. Terry's a tall man in his late fifties with a haircut that went out of style years ago. Milquetoast all the way. Men like that always have dark hearts, and I know Terry's pretty well. I keep tabs on him. I have all his usernames, all his passwords. By all accounts, he's stayed clear of kiddie porn since I threatened to bust him five years ago. If I thought he'd actually touched a child, he'd be joining Haby in jail. But I really don't think it went that far with Terry, and he wasn't paying for the garbage. He wasn't an active supporter of the world's true sickness, which no mysterious, part-time savior hanging out in the clouds was going to fix. But Terry's fantasies took him right to the edge, and when I confronted him, he surrendered all his privacy to me in exchange for a second chance.

And all the free beer I want.

I'm finishing my first swallow when Terry leans down to me, his jocularity suddenly gone. "There's a man in the corner, Bill."

"So?"

"He *knows* about me—about us."

"There's no *us*, Terry."

"He knows. . .our arrangement."

I pivot on the stool, following the bartender's gaze. Sure enough, a guy sits at one of the booths, hands clasped on the table, no glass in sight.

"How long has he been here?"

"An hour."

"Has he had a drink?"

"Yes."

"I presume you gave it to him for free?"

"I—I offered, but get this. He insisted on paying. In fact, he opened a goddamn tab."

"Tab? Moronic fucker. What's the name on the card?"

Terry sidled over to the cash register and looked. Returning, he whispered, "It's a Visa gift card."

I laugh at him, standing. "You let someone open a tab with that? Shit, I take it back. *You're* the moronic fucker."

"He said his name was Sorcell. I'm *scared,* Bill. You know I'm clean, but this guy—"

"Yeah, yeah. I'll take care of it."

"Just be careful, okay? I think he must be a mind reader."

"Then God help him."

Leaving my beer, I walk over to the booth and sit down opposite him. The man's a little more impressive up close. Probably in his thirties, younger than me by twenty years. Real sharp eyes. Thin face, strong chin, fairly fit—someone women and gay guys likely find attractive. Kind of guy who thinks he's in charge of everything. Let him have a good, sudden tachycardia. Once you learn you're not in charge of your own heartbeat, all illusions of power fade.

"Your name Sorcell?"

"Yes."

"My friend Terry says you're bothering him. Did he molest you as a kid? You here to get revenge?"

"Disgusting."

A refined tone of voice. East coast. Prefers musicals to NFL games, but not fey in the slightest. I say, "Got that right. But I've made getting rid of *disgusting* my life's work."

"Then why didn't you report him to the police when you knew what he was looking at?"

"How do you know?"

"A gift of mild telepathy," he says.

"Terry figured as much. Whose mind have you been reading—his or mine?"

"Both."

"I'll give you the shorthand version of my thoughts right now. *Go fuck yourself.*"

Sorcell answers with a smile and a squint. Then I feel it: a pressure mounting behind the front of my skull. I grunt, and his eyebrows shoot up as if in surprise. As soon as they do, the pressure goes away.

Resisting the urge to rub the spot, I ask what he wants.

"The same thing you do," Sorcell says. "To solve the mystery."

"You'll have to be more precise, since I definitely *can't* read minds."

"There's only one mystery, Mr. Brawson."

"I didn't report Terry because fantasies aren't illegal. Plus I had other reasons."

"It gives you pleasure to put faith in someone."

"If you sense even a drop of pleasure in me, you must be reading someone else's head."

"No," he says. "The opportunity to offer to put faith in him *did* give you pleasure. I take it such opportunities are rare in your line of work?"

"Exceedingly."

"And he's not betrayed your confidence yet. This gives you hope."

I shrug. "When you explain my psychology to me, I feel like such a damn loser."

"I don't think you're a loser at all. In fact, I think you're the best detective around. Just the man I need to solve the one true mystery."

"But you said—"

"I said nothing. You assumed I was asking about the mystery of your faith, but I find nothing interesting in an old cynic still clinging to hope."

"Then what?"

"Wait for it," Sorcell says, and puts his palms flat to the table as he closes his eyes. His expression verges on serene.

A Buddhist walks into a bar and says, "Do you serve beers with a lot of hops?"

"Of course," the bartender says. "Just look at all these IPAs."

"I'll take a Hefeweizen then."

The bartender pours him a pint and says, "I'm confused. That beer has the fewest hops around."

"It doesn't matter," the Buddhist says, smiling and touching his chest. "Hoppiness comes from within."

The table rattles. All the tables do—for a split second. The man opens his eyes. "I sense his approach."

I suppose I've gotten used to it over twenty years, how the speed of his travel disrupts our daily lives—the jiggle of plates in the cabinet, a brief hum in the ears. Then everything goes back to normal in a world where normal means one man is a god among men.

"Who is he?" Sorcell whispers. His right hand clutches into a fist.

"Unless he ever tells us, we'll never know," I say.

"Not true. *You* can find out. I'm certain."

"You're the telepath. Read his mind."

"I've tried."

"You couldn't do it?"

"I *could*."

I lean forward. "Tell me."

"It was unlike anything I've ever experienced. I sensed more than one thought pattern."

"So he's schizophrenic?"

"It wasn't like that at all. His mind is too fragmented to comprehend. But my own abilities aren't enough. Answering the question requires an old-fashioned approach, and you, Mr. William Brawson, are the most old-fashioned of them all. Deep down, nearly a knight."

"News to me."

"Discover his identity. He claims to belong to the world, yet he calls this city home. Surely he must live here in some disguise."

"As fast as he moves, he could live in Europe and no one would be the wiser."

"I've thought of that. Every city has detectives, Mr. Brawson."

I sit back. "Are you saying you've hired a PI in every—"

"I'm saying I believe in overkill. Nevertheless, I know this city—and you—hold the key. There's payment, of course."

Sorcell names a figure so high I make him repeat it.

Then I tell him I'm retiring. Get up, walk past the bar, wave at Terry without glancing at him, and head for the bathroom.

The thing about mind readers is, sometimes they can be mind writers.

In hindsight, what else explains the decision I make in the two-minute span between zipping my fly down and back up?

Surely not free will.

An alcoholic walks out of a bar a hell of a lot richer than he was when he entered.

And the punchline is he leaves more sober than when he came.

Ever looked at a god? Really studied every perfection? Ours has blue eyes and coal-black hair. A classically beautiful figure. No form-fitting outfit ever fit such a form as his. He stands six-foot-five on size-twelve feet (this data point, listed on the various websites dedicated to his worship, comes courtesy of footprints left in the dirt). The Internet has thousands of pictures of his face and thousands more of him streaking overhead. But nothing compromising. Not that his suit leaves much to the imagination. There are, of course, message boards full of posts debating the size of his penis. On this point, he seems more grower than shower, though no one believes he could be ill-endowed.

I make a call to an old friend at the FBI, and we talk about facial-recognition software.

"We've tried discovering his identity, Bill. There's been a global cross-agency effort dedicated to figuring it out for two decades. DNA, voice and face recognition, cell phone and Internet intrusions, scans of every single high-school yearbook produced in the country. Drones and satellites, blanket surveillance. . ."

"I get it."

How am I, a solitary old gumshoe, supposed to succeed where other such attempts have failed?

OUR HERO

It's said he can hear a kitten trapped in a tree from half a world away and will come to rescue it.

Maybe the thing to do is plant a lot of kittens in a lot of trees.

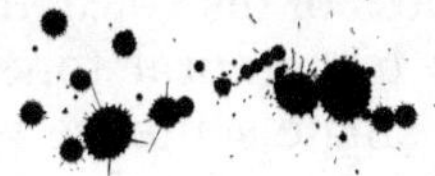

An amateur domestic terrorist walks into a bar, nervous and sweating as the clock ticks down on his plans. The bartender says, "Hey buddy, you look like you could use an Irish Car Bomb."

And the terrorist says, "Don't be ridiculous. Who has time for imports?"

I walk into a bar and order a double shot of bourbon. I've got a timer going in my head.

Three minutes, twenty seconds.

"Here you go, pal. I made it a triple. You look beaten down."

Two minutes, thirty seconds.

"Thanks," I say, throwing back the drink.

One minute, fifteen seconds.

The explosion rocks the bar, though the blast is a few blocks away. The bartender and his customers rush to the door. I reach for the bottle on the counter and help myself. They gasp and turn north, since that's where the worst damage will be. It's the screams that make me take the first deep pull. It's been years since hard liquor made me cough, but I cough now.

And stare hard at the rows of glasses on the wall.

Not more than two minutes pass before they start to vibrate. What was he doing before this tragedy? Watching the evening news in some apartment? Flying over the ocean? What alias could such a man have, what work could he do that would let him escape an office, a meeting, or a deadline on a second's notice without giving his true identity away? Few careers spring to mind.

Time to go.

I mull over the question as I shoulder through the horrified onlookers, flashing a fake police badge.

The bomb has destroyed a car and blown out a nearby building's windows.

Designed to get his attention. Designed to see if he'd come.

And he has. He extinguishes the fire with several fantastic gobs of spit. How great would the flames have to get before this tactic wouldn't work? What if step two involved pissing?

"Is everyone all right? Have there been any injuries?"

That distinct deepness of his voice, the casual masculinity of every syllable. Clearly his natural tone, no hint of forced or technical alteration. A single sentence would blow his cover in almost any job. More support for the work-from-home theory. Probably communicates strictly by email. Or he could pretend to be mute. Grunt and talk in sign language.

The police have arrived, and since no one was killed and the situation seems under control, he says he must go. "There's trouble in Texas."

Hell, there's trouble everywhere.

As he flies off and the crowd begins to thin, I notice Sorcell. He's walking away, but he stops, offering a simple nod.

He needs larger cats. And larger trees.

A man walks into a bar and takes a seat on the stool. "Jesus, mister," the bartender says. "You're the grimmest looking bastard I've ever seen."

"I should be," the man says. "I just exploded a bomb that killed twenty-five people."

"Twenty-five people! Holy shit, I hope they were all married women!"

"Why would you hope that?"

"Because widowers always tip me the best."

There was a countdown in my head again. I tried to reverse it, to add time rather than subtract it. But the numbers dwindled until—

Until.

What can our god do except put out fires, lift the heavy debris, offer emotional support? Power flourishes best when glimpsed; power that lingers long enough to be stared at exposes itself to comparison, and then to critique, and finally to diminishment. He realizes it. What else explains that pensive look on his face, that awkward smile as the paramedics and the doctors try to save the lives he cannot?

What else explains it except that, perhaps, he worries and cares?

Though pushed back from the crime scene of my creation, I stand close enough to study his mannerisms. There's a moment when he seems to notice me and his lips press tight, imitating my own expression.

As if we both hold ourselves accountable.

One of the detectives is an old drinking buddy named Stan, and when he sees me, he breaks protocol and motions me forward. I'm allowed to pass through.

"Second bombing in a week. Can you believe this, Bill?"

"Yes."

"I wish to hell we could have you on the case."

"Why, Stan?"

"Because you're a goddamn bulldog. And you understand the heart."

Perhaps overhearing, our hero turns to us and says in that wonderful voice, "I can see through solid objects, but I don't know if I'll ever detect the evil in some men's hearts."

A priest walks into a bar and says, "I just sat through ten hours of confessions, and I'm still not sure if I understand the first thing about sin."

"Well," the bartender answers, "I sit through ten hours of confessions every damn day, and I can tell you everything you need to know."

Offended, the priest says, "I don't know why they'd confess to you. You can't forgive them."

"I can do better than forgive," the bartender says, taking down a bottle of Scotch. "I can make them forget."

"Don't worry about detecting it," I say. "Just assume deceit and deception are always there. Then when you find them, you won't be surprised."

Our god flinches at this. Maybe it's for my eyes only, because I ask Stan about it later, after Terry serves us both on the house.

"Bullets and knives ricochet off his body. He can crash headfirst into a mountainside and not have a hair out of place. What the hell could you do to make him flinch?"

"Offer a glimpse of truth about the world?"

Stan's laughter follows me all the way to the bathroom. I see shoes under the single stall door as I stand before the only urinal.

"Making headway, Mr. Brawson?"

"Sorcell?"

"Ingenious way of getting close to him."

"What do you mean?"

He flushes and comes out and washes his hands in the sink.

I repeat my question only after he's gone.

Monsters are the inverse of heroes. Monsters return to the places they succeeded. Heroes return to the places they failed.

The second bombing happened in our city's financial district, and the media seeks meaning in this. Word has it the publisher of our newspaper expects a rambling manifesto to arrive any day. The next day there's still plenty of nervous foot traffic, good for a private investigator to get lost in as he watches people.

And records them.

In my hat and jacket, I'm a walking surveillance system. Tiny DVR camera fastened to the back of my collar. The earring clipped on my right lobe is a camera. My fake glasses offer 8GB of HD video and a 90-minute battery life. My cufflinks are old school Bond, James Bond snapshot lenses. I've got microphones on me too. Maybe I'll pick up that distinct voice, whispering in private agony, and figure out it's coming from the man in the business suit walking east, briefcase in hand.

A spy walks into a bar and demands all the bartender's secrets.

"Fine," the bartender says. "Your wife is a lesbian, and she's been caught in bed with another woman."

"I said to tell me your *secrets."*

"Okay. I just found out my wife is a lesbian, too."

That evening, while scanning through all my footage, I discover the woman.

I don't remember her, but she passed close by me about one hour into my surveillance. I do recall noticing other people I filmed and photographed around the same time: the obese man in the purple track gear, the older woman with her yapping Bichon Frise, the teenaged couple who should have been in school except all the schools were closed out of an abundance of caution. But I don't remember her.

OUR HERO

"Who the hell is she?" I say, noting the time of her appearance and switching video files to inspect different angles. Some don't capture her at all. At one point, the camera on my collar took several seconds of grainy, silent footage. She stands looking at the rubble two blocks away, since this is as close as the police will let anyone get. She touches the base of her throat as if in contemplation. This action isn't unusual. Many people throughout the recordings do exactly the same thing, often with their hands over their mouths, shaking their heads. It comes across like shallow people performing their grief for each other, though maybe they're genuinely horrified knowing twenty-five people were killed such a short distance away, such a short time ago.

But none of them are like her.

There's no purpose to her walk. She approaches the police barricade, peers, walks away—circles back. This happens several times, as if she's afraid to simply stand and stare. She keeps her head down, self-esteem and confidence perhaps running a little slim, except when she stops to look at the destruction. I wish my cameras had captured the details of her face, like the color of her eyes. All I get is she has fine features, dark hair, and a yellow turtleneck.

My first thought is one of the twenty-five dead must belong to her. A relative, a lover, a friend, and she refuses to accept she can get no closer to the place of loss, so she keeps returning to the barricade to stare a minute. Depart and come back, depart and come back. This is the slow-motion, drawn-out, excruciating equivalent of a caged animal throwing its body against unacceptable bars.

Then come the frames that send me out of my chair, eyeballs almost pressed to the monitor. I pause the video, calculate the elapsed time, and pull up the audio files on a separate computer. It's damn near impossible to sync them, and most of what's captured consists of footsteps and traffic and wind. But there are voices. Snippets. A child whining to go home. A man swearing about a business deal. Someone wishing he could kill the son of a bitch who murdered all those people.

And then—

"It's too bad he didn't get there in time."

It takes over an hour of trial and error, but I finally piece together who might have said it. I'm standing off to the right, and two women are approaching from behind. They're looking toward the rubble. One clearly mouths the words on the audio. It could reference anything. The pizza delivery man. A business client who missed his flight.

But the woman at the barricade must interpret the meaning the same way I do.

And she flinches.

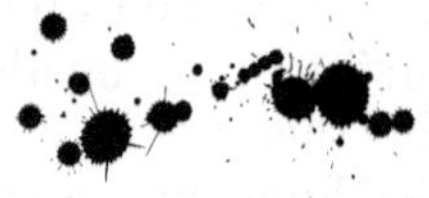

A stalker follows a woman into a bar and watches her sit alone at a table while he takes a seat at a booth and pretends to talk to his girlfriend on the phone.

I'm still pretending when the waitress walks over to me. "Okay honey, I'll see you in about ten minutes," I say, and put the phone aside.

"Like a drink?"

I gesture to the woman. "Did she order?"

"Yes."

"What was it? I'd like to buy."

The waitress jerks her head back a little. Her gaze darts over to my cell phone. Neurons misfire.

"Gin and tonic," she says, glancing back at the woman, perhaps not sure if she should have told me. She shouldn't have, but bar employees aren't the sharpest knives.

"Make it two and bring the bill to me."

A few minutes pass with me studying the woman in my peripheral vision. Lonely heart? Down on her luck? She's wearing another turtleneck, which doesn't do her any favors. Christ, this is crazy. Can I really be thinking she is some kind of lead, some kind of answer?

The waitress brings her the drink. It's been a while since my pulse jumped like it does now, as she gestures over at me, explaining the situation. The woman blinks, doesn't smile. Doesn't frown either. The waitress then brings me my gin and tonic and leans in.

"Helped you out as much as I could."

"Nice of you."

"Seems pretty shy," she says, bending close to my ear. "You're going to have to go to her. Sorry I didn't get her name for you, but then I didn't have yours either."

"That's okay. The booze and I will take it from here."

Her name is Diana Clarke. That's assuming the facial recognition database turned up an accurate match and my pal at the FBI isn't lying to me. But he's never let me down before. God bless him and his loose ethics.

I sip my glass half empty, roughly on par with her own pace, then I make my move.

"This is so awkward, but I just had to come over and ask if I could finish my drink with you. Please don't say no."

Her voice is low, hesitant. "I don't think so."

I sit down anyway. "Do you ever feel like your best intentions just add up to a bunch of failures?"

"I'd rather drink alone right now."

But I persist. "I'm in law enforcement. I do what I can to make things right, and at the end of the day I usually feel I should have just started my day in the bar rather than ended it here."

I'm looking off to the right, but I've practiced sidelong glances for so many years I can see her expression clearly. Pained. And interested.

Understanding.

"You're in law enforcement?"

"I'm a detective. We're running ourselves ragged trying to catch the bomber. You just feel so helpless, you know?"

She polishes off her drink in a gulp. "Yeah."

Smiling, I say, "You sound like you really do. Are you with the police too? I don't recall seeing you."

"No. I've got a home-based business. But I can imagine what it must be like. Thank you for everything you do to help."

She's talking to the table, no eye contact at all.

"Usually I deal with a different kind of sicko. The kind who likes little kids. It takes a different mindset to dwell in that muck. It wasn't a desirable job when I started, and it's even less so now when everyone's idea of justice is a man streaking across the sky."

"I'm sure he wants to help like everyone else. How can he help it if his abilities are. . . different?"

"It's not really the abilities. It's the mindset."

"What do you mean?"

"I mean what sort of savior does the world want? The kind who stays above it all or the kind who gets down in the filth? The kind who reaches down a hand to pull you up, or the sort who links his fingers together under your foot and boosts you out of it?"

She says nothing to this but seems lost in thought. Then her lips press tight, and I'm startled by a similarity. Could this woman be related to our hero? Perhaps his sister?

Or could she be—*somehow*—

"I need to tell you something," I say.

A gambler walks into a bar and tells the bartender, "Let's play Blackjack for a free round of beers."

"I know for a fact there's going to be another bomb. It's going to go off in twenty minutes."

"Okay," the bartender says. "I'll be the dealer."

She jolts out of her ruminations. And her response confirms every suspicion. There's nothing about calling the police. No interrogation about the basis for my claim. Only: "Where?"

And the bartender deals his customer a ten and a nine. He deals himself a five and a queen.

"The Republic Plaza."

"Looks like I'll be staying," the man says.

"I'm sorry, can you excuse me? I've got to go," she says.

"Where?"

"Just the bathroom."

Frowning, the bartender deals himself another card. A king. He's busted.

"Of course," I say, watching her head quickly to the back.

"I'll take my free beer now," the man says. "The most expensive thing you've got."

If I'm right, she's not coming back.

If I'm right, I'll feel the vibrations here in a moment.

I put my palms flat on the table.

"You might have won, but I'm still not going to serve you," the bartender says.

"And why is that?"

All the tables rattle just a second. I lean forward, eyes wide, and gnaw on one knuckle.

The bartender smiles, pointing to the cards. "It's illegal for me to serve anyone who's under 21."

OUR HERO

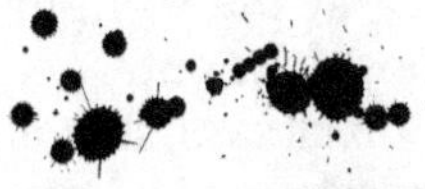

There had to be a bomb. I remember spending hours carefully planting the explosives.

Yet on the car radio, the police are saying they were summoned to the Republic Plaza on an anonymous tip, and the building checked out clean.

I park up the road from Diana Clarke's house and get out with a package in my hand. I walk down, go up her driveway, ring the doorbell.

She opens the door.

"You."

I present her with the package. "They're your clothes. It seems you left them in the bathroom stall. You're him in all his glorious perfection, aren't you? All that powerful muscle, all that unbreakable bone—it's all there under your skin."

Then I'm shoving in, breaking through. What the hell am I doing? She cries out as I tear at her shirt, another goddamn turtleneck. The rip reveals a fine white throat and an unusual golden necklace she seems desperate to clutch.

"Stop her, Brawson."

What's happening?

A hang glider question that my sanity rides, spiraling down a dark chasm.

"Kneel on her arms! Don't let her touch that necklace! I thought there'd be something like that when you mentioned her fondness for turtlenecks."

Sorcell stands behind me. I scrunch up my face as she screams at me to fight back. And then her eyes go lidless and watery.

"Yes. It is you. *You're* the other person I sensed when I tried to read *his* mind. No wonder it proved so confusing. But now, thanks to old-fashioned detective work, I know the truth. As long as I keep you in your proper place, I'll enjoy learning so much about you."

Sorcell reaches for the necklace, but it won't come off.

"Well then," he says. "Plan B."

Pressure in my head, almost blinding me.

I help bind her hands behind her back.

What am I doing? Why?

She keeps screaming at me to fight him. We're both in the muck. Boost her out. Boost *him* out.

"Lovely squirming," Sorcell says, standing over her. "Mr. Brawson, you have exceeded my expectations. I knew your ingenuity—with my help—would give us the answer. Enjoy the money."

I stare down at her.

"Your mind's troubled," Sorcell says to me. "You're wondering what you've done on your own and what I might have done through you. What if I were to tell you that I had no influence over you at all? Or that none of your horrible actions were done of your own volition? The problem with compulsion is that, pushed hard enough, it excuses everything. The problem with free will is it leaves you feeling utterly hopeless. In both cases there are urges, and in both cases there is dark surrender."

"Not everyone gives in!" I shout.

"No?" Sorcell asks. "Let me prove it."

He taps the middle of my forehead, and I gasp as tears begin to well.

"*No.*"

"As I said at our first meeting, sentimentality and hope are such banal things."

The son of a bitch.

A hopeful fool walks into a bar run by a pedophile.

"Bill!" Terry says, all smiles. "Haven't seen you for a while. Everything okay?"

Three regulars look up at me and nod.

"Let's go in your office, Terry."

His voice drops. "My office? Why?"

"Want to see how you do business."

"Bill, let me get you a drink. Anything you want. You know your money's no good here."

I head for the back. There's a door that says Management. That would be Terry.

"You can't go back there!"

Terry tries to stop me, and I punch him right in the gut. He goes down, and the regulars gape at us. I try the knob. It's locked.

OUR HERO

"Give me the goddamn key," I say, then lunge forward and shove my hands into his pockets. It takes half a minute to find the right key, and the door opens on a boy, maybe twelve, sleeping on a cot. *Someone's son.*

There are empty beer cans all around him.

"Please, Bill," Terry rasps from the floor. "I swear to God—"

I kick him in the mouth.

Two customers have fled, leaving the front door open behind them. That leaves one. I point at him. "You want to call the police, be my guest."

"I—I reckon you've given him the justice he deserves."

The justice he deserves? Probably. The only justice left in a world where our god has fallen?

That remains to be seen.

A drunken superhero stumbles into a bar during the middle of a fight and accidentally restores law and order. Slurring, all he asks in return is a refill of his flask. The grateful bartender eagerly obliges and fills it full of whiskey. The superhero staggers out, leaving the bartender shaking his head at all the unconscious people on the floor. His wife emerges from the back where she'd been hiding and says, "Who was that flasked man?"

I sit down at the bar and drink and wonder what Sorcell plans to do to Diana Clark, and whether I care enough to stop him, and if his success or failure means anything at all. As I drink, I stare at the glasses and wait to hear the delicate tinkle they make when *he* streaks overhead.

I may be waiting a long, long time.

STRAIGHT TO THE TOP

"**G**ET IN."

Mallard was shoved into the back seat. Weasel Face, the goon who manhandled him, climbed in beside him and shut the door. He rapped his pistol against the tinted glass partition in front of the passenger compartment. Right away, the engine started.

"Guess I shouldn't bother with the seat belt, right?" Mallard asked. He knew Weasel Face was Mr. Robert's number one thug and this ride wasn't for fun.

Weasel Face didn't look at him. "Keep making jokes, smart guy."

"You're going to use a gun, right? A gun's a sure thing."

Son, only suckers bet on a sure thing.

"Not this time, Dad," Mallard said softly.

This remark drew Weasel Face's attention. Whatever the man's real name was, Weasel Face still fit better. Jesus Christ, what a pointy mug.

"Are you calling me your dad?" Weasel Face pressed.

"No."

"Then why the hell did you say it?"

"I always talk to my dad when I'm in trouble."

"Talk to him?"

"It's just a thing. When my dad and I can't talk in person, I talk to him in my head."

Weasel Face raised his eyebrows. "Daddy going to leak out with your brains, then?"

Changed my mind, Son. From the sound of things, definitely bet on a gun.

They sat in the back of a black Lincoln Continental. 2017 model, must have cost around $45K—a good quarter of Mallard's gambling losses this month alone. The driver had the radio on a Top 40 station.

"Is this Ariana Grande? I don't want to die to this. I want to hear real music," Mallard said.

"What's real music to you, Mr. *Duck*?"

Mallard considered the question and realized he couldn't think of an actual song. He knew only the soft, stereotypical vibraphone notes found in the background of casino high-roller tables. Christ, what he'd give for about five minutes of that ambience now. It might actually calm his nerves.

When Mallard didn't answer, Weasel Face said, "You know what's real music to *me?*"

Jesus, this guy. Four to one odds he actually says—

"The screams of your victims?"

Smiling didn't help Weasel Face's expression.

"Executions are like guitar solos to me. Some deaths, they just go on too damn long. Think of Neil Young and 'Down by the River.' It's overindulgent. I appreciate guitar solos that capture everything in two minutes. Slash is a good example. He solos, it's done, and the song moves on. That's the kind of scream and moan I like. If I want to hear Neil Young, I shoot the kneecaps first."

"And if you want to hear Slash?"

Weasel Face pointed to his stomach.

Mallard pressed his lips together. "Where's our game?"

"There's a little spot up in the mountains I like."

What is it with psychopaths and little spots up in the mountains?

"I don't know, Dad."

"Quit talking to yourself like that, Duck. It's fucking creepy." He tapped the muzzle of his pistol against Mallard's chest. "And I don't like creepy."

Mallard went quiet. He stared out the window. The glass was tinted, making the night even blacker. The ride was smooth, but as the Lincoln wound its way up the crooked mountain roads, the constant side-to-side motion made him queasy.

"Oh God," he said.

"What?"

"Mr. Roberts shouldn't have bothered taking me to dinner before sending you after me."

"He's a gentleman. Even treats you to a last meal."

Mallard hunched forward. "That last meal is about to be all over the backseat."

Weasel Face twisted toward him. "Don't you dare."

"Or what? You'll kill me?"

"I'll go Neil Young on your ass."

Mallard hunched forward. "Spill my blood all you want, but my guts are about to spill themselves."

Weasel Face leaned forward and tapped on the glass partition. It cracked open.

"Pull over," Weasel Face said to the back of the driver's head.

"There's no side to pull over to. We're halfway up the mountain."

"You want to be the one to tell Mr. Roberts his car's covered in puke?"

The partition closed. The car veered right and slowed.

Mallard made a retching sound and clutched his stomach. His peripheral vision caught Weasel Face inching away.

The psychopath is squeamish. Who knew?

The car stopped. Weasel Face locked gazes with him. "Get out. I'll wait."

"You're not worried I'll run?"

Weasel Face gestured toward the back window. Mallard saw endless darkness beyond the bloody glow of the brake lights and understood at once.

"You going to puke or what?"

"I think if I just sit here the nausea will pass."

They waited. The music must have become too much for even Weasel Face, who beat on the partition again.

"Change that shit," he ordered when the glass lowered. "An old guy like you should be into the Beatles or something."

The glass rose again. The music changed a few seconds later.

"Eagles," Weasel Face said. "That's more like it."

"I don't know them."

"Seriously? What the hell *do* you know?"

"Poker."

Weasel Face laughed. "You must know poker like you know the Eagles. Who taught you?"

"My dad."

"Does he exist anywhere besides your head?"

"He lives in New Jersey. Taught me to gamble in Atlantic City."

"Must have been a shit player, or you wouldn't be in this predicament."

Mallard forced a laugh. "You think I owe Mr. Roberts *money?*"

"I've never killed anyone yet who wasn't up to their neck in debt and excuses."

"So says Mr. Roberts."

A trace of suspicion entered Weasel Face's expression. "You saying Mr. Roberts is a liar?"

"How many guitar solos have you taken working for him?"

"Six."

"Bet they were all Jews like me."

"Maybe one was."

You hear the note of caution in his voice, Son?

"I hear it, Dad."

Weasel Face frowned. "Sure you're not schizo?"

"I don't know."

"What happens when you talk to your dad in person?"

"I don't. The dad in my head's a lot nicer than the real one."

"You're a strange duck. Maybe I'm doing you a favor."

"Some of what's between my dad and me is my fault. He taught me poker and craps and roulette and all of that when I was just ten. He taught me well, leading me to think he's this expert. And when I ask him about it, he tells me that he sits on the State of New Jersey Casino Control Commission and he's got all of these connections and he's Mr. Big. Meanwhile we're living in this fleabag apartment. But I'm a kid at the time, what do I know? Then comes the day I stroll into the Borgata with some friends. It's my twenty-first birthday. First time I'm there because I'm legal, and who comes out of the service elevator pushing a mop bucket and wearing this janitor's outfit?"

"Your dad? That's hilarious." Weasel Face slapped his leg.

"We saw each other. Don't know whose face was redder. Don't know who was in more shock. And after that, he hated me. I tried to tell him I didn't care. But it didn't matter. He'd been exposed as a fraud and couldn't deal with it. He felt like a failure."

"He was mopping the floor in a goddamn casino. Sounds like a loser to me."

"I wouldn't mind being in his shoes right now, cleaning the shit off some linoleum."

"You going to throw up or what?"

Mallard glanced down at his stomach. "No, I think I'm good now."

Weasel Face smacked the partition and shouted, "Let's go!"

You're doing fine, Son. I believe in you.

"Thanks, Dad."

The car accelerated.

Mallard took a careful glance at Weasel Face to guess what he might be thinking. A man doles his thoughts out before him like a deck of cards. The trick was getting him to play the right one.

"What was that shit about the Jews?"

"Sorry?" Mallard said.

"Don't play dumb. You asked if I'd killed any Jews. What if they were?"

"Mr. Roberts likes his Jew boys. Up to a point."

"What point would that be?"

"Puberty."

Weasel Face stared at him. Mallard shrugged and added, "Guess I was an exception to the rule."

Weasel Face's eyes darted back and forth like someone trying to see something that wasn't there.

"You're full of shit. I haven't been killing boys," he said.

"No, you've been killing men who helped him get boys. The men who figured they could make a nice penny turning it back on him for blackmail."

"Mr. Roberts isn't like that. Word would get out."

"It can't, thanks to you. What do you care anyway?"

"I've got standards. Mr. Roberts could be a faggot. Doesn't bother me. But a pedo? Fuck that."

Mallard chuckled. "Would you keep working for him if what I'm saying is true?"

"Don't know."

"So there's no problem killing gamblers in hock to Mr. Roberts, but there's a moral issue with greasing his humps? That's progressive."

Weasel Face scowled and slapped the partition. It lowered.

"Pull over."

"Why?" the driver said.

"I'm wasting this guy right here."

"But we're ten miles from the spot."

"I don't care. Pull over!"

The glass rose again.

Shit, Son. This round's taken a bad turn.

"Look, I'm sorry," Mallard said. "Dad just told me I shouldn't have lied to you."

"So you *are* lying about Mr. Roberts?"

"Of course I am."

"I knew Mr. Roberts wasn't fucking boys."

Mallard made an exaggerated sigh. "I can't say how happy I am for you."

"Happy?"

"You passed the test."

"What test?"

"Mr. Roberts doesn't like idiots. He put us into this situation to test your loyalty. But you need to call him now, okay?"

Weasel Face just stared.

"Go ahead," Mallard continued, adding a slight chuckle. "Seriously. Mr. Roberts is expecting it. He doesn't really want you to kill me."

"This guy," Weasel Face muttered toward the partition, as if the driver could hear. "Can you *believe* this shit?"

He rapped on the glass. This time it lowered about halfway. Mallard watched the driver making eye contact with Weasel Face in the rearview mirror.

"I'm still trying to find a place to stop. There hasn't been a shoulder."

"Then never mind. Just get us straight to the top."

"Yes, sir."

The partition closed again, and the Lincoln accelerated, pressing Mallard into his seat. He swallowed. "You're going to call Mr. Roberts when we get there right? To confirm what I said?"

"Mr. Duck, you're just how Mr. Roberts described you."

"Oh?"

"He said you talked your way out of this trip a couple of times before and that you'd try talking your way out of it tonight. He said I shouldn't listen to a word. You're pretty good. But in this world, there are only two kinds of speech that get results: the whisper of cash and the shout of a gun."

You got to know when to hold 'em, know when to fold 'em—

"Jesus Christ, Dad. That's so cliché," Mallard said.

"So what's your dad really do? The one who's not in your head."

"He's a delivery driver."

Weasel Face laughed. "I guess that's a step up from being a janitor."

"A small one."

They were both thrown when the car suddenly jerked left.

The glass lowered. "Sorry about that. Deer in the road."

"Watch what the fuck you're doing. You don't want to get Duck killed on the way to his execution, right?"

The partition closed again as Mallard watched Weasel Face settle back. "What if I told you I just lied about my father?"

"Wouldn't surprise me at all."

"What if I told you that Mr. Roberts is my father?"

Mallard backed up his assertion with a stare. He threw everything he had into it, Poker Face versus Weasel Face.

Interesting play, Son. Mr. Roberts' garbage man isn't about to believe something so audacious at this point. But he might if you'd played the card earlier. You had him going just a little bit with that pedophile shit. You made it real enough in the guy's head to get him stirred up. At least for a minute. So tell me what that says about this guy?

"He's got a button to push."

Hell, everyone has at least one button. But this guy, he—

"Doesn't trust Mr. Roberts."

Weasel Face said, "I trust him to pay me a lot for what I do."

"What if I could guarantee you more money?"

"Reality check, Duck. You're in this situation because you couldn't repay the money you owe Mr. Roberts."

"That's not true at all."

Once again Weasel Face proved that smiling added no charm to his looks. "Go on, tell me another story. Make it fast, though, because we'll be reaching the top soon."

"I owe Mr. Roberts about a hundred grand. But that's chump change to a man like him. He wouldn't have me killed over it. It's not that I can't pay him back, it's that I'm not going to pay him back. Big difference."

"Dumb strategy."

"The problem was with tactics, not strategy. Owing someone money and finding a way to not pay it back is always worth the effort. I figured a man like Mr. Roberts would have some incriminating shit *somewhere.* So I got a buddy to help me run a phishing scheme on him. Totally worked. If his Gmail account was his asshole, I'd have been his proctologist. I was up to my elbow in his private stuff."

"Yeah?" The excited lilt in Weasel Face's voice proved a pleasant surprise.

"Let's just say what I found would have him behind bars sharing a foot-long with Subway's Jared."

Weasel Face shook his head in disgust. "Not the pedophilia bullshit again."

"You can believe it or not. The point is I was looking for blackmail material, and I thought I had it. Enough to cancel out my debt. The thing is I'd discovered too much. One ace would have been enough for my purposes. I came at Mr. Roberts with a handful of them, and in life, it's possible to overplay a strong hand."

"You thought he'd do everything you wanted?"

"Between relieving my menial debt or going to jail, I figured he'd fold. Instead, he called your ass."

"Texted, actually," Weasel Face said.

The road leveled out. The Lincoln slowed and stopped.

Running out of cards to play, Son. You may have to try roulette instead.

Mallard laughed. "Yeah, Dad. Russian roulette."

"Need a revolver for that." Weasel Face jabbed his pistol. "This here is a Beretta, an automatic."

The partition descended all the way, and the driver said, "We're here."

Weasel Face and Mallard got out. Weasel Face pointed his gun and motioned for Mallard to walk into the darkness.

"Get moving," he said.

"Dad was just saying I should have gone for roulette rather than poker. But it's a boring game," Mallard said as he walked away from the car.

"Wouldn't know. I don't gamble."

"Not even a little?"

"Not on nothin'. Not even the ponies."

Mallard looked up at the sky. A magnificent star field capped the world up this high. For just a moment, he thought he could raise his hands, spread his arms, and take flight into the universe.

"That's a shame," he said, looking back at Weasel Face.

"Why? It's just wasting money."

"Oh, it's so much more than that."

Mallard saw a trail ahead of him in the moonlight and followed.

"That's good," Weasel Face said. "That's just the direction I want you to go. Nice acoustics up here for a guitar solo."

"Much more," Mallard continued. "Gambling is tension, and in the space of that tension, you feel yourself wrestling with implications of fate and self-determination. *Luck* is the most powerful aphrodisiac in the world. It's the greatest prize."

Keep talking, Son. Get it all out. Maybe you'll bore him to death and he'll forget to kill you.

"That so?" Weasel Face said.

"Do you know what Napoleon used to ask about his generals?"

Weasel Face chuckled. "So now you're a history major?"

"He'd ask, 'Is he lucky?' Isn't that amazing? All the possible skills for a general to have, and Napoleon only cared about luck. But what it really says—"

Mallard heard footsteps behind him, closing space. He couldn't see exactly how much land he had ahead of him or where he might flee, though of course, Mallard knew he wasn't running anywhere. Not at this point. But he kept walking.

"What it really says—"

"Well, spit it out, Duck. Tell me what it says."

"The illusion of being in control. No one ever is. Even a man like Mr. Roberts. We're all losers who think we have our hands on the steering wheel. But it's the road that determines whether we turn left or right, or keep it in the middle. The road was there before we were born."

"How very philosophical."

Mallard smiled into the dark. "The casino graduates a thousand doctorates a day."

"You can stop right there," Weasel Face said.

Mallard did. He stared up at the stars. Not a bad parting vision if it came to that.

"Any last words?"

I'm never going to let you down, Son.

"Just that I wish you'd gambled at least once. Because for all illusion, there comes a moment—a round—when you realize you *are* in control. When you know you've played your hand perfectly even if it wasn't your strongest, and everyone's in, and your hole card is the ace of all aces, and all the money is yours."

Mallard flinched when the gun fired. Weasel Face was right about the acoustics. The sound echoed magnificently and worked such a strong effect on Mallard's mind that he felt the impact and collapsed to his knees.

He was still kneeling when the hand appeared before him.

He took it and was pulled to his feet, just as his father had done for him ever since Mallard could remember.

"Don't know which of us played that better, Dad," he said and started working the audio receiver out of his ear. It was a pesky little thing that had been driving him nuts since he inserted it before dinner with Mr. Roberts. Weasel Face was crumpled on the ground, blood spreading beneath him.

Dad grinned and spoke into a little microphone concealed in his jacket. The words piped out of the receiver clearly—

"I did, of course," he said.

"But I was the one whose life was on the line," Mallard said.

"Well, I was the one who had to sit up front listening to you describe me as some sort of asshole. I got so pissed I almost ran the goddamn car off the road."

They looked down at Weasel Face.

"If that dumb bastard had any experience in the casinos, he'd have known the greatest threat comes from the employee who's been turned or compromised," Dad said.

"In an odd way, I think he was too personally loyal to even consider the idea. I really don't think he could have been bribed. Noble, I guess," Mallard said.

"More like stupid."

"It says something about the quality of men Mr. Roberts hires."

Dad raised his eyebrows. "Oh yeah? He was dumb enough to hire me as a chauffeur. Sorry, Son, but this guy's HR department isn't running any detailed background checks. Which is mighty lucky for both of us."

They started stoward the Lincoln, and Mallard gave a final glance at the stars. If they were just a little bit flashier, he could imagine himself inside some dome-capped gambling resort. He said as much to his dad.

"Get your head out of the clouds, son. Keeping your feet

planted on the ground is the surest way to keep them from being planted under it. Got it?"

"I got it."

"Good," he said. They got into the car, Dad behind the wheel. He turned the ignition, and the Lincoln started almost noiselessly. "Now let's go kill Mr. Roberts."

THE SOMMELIER

R ICK MORTON STOOD across the street from Mneme and indulged in a memory of honeybees. The persistent hum of the building's neon sign and the low but excited murmur of the gathered patrons abetted his memory. He shoved his hands in his coat pockets and started counting the people whose line stretched down the street. Those nearest the entrance had been camping out for days like pharmafans determined to get their next fix. This crowd consisted of middle-aged and older men and women dressed in suits and dresses. Daubner must be quite the sadist, Morton thought. Not only did his winery lack a reservation system, he also insisted on a rigorous dress code.

Morton sucked in his stomach as he looked down at the grime on his dark shoes. Filth from the sublevel streets blackened the hem of his pants. His friends in the department always joked that he put the *plain* in plainclothes detective, and Morton supposed that was true. His outfit wouldn't hold up to Mneme's high standards.

But then he wasn't going in through the front door.

The winery was set to open in an hour, at 9 pm. It would close four hours later. Despite the long waiting line of hopefuls, Morton knew its serving room could accommodate only fifty people, and those fifty tended to stay the entire four hours. The winery's slogan was, "One night, a lifetime of memories."

A tram silently slid by on magnetic rails, hauling the district's dregs from one sector to the next. The faces looking out belonged to those who drank to forget—alcoholics almost as old-fashioned as the business card in Morton's front pocket. The card's edges were furred from many inspections, long stretches spent turning it over in his fingers. The card had arrived in an envelope, almost

265

a relic inside of a relic. The accompanying letter also seemed antiquated, handwritten in cursive. God, how Morton had stared at it in his office, remembering the grieving parents of Luca Garcia and Amanda Ryerson, and the crying, orphaned daughters of Steven and Rebecca Griegs. Those girls, ten and twelve at the time, were in their thirties now—almost the age Morton had been when the original cursive letter arrived to taunt him.

Dear Detective Salt—

Morton swallowed, refusing to let the entire memory resurface, though he'd always have a perfect recollection of the original letter. Cursive was unusual even decades ago, something no longer taught in schools. He'd sat at his desk transcribing the antiquated script into print like some British archaeologist deciphering Akkadian clay tablets in a museum basement, each sentence a slow-budding flower of terrible revelation, the totality a bouquet of thorns.

After the tram passed, Morton crossed the street, head down as he slipped by the crowd. Excitement and anticipation gathered in their conversation—

"Something from the 1920s. Maybe a flapper! Could you imagine?"

"Anything from 2030 works for me. My parents used to say every single day of 2030 felt like the world was on the verge of something awful or something awesome."

Morton fought the urge to identify the man who said that and shake some sense into him. Every year has its balance of births and deaths, but 2030 was the year of *the* deaths—the year of the letter.

None of these people had a reason to remember and ruminate upon the victims, of course, any more than he felt grief over Annie Chapman or the Black Dahlia or JonBenet Ramsey or Stephanie Duggan. They might have been cultural icons in their day, convenient symbols for the social headshakers and religious scolders, but time had added their names to its greater, endless death scroll. How they came to be inscribed no longer mattered.

Morton kept moving, putting the crowd behind him. Mneme occupied a refurbished building in a former industrial sector, making it far larger than its limited serving space suggested. Morton got the floor plan from the district assessor's office and knew the entire space to be 60,000 square feet. But what occupied all that area? Casks? Bottles?

A laboratory?

THE SOMMELIER

He came around to the hidden side of the building, where windowless garage panels and a steel security door gave evidence of its past life as a warehouse. Morton sighed, and the air had chilled just enough to cloud his breath. He stepped up to the door, wondering if its burgundy color was meant to suggest a red wine. Morton wouldn't hazard a guess at how many layers of paint had preceded it.

He turned the business card over and studied the twelve digits written there. The handwriting on the card was different from the letter. The numbers were written with a shakier hand—perhaps fearful, perhaps stricken. But a forensics analysis revealed the same pen was used for both.

Morton punched in the code.

A subtle *click* came from the lock. He pulled the door open and stood looking at a space lined with several hospital beds. It'd been years since any discovery startled him into pulling his taser, but Morton did so now. It took a moment to realize some of the beds were occupied, and the people were awake. Or at least their eyes were open. Many seemed to be whispering.

"Shut the door behind you, Detective," an unseen man said. "This part of the winery needs temperature control just as much as the barrel room."

The voice's cadence carried erudition, the unhurried affect of a butler. Morton gave a quick scan of the vaulted ceiling and saw multiple security cameras.

"I recognize your voice, Daubner."

"I'm not trying to disguise it. Now please shut the door. The memory's not as clear if the donor is too hot or too cold."

Morton holstered his taser and closed the door. He entered the room and got an immediate, complete look at the scene. There were fifteen beds in all. Four were in use—two men and two women. A very tall and lanky man who appeared to be in his late thirties stood observing each of them, moving back and forth between monitors. Each bed had a dedicated array of attending apparatus, with white pads attached at each occupant's temples, forehead, cheeks, and throat. Morton also saw IV drips, though the tubes appeared to drain into the back of each patient's neck. Two of the IV bags contained a pale yellow liquid, the other two ruby red.

"Is that—"

"Wine?" the tall man said, still not looking at him. "Yes."

Morton took two steps forward. "If I hadn't done my research, I'd think you catered to hardcore drunks, Daubner. Why bother tasting anything when you can have the mother's milk put right into your veins?"

"But you have done your research and know better about these—"

"Guinea pigs?"

Daubner cast a critical glance at him. "Perhaps you've not researched me after all."

"It doesn't take detective skills to read about you in the media, Daubner. You'd be hard to escape notice even if I wasn't trying to learn about you."

Now the tall man, Mneme's unmistakable owner and sommelier, left the monitors and approached Morton with his hand extended. Morton shook it.

"I wasn't sure if you'd come at all, but I never expected you to come alone."

"Who says I did?"

"Ah," Daubner said. From one of the beds a woman began whispering, and he excused himself to attend to her.

Morton followed. "Is something wrong?"

"Some people verbalize their memories during the transfer. I prefer that doesn't happen if possible. Not that I have any proof, but I believe speaking dilutes the quality of what gets imprinted into the wine."

Morton studied the woman's face. Her eyes stared at the ceiling, but he did not think that's what she saw if her words were indicative. *"Yes, Adam, of course I will. I've been waiting so long for you to ask. I love you."* Morton judged her to be in her eighties. Her thin lips smiled, and her delicate arms were crossed over one another at the stomach. She looked happy and peaceful, though similar observations had been made by people looking into many an open casket.

"I've read about your process a handful of times, but I still don't understand exactly what's happening here."

"But that is everyone's experience about most things in life, Detective. What percentage of drivers can explain the chemical reactions that power their car engine? How many people could send email if doing so required the knowledge to construct a network first? Experiencing my wine requires nothing more on the user's part than a willingness to swallow what I and my memory vintners create."

"Memory vintners?"

"A recent coinage," Daubner said. "I wanted to be as inclusive—and accurate—about my product as possible. Where would I be without people willing to share their memories?"

"Share? I understand you pay quite well."

"But it's hardly the same thing as selling blood plasma or eggs. Each memory needs to be special, a unique experience. So yes, these people are vintners just as much as I am."

Daubner began to wax about the philosophical and ethical aspects of his business, and under other circumstances, Morton might have been content listening all night, even though much of it rehashed considerations discussed countless times in prior interviews. Daubner billed himself as a sommelier of the mind, an expert at pairing the right memory with his customers' specific needs and desires. The crowd outside had come to experience some aspect of another person's life. An evolutionary step, perhaps, in virtual reality.

"Mrs. Palmer here lived much of her life among the Amish," Daubner said, pointing to the old woman who was still whispering. "The story of her husband's courtship is as gentle and endearing as any romance novel. No fiction writer could capture the reality of it, yet the audience for that reality remains just as popular as when Beverly Lewis launched the genre almost a century ago."

He always sells the sweet side, Morton thought as Daubner asked him to come and see the cellar. The recaptured romance, a warm parental experience, a dazzling historical foray. Staring up at the back of the sommelier's head, Morton could only wonder where the grey area began and what the red line might be. If Daubner had ever been posed the question in the media, the detective was unaware of it. But when it came to the latest technology trends and breakthroughs, journalists always wanted to keep the picture rosy.

Or in this case, he thought, *rosé*.

Daubner ushered him into a room isolated by a glass wall. It was lined with racks made from walnut that went twenty feet from floor to ceiling. Bottles after bottles—more than a few thousand, at least—almost overwhelmed his vision, though Morton did notice certain color distinctions in the wax seals, which included red, blue, green, yellow, and orange. Afraid he'd been silent too long, he decided to question their relevance.

"Here we don't classify the way a traditional winery would," Daubner said. "There isn't much concern as to Merlot or Shiraz, or to the year of the grape."

"You categorize by memory?"

"Precisely."

Daubner went to the nearest rack and swept his finger along the bottlenecks. "Yellow for love and safety. Green for comedy. Blue for adventure, and so on. Of course, these are broad categorizations. We drill down with far more specificity than that when the customer's deciding time comes."

Morton reached for a bottle, but just as he did, he heard a loud whir come from the ceiling. An articulated metallic arm moved fast down a track affixed to the walnut wine rack and delicately slid the bottle from its spot, handing it to Morton with laser-guided precision. The glass was a rich green and unlabeled except for a barcode. The detective held it in both hands and turned to Daubner as if offering it.

"What's this one?"

"I couldn't tell you without consulting the database."

"The wax seal is red."

"Yes."

"What does red mean?"

Daubner cocked his head to the left. "What does red usually mean, Detective?"

"Danger. Aggression."

"Or a Valentine's Day heart, or—"

"Sex."

"Certainly sex," Daubner said.

"Then you cater to the whole range of. . .experience?"

"Not yet. The spectrum you're talking about is as vast as the population, after all. But in time, when enough suitable candidates have been contracted as memory vintners—yes."

"What counts as *suitable*?"

Daubner reached forward to take the bottle from Morton's grasp. He held it up to his face using both hands, the way someone would lift a child.

"I would *love* to bottle some of your memories, Detective."

THE SOMMELIER

"They'd turn the wine to vinegar in an instant."

The sommelier's face became pale. He pivoted to the rack and returned the bottle to its place. Without looking back at Morton, he said, "It's been good of you to let me talk in order to avoid the conversation you came here to have. I doubt a man like you tolerates prevaricators under normal circumstances."

"There's nothing normal about what brought me here."

"The letter," Daubner said.

"Are you confessing to sending it?"

Daubner turned back to him. "Confirming. Confessing is too loaded. After all, I've done nothing wrong."

"The law might disagree. I know I do."

Sweat broke out on the sommelier's forehead. There was a moment when Morton thought Daubner would faint, and stepped forward, prepared to catch him. Instead, the man leaned against the bottle rack and held up a conciliatory hand.

"After I mailed the letter, I had almost no notion of what I'd done. I remember trying to fight it."

"Fight *what?*"

"The memory, Detective Morton. A memory unlike any other. More like a demon than a recollection."

"Whose memory?"

"Slipping in my business card was a supreme act of resistance. Giving you the access code to our back door was as close as my mind could come at the time to a plea."

"I said *whose memory?*"

"Now I realize I was begging you to come. The part of me that was subsumed by the overpowering memory cried out for rescue. Maybe I feared the memory wouldn't leave—that should be impossible, of course, but then I thought what had already happened to me was impossible. The shadow that seized control of my mind saw you as a direct threat. I must have latched onto that feeling. One man's threat is another man's hope, after all."

"The handwriting was a perfect match to the original letter. Are you telling me—"

"Yes, I'm telling you that the memory was so powerful that I became the man it belonged to. I felt his thrill and his dread, his anticipation and his giddiness as the two of us spelled out every word, both thirty years ago—and last week. You can't understand the elation he felt when he placed the envelope into the mailbox."

"Damnit, tell me whose memory it was!"

Daubner's eyes watered. He shook his head.

"If you don't," Morton said, stepping nearer, "I'll make sure every one of these bottles gets smashed. It'll be like a raid out of Prohibition. And then I'll track down every single *vintner* you've ever sampled because one of them has to be the man who wrote that letter. The man who killed all those. . ."

Morton squeezed his eyes shut and bowed his face into his right palm.

"I'm so very sorry," the sommelier said. "When the memory finally died away, leaving me a wreck, I sat in my office debating how to proceed. The letter had been mailed, and my business card with it. Should I wait for you to visit? Should I make a preemptive explanatory call to you? A week passed. I began to entertain the hope the letter was never received."

"Oh, I definitely got it."

"Then I must confess I'm surprised you simply showed up like this. For all you knew, this could have been an elaborate ambush."

"If it was, and I happened to die a bit earlier than the actuarial tables predict, it's no great loss. The truth is no one but me knows about your letter, Daubner."

"*Don't* call it mine!"

"Most of the people on the force were children when I got the original, but there are still a few old guys around who remember. It's not something we go reminiscing about. After thirty years, why should they care? They never got taunted. They never failed. Now tell me his name, Daubner."

The sommelier's throat bobbed. Morton thought he could strangle the man if he tried to obfuscate any longer. He pictured himself taking one of the bottles and smashing it across Daubner's stricken face.

"Come to my office, Detective."

"Another damn delay?"

"No—*no*. I'll tell you. But I need to show you, too."

Morton frowned and shrugged. "Make it quick."

"I will. I promise. Thirty years might be a fine age for a wine, but this memory should have been uncorked a long time ago."

Daubner led him from the bottle room and up a flight of stairs. Morton's hackles raised, wondering if there might yet be a trap waiting. His suspicions ebbed when Daubner opened the door to an office that had no walls other than a railing. The open-air office was positioned some twenty feet above the serving area. The doors had been unlocked, the lucky few ushered in. Morton gripped the railing and watched Daubner's staff attending to each table. He saw smiles. He heard warm laughter.

"Detective."

Morton turned as Daubner took a seat at his desk. He opened a drawer and pulled out a bottle.

"A true pinot noir," he said as Morton came to sit across from him. "The contents of this bottle came from the blackest of grapes."

God, Morton thought, unable to move. The bottle was dark with no trace of a label or sticker of any kind. He couldn't quite explain his own emotions to himself just then. He felt as if there was a personality emanating from the bottle, an essence, a consciousness. If this really was the distillation of a person, Morton felt he could pour the wine into the air and have it take shape. He sat and stared at the bottle, squaring off against it as he would any suspect in an interrogation room, until the glimpse of a dim cameo of his face in the glass made him flinch like a rookie.

"You'll know from my interviews that my first career was in memory care and technology. The goal was to imprint one's own key memories in a consumable form—sipping the past, saving time in a bottle as the old song goes. The concept of sampling someone else's experiences came much later."

"As you said, I know the background."

"But not all of it. I've never been truthful about my first patient—my first successful breakthrough."

Morton shook his head. Daubner stood and held the bottle up by its neck.

"My father," he said.

Morton wondered if anything about his face revealed how fast his pulse was going. He swallowed against an immediate, sharp dryness in his throat.

"He was always an enigma to me, Detective. He was distant—he traveled often for his job. I knew he had a dark side. I found a stash of his pornography when I was fifteen."

"Did he know you found it?"

"Oh, I doubt it, based on how he'd punish me for even minor infractions. I lived in fear of him until he grew old. Dementia changed him—softened him. Illness made him more like a father to me and triggered my forgiveness. I'd ask him to tell me stories, tell me all the things about him I never knew as a child."

"He told you about the murders?"

"God, no," Daubner said, looking at the bottle. "He told me memories that didn't seem real. It was as if he had enough awareness to change the details, or perhaps he was just relaying the truth of his life as he saw it in the fog of his condition. Regardless, I could tell there was something artificial about what he told me, and it made me greedy for the real thing. So, against all medical ethics, I brought my lab equipment home and began to use it on my father. He could not consent. He did not know what I was doing, and in a very real way, I didn't know what I was doing either. My memory capture and transfer process wasn't anywhere near as precise as it became. This bottle represents a jumble of memories. Each glass is unpredictable—and based on my experience, far more powerful than anything being served to the customers below us."

Morton asked to see the bottle. Daubner extended it but did not surrender it entirely into the detective's grip. Morton guessed the sommelier was afraid he'd smash the bottle on the ground.

But Morton was just interested in seeing how much of the wine had been drunk. What he saw suggested less than a glass.

"Is he still alive?"

"No," Daubner said. "He's been dead almost two years."

At least the monster's dead, Morton thought.

"When did you uncork the bottle?"

"Three months ago."

"Why did you wait?"'

"Fear, perhaps."

"Not grief?"

"No. The warm relationship we had toward the end didn't make up for years of pain."

"Then why open it at all? I don't understand."

"Like wine, all relationships have an aftertaste, Detective. Some are very complex. As I came into my new career as a sommelier of other people's lives, I decided I wanted to sip at my father's memories and understand him. Maybe I was looking for a better comprehension of myself. The first few tries were unusually strong, but not terrifying. Then came the night I had half a glass— the rest you know about."

THE SOMMELIER

Morton took his hands off the bottle and rubbed his temples. "Well," he said, and for a minute or so he found he had no other words or notion of how to proceed. The killer had died of old age, perhaps forgetting he was even a murderer. It wasn't fair, but when had fairness played any part in the world's affairs?

"I can't arrest a bottle," he said. "But it must be confiscated. There could be other memories—memories of other crimes."

"The only way to know is to drink."

"So be it. If nothing else, there'll be closure for the relatives of the people he killed."

"What about for you, Detective?"

Morton shook his head. "Not after receiving that letter. Even if he didn't kill again the rest of his life, I'll never be able to forget that he escaped. There's more than wine and memory in that bottle. It's also got the last drop of my blood, and more than a few tears."

Daubner hung his head at this, and Morton found the sommelier wouldn't even meet his eye for the rest of their encounter. They waited for Mneme to close before summoning an evidence response team to take possession of the bottle. Morton then took a full deposition from the sommelier that went into the early morning hours.

When it was over, Daubner said, "What happens next?"

"We go on living with the past until we die. I'm glad I'm old-fashioned and only drink to forget."

Morton went downstairs and headed for the security door. It didn't seem like Daubner was going to follow him. But as he reached the door, the sommelier called to him.

"Yes?"

"I'm sorry," Daubner said. "I feel like my father ruined your life."

"He ruined the lives of the people he killed. He only soured mine."

"Thirty years is a long time to live with the feelings you've endured. The last drop of blood and the tears, you said."

Morton nodded and stared.

"Forgive me, Detective. There's something I'd like to offer you. A new vintage. Something different than any other bottle in this building. Not a human memory, you see, but an invented one. One I'll invent for you. Call it *Perfect Happiness*."

"There's no such thing."

"Since my career change, I've been focused on listening to people and pairing them with the perfect memory. The best thing to pair with failure is success. If that has to mean pairing reality with fantasy, then so be it. Mankind was doing that long before the first grape was ever harvested."

Morton squinted. "Just what the hell are you offering me, Daubner? A wine that will make me think I caught your father?"

"The world would have been better if you had. You can live in that world one glass at a time, Detective. I'll make sure you have an unlimited supply. Please, let me do this for you."

Morton took a deep breath. He didn't have a fireplace in his home, but he could imagine himself beside one, alone and weary in the early morning hours, ruminating on failure while his fingertips rolled the delicate stem of an empty wineglass back and forth. Where was the promised bottle in his fantasy? Was it lying empty on the floor? Was it sitting on the table untouched containing the genie of an alternate reality just waiting to be uncorked? God help him, wouldn't he drink? Wouldn't he drink deep?

"I don't mind a good Shiraz," he said and hurried out the door.

FOR WANT OF THREAD

LOOK AT THAT GOWN. *Must be a hospital patient. Let's see what's underneath.*

She was in a place that knew no softness.

Underneath. Let's see. Push it up. Nice. Very nice.

Even the laughter was hard, so too the ground. So many bits of sharpness—glass shards, gravel, nails, and screws. Rat claws. Cat claws. The length of each man, their predatory faces flashing over her like black ribbons. Some fading part of her pitied them. How was it their fault? They were made this way. They were destined to do this. A sister's revenge on a sister performed through the flesh of men.

She knew her name before she shut her eyes. When she opened them, she did not. Her attackers were gone. The white sheet that draped about her body was no longer white. Not bloody at all, but not white and not whole. Somehow the rips in the fabric sent a deep revulsion through her, a greater offense than any attempted against her flesh. The fabric was delicate but strong, like cloth woven out of wind. Cloth, she thought, uncertain why the word came to mind with such significance. She felt on the threshold of understanding something.

Well, well. Awake already. Ready for round two?

Three men crowded the entrance. Their presence confirmed the walls on either side of her, stretching so high. This was an alleyway. A narrow place. Walls of rough brick and rock. A hard world. A mason's world.

She pulled herself up as the men laughed. Their faces weren't black ribbons to her anymore. She saw eyes with hard gazes, mouths with hard, sharp teeth. Her bare feet brushed something shiny and silver. A pair of scissors, or perhaps something a little larger, like shears. They meant nothing to her, yet something told her they *should* be of great significance. Hers but not *hers*. A weapon. A defense. A threat.

She stooped to get them.

Now, no need for all that. We'll just take them away again. Might even have to use them on you.

The cuts in her sheet. Were the scissors responsible? She considered the possibility even as the men swarmed her. As promised, they knocked the tool out of her hand, and it made a *clink* against the concrete. They had her on her back, hardness everywhere again, the world hard and cold and sharp, a threadbare and fraying place. The first assault began, and again she felt the strange disconnect of pity. They were always going to do this; they were made this way. Someone knew it a long time ago. Did she know it? Was she supposed to?

There's the assholes. We're going to fuck you up good.

Footsteps, shouts, screams. All the world's beauty and softness blanketing her in warm down. Salvation and kindness are rounded things, like the runners of a rocking chair, like the globe of the world. Gentle but firm arms pulled her up to a seated position and held her about the shoulders, cradling, shushing.

You're safe now. Jason, Chris-cat, and Philly Freedom are going to get those fucks. Don't worry about the police. They're good for when it comes to finding the bodies. Until there's a body for them to find and cart away, they're worthless. That sounds terrible, I know. Or maybe not. You must want them dead more than I do. Look at what they were trying to do. Bastards.

Something about this woman stirred an urgent memory, like a face she'd been waiting her entire life to see. Was this a long-lost sister? Was she in search of a sister? How could she forget such a thing? Her name, yes, that was unimportant. But a missing sister?

She touched the woman's face, causing her to flinch back a second and then offer a nervous little laugh.

Hey, that's okay. Just glad you're safe and we could help. You got a name?

Yes, she supposed she did. She must have one. Maybe if she thought hard enough. But she wasn't thinking about much of anything except curves and softness and kindness. This woman embodied all three, though she was very dirty. Pressing against her only added to the stains on the sheet, but it was no matter. The woman wore blue pants with rips in them and a black shirt that left her shoulders and arms bare. Both arms were covered in patterns and images that bled into each other in the most wonderful way, as if she'd tried to weave a tapestry into her skin. Her left arm blossomed with roses stemming along the length of her forearm and surrounded by bouquets of bluebells and clusters of carnations and bright, green leaves. She reached to touch the petals, and this time the woman did not flinch. The smoothness of her unwashed skin more than answered the expectation of floral silk.

You act like you've never seen tats before. Let me guess. Catholic school girl, right? You run away from a convent?

The other arm had no flowers. She found names and numbers there. Fittzy Pie 12-5-16. Mel 4-25-19. Dana Est 7-9-00 Closed __________. An arm's length of others. The woman noticed her interest.

I'm a walking memorial wall. The crazy shit that happens out here. When you make a real friend, you don't forget them. You don't let yourself forget, so you put it on your skin because you can't trust your mind to keep shit. I'd write their obituaries on me if I had room. This one here is my first. I'm Dana. That's my birthday. When I die, I want someone to fill in the blank. If not the day I died, then at least the day I was found. Then they can just burn the whole thing. Don't just close up shop, light the whole fucking building on fire. So, like I asked, do you have a name?

Everyone had a name. The question was who gave it to them. She felt an old, bitter argument echoing at her from the sky. She looked up into all that blue. Her vision was narrowed by the alleyway walls, but still—*all that blue.*

"Clo. . .clo. . .clo—"

Hey, you coughing or talking? It's cool. Just take a bit.

"Clo. . .clo—"

Chloe.

Sure. Chloe. Not right but right enough. Everything Dana said was right enough.

I really like that. It's a great name. Pretty. I had a doll named Chloe. Probably rotting away in a landfill. I should add a tattoo.

How could laughter be so soft and so bitter?

The men returned—Dana's men and not the ones they chased off.

Beat the shit out of them.
Hell yeah, we did.
Bitterness left Dana's laugh.
Hell yeah, you did!
Kicked the big one so hard in the balls he'll be seeing stars for the next twenty years.
How about her? She okay?
I think we got here in time. Boys, this is Chloe. Chloe, this is the Three Splooges. Jason, Chris-cat, and Philly Freedom. You'll get used to the smell.
Like you're any better.
I'm a girl. Trust me, I smell better.
That got a lot of laughs and nudges. No one laughed louder than Dana.
Chloe, can you walk? Our camp's not far from here.
"I can walk."
Dana stood up with her, holding on, stabilizing. After a few steps, Jason pointed at the ground.
Hey, look at that. Scissors. Always handy. Maybe we could give ourselves haircuts. Want to lose those dreads?
Want to lose your balls?
The scissors went into his pocket. She thought to ask him for them. Scissors or shears. Whatever they were, they had an importance she felt rather than knew. Best kept in hand. She held hers out.
What is it, Chloe?
You want the scissors? Fuck no, bitch. Finders, keepers.
Not if they're hers, asshole.
Why would they be hers?
Maybe because they were on the ground right fucking beside her?
Nope, all mine.
Christ, Jason, quit being a dick.
There he goes.
Dana sighed and shook her head. They all stood watching Jason stalk away in a cloud of petulant mutterings. His scissors now. His. Finders, keepers.
He's like that. Don't worry, Chloe. We'll get you another pair of scissors.
He'll get tired of them or forget about them in a day or two.

FOR WANT OF THREAD

As soon as he does, I'll steal them back for you. Better just let him go for now, or he'll be fighting head demons all night.

She understood none of what she heard. What she knew was Dana's touch, its rightness, its sincerity and firmness. She submitted to its guidance out of the alleyway, through more narrow passages, and then into a world of noise and crowds. She looked back, unsure about how or why she ever came to be there. In pursuit of something. Dana, perhaps. Yes, that must be it. How would Dana ever be made to understand?

Shit, Jason really took off, didn't he?

His figure was small in the distance, but his walk remained distinct in its fits-and-starts erraticism. Some people walk like they move the earth, others like the earth moves beneath them, neither characteristic nor their implications a matter of fault or achievement, but something bred in the bone—or sewn there. She tried to understand her sudden shiver, for she was not cold.

So, we're going up six blocks to the camp. It's safe there. There's room in my tent. We can score some food for you and something to wear besides whatever the hell it is you've got on. Our feet look to be the same size. I've got some tennis shoes you can have. Some holes in them but better than walking around barefoot. Shit, Chloe, now that I look at you, you sure do look like you ran away from an insane asylum.

They started walking. Dana had her right arm draped around her, forever the steadying force. Sheltering her in memories of dead friends. She thought of the scissors. Scissors or shears. Her thoughts moved fast but without pattern. Everything moved fast except for the four of them, everything else part of a world they knew not. Snarling sounds, hardship sounds, a world of hammering noise and only Dana's voice to soften it in her ears. Who was she? The arm across her shoulder felt heavier. The weight of appointed times. The sensation was too great and she tore herself out from under it.

Hey—

And fled to Dana's left side and took the arm and snuggled herself under the roses and the bluebells, the carnations, the leaves.

Well, just make yourself at home, Chloe.

Laughter as soft as rain water.

I like it that you don't talk so much. It's not so much that you're a good listener, it's just that I like talking to myself but hate the whole stigma attached to it. This is a best-of-both-worlds situation.

"I talk sometimes," she said.

Chatterbox. Now shut up and hold my hand. It'll help keep my arm still while I do this.

Dana's right arm was out with the palm facing up, a thin piece of rubber hose tied just below her bicep. Watching her knot the hose, pulling one end tight with her teeth, proved fascinating. Somewhere inside her lay the knowledge of many knots. Not names, to be exact, but types. Steps to create them. Reasons and purposes.

Watching Dana now was like watching a beautiful dance whose gestures took place everywhere but the feet. Those were planted flat on the bottom of the tent, which was red and identical to forty other tents, all lined up in rows and columns in the parking lot of a church. She understood this to be holy ground, though in the three days she'd been here there'd been no sense of the sacred until this moment of revelation. Dana's motions leading up to this moment had a sacramental air. An offering of brown powder was placed in the rounded little bowl of a spoon, transforming it into a handheld altar, silver and perfect everywhere except along the delicate curve of its belly, blackened by flame. Dana added liquid to the bowl in precious drops, each falling into place and accumulating under her practiced gaze.

Fascinating, right? I could have been a chemist. We can all be anything we want unless our parents die in a car crash and we end up in the care of an uncle who's a pervert who knows he can get away with it, because a traumatized orphan is a hundred percent pure drama queen, and her crazy stories are not to be believed. Is that what happened to you, Chloe? Your parents die on the highway?

"I don't know them."

Lucky bitch.

"I mean it. I can't remember them."

I mean it too. Lucky bitch.

Hard dry wit, soft summer-shower smile.

Dana now brought the oval flame under the spoon, the liquid bubbling soon after. A boiled offering. The lighter was put aside and the needle taken up. Dana gave the liquid three gentle stirs and drew the offering into the barrel.

This can be hard to watch.

"I'll never turn my head from you."

Dana's fingers curled around hers. Palm to palm, one prayer held tight between separate hands.

The needle was brought above a throbbing spot. Despite all she said, she did want to look away. The act of injection baffled her. It was like a goddess making an offering to herself. Was Dana deity or offering? Was divinity always both in equal parts?

There. Feel better already. I'll go to sleep for a while. I always do. You don't have to stay, but I'd be happy if you did.

"I'll stay."

Dana set the spoon and the needle aside. She untied the strip of hose and laid down. The red tent had two cots and two sleeping bags. The cots and bags were red too, and all had the same white logo stamped on them. Eskimo Quickfish. She didn't understand the reference, but Dana had joked about it when they entered the tent together for the first time.

They're not really tents. They're called pop-up shelters. I guess these were designed for people out ice fishing. I want that to be true. There should be a hole in the concrete for us to sit around.

Soon, Dana's eyelids fluttered, fifty quarter blinks a minute, their restive motion so at odds with the long and luxurious rise and fall of her chest. She preferred to watch the slower motions of Dana's body, the relaxed breathing that seemed to take place outside of any concern or even awareness of time. Why rush a breath? Oxygen is a food best savored forever. She looked at the red walls before taking up the rubber hose, surrendering to an immediate urge to stretch and lengthen it. She made motions with it in the air. Up, down, in, out. What was she doing? Why did the action comfort and please her?

She put the hose down out of a most curious fear. It seemed she began to remember something—everything, maybe—and the idea of rediscovering herself held too much dread. Amnesia had perfected her; why mar perfection with memory?

Hours passed without any notice. Even Dana's waking moments, signaled by yawns and contented stretching, made but the vaguest of silhouettes against the veil of her new obsession. At some point after setting down the piece of tubing, she walked back and forth in the space between their cots. The shelter was not designed for pacing. Five steps in one direction, about-face, five steps back. Sometimes heel-to-toe, sometimes crossing her feet over the ankles. The routine had its comforts. She felt like she was making something. Warp-and-weft walking.

The red imperfection would catch the eye of very few people, just a tongue of thread at the foot of the sleeping bag. Less than the length of a fingernail, one of those little protruding snags left behind when the soft scrapes against the hard. The human fabric was full of them. She made a pained "Oh!" and sat on the cot, bunching the wounded sleeping back into her lap, her fingertips pushing the loose fiber down as if it were wet clay that could be smoothed, perfected. She did not know why the thread defied her, why all her efforts to reconcile only resulted in further unraveling. The scissors came to mind. She'd not seen them in four days, but Dana assured her she'd get them back as soon as Jason forgot about them.

You have to feel for the guy. Total schizo. The shit he hears and sees when he's off his meds, the shit he says and believes and obsesses over. . .you could write a novel. There's no trip more powerful than a fucked-up brain. The rest of us have to buy drugs for the experience. He quits taking drugs and gets it for free. Never known him to be dangerous, so at least there's that.

A fucked-up brain. Nothing earned, nothing deserved. Fate. One of those little complications, one of life's added knots.

She began pulling on the thread. The fiber was silky, strong, unusual. The word she wanted was synthetic. Whoever she'd once been, she sensed it was not a talker. Maybe she suffered now over the want of a word. She knew it couldn't be for the want of thread. It was always falling into her hands, wasn't it? Whoever she'd been, thread was there. She looked at her palms buried in great spools and tangles of red threads. Hands bloody with thread, thread trailing back like innards to the corpse still eager to offer them. Her fingers flexed and worked their way through the tangles, with little preference for anything else except Dana's thick, matted hair. Dana, her eyelids still in that rapid half-flutter of chased dreams, sweat pooling in the perfect hollow of her throat, moaned.

FOR WANT OF THREAD

Don't. . .don't. . .

She listened to mumbled pleas, old panics, and traumas no one ever outruns. You can't escape your life's knots. Wherever they occur, that is where they'll remain. There's no cut and mend. The scissors snip one time only, at the end.

"This is not my fault," she said.

She saw the hypodermic needle on the little folding table next to Dana's cot, propped atop the spoon. Clutching all the red thread to her breast with her left hand, she got up, leaned over, and pinched it up. How did one sew with this? She touched the base and, with a little wiggle, the needle came free of the barrel. How was the thread hooked and tied? She took the needle and punctured part of the sleeping bag, taking it in and out. She found the end of the unraveled thread and placed it to the end of the shaft, willing them to merge. Why didn't they? She brought them together again and again.

The flaps to the tent moved.

Dana, you up? I have to show you something. I've never seen anything like it.

She started to speak on Dana's behalf, but her voice came out too low, too shy, and Jason came in. They stared at each other. His brow creased, his eyes narrowed. His attention moved between Dana and the needle.

What are you doing? Is that her. . . ? Don't you know you can't just do that. . . ?

As he reached his hand forward, so did she, and he drew back, wringing his fingers in a close call. Had there been one? How did a needle threaten him?

Just put it down on the table. What the fuck is wrong with you? She'll get thrown out of here if they know she's using.

Jason opened and closed the scissors as he spoke, as if to cut up the words as he went.

When did she shoot up?

"I don't know."

Hours ago or just now?

"I think hours."

He gestured for her to surrender the needle. She put it on the little table and returned to the cot. Jason sat down beside her. He kept working the scissors, the blades noiseless. They once made sounds upon closing. Screams, cries. Sometimes a fit of laughter.

Where did you get these?

"I don't know."

You don't know?

"I just had them. I'd like them back."

I bet you would. I've made some discoveries.

She stared at him.

We've got something in common. I'm an Edgewood Arsenal baby. My dad had so much shit pumped through his veins to warp his DNA. The whole point was to speed evolution. Why wait around for humankind to drop its tail when science can just lop it off and keep it off?

Scissors open, scissors shut.

I hear the thoughts of everyone around me. That's my gift. You can say whatever you want, but I know what you're thinking. Voices bombard me. Sometimes it's too much. I never wish I hadn't been born. I wish my father hadn't been born. Then I'd have a different father. Different everything. It's a curse to be special and know everyone's got a Mason—Dixon line in them: one side talk, the other side thought, the two seldom in accord. Much of the time it's as you'd expect. They're saying nice things and thinking the ugly. But every so often the opposite is true. Once a stranger ambushed me and hurt me so bad. I was on the ground getting kicked, and he was standing over me shouting, "Mother fucker!" and "Die, you goddamn Jew!" But he was thinking, "I wish I didn't have to do this. I saw you from afar, and I fell in love with you. If only we could be together. You and I. Together." I didn't feel his kicks, but I cried over his pain.

Dana stirred, shifting on her cot, bringing her hands to her chest.

Oh. You. I thought I heard you.

You were having a good dream.

You shouldn't listen.

It's not eavesdropping when it's broadcasted. You and her, her and you. A good thing.

She saw Dana blush.

I wasn't dreaming about Chloe. I don't know what I was dreaming about. No, that's not true. I had the lawyer dream again.

I know you did. That's why I lied about you dreaming of Chloe. I knew the lawyer dream would embarrass you.

FOR WANT OF THREAD

Dana sat up. She moved like the substance of everything must be doubted, no real firmness anywhere. Swung her feet to the floor, tapping with her toes, her hands taloned around the edge of the cot, the limit of her nest.

Got something metal?

Dana blinked her eyes.

No. Well, yes. Here.

She handed him the spoon. Jason opened the scissors and placed the neck of the bowl between the blades.

The bowl fell between their feet.

What the fuck.

A statement, not a question.

Everything's paper. Even rock.

He reached into his coat pocket and pulled out two halves of a piece of river rock a little smaller than his fist.

No effort at all. Watch.

He took one of the halves and angled the open scissors to its middle. The quarter pieces fell on the floor next to the bowl of the spoon. Dana picked up all three, turning them over, looking for the trick.

Scissors just made rock its bitch.

Chloe, where the hell did you get these?

That's just what I came to ask. She needs to be isolated.

Isolated?

This is secret military shit, no question about it.

Calm down, Jason. Soldiers aren't going into battle with goddamn scissors.

These scissors are weapons-grade. Why would Chloe have them? Why was she wearing a sheet when we rescued her? Nothing adds up. She doesn't talk much, but I hear her thinking nonstop.

He stood up, the scissors open.

Dana got up and stood in front of him.

Nonstop thinking. Crazy shit. Satanic shit. She's worried.

Yeah? What's she worried about, Jason?

Her little super weapon fell into the wrong hands. There's maybe twenty people on Earth who'd recognize it for what it is because I'm a super weapon too, born and bred.

Why don't you put your dick between the blades and squeeze real hard. See which super weapon's strongest.

I want you to come to my tent, Dana. It's not safe in here with her. Who knows what else she might have?

Chloe had a sheet.

Where's it now?

Dumpster. How should I know?

I bet the sheet is the one thing the scissors can't cut. That would make sense. Goddamn, it's all making a lot of sense.

Nothing you're saying is making sense, Jason. You need to calm down.

I won't calm down.

Then you need to get the fuck out of here. You're upsetting Chloe.

She's not upset.

No? How do you know?

Because I hear her thoughts.

Christ. Get out, Jason. We'll talk more when you've settled down.

I'm taking the scissors.

They're not yours.

They're the property of the United States government, and when it comes right down to it, so am I. The scissors stay with me.

Dana didn't tell her why, but they folded their cots, set them aside, and put their sleeping bags on the floor. Then Dana put all her shirts, pants, socks, and underwear atop that.

Now take your clothes off and add them.

She did.

Dana guided her down onto the awkward pallet of softness.

So where did you get those scissors?

"I don't know. I just had them."

You really don't remember anything about your life?

"A face. Two faces. Sisters."

Your sisters?

"Two faces but the same face."

So twins?

"Three faces but the same face."

Dana leaned forward.

FOR WANT OF THREAD

Triplets. Hot damn. Chloe Cubed. I wouldn't know where to start.

"I don't think we're much alike."

Maybe they're evangelicals. Maybe that's why you ran off. They're bigots.

"People can't help what they believe."

That's not true. That's never true. Don't say that. In fact, just quit talking. You're better when you're quiet. Beautiful and quiet. Just let me maneuver. All this talk of scissors has me hot and bothered.

She let Dana move her legs. Thigh on thigh. Then. . .then—

"We're one!"

I love how sensitive you are. But shhh. The walls aren't walls, right? Just relax into me. I'm feeling really comfortable with you. I trust you. Ever get a feeling like all the bad things in your life are there to lead you to one good thing? That there's a purpose to misery? You know?

"I don't think—"

Chloe, sometimes you should just nod and pretend.

Mid-afternoons were her favorite time because they went to the park or walked downtown. Sometimes Dana and herself, sometimes in the company of Chris-cat and Philly Freedom. A few times the whole camp's population, all forty people, seemed to stroll with them. Jason was gone. The scissors were gone too.

Philly Freedom said his brother came and talked him into leaving. Dana frowned.

He should have left the scissors.

The magic scissors?

You see them in action?

Hell yeah, I did. I watched him snip a triangle of concrete right out of the curb.

Shit.

They no longer asked about her relationship to the scissors. The scissors now had a life and mythology of their own, like something that fell among them from out of the sky. Strange artifacts, strange visitations, and visions, all the power of myth in a pair of scissors. Her role in that story faded to make room for character development in the new tale of Dana and Chloe. They held hands as they walked down the street, but no one protested or commented. No one noticed.

You think we'll see him again?

I've known him three years now. Longest stretch of sanity was five months.

Guess we're the Two Splooges until he comes back.

They all laughed. So much laughter. Philly Freedom's always ended in a hacking cough that went on and on until everyone stood in awkward silence. He'd been dying for some time. Lung cancer. Everyone knew, but when he coughed, Dana or someone else always pounded him on the back like they meant to help him clear his throat. He could run short distances and exert himself in various ways, like saving women from alleyway rapists. But laughing had a peculiar way of bringing his infirmities to the fore.

It's a really weird thing. The morning we found Chloe, I woke up certain I was dying. My heart was going so fast, I couldn't get any air. The Marlborough Man had come to claim my soul. I was preparing to go to the light the moment I saw it. Then, all of a sudden, I felt fine. Fine's not the best word for it. Hell, I don't know what I feel half the time. But I'm sure I should be dead. I mean I should have died.

Philly Freedom confessed this while he and Dana passed a vape pen back and forth. They all sat bored and tired in a somewhat cleaner city park. On this particular day, they'd been on a required mission of community service, issued a shopping cart they were to fill with litter. They might be homeless but not worthless. Trash picking up trash. The cart was full of cardboard, moldy newspapers and yellowed receipts, crushed aluminum cans, fast food wrappers, and six-pack yokes, the kind always ensnaring birds and sea turtles.

She listened to Philly's story with great interest, really leaning into it. No one laughed at the end. Strange things happened in the world, and stranger things happened in the streets. Like an amnesiac dyke showing up in nothing but a sheet, armed with magic scissors. Dana said this as she put her left arm around Chloe's shoulder and drew her head down to kiss the top of it. She liked the shelter of Dana's floral arm.

Do I get a spot on your skin, Dee?

FOR WANT OF THREAD

Like you need to ask.

I want more than a name and a date. I want my face on your right tit.

Dana jerked her right hand around the back of his neck and rubbed his nose in her cleavage.

Just like a silly putty transfer, you dirty old man. Filthy Philly Freedom.

Everyone laughed until Philly Freedom started coughing.

But he's not going to die, she thought, her certainty incomprehensible but no less sure.

They stayed in their park until almost dusk and headed back as a group, eight or nine people in all. Walking together like that made them all feel like it was their world and everyone else just lived in it.

Then the man fell out of the sky in front of them, a horrific split of skin, broken bones protruding through meat, teeth everywhere you looked. Dana screamed. Lots of people did, just about everyone who didn't have both hands over their mouths. Crowds gathered. So many different existences and realities exist beside each other like the flags of separate countries sharing the same pole. Moments of graphic brutality plait them. No equality can surpass what's found among sudden witnesses to atrocity.

She tried to comfort Dana, to move her away. Dana and a few others now directed their attention to the seventh story of the building to their right and the open window. A woman leaning her head from the window was shouting.

He jumped! I tried to stop him, but he wouldn't listen! He kept saying he couldn't die!

Within minutes, the woman was outside saying the same thing to anyone who'd listen. Few were. Why bother with words when a picture paints thousands of them? The crowd this dusk stood gifted with *Guernica* and *The Scream* and *Saturn Devouring His Son.* All the world's art in a suicide.

But not one. Not a successful one, at any rate. To the surprise of all, the paramedics said the man was alive.

His heart's only sort of in his chest.

He must be brain dead at least.

The crowd's skepticism grew. They became art critics finding flaws in the work that first mesmerized them. Then, from the not-corpse, from the concrete canvas—

Told you, Stacy. Told you. Slit my wrist and didn't bleed out. Now this. I'm immortal.

They gathered him and his fragments and put them into the ambulance and drove away. Dana stared at Philly Freedom.

Looks like your condition is spreading. We're having an outbreak of immortality in these parts.

Jesus.

He walked on. So did everyone, leaving them alone with the shopping cart. Dana turned to her.

That was something. You okay?

"I don't know."

Thanks for the definitive. Let's go back to the tent. I need some downtime after all that.

Dana seldom sounded like she needed care, but tonight proved different. They undressed. Dana tied the piece of hose around her arm again.

You don't mind, do you?

She shook her head.

I never thought I could find a replacement in my life for heroin. But I look at you and have dreams.

"Dreams?"

Of us. Together. Somewhere else. What do you think?

"I think that's all I've ever wanted."

Dreams are the only thing that keep sleeping from being like death.

She watched the routine. A new spoon had been acquired. A new needle as well. Dana sewed the drug into herself and gave the warmest, slowest smile and sank onto the pallet. They pressed their naked flesh together in the pocket of her sleeping bag. Face to face in the darkness, they looked into each other's unseen eyes.

I'm really sorry, Chloe.

"About what?"

Everything. Being weak. I'm going to get off of it. Maybe I'll get a law degree. Become an advocate. I can do anything with you. You're my drug now.

"As you are mine."

Hardness edged Dana's laughter.

You come across as the very last person in the world to do drugs.

"I'm not sure they'd work on me."

FOR WANT OF THREAD

Trust me, they work on everyone.

The desire to dispute Dana was very strong. She wanted to say drugs could not work on people unless they were destined to take them. Her mind clouded with conflicting images. She saw a skein of red yarn threatened by golden scissors. She saw the jumper's body strewn all over a cosmic loom. She saw a thread vibrating as if plucked, vibrating from coughing fits that ended everyone's laughter.

"I think I did something I shouldn't have."

You're tripping. I sure as hell am. Good night.

"I stole something."

No judgment here. I'm fading out. Kiss me into unconsciousness.

And so she did. The night deepened. Dana slept, leaving her with a curious sense of abandonment. Her life would not resume until Dana's eyes opened again. No one knew, because no one could, but she hadn't slept once her entire time at the camp. If sleep is an imitation of death, what is an imitation of sleep? Closing one's eyes? She understood sleep was meant to be restorative. What restored her?

She left the sleeping bag, fighting out of it with little stealth. Dana was beyond the reach of casual interruption. She sat in the dark, considering what she might do. Her fingers weaved through each other. They knew the answer. Their work was her leisure, her rest.

They rose from her lap and seemed to lift her whole body. She stood, walked out of the tent, and went to the shopping cart. She watched herself plunder it. The loot was brought into the tent, and she sat in the dark, eyes shut, fingers folding, pressing, twisting, slitting, weaving. She forgot everything as she worked. Understanding she had something to forget made her realize she was not amnesiac at all. There was a willful curtain between what she knew and what she pretended not to know. This curtain had to be maintained. It allowed her situation here to continue. She understood this only by forgetting it was a fact. When her fingers finished, she remembered the curtain. It reinforced her will to keep it closed and therefore left her less of her true self than ever.

Jesus Christ. What's all this? Where did it come from?

Dana blinked and rubbed her eyes at the assortment of baskets, bowls, welcome mats, wind chimes, potholders, and jewelry stacked around her

Who gave us these, Chloe? Oh my God, they're beautiful.

"I made them."

What?

"I made them last night. From what we collected."

Dana staggered up, wobbled out of the tent. She sat where she'd been sitting for the last few hours, the last finished basket on her knees. She smiled when Dana returned. Dana did not smile back.

The cart's almost empty.

Dana looked at all the creations. Her lips moved like she was counting. Not the new works of art but all the little things that went into making them. Reconciling the cart's emptiness with this transubstantiation.

That's fucking crazy. Was I knocked out for a week?

"No."

Well, you didn't do all this in one night! I don't want to hear it!

"Why are you mad?"

I'm not mad, I'm. . .freaked.

They sat in silence while Dana picked up one object and then another. She shook her head.

I don't even see how you managed to. . .how is any of this shit staying together? If it's glue, hand it over. I want to huff the shit out of it.

Dana went and got Chris-cat and Philly Freedom to offer their perspective. Chris-cat whistled.

I know six stores that will buy every piece right now. This stuff is the new trend. Upcycling.

More like up-yours cycling.

I'm serious, Dana. If upcycling wasn't already a thing, all of this would make *it one. Chloe, you're amazing.*

Hell yeah, she is. That's why I fell in love with her. The Leonardo da Vinci of upcycling.

Chris-cat led them to the first store, Junxploits, with Dana pushing the shopping cart of *art, pure art.* That's what the Junxploits owner called the collection. He bought the whole collection of *art, pure art* for three hundred dollars. Dana put the money into her hand. She noticed Chris-cat and Philly Freedom staring at the cash. Dana noticed it too.

We good, guys?

I found all those newspapers.
I found those Taco Bell wrappers.
Okay. What's your point?
Like you don't know.

Dana made a little motion with her fingers and handed over the money. Then she sifted through the bills and passed some over to the two men.

Good?
Good.
Chloe, want us to get you some more junk? We mine the coal, you make the diamonds.

"I'd like that."

Dana moved in front of her.

You get five percent each.
That's bullshit.
Hey, Cat, anyone can find trash. It isn't hard work.
It was my idea to sell it in the first place. The shit would still be sitting in your tent without my vision.
Thank you for your vision. It's ours now.
You're kind of a cunt, Dee.
I am when it comes to protecting my girl. Here's the cart. Come back when it's full.

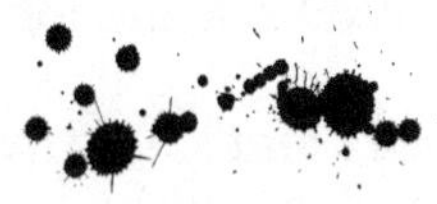

You don't mind, do you?

"I don't mind."

I just want one more score. Then I quit. But I can't quit until I've done it one last time. There's got to be a last time, right? And we've got all this money.

Dana led her to the place where some of *all this money* was exchanged for a baggie of brown powder. Another alleyway where several men stood loitering around a figure named Bairstow. Little said, lots of looks. Who is this chick they've never seen before? Why's she with Dee? What's the deal? Oh, *that's* the deal. Pure rich white girl dyking out with a mixed-race junkie. A bar of soap in dry, dirty hands. Just add spit. One man had a rat on his shoulder. He offered her a chance to pet it, leaning his shoulder toward her. The rat enjoyed her attention until it didn't. Dana took her home.

Alone together back in the tent, Dana began tapping the powder into the spoon.

Bairstow's shit isn't good even for street grade, but it's what I have to work with. I'm sorry, Chloe, but I really need it. Things have been so nuts around here.

"There's a last time for everything."

That's right. A last time. Or next-to-last time. I sort of bought more than I meant. Can't use it all tonight.

She watched Dana work. The preparation never failed to fascinate. The complicated simpleness of it. The line of rubber hose. The needle. The invisible thread sewn into the flesh. This she understood. The understanding made her tremble.

You okay? Hell, you want to shoot up? Make you feel great. I'm just kidding.

"There's a first time for everything."

Not for you and heroin. Not happening. Besides, you've got me. We're each other's drugs, or we will be once I've quit this shit. Really soon, you know? This feels like it was meant to be. You and me. I've been thinking. The amount we made today for your art. . .and you did it all in one night. We can go into business. Online or a store like that guy has. We'll get out of here. Have a home.

She stood up and paced back and forth. Heel-to-toe or cross-ankled.

What's wrong? Doesn't that sound like a good idea? Chloe?

A good idea, a great idea. But impossible. Why impossible? Wasn't she here to make the impossible possible? Isn't that what she'd been doing all this time?

Hey. Come here. Hold my hand so I don't screw up. Then we'll really talk.

She nodded. Dana brought the needle tip to her skin.

What's that?

Commotion outside their tent. Lots of shouting and swearing. They looked at each other. Dana put the needle down. Untied herself. They hurried outside.

Jason stood there calling the camp population around him. He had both hands raised high. The right hand held the scissors, the index finger of his left hand reduced to a stubbed wad of gauze.

Everyone! Everyone! I've come to let the cat out of the bag. No more secrets! The government can't keep you under its thumb forever, and now we have the power to fight back! The revolution starts here! I am your Prometheus, and here—HERE—is the stolen fire!

"Prometheus."

Dana asked who that was.

Not everyone came out of their tents. Not everyone was even around. Some additional people came out of the church. Cell phones to ears.

Shut up, Jason, or you're going to get us all thrown out of here.

We're not getting thrown out of anywhere. I have the power to stop the world.

You got the power to trim my beard, asshole? I've got a job interview next year.

The man who asked stepped in front of Jason, all smiles, head jutted forward, chin up and out.

Don't take too much. Just an inch.

Everyone laughed. That's what they always do. That's what they were always going to do, just as they were always going to be standing here. Jason opened the scissors wide.

"Oh, no."

Dana screamed first. Screamed only. The others stood astonished, their thoughts almost written above their heads. *Magic show. Fake. WTF?*

The decapitated body standing in place, the head on the ground looking up.

I ain't dead I ain't dead I ain't dead

Jason took it in the four good fingers of his left hand. Everyone stayed still and hushed, their thoughts unchanged. *Fake. Theater. Magic show. Possibility.* Even Dana stood quiet, hands over her mouth, waiting for Jason's pronouncement.

I give you immortality. Death by scissors grants eternal life by scissors. I have bared my own finger to the scissors. This is the secret the government protects. They've all done it. They killed themselves with these scissors, and now they live forever.

Faith or skepticism, madness or sanity, the quality and quantity of all vested in the womb, unearned. Not grown or nurtured, not overcome, not lost or gained by experiences of personal tragedy. All such notions of self-determination are mere illusions, food for the poets. They should not be. She knew that.

Had argued that. Memories of the argument existed behind the curtain that kept her from her memories. The curtain needed to be torn down now. It needed to fall as the heads were falling, without ceremony.

She tried. She was sure she tried. When she'd weaved the pieces of trash last night and lost herself in the weaving, she thought the curtain was an act and construction of will. Why couldn't will defeat it now? *Fall*, she thought. *Fall and let what happens happen. Let happen what I was here to keep from happening.*

She didn't know what that was. She had a suspicion. The fall of the curtain would confirm it. She feared the confirmation. Did fear keep the curtain in place? Was the curtain always an act of fear rather than will?

Almost dazed, she wandered through the chaos of roaming bodies, some with their heads still intact. She entered the tent and took the rubber hose, knotting it around her left arm with magnificent ease. Those same dexterous fingers took up the waiting needle.

Chloe, you in here? We have to get out of here, girl. I don't know what the fuck is going on, but. . .Chloe? Oh, Jesus. What are you doing? What have you done?

She felt the drug moving through her like some alien thread. She was on the floor, Dana crying over her.

You don't even know how. You don't even know how. Oh God.

She reached up to two things at once. Her face. The curtain. Grasping fingers found her face. Found the curtain. Caressed. Pulled. Both fell atop her. The cosmos split open in the instant. She saw the tent as thousands upon thousands of individual threads. She saw through the fibers to the sky. Or no, she did not see through the fabric. The tent itself was torn open as Jason plunged the scissors down and sheared himself an opening. *Here's Johnny!* Beyond his face, in the square opening, she beheld skeins of clouds against the great loom of heaven, inactive, cold like a paused tapestry. A work abandoned. All of history there in infinite detail, every thread a life.

Beyond the loom, two identical faces with glaring eyes.

"Sisters, we see each other again at last. I am done hiding."

Dana, get away from her.

Jason, for the love of God, do something. She's going to overdose.

FOR WANT OF THREAD

Is she? Do you think she can die? She has the scissors of immortality.

You've got them.

So I do. Let me kill you both so you may live forever.

Stay away from us, Jason!

Dana cradled her head and went on shouting at him. She now experienced Dana's body as a tapestry, dirty, tattered in places but still the most beautiful ever made. The most beautiful she ever made. Where Jason had stood, she now witnessed a tall, strained tapestry on the verge of flying apart. Then he was flesh again, cutting out his path to reach them. Two faces appeared behind him. He seemed not to notice even though they looked over his left and right shoulder. Their hard stares had not softened with proximity.

"Sister Atropos. Sister Lachesis."

"Sister Clotho, we have come."

Yes, the curtain has fallen.

Now Jason turned. A panicked motion, the scissors swinging. What did he perceive? Two women? A sudden breath on the nape of his neck? A gusting breeze? Atropos caught his wrist, squeezed until his fingers opened. Reclaimed her scissors. Exulted in having her birthright restored.

"So many threads to cut. Your theft was foolish, Clotho."

Atropos lifted a single strand of hair from the top of Jason's head and snipped. He crumpled at once and landed on the tent floor. He became a tapestry again, a grim and sad piece, so full of knots and tangles. Looking at it robbed her of speech. Sister Atropos was not tongue-tied.

"Thread you were, to thread you return. I have much work to do."

She watched Atropos as much as she could through the hole Jason had made. Her sister collected severed heads whose eyes had gone on seeing, brains thinking. On each she plucked up a single strand of hair, and a simple snip resolved their fates.

She looked down at Dana. Sometimes she was a body, sometimes a tapestry. When she was a body, she lay on her back. Her eyes shifted back and forth. Her throat bobbed but she made no sound.

Lachesis knelt beside her. "This is the one who caused your rebellion?"

She nodded.

"I guess I'll never understand. Why her?"

"I wove her perfectly. Of all the billions, her thread called to me even as I shaped it."

"You wove her for yourself?"

"No—*no*. I wove her for herself. And then you ruined it."

"I added the knots. Made the rips and tears."

"You determined her."

"All are determined, Clotho."

"It isn't right."

"Dear sister," Lachesis said, not without tenderness. "How can an artisan so misunderstand her own work? You confuse perfection with lack of blemish. My knots and tangles give each of your creations a beauty you cannot see."

Atropos returned.

"I have blurred myself across the world, in homes and hospitals, on streets, on farmland, on boats at sea. The work is denied no longer. All threads, due and overdue their cutting, are cut. Save one."

"Our sister Clotho still resists."

"Let her."

"She does not understand."

"If eternity hasn't brought comprehension, nothing will."

Atropos moved toward Dana. "Let me see her hair."

"Never!"

"You've sheltered her thread from me for far too long."

"I will never stop."

She looked down at Dana, caressed her face, wondering at her thoughts. It seemed Dana might somehow understand. Her eyes brimmed. Not the eyes of one looking upon her lover. Rather the eyes of one looking upon her mother.

Dana became a bunched tapestry in her hand, the events of her life flowing in pictograms interrupted by ugly knots and tangles forced into the weave by other hands.

"All the pain you gave her, Lachesis. She deserved so much better."

"I will never convince you, Clotho. Atropos is right. If you don't understand now, you never will."

The tapestry ended in a single loose thread. Atropos stooped to cut it even as Clotho tried to yank it out of her reach. Their fingernails dug into the end of Dana's life, the final image from a week earlier. The rubber hose, the brown powder. The fire under the spoon. The needle that proffered the offering. The offering to the goddess of self that killed the goddess.

She could not stop Atropos from making the cut. The dangling last strand of thread fell away from the tapestry. The tapestry itself seemed to grow cold, turn gray.

"Now it is done. Come, Clotho. We must resume our task."

She cursed them and pulled the needle from her arm. She broke it away from the barrel and waved her left hand. The tent fell apart around them, reduced to millions of single threads. She called them to join together and she called them to the needle, joining them there in a seamless unity. She took up the end of Dana's tapestry and sewed. New life flowed; new moments arose. Lachesis bent near, trying to disrupt the pattern, but Clotho fought her off. Her sister stood watching. Hint of regret. Hint of understanding.

Atropos, however, would not be denied. The more Clotho sewed, the more her sister attacked with the scissors. The tapestry grew and shrank, grew and shrank, the adding and subtracting hands working with equal speed and determination. The thread diminished. She ripped her hair out and bonded it to the needle. Anything to feed the tapestry.

"Sister," Lachesis said. "*Please.*"

She knew she could not continue. Atropos would never stop, and her job was simple. An idea came to her. She thought of Callisto, eternal in the heavens. She could not raise someone to the stars. But there might be safety for Dana after all.

She shoved a wad of the tapestry into her mouth and swallowed. Kept swallowing, kept stuffing. Never chewing. Swallowing as she sewed. Even Atropos was stunned, the scissors hanging impotent at her side. Lachesis cried. She swallowed. The fabric went down. Dana inside her. Protected. Warm.

Eternal.

"What have you done, Clotho?"

"We are one."

"We three are one," Lachesis said. "There can be no fourth."

"Dana is inside me now. I will keep her there forever in the skein of my being. The lives I weave going forward will bear her spirit. Their fibers will make or solve their own knots and tangles. This is how it always should have been. I'm sorry, sister."

"Am I to have no purpose?" Lachesis said.

"The idea of fate has left you blind. Purpose should be discovered, not accepted."

They joined hands and looked at Atropos. She held up the scissors. She opened and closed them.

"I will never change," she said. "I will never stay my hand, nor will I ever act before it's time. But I *will* make my cuts."

"Nor will you suffer from want of threads," she said.

She touched her stomach and felt Dana there.

Come, she thought. Let me teach you how to weave.

MOM

  THEY WERE ALL *about the same age, pretty young, but she considered her neighbors to be a bunch of listless, narrow-minded old poops. Each acted like the universe revolved around them, and no one engaged too much. It wasn't a great neighborhood, but she'd grown up there and wanted to make a go of things, make it better, leave her mark. And the best way to do that, she decided, was having children.*

It was a wish nurtured from the days of her girlhood. First, she had pet rocks, and then she moved on to plants and bugs before her interest turned to animals. Pets made good practice for motherhood, and she worked hard to protect and look after them. Mistakes nevertheless happened, and the results could be chilling. She hated making them, but the errors helped her become a better mom. Anyone could see that. The problem was that all her neighbors noticed these accidents, and their judgment proved immediate and harsh.

—What she's doing is so cruel.

—Complete waste of time.

—Look, honey, if you're going to do something like that, do it right. You can't be so absent-minded. It's disgusting.

In the end, she knew the problem was the neighborhood itself. She'd been there all her life, and they all hated her. The old poops. So, she moved. It took a while, but she found a different place that was just perfect. The new neighbors seemed interesting. There was the sun worshipper who liked to bake all day and a gal with dreamy clouds in her eyes. A guy who was red in the face and another with a big ugly birthmark she tried not to notice. She felt she could get along with everyone except the three ice queens at the end of the block, but after her last experience, she didn't mind being ignored.

SEAN EADS AND JOSHUA VIOLA

New neighborhood, new start. Clean face, clean record. Two neighbors even said they wouldn't mind having children too but were very frank about their sterility. It surprised her when they objected the loudest to her plans. Then she realized that since they couldn't have children, they didn't want anyone else doing it either. That seemed to be the attitude of the entire neighborhood. No kids wanted. Not in their backyards.

But she'd show these new old poops.

And she did.

Earth took up all seven windows in *Hanno*'s observation deck, and Captain Jeremiah Miller found three of his four-member crew clustered in a corner while the six members of the *cargo* groped each other and made out in front of the center pane. Three men, three women, none older than twenty-five. Though he considered it unprofessional, Miller had taken to using the nicknames his second officer, Lieutenant Manzanares, had given the men. Andrew Wellington was *Randy Andy;* Yukito Kimura was *Mr. Drippy*; and Gerhard Nichter was *Get Hard Quicker*. The women—Delphine Adisa, Cosima Minucci, and Becca Reed—hadn't been given nicknames except for *Whore 1, Whore 2,* and *Whore 3*. Miller chalked up this aggressive resentment to the lieutenant's suppressed homosexuality, made clear in his psychological profile.

The final crew member, Dr. Amma Clarion, announced her presence at Miller's back, and he stepped aside to let her into the room. The ship's medical officer carried a tray of chilled champagne and six glasses. "Courtesy of Mission Command," she said, approaching the *cargo*, who hooted and hollered as they gathered around her. They took up the glasses, and Dr. Clarion started to pour.

"Here's to success for each of you and the task ahead," she said. "The future of humanity may be in your hands."

"More like in our glands," Mr. Drippy said, and his male counterparts just about fell into each other as they laughed. Captain Miller side-eyed his crew—Manzanares, Bettes, and Pizer—and found them stewing.

"So do we start fucking here and now?" Randy Andy said.

Get Hard smirked, hooked his right arm around the shoulder of his assignment, and kissed her cheek. "Does Earth get you horny?"

"I don't know, does *this* get Earth horny?" Randy Andy shoved both his pants and his underwear to his ankles, pressed his ass against the glass, and bent forward to give the homeworld a little wink.

Manzanares stepped forward, grabbed Randy Andy by the shoulder, and forced him away. He shuffled into the waiting arms of his assignment, and they fell on the floor and started laughing as they began making out.

"You don't get it, do you, soldier boy? We're all that matters. We're the stars here, not you."

Miller and Clarion intercepted Manzanares before he could respond to the goading. *Hanno*'s command crew had been together for more than two years of training, and Miller had never seen his first officer lose his composure.

"Manz," he said as Doctor Clarion added in a low voice. "You could be court-martialed if you were to harm any of them, Lieutenant. Remember *CHCB*."

Manzanares closed his eyes for a moment and nodded. "CHCB," he said. "I still can't stand it, sir. Is this ship called *Hanno* or *Whorehouse*?"

"You knew the mission well in advance, Lieutenant."

"Nothing says they have to rub it in our faces."

Miller shrugged. "I wish I had a solution for you."

"I have one for myself, Captain," Manzanares said, causing Miller to lift his eyebrows. "Permission to enter suspended animation now."

Bettes and Pizer said, "Us too, sir."

Miller met each of their gazes. "Protocol says SA systems aren't to be engaged until we pass Mars. You can't wait fourteen days?"

"Have mercy, Captain," Bettes said. "All of the ship's operations went automated once we left Earth's orbit. Short of a catastrophe, I don't see what our role is except to watch the *cargo* fuck around and insult us."

"The mission's more than that. Think of them as soldiers."

Manzanares laughed.

Pizer was more diplomatic. "Sure, Captain, in a sense. In the big picture. The problem is, we're having to sit through the gritty details, and meanwhile, we're supposed to keep our hands to ourselves."

They looked behind them. All three couples were now screwing right on the metal floor, with Dr. Clarion standing off to the side, observing with the champagne bottle in her right hand. She took a casual swig and smiled at Miller.

"We're off to a vigorous start, Captain."

Soldiers in their first battle, Miller thought.

He sighed and regarded his bridge crew. "Permission granted to sleep away the next thirteen months of your lives. Short of a disaster, I'll leave you in suspended animation until we're three-quarters of the way back to Earth. With any luck, you'll wake up to a ship with at least three new crew members."

Pale blue dot.

Earth was still too large to be called a dot, but after a week they were one hundred twenty-one million kilometers away, and the planet was less than the size of Miller's fist as he held it up to the center pane. Up close, Earth was nothing but shades of silver and slate and flashes of taupe. No trace of the blue and white marble captured in so many photos and videos. Earth from space looked more like the face of an old gray lady with the blackness of the universe gathered about her shoulders like a shawl. It felt and looked like an old and dying world.

The homeworld seemed to have more of its traditional color from this distance, and thinking of Earth as it had been in pictures from centuries ago added to Miller's immediate melancholy. He did not have time to indulge it further, though, as yet again the *cargo* came running in for more theatrics. The three couples were naked and giggling, playing a game they no doubt called *Humiliate the Captain.*

He'd almost pulled a Manzanares an hour ago, when he found Get Hard having sex with his assignment on the bridge. Miller started toward them, damn near ready to haul them off to the airlock, when the couple flashed him the most arrogant look of unconcern. And they were right. The mission parameters empowered them to have sex almost anywhere they chose.

Even in his command chair.

Now that all three couples were here, Miller knew he was being taunted and stalked, and his anger started to rise again. He could almost hear Dr. Clarion giving him a warning reminder.

CHCB.

The Cargo Has Carte Blanche.

He thought of his crew nice and snug in their suspended animation pods and grew jealous. Watching the virile young bucks press their sumptuous assignments up against the windows and start grinding, he had to admit he was jealous of many things.

"You all do have assigned quarters for this," he said, though not very loud, and his tone came across as helpless and tired.

Dr. Clarion entered, carrying a computer tablet and a cup of coffee. She smiled at Miller and came to stand beside him.

"I didn't expect to find you here getting an eyeful."

"I was trying to escape them."

He liked the doctor's smile. At 40, she was a decade younger than him, and her dark hair hadn't a trace of gray. His own hair used to be black, but now it looked like Earth from space.

Clarion sipped her coffee and watched the pairings go at it. She sometimes consulted her computer, which Miller saw had live data on each individual: body temperature, blood pressure, an array of fluctuating hormone levels.

"How are they doing?"

"Oh," she said, "I think they're doing just fine. Of course, no one is pregnant yet."

"Do those readings indicate what might be wrong?"

She put the computer aside. "If you're asking me, the women don't want it bad enough."

"*What?*"

"They don't really want to be mothers," she said, and Miller thought she was making another of her deadpan jokes. Then he realized she was very serious.

"Isn't that like some ancient judge telling a raped woman they must have enjoyed it because they got pregnant?"

Her stare was as icy as space itself. "I'm telling you they're here for the excitement, not the mission."

"What about the men? They're not exactly the model of—"

"The men are here as breeding studs, Captain. The only

personality trait required is willingness, and they've got plenty of that. It's more complex on the woman's side."

"I see," Miller said. "I didn't realize emotions could be such a crucial factor in fertilization."

"Maybe it didn't use to be but now, for some reason, it *is*."

A month later, as Hanno neared Jupiter, Captain Miller noted a distinct dispiritedness taking over the cargo. Randy Andy, Mr. Drippy, and Get Hard had taken to hanging out by themselves in the observation deck, playing cards and making bitter complaints about the women and their failure to conceive. Captain Miller sat in his command chair on the bridge, bored into eavesdropping on their conversation through the speaker system.

"They made a big mistake with that bitch. She's got bad eggs."

"Same with Becca. I know I'm potent. I wouldn't be here if I wasn't verified stud material. She and I have fucked a lot. There's no way I'm the reason she's not pregnant."

If the mission stakes weren't so high, Miller could have indulged in a bit of schadenfreude over their emotional state. Maybe he *did* indulge, just a little.

"Hey Amma, how far are we from Earth now?"

Miller sat up straighter. He hadn't realized Dr. Clarion was on the observation deck. Why would she be if the women weren't there too?

"Seven hundred million kilometers, give or take."

"You think the radiation can reach us all the way out here?"

"Space is full of radiation."

"But what about the stuff that's causing us all the problems?"

"Thorium 236. No, it shouldn't be reaching us out here. It shouldn't be reaching us even in Earth orbit, for that matter. Going all the way to the Kuiper Belt is what we scientists call an abundance of caution. Or overkill. Now I've come to tell you the bad news. You drew the short straw, Yukito. You're up first in the Box. Cosima is already waiting for you."

Mr. Drippy made a passionate plea while Randy Andy, and Get Hard laughed at him.

"See you in a month, man."

MOM

"The Box. More like the Hole. A month in isolation? Forget it, Doctor!"

"That's not an option. Since conception hasn't happened thirty days into the trip, one couple has to spend the next thirty in the same Thorium 236-shielded room we have on Earth. You can't leave it, but all you have to do for the next thirty days is eat, drink, breathe, and have sex as much as possible, until Cosima gets pregnant."

"What if she doesn't?"

"Didn't you read the mission parameters, Yukito? Failure means you both go out the airlock."

Captain Miller went to the medical bay the next day and found Dr. Clarion at her desk, giving a dazed stare at the monitor. She didn't seem to realize his presence, and as Miller came forward, he heard sounds of passion and despair in equal measure.

"What the hell?" he said.

Clarion motioned him over, and he was a little shocked to realize the doctor was watching Mr. Drippy and his assignment going at it in the Box.

"Is your degree in voyeurism?"

"Scientific observation was never more tedious," Clarion said, gesturing to a secondary screen on her right. Two sets of bioanalytics were displayed there, a rainbow of charts and telemetry. "Everything is looking as perfect as can be. We have a man and woman in their sexual prime, each among the most genetically superior subjects Earth has to offer. And they're going at it as often as they can in a controlled environment—"

"I'm close, Cosima. I'm so close, baby."

"Yes, Yukito, God yes."

Clarion leaned toward the larger monitor and tapped on her keyboard.

"They're both reaching climax."

"So I gathered."

"Cosima is in her twelfth day of ovulation. Scans show an egg in her fallopian tube. Conditions could not be more perfect."

His orgasm happened a moment later, and Clarion swung into

motion, inputting several commands. "Now for the real show," she said as the larger monitor changed to show a pulsating canal of dense fibromuscular tissue. All members of the cargo had microscopic cameras implanted throughout their bodies, allowing a live cellular view whenever Clarion called for it. Just now an uncountable number of sperm were bullying and thrashing their way into view. The footage was silent, but Miller had no problem imagining the sound of spawning salmon.

"Come on, come on," the doctor said, whispering as she leaned further toward the screen. Miller looked between her and the monitor, which now shifted to a different camera. Mr. Drippy's sperm cells came into view like a herd of wild stallions appearing around a bend and thundering through a canyon. The furious thrashing of their axial filaments battered the camera lens.

"So far, so good?" Miller said.

"Yes, I think. No—wait. *Wait.*"

Clarion made a fist and hit the table. Miller didn't need her to explain. Many of the sperm were deteriorating, their tails crumbling and breaking into pieces, leaving the heads to tumble and crash into the uterine wall like asteroids pelting the face of the moon. Again Miller found himself imagining the sound of impact despite the mute footage.

"Report," he said.

"I'd put the losses at thirty percent. *Ninety seconds* after ejaculation, and a third of the sperm has failed. That's almost equal to what a couple would experience trying to conceive on Earth's surface without any protection from Thorium 236. The protected environment in a Conceiving Room has been shown to boost natural conception up to sixty percent, and that's on a planet otherwise saturated with the radiation. They shouldn't even need it out here."

Clarion toggled to another camera. About one hundred sperm kept trudging toward the waiting egg, which looked unblemished in the captain's estimation.

"It's a horse race now," Miller said, embracing his own rising urgency. He may not like any of the *cargo* for their entitled attitude, but as he watched more sperm fall away, leaving just a few on final approach to the egg, the captain had to cheer. He was rooting for the future of humanity.

That future collapsed in front of him. One lone sperm cell

reached the egg, and its fragile head shattered on impact, sending the nucleus ricocheting away like so much refuse. The egg remained like a dead planet moving through space, with no further purpose to its brief existence.

"I think it's going to happen this time, Yukio. I just feel it."

Clarion shifted back to the Box camera, which showed Mr. Drippy and Cosima holding each other while they recovered. Her head rested on his chest while he was staring at the ceiling and, perhaps, at the universe beyond its walls.

"Do we tell them to recharge for another round? How long will the egg be in prime position?"

Silence as deep and vast as space itself had settled over the room.

"Dr. Clarion, did you hear me?"

When she answered with a small sob, the sound seemed as amplified as a supernova, jolting Miller into putting one hand on her shoulder.

"Amma?"

She replied with silent tears.

Seventy-five days into the mission, and Captain Miller watched Saturn dwindling behind them in the observation deck windows. Behind him, the cargo stood in a dispirited mood as Dr. Clarion told Randy Andy and his assignment that it was now their turn in the Box. All three couples were grumbling and sniping at each other now. *Hanno* was pregnant with acrimony.

"The mission will never succeed with that mindset," Clarion said. "Try to stay calm. It's still about nine months to the Kuiper belt, and then another eleven months back to Earth. Plenty of time to conceive—"

"I want out," Mr. Drippy said.

Miller turned around. "Out? What do you think that means? We're in deep space."

"Put me in suspended animation like the rest of the crew."

"Failure to participate means—"

"I'm not saying I won't participate anymore. Put me in suspended animation, and let me store up some good-quality sperm. Maybe then I won't be shooting blanks."

Dr. Clarion said, "You can stop with this performative bitterness," when Miller decided to cut her off.

"Done," he said. "Delphine, do you want to join him? Rest up for a couple of months?"

She nodded.

Get Hard and Cosima said they'd like to as well.

"Fine," the captain said. "Dr. Clarion will see to it."

"The hell I will."

"What about us?" Randy Andy said. "We could use a break."

Miller shook his head. "You and Becca are due for one month in the Box as part of the controlled experiment. After that, you're both welcome to a turn in suspended animation. The rest of you can go get ready."

As the three couples left, Clarion stepped in front of him. "Are you out of your mind? We can't have two-thirds of the cargo sleeping away the trip."

"They need a break. You can see they're cracking under the stress. Maybe all of us are, whether or not we want to admit it."

It was the closest he'd come to even alluding to her crying. Miller could tell that's just how she took it, and the doctor turned and left without another word. He watched her go and then pivoted back to stare at Saturn.

Even if we fail, it's not the end of humanity, he thought. Since the sudden emanation of Thorium 236 radiation from within the Earth's mantle and its increasing saturation over the last century, no solution was considered too improbable to try. In another fifty years, construction would be complete on the shielded artificial insemination chambers that were projected to generate one hundred sixty million new births a year. Many argued this solution alone was so satisfactory no other option needed to be tested.

"Captain."

He flinched out of his reflection and found Dr. Clarion had returned. Back to get a last word? Back to make a threat? His decision *was* contradictory to the point of the trip, and it was very possible Mission Command would override him. But they had to know about it first.

Fixing his stare on Saturn, he said, "What is it, Doctor?"

She came to stand beside him. "It's hard to believe Earth is out there, isn't it?"

He looked askance at her. What gambit was this?

MOM

"It's a little over a billion kilometers in that direction," he said, tapping the window.

"Have you ever considered how unfair this is?"

"If you're referring to my decision—"

"I'm referring to the entire mission, Captain. We're ranging to the limit of the solar system in a ship of our own design, a ship that can hypothetically operate for a thousand years with a crew this size and be self-sufficient. In *any* other context, we'd be hailed as the next big step for Mankind. But we're not a step. We're a crib, and an empty one at that."

He started to tell her there was plenty of time left, but stopped himself, calculating what words could be used against him.

"It's a long trip," he said. "I have every confidence *Hanno* will return to Earth with four newborns."

"Four?"

Miller smiled. "Twins run in Get Hard's family."

Clarion returned a cold stare. "There won't be any children born on board."

"I promise the cargo won't be in suspended animation for very—"

"It doesn't matter," she said. "I'm trying to make myself accept what many, many tests are telling us. The simple fact is that these three men are producing sperm too fragile for natural conception, and verging on being too fragile for artificial conception as well. Their sperm is actually stronger on Earth under Thorium 236 exposure."

"I'm not following the implications."

"I don't know that I'm implying anything. We may be seeing an evolutionary response to Earth's environmental change. The radiation is interfering with natural conception on Earth, yet it seems the cells themselves are adapting to need the radiation to survive at all. That's my hypothesis at any rate. It's not just sperm cells, either. Every ovum sample shows the same problems."

Miller mulled over this.

"Maybe we should just request permission to turn the ship around," he said.

"Not yet. If my hypothesis is to be tested, a control group is required. Subjects who aren't in the same demographics as the subject group."

She touched his hand, and Miller looked down and laughed.

"Your deadpan humor is really something. That's the longest setup for a joke I've ever heard."

"I'm not joking. You're 50, I'm 45. . .and still capable."

"But everyone—"

"*Almost* everyone is going into suspended animation. Wellington and his assignment are due to spend thirty days in the Box, but they want to be in suspended animation too. We can make that happen. Then we have the ship to ourselves."

Miller looked at his wrist as he felt the doctor seize it.

"So, Captain," she said. "What do you say?"

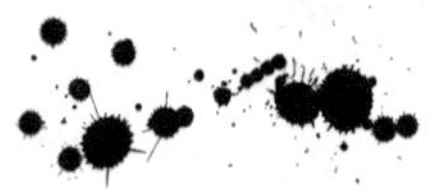

"Yes, yes, God yes," Miller whispered as he reached orgasm for the twentieth time in eight days. Amma gasped and went rigid beneath him, her nice legs wrapped around the small of his back. He rocked back and forth a little inside her, finishing, and then rolled onto his side.

"Think it'll happen this time?"

She nodded, grinning.

"Shame about your lack of internal cameras," he continued. "We could watch the progress or lack thereof for ourselves."

He kissed her mouth. She kissed back with even greater passion, her eyes shut tight. They were often like this in the minutes following their coupling, and he could almost read her thoughts as if they were written on the lines of her forehead creases. *I have to want it bad enough.* Miller wasn't sure why this notion came to him, and he didn't ask questions.

If she held to her previous pattern, Amma's mood would turn sour in about fifteen minutes. She'd start talking about her own mother in astonishing tones of disdain.

"If I'd been conceived before the Thorium 236 crisis, I'm sure she would have aborted me. Her maternal instincts were never good. She liked the idea of being a mom, but only the idea. It was so obvious how bad she was that there were constant complaints to the authorities from school officials and neighbors. Sometimes it seemed she forgot she had a daughter."

Amma never failed to bring this up again and again, like some dementia patient anchored to a final memory. Miller didn't mind hearing it repeated, though. His own mother had been an alcoholic wreck, and he'd joined the army to escape her.

"You know," she now said, caressing his chest, "for the longest time I was poisoned against the idea of having children of my own. Because of *her*. I was sure I'd be a terrible mom, just like my own. I had my career as a military doctor—no other focus allowed. I told myself I would only attempt conception out of scientific necessity. But that was a lie. I have to admit it. I wanted this. I *want* a child, Jeremiah."

He started to say, "I do, too," but couldn't bring himself to speak. It didn't seem like a lie. His mouth opened and shut and opened again.

"You have to want it, don't you?"

"Metaphysics shouldn't play a part in conception, but maybe it does now. Somehow."

"I never thought of it like that. Like every other man my age, I donated four milliliters of semen to the government, and they froze it and locked it away in a Thorium 236-proof container. I may have children right now. I might father a hundred long after I'm dead. Who's to say?"

"I'm not talking about being a father, Jeremiah. I'm talking about being a *dad*. They're just different, the way a mother and a mom are different. So. . .do you want that?"

Once again, the answer he wanted to give just wouldn't come out. *Yes* was perched on his lips but refused to fly forth. The lie lacked wings.

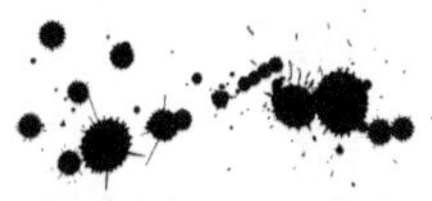

After years and years of ignoring her and her attempts at motherhood, the old poops had become furious. She heard them yelling up and down the neighborhood, talking about the incessant crying, the obvious neglect.

—Why does she even want children if she won't bother looking out for them?

—Where's the discipline? Her kids are leaving trash in my yard, and she looks the other way.

—She's getting old before her time. She's gone senile, but she keeps popping them out.

Their ridicule now became as persistent as it had been in the old neighborhood. No doubt there had been more of the same mistakes she'd vowed not to make again. It's easy to forget to feed children, it's easy to get mad at them, it's easy to shake them a little too much. None of her neighbors had any children and they didn't know the difficulty of being a good mom. That was even more true now, when the kids were getting a little older and wanting to assert their independence. Some of the little brats even talked about leaving home, but so far none of them had tried anything beyond a little backyard adventure. It was true some of the garbage from these campouts blew into neighboring yards. But everyone had a big space. The complaints were just an excuse for nastiness. A good mom stands up for her children, and that's what she started to do.

Her little babies were perfect.

Her little babies had imagination and creativity.

They added *to the neighborhood no matter what the old poops said.*

The more she argued, the angrier she got. Sometimes her insides felt like a furnace after the righteous defense of her children. The old poops started going silent on her. She shut them up again. They were just jealous because she had children when they didn't. She was contributing to the growth of the neighborhood, and they were just standing around growing old and being pointless.

Yes, she shut them up.

Until.

—Well, look at that.

—Look at what?

—Looks like the kids are running away from home.

—It's true. You must be such a wonderful and caring mom if you didn't even notice.

—Maybe you should lock the doors and windows when you decide to nap.

She was shocked to find some of the kids weren't in the backyard anymore. They were making a beeline across the neighborhood. This hurt. She got angry. Why would her children want to leave? She'd given them everything she had to give. She'd never failed to defend them against the old poops. She had called them perfect.

MOM

Yes, perfect.

But some were running away from home, there was no doubt about that, and this behavior embarrassed her in front of the whole neighborhood. The old poops were having great fun at her expense.

And she had to decide just what she wanted to do about the situation.

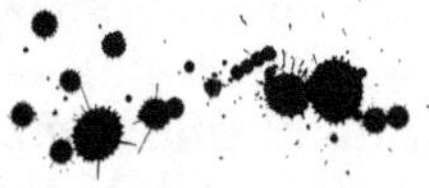

Amma hadn't made a sound in an hour, but Miller didn't think she was asleep. She rested on her side, snugged up against him but facing away. They had taken the mattress off his rack and placed it on the floor along with a mattress from Pizer's quarters to make a more sizable bed, though Amma was now having trouble getting up and down. She didn't complain. In fact, she said she was happier than she'd ever been and had taken to placing his right hand against her stomach, which is where it was now.

The baby was kicking again.

No.

Babies.

Miller remembered how they'd celebrated when she told him. They had *Hanno* to themselves by then, with everyone else in suspended animation. His thoughts were almost drowned by calculations and figures. She was already three months pregnant when she discovered the twins, and the news fell on the seven-month mark of the mission, two hundred ten days since they'd escaped Earth's ashen face. Maybe it was simpler to think of his chronology in terms of whatever planet they were passing. Saturn had been in the observation deck's windows when Amma made her proposal. They were a month away from Neptune when she told him about the twins. That meant *Hanno* would have rocketed past Pluto in the Kuiper Belt and was preparing to start the return trip when the twins were born.

Many, many reckonings were starting to realize themselves in his mind. Miller stroked her hair and tried to smile despite the gloom occupying his thoughts. Decisions were going to have to be made very soon now.

Amma moaned a little. She whispered, "No, Mom. Don't. . .don't—"

Then she spasmed and came awake, panting a little.

"You okay?"

"Bad dream."

"Seemed to be about your mom."

"I think my own pregnancy is making me remember her more. When I was 12, I decided to run away from home. Snuck out of the house one night while she was asleep. Crossed the yard, climbed the fence. I guess one of the neighbors saw me and said something. She came after me. She was screaming, and I was screaming back. She was calling me ungrateful, and I remember shouting, 'I don't need you! I don't need you!' All of this in the middle of the neighborhood. Just crazy."

Miller wasn't sure if he was supposed to laugh, but he risked a chuckle. "You were headstrong."

"I was desperate. She was so smothering, overcompensating because she knew how awful she was. She had a big ego, and her ego told her she was the perfect mom. She always doubled down when faced with reality. She'd hug like she meant to squeeze the life out of me. Hugging to hurt."

The captain made sure his own embrace was firm but tender.

"You're worried you'll be like that?"

"I'm worried I won't even get the chance."

So we're thinking the same thing, he told himself. The repercussions of their actions and how they'd hidden them from Mission Control. He wasn't so impulsive or careless as to ignore the consequences from the beginning. The considerations had been there like a shadow from the moment of first penetration and through the quick act of sex. It had made him feel like he was ejaculating poison into Amma's body. But after the third or fourth time, these sensations ebbed. He thought they were both too old to become parents, that her pregnancy couldn't happen, so what was the harm?

But here they were.

"I won't let them have the children," she said.

"Maybe we can hide them. Sneak them off the ship once we return—"

Her laughter was harsh and almost hysterical. It felt like a deserved slap in the face.

"There's no going back, Jeremiah. We both know that. You've forged your logs, I've forged my medical records. Mission Control thinks we've never stopped running experiments with the cargo. Court martial would be inevitable even if the conception hadn't happened."

"I know."

"Our children will be doomed to be medical experiments for the rest of their lives. I'm a hypocrite. I had no problem accepting the fate of any child born during this mission. They'd be confiscated and studied and probed in every possible way, including dissection."

"They wouldn't—"

"I was told I might be ordered to do it *myself* during the trip if circumstances warranted it."

"Could you have?"

"At the start of the trip, *yes*. I was a scientist focused on the continuation of humanity."

"And now?"

She let out a small sob. "Now I'm about to be a mom."

Miller told her he could commit.

Amma had worked it all out. *Hanno* could be self-sufficient and self-directed for hundreds of years, and with just four people to feed and extended bouts of suspended animation, they might find some inhabitable world in a century or two and live out their lives. These flights of fancy were unlike anything he'd ever known, bursts of liberating imagination that seemed to expand his appreciation of the universe and his special place in it as the new father of humanity.

"We'll need more than just our own DNA," she said. "Unless our children are going to breed with each other, there'll have to be additional options. It's logical to harvest them before we proceed with the rest of the plan."

Miller was in the observation lounge, meditating on the black vastness of space when she messaged him that the extraction was complete. She'd taken and secured sperm and eggs from all the members of the crew and cargo in suspended animation. They could now move on to the next stage of the plan.

Jettisoning the suspended animation pods would require a

command code only he could provide. His imagination painted the suspension pods floating past, their occupants asleep for a few more days, until their power supplies dwindled. When the power was at ten percent, the pods were programmed to end the suspension cycle at once and blow the doors. The designers of this failsafe had assumed such actions would take place aboard the ship.

Miller's gorge rose, and he doubled over, gulping it back down. He staggered into the hallway and got onto the automated walkway that sped him down *Hanno's* three-hundred-meter length to the forward bridge. He collapsed into his command chair and wiped his eyes as he observed the room, which seemed populated by the ghosts of Manzanares, Pizer, and Bettes. The bridge was designed as a semi-circle with seven operational stations. Telemetry ran across various screens, and the largest showed navigational data and projected *Hanno's* course into the Kuiper Belt. They were now almost four billion kilometers from Earth. Farther out than any human had ever traveled by a considerable degree.

Never returning, he thought. A litany of history's most fateful decisions could be categorized as either *Turning Back* or *Going Forward, Heading Home,* or *Fleeing Home.* Alexander the Great had relented to his mutiny-minded soldiers and pivoted away from India. Miller at that moment felt like Caesar pondering the banks of the Rubicon. He and Caesar were both faced with a treacherous homecoming, and Miller realized the Kuiper Belt was his Rubicon in reverse, and once *Hanno* entered it, all concepts of Earth had to be purged from his mind. He would never see the homeworld again.

You're doing this for your children, he told himself. No, more than that: for a new branch of the human race, insurance against the situation worsening on Earth. What were the lives of his bridge crew and the cargo if it guaranteed humanity's survival?

Shaking, he rose and made his way to the communications station. *Hanno's* operational systems sent regular automated status updates to Mission Control, and Miller dispatched a log entry per day. At this distance, *Hanno's* powerful laser pulse communication system still took five hours to get messages to Earth and five more hours for a reply. The console itself required little user skill to operate. Just press the red *Transmit* button and start talking.

MOM

The captain's right index finger now hovered over the button.

What was the point in saying anything? The ship's telemetry would report the expulsion of the suspended animation pods. Once he did it, there'd be a ten-hour reprieve before the emergency queries arrived. What lie could he give to explain it? Did Mission Control deserve an explanation at all?

Miller licked his arid lips.

They need to understand why, he told himself. They need to know the logic, the reason, the plain common sense of why Amma, the children, and I aren't coming back. They have to be assured that I'm not crazy.

I have to justify myself, he thought.

Miller shut his eyes.

Let the die be cast.

Rubicon.

Kuiper Belt.

One step.

For all mankind.

He pressed the button, his lower lip trembling as the silence lengthened.

"Mission Control," he said. "This will be my final log in my capacity as ship's captain. I hope you're all sitting down."

Amma was screaming at him as she cradled her stomach, calling him a fool and much worse. Calling him a murderer. A baby killer. Her face was red and slicked with sweat. Miller's efforts at calming her were in vain, but he went on anyway.

"The fault in your plan is now realizing just how automated *Hanno* is. Mission Control could send a signal and shut us down from Earth. They can and *will* turn us around."

"There has to be a way to disengage those systems."

"Not without risking damage to the ship itself," he said. "Don't you see? I *had* to come clean. But I've protected you. My log entry maximizes my criminality. Makes it seem like impregnating you was my idea, and you never had a choice."

"At this point, Jeremiah, I don't really care if you go around calling yourself a rapist. It won't protect the twins."

She gritted her teeth, bending forward and panting. Miller thought she was going into premature labor, but she waved him off. She straightened up as the door opened and Lt. Manzanares entered with Pizer and Bettes. Miller imagined their utter confusion. They were just twenty minutes out of suspended animation, and now they found Dr. Clarion pregnant and in a shouting match with their captain. They waited in mute astonishment, and Miller gave the lieutenant a nod.

"Sir, what's happened? Where are we?"

"Approaching the Kuiper Belt."

Manzanares's gaze kept darting to Dr. Clarion's stomach.

"Has the mission been. . .successful?"

"Yes, but not as intended."

"Bastard," Amma said. "Utter bastard."

She nudged her way past them and left. The bridge officers looked at him.

"Lieutenant, I'm turning command of *Hanno* over to you. It will be easier if you just go to the bridge now and listen to my latest log. It is almost my confession. I dispatched it to Mission Control three hours ago, and you can believe their response will be forthcoming at the soonest possible moment."

"Yes, sir," Manzanares said, sounding lost.

"Since we have no brig, I'm confining myself to my quarters until you receive orders about what to do to me."

The lieutenant nodded, seemed speechless for a moment, and then managed, "What about Doctor Clarion?"

"She's best qualified to deal with her situation on her own."

When Captain Miller was called to the bridge a few hours later, he pictured the crew waiting with whatever makeshift shackles they could arrange. He expected Manzanares to order him into suspended animation at once. He thought of the long, dreamless sleep with something like longing.

He was about to enter the bridge when *Hanno* made a sudden wild pitch that threw him to the floor and sent him sprawling against the wall. Then the ship made a reverse swing that sent him sliding and scrambling.

MOM

What in hell?

He got himself up and found the bridge in pure chaos. Bettes was at the communication station, trying to make sense of a scrambled screen and shouting into the receiver as if there were some expectation of immediate communication. Pizer stood braced at the helm and seemed to be fighting the controls.

"*Hanno*'s lateral thrusters are about to fire again. I can't—"

The ship made a vicious shift that would have thrown everyone from their station if not for the guard rails.

Mission Control is trying to override the navigation system, Miller thought. Has to be.

"Ventral thrusters activating. Bracc yourselves!"

The ship's momentum broke and changed. Miller gripped the guard rail tight as the ship threatened to execute a barrel road.

"Manzanares, report!"

"A transmission came from Earth, Captain. Emergency alerts—gibberish—and a navigation override command that appears to be corrupted or incomplete. *Hanno*'s navigation system doesn't know how to interpret it, and we're locked in an erratic thruster firing cycle. Pizer, any updates?"

"No, sir," Pizer said, voice strained as he fought the ship for control.

Miller inched his way to Manzanares in the command chair.

"You said gibberish. Weren't they responding to my log transmission?"

"No, Captain. Bettes, replay the transmission."

There were several bursts of static before Miller made out the first phrase.

"*. . .Massive death. . .inexplicable. . .*"

"*Extinction-level event. . .atmosphere. . .sheared away. . .*"

Miller and Manzanares exchanged looks. *Hanno* shifted and pitched again.

"*Apocalyptic. . .impossible. . .Doomed.*"

"That's the end of it, sir," Bettes said.

Miller and Manzanares exchanged glances. In the next instant, the lieutenant got out of the command chair. Miller gave the grimmest of nods and sat down.

Hanno banked again. Miller spared a thought for Amma and the twins, hoping all three were safe.

"Extinction-level event. What could it be?"

"Perhaps an uncharted asteroid?"

Hanno shifted again, throwing Miller hard against his right armrest.

"We've been turned into something between a spinning top and a pendulum. Pizer, if you can't regain control in the next five minutes, we're going to shut the reactor down. That will kill the engines and the thrusters and leave us adrift."

"Captain, the reactor would take at least three months to restart—"

"We can't enter the Kuiper Belt going back and forth like a schizophrenic. Get to work."

Manzanares leaned forward to speak low into Miller's ear. "Three months may be wishful thinking, sir. Are you sure you want to take that chance? We'd be at almost minimal power and *no* guarantee of—"

The ship shifted again, throwing Manzanares into Miller's lap. For a moment they were staring at each other, their noses almost touching. The captain saw blame in the lieutenant's eyes. Blame and judgment, regardless of the circumstances. Manzanares's eyes were mirrors.

"Shut it down!"

With the ship drifting but stabilized, Miller began focusing on the final message from Mission Control. The bridge crew listened to it several times and made conjectures.

"A supernova could rip the atmosphere away if Earth was in its direct path," Pizer said.

"Or the eruption of the Yellowstone caldera," Bettes said.

Miller shook his head. "These things are explicable. The message said *inexplicable.*"

"Maybe in the sudden chaos no one had a firm understanding," Manzanares said.

Miller was about to agree when Dr. Clarion's message arrived from the medical bay. A summons for the captain. His bridge crew became shy. Even Manzanares wouldn't look at him.

"Keep reviewing the final transmission and speculating until I return," he said. "We can't ignore any possibility at this point."

But what *is* the point? Miller thought as he left the bridge. The medical bay was in the middle of the ship, and he jogged the distance since the automated walkway was off. He stopped just outside the door and tried to listen for any sound. The noise of his own heartbeat made it difficult.

Was that a baby's wailing? Two babies?

Was it a figment of fevered imagination?

He waited outside the medical bay and counted out a hundred and twenty seconds, all the while trying to hear anything from the other side of the door. When he did enter, he found Amma sitting at her desk, her eyes somewhat vacant. Both hands clutched her stomach as if they were trying to hold together something on the verge of cracking.

They looked at each other. Uncertain what to say, Miller opted to give her a status report. How strange it was to relay the apparent end of the world and the ship's distressing status in less than a minute.

She listened. A long moment passed, and she said, "I'm having contractions, Jeremiah. This may be prodromal labor, but my intuition tells me it's the real thing. I'm at twenty-four weeks. The babies are in danger if they're born this soon, but the ship's mission meant I was supplied with the best neonatal facilities possible. . .as long as they have power."

"You'll have it," he said, clenching both hands into fists.

She got to her feet and grimaced.

"Yes," she said. "Now I'm certain it's the real thing."

Amma began to disrobe even as they walked over to one of three birthing beds. She settled onto it and began affixing monitoring devices to her skin. The screens behind her flickered with a glow so dull and low it was almost painful for Miller to see.

"Maybe if we bring the cargo out of suspended animation and shut those pods down—"

"No, I'd prefer they remain asleep. Less stress to manage for all of us. This will be okay."

She settled onto the bed and began instructing him. Miller followed her orders as best he could and was relieved when she gave a little laugh. He smiled from his position until he saw the serious look on her face.

"I was going to kill them," she said, wincing as another contraction hit. "Once I knew about your betrayal. I could only think about the fates of our children on Earth, and I knew I'd rather end their lives before they began. But I couldn't. There's a strange, unaccountable madness that comes with being a mom. You can be in total darkness, yet you can't stop yourself imagining the possibility of light."

"Some would call that hope," he said.

"Depends on context and circumstance, doesn't it?"

She laughed again.

"What's so funny?"

"If Earth is gone," Amma said, "then all of my hopes have come true."

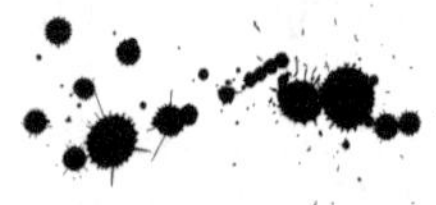

He returned to the bridge many hours later, walking in a daze with the sight of his newborn boy and girl stamped onto his memory. He didn't know what to think or feel. He was a dad. Amma was a mom.

When should he announce the births of Hannah and Hanno?

They were so small, so underweight and fragile, but Amma said the nursing chambers would see them through. As they'd stood beside each other, looking down on the two lives they'd created, Amma had said, "I'll never be like my own mother. Smothering. Inescapable. There'll never be a shouting match. These children will never feel the need to run away from me, to shout, 'I don't need you! I've outgrown you!' the way I did when I tried to flee."

He'd just nodded, understanding her vow and refusing to give voice to the immediate thought that entered his mind.

Where would any of them go if they wanted to run away? Their world was the length of the ship now—nothing more.

He stood there on the bridge like a shadow, lost in thought until Manzanares said, "Captain, we're detecting something on our infrared scans."

He stirred. "How far ahead?"

"It's not in front of us, sir."

He joined the lieutenant in front of his display. A blob of color showed on the dim screen. Miller had never seen anything like it, but at once he knew what it had to be.

"Sir, we appear to have captured evidence of a massive object of unknown—"

MOM

"It's a planet," he said, swallowing against the sudden dryness of his throat. "A rogue planet. I think we now know what happened to Earth. This body must have come at us from behind the sun. That's the only possible way we could have been blindsided. Maybe there was a collision. Christ."

"It's really moving, sir. Coming in at almost one hundred kilometers a second. Five times our own celerity before we shut down the reactor."

"Can we extrapolate its trajectory?"

"Already done, sir. It appears to be coming straight for us. At its current speed, the rogue will enter this sector by 2354.7. We've just been given a three-month warning, sir. If we don't have our reactor up by then, we could end up like a bug on a windshield."

Analysis showed the planet was picking up speed, though no one could account for it. They studied the data in mute horror. In another week, a faint red dot showed in the observation deck windows. It was like a pulsing dot, like a wink, and the bridge crew gathered to stare at it. Pizer said, "It's like we're the last humans in the universe, and this thing is tracking us down."

"I doubt it's personal," Manzanares said.

"But the trajectory—"

"Unfortunate coincidence," Miller said. "Nothing more."

"Captain," Bettes said. "Isn't it time we brought the cargo out of suspended animation? Shouldn't they know what's happening?"

"Would you want to know?" Manzanares said. "Would you want to be woken up just to be told you're going to die?"

Miller flinched at the fatalism. He surveyed his crew and found no hope among them. It felt so perverse to have such an inexhaustible amount of it in himself. His wellspring flowed from the medical bay.

There has to be a way to restart the reactor now, he thought. We're all ingenious people. Our creativity just needs a spur.

He knew where it could be found.

Amma had told him not to announce anything about the birth of the twins. She had all but locked herself in the medical bay to watch over the babies non-stop, and his bridge crew was so occupied that they seemed to have forgotten she existed. Whenever Miller snuck away to visit his family, he found Amma standing over the nursing pods with a sort of manic zeal. She refused to listen to anything he said and just repeated, "Aren't they perfect? Aren't they beautiful? Humanity's future, and we produced them, Jeremiah. The mom and dad of tomorrow."

Maybe if the crew understood the fullest measure of the stakes, they would somehow unlock new reservoirs of brilliance and figure out a pathway to jumpstart the reactor in record time. Nothing so empowered the mind like desperation, and nothing so hindered it like despair.

The sight of the twins would burn away that despair.

He ordered them to follow him, and they trekked down *Hanno*'s almost dark main corridor to the medical bay. Amma gasped when she saw them and put herself in front of the nursing pods with her hands stretched out on either side.

"No," she said. "No."

"Amma," he began, before correcting himself. "Dr. Clarion, I want to show the crew just how successful our mission has been. We've achieved what we set out to achieve. Come and look at the future."

He moved Amma aside. She trembled in his arms as Manzanares, Bettes, and Pizer crowded around the twins. None of them said a word. The babies were asleep, and the room became pregnant with a deep, heavy silence quite unlike what Miller had imagined. Where was the applause, the awe, the renewed spirit? Where was the burst of determination, the can-do attitude, the fresh, unfathomed solutions?

"Why, Jeremiah? Why did you let them see?"

Amma started sobbing. Miller couldn't account for her reaction at all. Then, to his complete astonishment, his officers rubbed their eyes. They were weeping. He raised his hands at them and said, "We've accomplished the mission. Just not in the way it was intended. Here is our survival. Hannah and Hanno. In a way, we're all their parents. Now is the time to be brilliant for them."

Bettes walked out first, followed by Pizer. When Manzanares turned without saying a word, Miller seized his shoulder.

"What is it?"

"Remember what I said about the cargo being left asleep, sir?"

"Yes."

"Not knowing about the babies is the same thing, Captain."

MOM

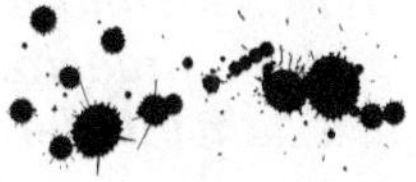

He could not implore his crew any harder, and they did not respond. They began not reporting to the bridge at all. A month after the last transmission from Earth, Manzanares stood in front of Miller and requested permission to enter suspended animation. So did Pizer and Bettes.

"No," Miller said. "Permission isn't granted."

They did it anyway. Miller considered ending the sleep cycle even as it began, then thought better of it. What was the use of waging such a tug of war?

He returned to the medical bay to see his children. Amma almost screamed at him to come no closer than two meters.

"Can't I hold them?"

"Out of the question," she said, snapping at him. "You must be insane."

He supposed it was enough just to see them, and he made frequent visits. Otherwise, he began spending most of his time in the engine room, willing the reactor's cold mass to complete its restart cycle sooner than the laws of physics mandated. Then he'd walk to the observation deck and look at the glowing orb pursuing them. It was like Hannah and Hanno in a way, getting larger and larger every time he saw it.

By the end of the second month, the rogue planet had recognizable features. It seemed to be producing its own inner light, no longer red but blue as the sea, and familiar continents stood out against that light like bas reliefs. Pale blue dot, Miller thought. He was staring down at North America. The skies were gone, the oceans were gone, but the blue light remained.

How?

How?

The old poops were having a field day at her expense because she had no choice but to make a public scene. She had to show everyone she wasn't the sort of mom who didn't look after her

kids, who didn't care about them, and who never gave each and every child all that she had, no favoritism. Any mom would do that, and the neighbors just didn't understand the strength of her commitment.

—What is she thinking?

—It's horrific. Talk about throwing out the baby with the bathwater.

—This may be the most disturbing thing I've ever seen.

—I'll say again: What is she thinking?

She heard the criticisms and was stung by them; the truth has a way of stinging. Once she set off after her runaways, somewhere around the halfway mark, she realized how impulsive her actions had been. It'd been a long time since she'd made so grave a mistake as a mom. It filled her with such shame she knew that for the second time in her life, she had to move to a new neighborhood. Her failures before the neighbors were of too great a magnitude.

The funny thing was, as she approached her fleeing children, she could hear a voice. She was so accustomed to the cacophony of life that everything sort of blended together, but now she heard a single voice. Her child was staring at her as she reached him. He was shaking a fist at her and screaming, "We've outgrown you! We've outgrown you! We've outgrown you!"

Ungrateful brat.

Then it was over, and she came to a stop, pausing to gather her thoughts and take a look around. She felt the stares of her neighbors at her back, but of course, she already knew she wasn't turning around.

There was a new neighborhood on the horizon, not too far away. She set out in that direction with the certainty that all the errors she'd made could be taken to heart and would make her a much better mom when she started over.

AFTERWORD

WELL, LOOK AT YOU. You made it to the end.

Did you read them all?

If you didn't, it's not due to the quality of the writing. The Eads/Viola pen is indeed a mighty one and sumptuous phrases abound. Little asides, like *Free will is a grey concept at best, and outright illusion for a beggared man.* Or perhaps *The recaptured romance, a warm parental experience, a dazzling historical foray.* That's just lovely.

No, my guess is if you stopped reading a story or two, it's because you're too damn squeamish. Maybe you were lured by the rhythm of the prose and then suddenly came upon this:

A terrifying, fleshy string was attached to the infant's stomach, and as the feet came through, the cord brought with it a purple mass that reminded Alaster of a calf's liver sewn up by a drenched skein of yellow and red yarn.

Yikes.

Or you were there, on your cozy couch, a nice sandwich in hand, when this blindsided you:

Had I ever looked at a piece of dog shit and had its taste just explode in my mouth?

Therein lies the beauty of this collection. Some of the most elegant writing imaginable, bookended by imagery that will either horrify, disgust, or simply make you weep for humanity.

I love it.

I've known Sean and Josh for years and may have even been the person who introduced them. If so, I'll take some credit for the writing team they've become, if only to revel in the fact that there is indeed a synergy in these two, a sum greater than the parts, a virus that has mutated to a point of invincibility.

I'm ceaselessly impressed by co-writers. How they're able to work together to craft the finest possible tale, rather than let their individual egos tear their efforts asunder. I love picturing Sean and Josh sitting at a table, beers in hands, heatedly discussing whether or not the baby's entrails should metaphorically or literally wrap around the banister like a Christmas garland. They would each take their positions with utmost seriousness and defend them with the earnestness of a prosecutor. But I suspect they end up compromising for the betterment of the story.

Story first. Always story first.

And these stories? They're beautiful. Yes, they are intended to frighten, to anger, to repulse, to amuse. But they are not devices. They are *human*. Sean and Josh do not write with a formula in mind. Rather, they want a reaction from you. They want you to experience emotion, whatever that emotion may be. Don't tell me you didn't laugh out loud at *Eunuch's Code* or pee yourself just a little at *Many Carvings*. Don't tell me you didn't run to your bathroom and swirl some mouthwash after reading *The Jarheads*. Yeah. You did all those things.

If it sounds like I'm defending them, I'm not. The powerhouse of Eads/Viola doesn't need me convincing you they're good. You now know it for yourself. And I'm not sure they give a shit what you think anyway.

Besides, you know you're doing something right if Stephen Graham Jones calls you sick.

Carter Wilson
November 2022
Erie, Colorado

THE END?

Not if you want to dive into more of Crystal Lake Publishing's Tales from the Darkest Depths!

Check out our amazing website and online store
or download our latest catalog here.
https://geni.us/CLPCatalog

We always have great new projects and content on the website to dive into, as well as a newsletter, behind the scenes options, social media platforms, our own dark fiction shared-world series and our very own webstore. Our webstore even has categories specifically for KU books, non-fiction, anthologies, and of course more novels and novellas.

ABOUT THE AUTHORS

Joshua Viola is a Colorado Book Award winner and Splatterpunk Award nominee. He co-authored *Legacy of Kain: Soul Reaver—The Dead Shall Rise*, an official prequel to the beloved video game series, which became the 4th most funded graphic novel of all time on Kickstarter, raising over $1.4 million. He edited the *Denver Post* #1 bestselling horror anthology *Nightmares Unhinged* and co-edited *Cyber World*, named one of the best science fiction anthologies of 2016 by Barnes & Noble. He co-authored the comic book slasher series *True Believers* with Stephen Graham Jones, featuring official cameos from icons like Jamie Lee Curtis, R.L. Stine, Jeffrey Combs, and Barbara Crampton. As a producer, he has contributed to films such as *Aliens Expanded*, *The Thing Expanded*, *TerrorBytes*, *Shelby Oaks*, *Shrine of Abominations*, *Deathgasm II: Goremageddon*, and the recent *Deathstalker* reboot directed by Steven Kostanski (*The Void, Psycho Goreman*), starring Daniel Bernhardt (*The Matrix, John Wick*) and produced with Slash from Guns N' Roses. In 2024, he founded Bit Bot Media with musician Klayton (Celldweller), a multimedia company focused on original and licensed IP, including *The Terminator, Legacy of Kain, Evil Dead 2*, and more. Bit Bot also collaborates with Canadian film studio Raven Banner Entertainment on film productions, merchandise, and distribution, including titles like *The Autopsy of Jane Doe* and the documentary *Hate to Love: Nickelback*. Joshua's video game development includes work on titles such as *The Rocky Horror Show, Pirates of the Caribbean: Call of the Kraken, Unioverse, The Smurfs, TARGET: Terror*, and others. He is the owner and chief editor of Hex Publishers and resides in Denver, CO, with his husband and son.

Sean Eads is a writer and librarian living in Denver, Colorado. He is originally from Kentucky and has a Masters degree in literature from the University of Kentucky and a Masters degree in library science from the University of Illinois. His first novel, The Survivors, was a finalist for the Lambda Literary Award. His third novel, Lord Byron's Prophecy was a finalist for the Shirley Jackson Award and the Colorado Book Award. His fifth novel, Confessions, was also a finalist for the Colorado Book Award. His favorite writers are Ray Bradbury, Herman Melville, Cormac McCarthy and Ernest Hemingway.

Readers . . .

Thank you for reading *Midnight Vintage*. We hope you enjoyed this collection.

If you have a moment, please review *Midnight Vintage* at the store where you bought it.

Help other readers by telling them why you enjoyed this book. No need to write an in-depth discussion. Even a single sentence will be greatly appreciated. Reviews go a long way to helping a book sell, and is great for an author's career. It'll also help us to continue publishing quality books.

Thank you again for taking the time to journey with Crystal Lake Publishing.

Visit our Linktree page for a list of our social media platforms.
https://linktr.ee/CrystalLakePublishing

Follow us on Amazon:

MISSION STATEMENT:

Since its founding in August 2012, Crystal Lake has quickly become one of the world's leading publishers of Dark Fiction and Horror books. In 2023, Crystal Lake officially transitioned into an entertainment company, joining several other divisions, genres, and imprints, including Torrid Waters, Crystal Lake Comics, Crystal Lake Games, Crystal Lake Kids, and many more.

While we strive to present only the highest quality fiction and entertainment, we also endeavour to support authors along their writing journey. We offer our time and experience in non-fiction projects, as well as author mentoring and services, at competitive prices.

With several Bram Stoker Award wins and many other wins and nominations (including the HWA's Specialty Press Award), Crystal Lake Publishing puts integrity, honor, and respect at the forefront of our publishing operations.

We strive for each book and outreach program we spearhead to not only entertain and touch or comment on issues that affect our readers, but also to strengthen and support the Dark Fiction field and its authors.

Not only do we find and publish authors we believe are destined for greatness, but we strive to work with men and women who endeavour to be decent human beings who care more for others than themselves, while still being hard working, driven, and passionate artists and storytellers.

Crystal Lake Publishing is and will always be a beacon of what passion and dedication, combined with overwhelming teamwork and respect, can accomplish. We endeavour to know each and every one of our readers, while building personal relationships with our authors, reviewers, bloggers, podcasters, bookstores, and libraries.

We will be as trustworthy, forthright, and transparent as any business can be, while also keeping most of the headaches away from our authors, since it's our job to solve the problems so they can stay in a creative mind. Which of course also means paying our authors.

We do not just publish books, we present to you worlds within your world, doors within your mind, from talented authors who sacrifice so much for a moment of your time.

There are some amazing small presses out there, and through collaboration and open forums we will continue to support other presses in the goal of helping authors and showing the world what quality small presses are capable of accomplishing. No one wins when a small press goes down, so we will always be there to support hardworking, legitimate presses and their authors. We don't see Crystal Lake as the best press out there, but we will always strive to be the best, strive to be the most interactive and grateful, and even blessed press around. No matter what happens over time, we will also take our mission very seriously while appreciating where we are and enjoying the journey.

What do we offer our authors that they can't do for themselves through self-publishing?

We are big supporters of self-publishing (especially hybrid publishing), if done with care, patience, and planning. However, not every author has the time or inclination to do market research, advertise, and set up book launch strategies. Although a lot of authors are successful in doing it all, strong small presses will always be there for the authors who just want to do what they do best: write.

What we offer is experience, industry knowledge, contacts and trust built up over years. And due to our strong brand and trusting fanbase, every Crystal Lake Publishing book comes with weight of respect. In time our fans begin to trust our judgment and will try a new author purely based on our support of said author.

With each launch we strive to fine-tune our approach, learn from our mistakes, and increase our reach. We continue to assure our authors that we're here for them and that we'll carry the weight of the launch and dealing with third parties while they focus on their strengths—be it writing, interviews, blogs, signings, etc.

We also offer several mentoring packages to authors that include knowledge and skills they can use in both traditional and self-publishing endeavours.

We look forward to launching many new careers.

This is what we believe in. What we stand for. This will be our legacy.

Welcome to Crystal Lake Publishing—
Where stories come alive!